SOMEONE
TO
WATCH
OVER

WILLIAM SCHREIBER

Published in the United States by
Not a Pipe Publishing, Independence, Oregon.
www.NotAPipePublishing.com
Cover by Gigi Little

Trade Paperback Edition

ISBN-13: 978-1-948120-52-4

"Dimming Of The Day"
Words and Music by Richard Thompson
Copyright (c) 1975 Beeswing Music
Copyright Renewed
All Rights Administered by Songs Of Kobalt Music Publishing
All Rights Reserved Used by Permission
Reprinted by Permission of Hal Leonard LLC

Author photo by Brian Keogh

Dedication

For our parents and children, living and deceased.
Although they may have left for now,
they're never really gone.

SOMEONE
TO
WATCH
OVER

*There are years that ask questions
and years that answer.*

– Zora Neale Hurston

ONE

Yoke of Life

What do I look like? She couldn't remember. And she'd given up on mirrors long ago. Dang things never revealed anybody's true self anyhow. Folks would be better off ponderin' themselves in the surface of Chickamauga Lake during a Spring blow. The wavering image looking back at them from its wind-whipped water was more likely to reflect the peculiar forces at work on them every day of their natural-born lives.

She held fast to the notion that folks' bodies were the least interesting thing about them, mere pickle jars to the sprouts of life within. There was some comfort in that because she could no longer perceive her physical self. She couldn't remember the last time she'd felt the skin of another person brush hers. Or had been aware of her age.

She could be eight. Or twenty. Or fifty-seven. What did it matter? She was all of them at once, carried all the years of her life inside, along with the emotional baggage that had always fed the gossip mill, until folks had nothing left to whisper about.

No, ma'am. Age made no nevermind, especially in these grinding foothills of Tennessee's Great Smoky Mountains. Souls around here had their hands full merely bearing up under the circumstances with which the yoke of strenuous living had burdened them. This she knew.

Some were brave enough, some would say foolhardy enough, to stand their ground against a surefire destiny of deprivation. They squared off and schemed to get out. Others simply rolled over. Folks here either surrendered to fate or fought their way out of the corner into which it had jammed them.

She hadn't expected to come back to this place, but maybe it was fitting. After all, it held her beginnings ... as well as her end.

Without a sound, she made her way through the foggy dawn toward a sagging car cloaked in a muted gray akin to sodden field cotton.

The decrepit station wagon slumped all catawampus in front of the town's lovely bookstore; the former antebellum church, now home to a landmark bell steeple, brought a gust of memories, here and then gone.

The historic cobblestone town square of red-brick buildings stood as it had years and years ago, but she barely noticed it—she couldn't take her eyes off the car.

The rust bucket had never strayed from her sight. It drew her like a magnet, just like it always had, no matter where it went.

The bookstore's steeple rose above it, the glow from the tower's angelic stained-glass windows illuminating the murk, and vibrations whispered to her from the car's interior; not the kind that disturbed air and gave rise to sound, but vibrations that disturbed her soul and gave birth to yearning.

She harbored a connection with the woman she knew was sheltering in there, a bond perhaps only understood by two lives that had begun as one. Although they weren't twins, they had once shared a womb—now, they shared each other's dreams and, sometimes, the same feelings of despair. If they could only break free of the heartbreak in which fate had cornered them, she reckoned they just might share in each other's salvation.

The steeple bell rang the early hour as she picked up a pebble and peered through the station wagon's cargo-area window, streaked with grime.

Tick-tick-tick. She tapped the glass, prompting a dewdrop to flee and carve a valley through the window's matted clay rouge. The woman inside, clenched in a protective ball, didn't stir.

CLACK-CLACK-CLACK! The jarring sound of belligerent metal striking the window on the other side of the car caused her to drop the pebble, so consumed by the woman in the vehicle, she hadn't seen the cop with the steel flashlight arrive. Hadn't noticed the harshness of his patrol car's headlights that now bleached the station wagon's backside.

He looked her way, over the car roof, but obviously didn't see her, and she withdrew into the mist. Her frustration mixed with a sense of urgency. Something had to be done before it was too late.

TWO

Home Again

A noise grated inside Lennie Riley's head when she flexed her jaw inside the station wagon. Grains crunched between her teeth. Sand? Her mouth was bitter-dry as a bloodied desert. As her thirst welled up, something gurgled. Her lungs. Rising and falling.

A bell tolled low and slow somewhere. She willed her eyes open. In the dimness, what appeared to be a swath of skin hanging overhead came into focus. The ripped roof liner.

She was curled in the cargo area. Heat oozed from her sweaty skin, toes clenched into stubby fists. Rolling onto her side, she stretched her legs. She couldn't remember falling as—

—a sharp *CLACK-CLACK-CLACK* on the glass next to her head instinctively sent her skittering into an opposite corner like a spooked deer.

"Yeah, Dispatch. She's movin'."

She recoiled at the sound of a man's muffled voice outside. As she glanced at the window to which she had scrambled, she was startled by something in her peripheral vision. *What was THAT?* Her brain registered a glimpse of something—*someone*—there and gone.

The disorienting instant was avalanched by a rapid succession of sensory assaults: Her cheek burned. Heavy air weighed on her lungs. Scraped legs wept.

A glance around the caged space found her turquoise-dyed cowboy boots tossed on the other side. They instantly anchored her in the moment, and she clung to the sight of them.

"Mosely Police. I need you to open the door."

She squinted into his glaring flashlight outside as her sense of self-preservation kicked into high gear. *Police?*

Fractured thoughts converged as she unlocked the tailgate. "I'm okay," she said in the strongest tone she could muster. The lilt of her Southern voice was the only thing she recognized about herself.

She pushed the heavy swing-door open with a bare foot and ran her hand through her tangled hair, a finger catching in the white magnolia she'd clipped in last night. She unsnarled the tattered, blood-speckled flower and winced when she attempted to take a deep, calming breath.

Scooting on her backside to exit the tailgate, she welcomed the comfort of warm cobblestone under her feet. Her torn floral sundress was twisted around her like a wrung dishrag, and she tugged it back into place as she caught a throbbing glimpse of a police car.

The pealing bell was more pronounced out here, but she could scarcely make out the murky form in the center of the town-square's traffic roundabout—a colossal bronzed Confederate soldier brandishing an upthrust cavalry saber. It had defiantly stood its ground there as far back as she could remember, protecting this speed-bump town and its three-digit population.

She'd parked in a spot at A Likely Story Bookstore. Her station wagon wasn't between the lines. Not by a long shot. Was that why the cop was here? *He think I'm some kinda drunk driver?* He was young and thin. An angular face. Maybe mid-twenties. She tried to pull herself together as the bell fell silent.

"You know where you are?" His voice resonated with a throaty drawl that was as much a part of this place as hubcap birdbaths.

It was hard to look at him, partly because he was shining his light directly into her face, but mostly because she was deeply ashamed.

Last night thundered in, and she took refuge in her toes, where she could make out chipped lavender polish. She touched her blazing cheek and drew back fingers stained with blood.

He said, "I'm gonna transport you to Tri-County, then we'll talk."

The thought of the hospital caused her heartbeats to stumble over themselves, each pulse racing to overtake the one that preceded it. "No. Please, don't."

She couldn't live with being unloaded from a police car at the ER. She volunteered as a cuddler for preemies in the neonatal intensive care unit. Seeing her like this, the part of her life she kept hidden, they'd never let her near those precious infants again.

"I'm fine. I'll just ... drop in the QuikCare. The walk-in. I'm, um ... established there." Her fingers raked over a cut at her hairline, and she grimaced at a jagged dart of pain.

"You have a driver's license and registration?"

She dug her license from a funky yellow-over-orange wrist purse made to resemble a piece of Halloween candy corn and retrieved her registration from the glove box.

He scanned them. "Eleanor Grace Riley."

"Yessir. Only I go by Lennie." It felt odd addressing this kid as sir. But he was the law.

"Kodiak, Alaska?"

"Yessir." She rubbed her mouth, looked at her fingers to see a whisper of last night's coral lipstick. When she glanced at the bookstore, her gaze climbed the steeple's stained-glass windows. "And I know it says hazel eyes, because I tried to convince the guy otherwise at the DMV out there. Turned out, he wasn't too friendly. I think of them as green, like Granny Smith apples?"

She heard herself rambling and clamped down as the light behind the stained-glass angels washed over her and the cop.

A last-second thought tumbled through her mind, and she decided to appeal to him as her own character witness. "Plus, as you see on my license, I'm an organ donor, because, well, it's the right thing to do. Help others, as you'd like to be helped."

The officer adjusted the holster on his squeaky leather utility belt, then keyed the radio affixed at his shoulder. "Dispatch, forty-two."

His radio burped static. "Forty-two, Dispatch," a reedy voice replied.

He read from her license. "Occupant, Eleanor Grace Riley. White female. Forty-one years of age. Vehicle looks older'n I am."

I've got jeans older than you are.

He talked sideways to his shoulder radio. "You run that plate?"

"Nineteen eighty-three Bonneville Safari wagon is registered to her out in Alaska," the dispatcher said.

The young lawman cranked an eyebrow at Lennie. "You're a long way from home."

There was a hint of suspicion in his voice. Of course. Strangers around here were generally regarded with wariness. She rubbed her aching neck and shifted her weight on her feet.

"Actually, sir, *this* is home. I just ... took some time away, and now I've moved back. A couple months ago."

Her hopes of creating a so-called normal life here had just met a reality check. She studied his face. Tried to read his thoughts in his expression.

It was then she noticed his name badge, and it didn't matter a lick what he was thinking. What mattered was his pedigree: D. Mosely.

Her right ear rang as her pulse throbbed all the way from her left eye to her swollen ankles. The Moselys ran this town that was their birthright: Mosely, Tennessee. Five square miles of backcountry carved on the edge of endurance. It had always been that way, going back to the Confederacy.

Now, they'd apparently gone from simply owning the police chief with shady campaign money, to putting their own law-enforcement boots on the ground.

"I, um ... I'm trying to get some traction in my life back here. Back home."

"You need to get your license and tag transferred."

She knew her only play was to agree to everything. "Yessir. I'll see to it. I've just been—" she started to say but caught herself and lifted her hands to ward off the diversionary thought. "No. No excuses, I'll get on it."

She jacked up her twang, hoping to somehow connect with him as a local, one of his own kind. "Quicker'n a toupee in a dadgum tornado."

A smirk almost cracked his face. Almost. "Right ... Stand by." Officer Mosely walked back to his patrol car with her license and registration.

Brushing lightly over the gritty cobblestones with her toes, she stole glances at him under the cruiser's dome light, talking on the radio, and forced herself to relax her breathing.

After a few moments, a verdict was apparently rendered, and he returned. "I'm gonna have to transport you to Tri-County. You can get some treatment, and I can get to the bottom of this."

Her heart jackhammered her rib cage. "Please, sir, no." She crossed her arms and buried her hands in her armpits, thumbs flicking her fingernails. "I work here." She nodded at the bookstore.

He glanced at the misty brick building. "A Likely Story?"

"Yessir." She pressed her chin into her chest as if she were a contrite sinner. "And, sir, these are truly unfortunate circumstances you find me in."

At stake was something bigger than her and Officer Mosely, privileged native son. Surely, he could appreciate the price this hard land extracted from your hide, even if he was born above it all.

"Y'all are catchin' me at a tough time ... terrible time. But, y'see, sir, I'll bounce back, 'cause—"

"I've still gotta transport you."

"Please. What about my kids, sir? They're not mine, but I think of them as mine."

She pressed her stinging bloody palms to her chest and swam his eyes. "Me? I'm for the kids of Mosely. Y'see, what I do is ... I read to the little ones with seeking hearts in the summer program. Right inside those walls."

She pointed to the bookstore and tilted her head as she explained, hoping to convince him that she aspired to something more than what he saw before him.

"It's about the children, sir. The steeple bell calls 'em to the pages of those books, surely as they called lost souls to the Almighty in the wayback. I find joy that sustains me in firin' their imaginations. Their dreams. You transport me, and you'll take all that away from them. Please."

She watched his lips for the first twinge of a response, but there was none. His radio squawked on his shoulder. "Forty-two, Dispatch."

Officer Mosely hesitated and nibbled the inside of his bottom lip before keying his radio. "Forty-two, go ahead."

"Status on your possible 10-41?" the dispatcher said.

"Stand by." His tongue slowly ping-ponged back and forth behind his bulging lower lip as he remained silent. He scratched his sideburn. "You wanna file a report?"

She didn't know whether to laugh or cry. "Report?"

"Charges." He shone his light on her bare feet, then traced up her bloodied leg and her torso. "Assault? Battery? I'm thinkin' along the lines of a domestic dust-up."

A scowl etched his face, a look she'd seen before: the assumption that whoever had done this to her deserved to be tried and punished. That she was a victim. When in fact, she had just taken another foolish risk.

She stared straight into his eyes. "No, sir. I don't."

THREE

Walking Wounded

Alone in a sterile exam room at the QuikCare, Lennie sat on a stainless-steel table, a blue plastic bag of personal effects at her side.

The concrete walk-in clinic adjacent to the Mosely railyard was enshrined in the mountains' bare-knuckle grit. It did a steady business patching up barroom brawlers blowing their wages to escape the drudgery of life on the train docks, in the limestone quarry and on logging crews, all of which the Mosely family controlled through Mosely Enterprises. Members of a fight club, rumored to be somewhere outside town on Highway D, were also steady customers.

Her past hour had consisted of paperwork, a shower and topical medications to help begin the physical healing process. She slumped in exhaustion as the encounter with the cop waded into her mind. She was grateful he had let her slide on going to the hospital, but was there another person with him, at the opposite window?

It had seemed for an instant like somebody was there. A partner who took another call and left maybe? She tried to massage an aching knot out of her thigh. She could've just imagined it. After all, she had been woozy.

But what if there was a second observer who reported her to Tri-County and the staff in the preemie ward found out? That would be the end of her cuddler job. She shuddered at the thought.

Her mental sleuthing collided with her reflection in a mirror on the opposite wall, and she nearly gagged at the sight. Wet, clinging chestnut hair hung to her shoulders like soppy wheat linguini, and the purple half-moon under her left eye glistened with ointment in the fluorescent overheads.

Bare feet dangled toward her tasseled, turquoise cowboy boots, which she had long ago christened her cow-boho boots after winning them in a coffeehouse poetry slam in Anchorage. Boho. Bohemian. That life was behind her now. Had brought her full circle back to this place.

She resisted the urge to look in the mirror again out of fear for the condition of her cheekbones, which she cherished. Not because they were Reese Witherspoon glamorous or anything, but because they were Mom's, at least from the picture she'd seen of her as a child on Dad's bedroom wall.

From what she could tell, she had inherited Mom's graceful facial features, the only keepsake she had. But there had been no motherly presence to hold her hand through the maelstrom of growing up, no confidante to share the dreams, the yearnings, the insecurities of a young girl facing training bras, periods, and the dicey delights of boys.

A few minutes later, a doctor with cherubic cheeks and a gray mustache stood over her as he fingered the bottom of her chin with his latex glove. His breath betrayed an obvious taste for garlic bagels. "Tilt your head back for me."

She rolled her neck back and found herself looking up his nostrils, home to a gnarl of nose hair.

"A little sting." He squeezed a burning drop into her swollen left eye then snapped off his exam gloves. "You should be fine, but when we hit forty, the body takes a little more time to bounce back."

"Yeah, trust me," she replied, "I've kinda figured that out."

He gazed at her for a long moment. Made her uncomfortable. *God, I look like a mauler's mug shot.* There was a time she'd been called pretty as a moonlit night.

The doctor turned toward the door. "Emily's here."

Her shoulders sank as she blew her lungs clear and closed her eyes, trying to make it all go away. She recognized the brisk pace of Emily Parson's approaching stride echoing in the corridor and distracted herself by trying to guess which pair of sensible shoes she was wearing today.

She opened her eyes to see a pair of black Thom McAn flats. Probably from the Walmart down in Sweetwater. She lifted her gaze to find Emily pointing a digital SLR camera at her.

The earnest social worker in her first job a year out of college counted to three before the flash fired in Lennie's face. Emily set her camera on the counter, Lennie's ravaged image frozen in the preview screen on the back.

Though it would have been ungracious for her to admit, Lennie had grown irked by how together Emily always seemed. Bobbed raven hair that was perfect for the Southern heat, and a rotation of breezy linen jacket-and-skirt sets perfectly accented with comfortable shoes.

She pulled an offbeat tangerine bolero shrug from her personal effects bag and wrapped her shoulders, her tattered sundress suddenly no match for the room's chill.

"I have a bed for you," Emily said. "Same room as last time."

Lennie just stared down at her funky boots.

"Lennie." The tightness in the young woman's voice was the same a parent gives a teen who constantly battles boundaries.

Lennie looked up. She knew Emily's line of classroom reasoning would be textbook.

"This is the second time Derrick's done this since you moved back to town."

Lennie stared at her fingers in her lap, clasped as if in prayer. *Sometimes, life isn't textbook.*

"These relationships of yours?" Emily said. "There's a cycle." She opened Lennie's case file. "Texas, California, Alaska, when you were working the crabbing boat."

Lennie didn't say a word.

"You can't outrun the core issue we've been discussing."

The overhead light buzzed the dead air like a monstrous mosquito as she weighed a response. "I said some things I shouldn't of. He just lashed out is all."

Emily's expression softened. "I know you're afraid. That's completely understandable. But this is about taking the first step."

A bubble of grief rose from an unfathomable depth. Lennie's refusal to let it penetrate the surface made her shake her head involuntarily. Still, whatever smoldered in her deepest of deeps, the anguish that had drawn her back to Mosely, threatened to surge once more.

"Step to where, Emily?" She grimaced against a blade of pain in her ribs as she eased off the table, dogged by fatigue she knew in her bones a night's sleep wouldn't cure. "I've doubled back on myself so many times, where am I supposed to step to?"

Emily lifted Lennie's file from the counter and clutched it to her chest. "Anywhere other than where you are."

Lennie's gaze found her battered face in the preview screen of her caseworker's camera. Somehow, it looked even worse in miniature, as if her entire life had been compressed into a single, crushing image trapped in an inch-square cage. She barely recognized herself.

Emily said," You're hauling your past on your back, but the future starts just outside that door."

When Lennie walked out of the clinic, the morning mist still ringed the distant Smokies. But now, the verdant peaks punctured the fog like the knuckles of a fist straining to break free of an ashen skin that smothered them.

Spring 1986

Dear Mommy,

It's me, Lennie. It's my birthday again. Guess how old I am... eight! Daddy took me to Walmart in Sweetwater to pick a present (My Little Pony Crystal Rainbow Castle), and then we stopped to visit you at the graveyard to remember when you went to heaven. Do they have ages up there? Daddy says they don't. I say they do. It's heaven. You can have anything you want, right?

I know I should be happy on my birthday, but I get sad sometimes because of what happened with you. Miss Ellen at school said I should just sit down and tell you that. She helped me with the spelling. I get to sit in her chair and look out a big window. She helps me not feel so sad. She's my friend. Do you have friends up there? Did you ever know I had to wear a special shoe on one foot to straighten it when I was little? Did you have to wear one of those when you were my age?

I told Miss Ellen my heart made a wish that I could know you, and she said wishes are what dreams are made of. Her hair is black and hard as a rock. She says it's called Aqua Net. The color of mine is like a pretty pony I see sometimes in the field. Or maybe like a shiny penny. How is your hair? I wrote you something...

"My Footprint" by Lennie Riley, Age 8

My footprint is small, I wore a squiggly shoe,
My footprints follow me, these are for you.
My foot pointed that way, my foot had a curve,
But I got it fixed up, of that I am sure.
I walk through the mud, through the rain and the warm,
I hope that one day, I'll walk into your arms.

FOUR

Broken Pieces

A cloud of dust followed a metallic-blue convertible as it
cruised down the street outside Lennie's room at the New
Hope Women's Shelter. She watched it disappear around
the corner.

Had to be a tourist. They weren't hard to spot. These foothills
were home to muddy pickups and sag-ass sedans, not sparkling
convertibles.

During these summer months, Mosely rolled out the Southern hospitality and served as an authentic historic site for visitors
on the state's Civil War Trail. Those who scratched out a life
here, though, experienced something entirely different. The constant hardship showed itself in bowed porches, rutted roads and
the mumbled dreams of getting out.

Ignoring the rumble of the window air conditioner, she
peered through the glass and across the street. In a vacant lot,
three girls skipped rope. Two in sneakers and one barefoot.

Lennie fretted for the barefoot child because she had learned as a little girl that summer scorched all but the most calloused soles.

Coming from bone-cold Alaska, she'd managed to forget about the blistering temperatures in these hills. Every square inch sun-baked, heat seeped from the ground and fused with moisture flowing north from the Gulf of Mexico. The resulting humidity packed the power to banish laundry wrinkles from a clothesline like a preacher driving out the devil.

She mopped her forehead with a damp washcloth. Despite the overworked AC unit, her room was stifling, but she was beyond grateful to have it.

The shelter, a decommissioned World War II Army Supply Corps school, was surrounded by centuries-old oaks. Not exactly home, but at least a roof over her head. Somewhere to heal as she tried to work through things with Emily.

Three weeks of recuperation behind her, she had regained a toehold on life, tenuous as it was. Her job at A Likely Story Bookstore was the same one she'd had in high school, when she'd fled Mosely at seventeen. And she'd grown accustomed to the routine at the shelter.

As August neared its end, though, so did her allotted time there. That scared the bejesus out of her, because she had nowhere to go.

Lennie sat on a squeaky vinyl couch in Emily's office, her hair pulled into a ponytail through the back strap of a frayed ball cap from the *Trident Star*, the crab boat she'd worked out of Kodiak.

The couch faced her interrogator's chair, across a coffee table strewn with Dollar Store toys in an office outfitted with a mishmash of outlet furniture.

Her mind had wandered every which way during the last thirty minutes of Emily's probing, and a child's laughter drew Lennie's attention outside, where a gaggle of kids played in the shelter's dirt-patch play area as their young mothers kept an eye on them.

"Your mom died delivering you," Emily said.

Lennie continued to watch the children frolic, emotions crowding her chest. She responded with a vague nod.

"That must have been difficult to bear. Realizing the impact of that as you grew up."

Lennie hugged her knees to her chest in a protective ball. "When I was six or seven," she said, "I started to have dreams about drinking sweet mint tea with her on the back porch. Just the two of us. Little ceramic coffee mugs. Girl talk. Silly, right? I sometimes think about what ... about how life might have gone a different way, I guess."

"I ask because it seems to have fed a strained relationship with your dad."

There it was. The lynchpin of it all. "It's not strained." She rested her chin on her knees and stared at the empty space in front of her. "It's not *anything*."

As a girl, she could tell that Dad—a lifelong laborer at the Mosely Limestone Quarry—couldn't figure out what she needed as she stormed the waves of adolescence in search of deeper water.

Emily said, "Our relationships are interconnected. The struggle in your relationship with your father, and it would seem, your brother—"

"Look, I'm here because I messed up with Derrick. Can we just talk about that?"

"How did you mess up?"

"I told you. I said something that provoked him, and he went off."

She caught the young counselor studying her, flicking the corner of the stiff case folder beside her. Lennie heaved herself off the couch and began to pace. "That's a tremendous stress ball, Emily."

"We're just having a conversation."

"I mean the flicking. The file."

Emily stopped popping the corner of the folder. "Sorry."

Lennie was again drawn to the window where she watched a teen mom console a crying toddler who had fallen. She helped her daughter to stand, brushed her off and sent her on her way.

Lennie absorbed the tenderness of the moment before being swamped by memories of having had to rely solely on her own fighter's spirit to help herself up her whole life.

Emily's voice jarred her back into the room. "… won't cite the statistics about where this could very likely end, but I need to ask: do you have a healthcare directive?"

Her distracted mind shifting gears, Lennie turned from the window. "What?"

"A healthcare directive."

She tried to rub the tired from her face. "Stop. It's not—"

"You need to think about the measures you want, and don't want, to keep yourself alive."

"Seriously? You and your twenty-four years of experience in the ways'a the world are gonna try and scare me now?"

"It's not about scaring you. It's about you living your life with a sense of wholeness from this point forward. Not being afraid of it."

Lennie put her hands on the top of her head, fingers laced over her ball cap like an inmate being marched through the prison yard. "You're just a child," she muttered. "You can't fix me."

"Nobody can fix you. Except you. But you have to *want* to."

The muted children's laughter outside invaded her thoughts, yanking her back to a day with her father and older brother on their family driveway basketball court when she was twelve.

Their gravel driveway angled up from the crushed-rock street, leveling off at a concrete slab that served as Dad's beloved half-court. A pole-mounted backboard stood outside a kitchen door she could still hear slamming behind her. It had been her only common ground with Dad and Johnny, a hallowed family place where Dad had taught them how to play, insisting she not shoot "like a girl."

"None of those chest-heave shots," he used to drill into her. She swore she wasn't gonna shoot like a girl; she was gonna shoot like Lennie.

Emily said, "I'm suggesting you think about what you—"

"Placental abruption." Lennie scrubbed her lips with her hand, as if the outburst had burned them. Then she sank into the couch. Resting her elbows on her knees, she stared at her fingers as she incessantly intertwined and pulled them apart.

"I was seventeen." She closed her eyes, shook her head. *Say it.* Her eyes fluttered open. "There was a ... I got pregnant in high school and ... there was a—" She struggled with the word. "Complication."

She took a quivering breath. *Keep going.*

She could hear the nurse urging her to push. "The placenta ... it, um—" She licked the corners of her parched lips. Could feel the scratchy medical gown she wore at the clinic. "They said it detached from the uterine wall. I didn't ... I bled ... bad."

She exhaled. "The baby—" She squeezed her eyes tight, lost in the darkness behind her lids.

When she opened them, she had to fight to keep her voice from trembling. "I darkened Dad's door with a disgraceful pregnancy. That's what he said. He was so ... angry and ... crushed. Johnny was away at college. He never knew."

Clenching and relaxing her fists, she extended her fingers as wide as she could, as if warding off emotional rigor mortis. "I couldn't tell Dad who the father was because it would've put him and Johnny in danger."

Her bottom lip quivered, and her voice grew weaker with every word. "So, I ... I don't know. I ran. I didn't know what else to do." She backhanded a tear from her cheek, disappointed she had allowed it to breach her defenses.

As a teen, she'd been unable to grasp how frightening it would be out there on her own. The Bonneville's odometer had clicked off the loneliness as she roamed farther and farther west, working odd jobs to support herself, driven by a panic she kept well-hidden.

Her only chaperone had been the radio songs that spoke with the same heartbreak voice she heard inside. A voice that constantly reminded her of the enormity of her decision to run.

"I don't know if my baby had a chance to grow up. Never even had a chance to know the gender. Maybe he or she got in a car accident. Or cancer. Or might even be..." She couldn't bring herself to utter the word and took a moment to still her trembling voice.

"My child might not be alive for all I know." The hum of the air conditioner filled the room. "I still ... more than twenty years on, I haven't seen Dad. Haven't talked with him about the baby. Haven't tried to see him since I been back." She absorbed the weight of that in a crushing silence.

"And Johnny?" she said, lifting her hands. "He gave up on me long ago. Can't say as I blame him, I guess. But maybe, Dad and I ... my dream is we can get right with it one day. But, I can't ...

I mean, I'm so scared to finally know whether or not he can ever love me again after what I did." Her eyes rimmed with tears. "What if he can't, y'know? So, yeah ... I'm just ... and always will be, when it comes right down to it ... the shame of his life."

Emily handed her a box of tissue, and Lennie blew her nose. "God, look at me. What a mess."

The shelter counselor jotted a note on her pad. "Maybe you should reach out to him."

Lennie pushed her head back into the overstuffed couch pillow and stared at the ceiling, fumbling for a thought. When she felt Emily taking her measure, she gave her a sideways glance.

Emily tipped her head slightly and offered, "You could go see him."

Lennie sat forward, palms scrubbing her thighs as if trying to remove a stain. "I've seen him at the market, and I ... I just wig out and slip down another aisle. But I'll ... I know it's stupid, but I've watched him. I just stand there. Hiding. Watching him. He's gotta know I'm back as much as this town talks. He moved slower, like he was suddenly too old to be my Dad. That's as close as I've been able to get. I don't know if I can take that next—"

"You *can*." Emily's tone was one of iron-willed belief. "This constant cycle of abusive relationships ... they've endangered you physically and imprisoned you emotionally. You're depriving yourself of someone you very much love. And, I'll bet, depriving him, as well."

Lennie let the thought sink in. Slow-walked herself, tiptoeing up to the edge of a possible reunion.

She looked outside at the kids, currents of fear and bravery battling before a final rush of courage took her. "Okay." She nodded and slowly drew a breath. "Yeah ... Okay."

She had to tell him what happened. Had to hear his voice. Hug him for the first time in a lifetime.

She pictured her arrival at the old ridgeline house. Hearing her pull into the basketball driveway, he would come out of his backyard woodworking shop to glimpse who might be visiting. He'd pause, confused at first over what he was seeing: the old family station wagon she had left in. She'd step out. His face would drain of expression, then reshape itself into softer lines.

His eyes would well up, just like the secret she'd harbored all these years, and had even guarded from Emily. And the sound of her slamming the car door would set them walking toward each other to reclaim all that had been lost.

FIVE

Father-Daughter Reunion

A bead of sweat trickled down the middle of Lennie's back as she walked the five blocks from New Hope Shelter to the bookstore. She fluffed her hair to get some airflow on her neck, thankful she had chosen the light Camellia shift dress. She wanted to look especially good today—the day she would go see Dad.

Not even the heat radiating from the sidewalk could flatten the bounce in her step. She was finally able to go back to work reading to the kids at A Likely Story.

She might have been knocked down, but she had picked herself up and was now determined to hit the reset button on her life.

The prospect made her heart race with excitement, but when she thought about going to see him after work at the house where she grew up, her entire body tensed.

More than twenty years had passed since she left. She saw herself quietly packing in the middle of the night, remembered the way his shouts echoed in her head. The disgrace she'd brought to him, to the family. The whispers at church. Likely he assumed that was why she had gone.

As she headed west, though, her overriding need had been to avoid the question that would come up as surely as the sun rose over the horizon. *Who did this to you?*

With the passage of time, Lennie could see it through Dad's eyes. Under his roof, she had overstepped his boundaries of right and wrong. Maybe he'd never forgiven her for that. She had even tried to steel herself against the possibility he would tell her to stay the hell out of his life.

The August humidity glazed the historic square's shop windows with tendrils of condensation. Which, of course, meant blessedly cold air conditioning inside.

The bookstore's steeple bell rang the hour as Lennie arrived at nine a.m., averting her gaze from where she had slept in the station wagon a few weeks ago. The patch of oil-stained cobblestone glistened in the morning light, a stark reminder of how far she had come. And how far she still had to go.

She pulled open one of the towering double doors and it creaked on its original forged-iron hinges. The former church vestibule brimmed with 50-cent clearance paperbacks stacked on folding cafeteria tables. She dabbed perspiration from her face and neck and inhaled the musky aroma of old books, mingled with gardenia incense.

Making her way to the children's reading room, she heard the sound system's toe-tapping bluegrass music fill the cavernous space as early-bird shoppers browsed titles in various stages of aging: hardbacks, paperbacks, no backs at all.

Inside of ten minutes, she was sitting on an old milking stool, an oversized illustrated book perched on her knees as she read to a group of preschoolers gathered 'round.

She let her eyes flit from child to child, her story voice breathing life into their make-believe. The wonder in their eyes filled her with joy. There was fussy Priscilla, with her hair ribbons; Cutie Jacob, with his lazy eye drifting toward the Tennessee River when he looked up at her; and Sophie, with her darling little glasses.

The kids hung on every word, faces radiating awe as Lennie brought the tale's lumbering hippopotamus hero in for a smooth landing, reading, "... and Horatio the Hippo cried out, 'Of course I can fly home!'" She flapped the big book like a pair of wings. "'We all have wings that we can't see!' The End!"

The kids clapped, faces beaming—all except six-year-old Kacey, whose features crinkled with worry. "Will he make it home for sure, Miss Lennie? Will he *really* make it back to his mommy and daddy?"

"Of course he will, sweetheart," Lennie assured her. "What good are wings if you can't fly home with them?" She smiled at the little girl and closed the book.

Buzz-cut Bobby backhanded his runny nose. He apparently wasn't buying the far-fetched yarn. "Chickens have wings, but they can't fly home."

"That's why they get eaten!" said the boy next to him, laughing along with the roomful of rambunctious kids. So rambunctious, in fact, that Lennie barely heard the rapping on the glass separating the reading room from the retail space beyond.

Shelving the book, she looked over at Yolanda Simmons, a svelte African American woman. The two had been friends since meeting in the reading program when they were five. The current owner, Miss Bernie, had been their reader and plopped them on the floor together to foster friendships between the black kids and white kids in a town where the races barely tolerated each other.

Yolanda tapped with the store's cordless phone on the glass, then pointed to Lennie and palmed the mouthpiece. "It's your brother," she said through the sound-dampening partition window.

It took a second for the words to register. "John?" Lennie mumbled to herself. *How did he find out I came back?* She knew the Mosely grapevine stretched at least a country mile but had no idea the thing wound forty miles north to Knoxville.

She got up off the low-slung stool and met Yolanda in the doorway. Lennie took the phone. "Thanks." She pressed it to her ear. "Hello?"

"Hey, it's John."

"Okay," she replied, wariness creeping in. "How'd you know I was here?"

"I don't—" She heard the catch in his throat. "Lennie—" His voice trailed off and she looked down, trying to listen harder through the phone line because something seemed ... *off.* Her brother had always been hard to rattle.

"Dad died," he said as his lungs emptied into her ear. She kept blinking, the unthinkable sending shockwaves through her mind. Something deep inside rejected those two crushing words. *Dad. Died.*

Heat flushed her face and her legs weakened. She latched onto a bookcase to steady herself and slowly sank into a chair. She tried to say something, but there was only paralyzing blankness. Her scalp tingled, and she raked her fingers through her hair to try and make it stop.

"He's dead," John said in a thin and distant voice.

She shook her head at such an absurdity. "No, he's not." Hadn't she spied on him in the store just last week?

"He died, Lennie." John's words were measured and flat. "I was there."

She could see his face in the tone of his voice. But it wasn't his adult features she pictured. Instead, it was his desolate teenager's face, the last she had known of him, growing up on the ridge overlooking the railyard and the QuikCare.

A storm spun up inside her. Blew everything away. Past, present, future. It all collapsed into an emotional whirlpool that forced a single word from her mouth. "Johnny."

She knew his cobalt-blue eyes were closed, the dark lashes that all the high school girls used to like quivering as he concentrated on maintaining control. She knew he was choking back his hurt, just as Dad would've done.

She had a vague awareness of him continuing to string words together, explaining what happened in his methodical way, but it was just a droning in her peripheral senses.

Fleeting memories of Dad sparked like heat lightning in the clouds: her showing him a firefly she'd caught in a mason jar among the backyard pines ... him dropping her off with her lunch box on the first day of school ... the last sight of him as he sat reading his Bible in the light of the living room lamp the night she left.

" ... can you hear me?" John was saying. "Are you still there?"

"Yeah ... Yeah, I'm ... I'm here." She tried to swallow. "What do you—?" She held her jaw to keep it from shaking. "I mean, where? How?"

"I *just* told you." His voice was clipped with irritation. "I went down to Mosely to shoot some baskets with him at the house. Stevie and I. I left Knoxville—"

"Stevie?" Lennie cocked her head. She didn't recognize the name.

"My son."

She labored to concentrate on simply gathering information. "How did he—?" Lennie let the question die.

There was a pause on the other end. John's lips smack in her ear. "He collapsed ... doing that layup move he always did."

Layup move? Her frantic mind wrestled to pluck the basketball tidbit from her long-ago. And her childhood days on their driveway court crashed in. "The give'n'go one? With the bounce pass?"

"Yeah. Stevie bounced Dad the ball and he ... he drove to the basket and—" She heard him exhale into the phone. "He rose up ... and he ... he just came down."

Lennie drew her arms closer to her body and gripped the phone like it was a last-ditch handhold over a deadly pit.

"When?" She hardly recognized her own voice. Even during the darkest times on her own out in the world, she couldn't remember an instance it had ever sounded so lifeless.

"Yesterday afternoon."

Straightening in the chair, she raked the hair out of her face with her hand, squeezed it in a death grip, then turned it loose.

Her heart pulsed a rhythmic pressure in her ears as she stared at the nothingness in front of her. She lowered the phone, John's voice fading away from her. "Lennie, I think—"

She hung up. There would be no father. No daughter. No chance to set things right. To hope to know his love again.

Leaning forward, she placed the phone on the floor with her trembling hand and scooted it as far away as she possibly could with the toe of her rhinestone daisy sandal.

SIX

Undercurrents

He liked the feel of swiveling in his ergonomic chair as he positioned himself at his oak draftsman's table and settled his Italian leather wingtips on the footrest. After taking a sip of Perrier, John Riley twisted the barrel of his Swiss-made mechanical pencil to provide enough lead to complete his sketch of a mighty railroad truss bridge.

Nearly a mile in length, it was designed to cross the Mississippi River over in Memphis. Riley Engineering was a finalist bidder on the milestone project, which would be the most lucrative in company history. The personalized bridge elevation was John's finishing touch on the bid materials. Going the extra mile always impresses.

An accomplished structural engineer, he was well aware of the immutable breaking point of the 3mm pencil lead and knew he would exert the right amount of pressure to stay within its strength tolerance. It was simply a matter of applying the correct angle of attack.

He was still ticked off that Lennie had hung up on him four days ago—not only that she'd *done* it, but that he'd allowed himself to expect anything else from her. Of course she'd failed to listen as he struggled to explain what had happened, forcing him to repeat himself. Of course she mishandled the situation. She was Lennie.

As far back as he could recall, his sister had been undisciplined and lacked focus. Her entire take on the world was rooted in impulse. And he'd always had to be the responsible one. Dad had told him that Miss DeeDee, a gossipy cashier at the Mosely GasMart, had spotted Lennie filling up their old family station wagon a few weeks back. *What, and she couldn't call to let them know she was back?*

John had been forced to figure out how to get in touch with her; he had guessed that she might still be connected to that musty bookstore where she'd worked in high school. *And then she hangs up on me?*

He had handled all the funeral preparations, set for tomorrow. Sure, Lennie had called the day after she'd hung up. She wanted to help with the planning. Maybe he shouldn't have told her not to bother and curtly dismissed her.

At first he felt bad about that. But the more he thought about it, the more certain he was that excluding her from the arrangements wasn't his fault. You don't just vanish into the world and then suddenly show up and expect everybody to deal you back in. She *invited* exclusion.

A digital chirp from his desk phone broke his train of thought. "John?" a woman's voice said.

"Yes, Rachel." As he listened for what came next, he let his exasperation with Lennie dissipate.

"Mosely Monument wants to know if you'd like your dad's middle name or initial in the headstone engraving."

He rolled his mechanical pencil in his fingers and considered his executive assistant's question. He wasn't sure how to answer. *Middle name?* He didn't remember ever seeing or hearing a middle name. Not even an initial. A moment ticked by before he responded.

"Tell them I'll get back to them."

"Okay. They just need to know by next week." Another chirp ended the call.

He dragged his hand over the late-afternoon stubble on his jaw. His gears turned as he tried to piece together Dad's full name, a man who had scrimped and scraped to help him get where he was today. *And I don't even know if he has a middle name.*

Getting to his feet, John gazed out floor-to-ceiling windows from his perch on the twenty-fifth floor of the iconic First Tennessee Plaza, Knoxville's most prestigious corporate address.

He peered at his reflection in the glass. Even in this muted version of himself, he could see that the jade seersucker dress shirt nicely offset his slacks. His athletic, six-foot frame could be attributed to his commitment at the gym and a sensible diet. He'd inherited Dad's coal-black hair as well as his conviction that a man should expect as much from those around him as he did from himself.

His father had toiled in the quarry all his life, managing to claw his way to the position of a shift foreman after twenty years. He led a six-man crew and ultimately fought recurring respiratory issues from the dank and dust.

He wanted more for John and pinned all his hopes on his son to pursue an education and career that would do him proud. Later on, he pointed out the importance of surrounding himself with the right people. *Make sure you have a rock-solid team, son. If you want to play A-level ball, don't surround yourself with B-level players.*

As he turned from the window, he mused how Dad's advice had served him well. His achievements lined the walls: two master's degrees from the University of Tennessee, one in structural engineering and one in construction management; the Governor's Award for Outstanding Achievement in Business; gleaming aerial photographs of his commercial construction projects; the "cover boy" of *Forbes* magazine's regional edition as a "Southern CEO to Watch."

He was proud of how quickly he'd built Riley Engineering into one of the most successful firms in the Southeast, with satellite offices in Atlanta and Charlotte. No doubt, he had risen above his beginnings.

Still, an unsettled feeling made him shift on his feet. Why didn't he know Dad's middle name? He took in the panorama— the Tennessee River below, the Smokies whitewashed with clouds beyond. *Dad never had this view.*

Guilt seeped through him when he realized he'd never brought Dad up to Knoxville to see what he'd built standing on the old man's shoulders. Mosely had defined Dad's entire existence. In fact, the only time John could recall him venturing beyond its borders was to take him and Lennie on a trip when they were kids to see a Space Shuttle launch in Florida.

He wanted Mosely to know how much Dad had meant to him, so he had spared no expense for the funeral, right down to the eight-thousand-dollar mahogany casket and the seven-thousand-dollar upright family monument grave marker.

Enough distraction. Back to work. That's what Dad would want. The possibility of a lucrative contract was now within his grasp. He sat back down at his drafting table, determined to submit the winning bid to replace the aging bridge that spanned the Mississippi from Memphis, Tennessee, to West Memphis, Arkansas.

"We're in." Momentarily startled, he turned to see Kyle Barker, the firm's attorney, at the door wearing a linen suit, a bow tie and a smug grin. "Carson-Briggs just withdrew from the bridge project."

Kyle ceremoniously whipped a houndstooth kerchief from his breast pocket, removed his glasses, breathed on one of the lenses and cleaned it.

"What are you talking about?"

Kyle slipped his glasses back on and checked the tilt of his bow tie in his reflection off the top of a lighted glass display case John had bought in a jewelry store bankruptcy sale.

The case housed John's collection of vintage 35mm SLR cameras, all painstakingly arranged by year and technical capability on white, lint-free cloth. John was most proud of the first camera he owned as a boy: an unassuming Nikon F3, which sat in a place of honor at the center.

The attorney grinned. "I worked a little of my legal magic and found a minuscule breach of the specs in their bid." His voice squeaked the word *minuscule* like a cartoon mouse.

Knowing his college fraternity brother tended to exaggerate his feats—legal, sexual and otherwise—John rolled his eyes. "Yeah, right." He got back to work, checking his bid numbers.

"I'm serious," Kyle said. "They're out. Hello, Memphis!"

John set his mechanical pencil down and slowly swiveled to face him. "A breach? Don't mess with me, Kyle. This is too important."

The corporate lawyer shrugged and lifted his palms. "Hey, like I always say, 'Life's a breach.' This is for real."

John felt like belting out a victorious "Woot-woot!" but opted for a quieter response in the interest of professional decorum: a single fist-thud to his chest.

"*Yes!* Guess that's why I pay you too much. Wait ... How did you see a competitor's bid? They were all sealed."

"*That's* why you pay me too much," Kyle replied as he checked out two childish crayon drawings taped over John's drafting table:

a stick man held a massive bridge over his head, like Superman. A title was scribbled on one of them. *Daddy Builds Bridges!*

"The kids did those at school," John said, beaming inside.

"Cute. Too bad Daddy can't play racquetball worth a damn."

"Puh-leese. That was a lucky kill shot and you know it."

The lawyer made a big deal of replaying the disputed shot with an air-swing. "Kill shots are never lucky. Just deadly, bro."

John let the comment go. A winning bid was a moment to relish. He held out a fist. Kyle knuckled up, disappeared out the door and yelled, "You da man!" for the office to hear.

"And don't you forget it!" John hollered back.

He picked up the mechanical pencil and tapped it on his draftsman's table. But he couldn't concentrate. Dad had always relished hearing about John's wins, and he wanted to call him with the news of his business coup. Only he couldn't. Ever again. The realization left him numb.

He also couldn't escape a tightening sense of shame for not knowing something as personal as Dad's middle name. *If* he even had one.

He glanced at his railway bridge sketch. *C'mon, stay focused. He'd expect nothing else.*

Soon, he lost himself in the intersecting crossbeams, struts and braces atop massive pilings submerged in the Mississippi River, and something made him pause. What about the seasonal fluid dynamics of the underwater currents?

He decided to re-check his calculations.

SEVEN

Of This Earth

Thunderheads bruised the sky to the south as a rising wind agitated funeral flags on the cars lining up for a procession. Lennie didn't like the look of the gathering clouds.

Maybe the storm would pass them by. *This, too, shall pass.* She'd read that in a book of poetry by Edward FitzGerald, which she'd picked up for a dime at a sidewalk sale in Santa Fe, New Mexico, during her wandering years. She'd latched onto the notion, and its promise had seen her through a lot. But she wasn't so sure anymore.

She eased her car behind John's Lincoln Navigator. The thing looked big enough to push over a small house. She was number two in the winding snake of cars behind the black hearse leaving Mosely's First Baptist Church of Deliverance.

True to form, John had staked out the first position behind the Cadillac funeral coach by parking behind it before the service. His brawny SUV gleamed like polished onyx amid the rust of the local mourners' rambling wrecks.

Although she was certain her car had more miles than any of the town's fleet of beaters, she refused to lump it with theirs. The Bonneville Grand Safari wagon had been her constant companion for twenty-odd years, and she considered it a road-wise *grande dame*.

She squinted against the sun that reflected off John's smoked back window, coated with heat-reflecting film. AC's probably nice in there.

Her windows were all down, her air conditioning of the four-sixty variety: four windows down, sixty miles an hour. Sitting still was a surefire invitation to heat stroke.

Through her rearview, she reassured herself with a glance at the gaggle of purple helium balloons tied off in the back seat. They pushed against the roof of her car, looking as anxious as she was to find some relief. "C'mon," she muttered. "Let's get moving."

She wanted to look good on Dad's final day on this earth, but her tunic dress was beginning to cling. She blotted her face and neck with a hand towel, then fanned herself with a full-color program John had produced for the service.

The prayers that had been offered on Dad's behalf filled her mind. She gazed up through the windshield for a final glimpse of the white steeple rising above the rustic church. The family church. Not just the Rileys', but every family in town that was God-fearing. Which was all of them.

She wondered what kind of heavenly influence the First Baptist Church of Deliverance had, since the congregation's prayers were the closing arguments on Dad's behalf before the ultimate Judge. Pastor Fisk had led their fervent appeals for the Lord's mercy. Would God hear their pleas? When it came to answered prayers, she lugged an empty bucket. Maybe she wasn't worthy.

Still, she mouthed a silent prayer that God reunite Dad with Mom in heaven. She harbored no doubt that was where Mom had gone—you don't lay down your life for another and not find your mansion in paradise. She decided to tack on an extra little Godly ask for the congregation's good standing with the Almighty. After all, applying for admission was one thing, making the cut quite another.

The hearse began to move. Headlights snapped on. Lennie noticed there was no police escort to keep the procession together as in other places she'd lived. It had slipped her memory that the cars' lights were enough to signal others in these flinty foothills to pull over and let a soul pass. Mosely always yielded death the right of way.

She slowly rolled with the procession down Barnett Shoals Road, a stretch that undulated like ribbon candy. She glanced in her side-view mirror at shimmering headlights wavering in the heat curtain behind her.

The caravan came upon a long-abandoned Sinclair gas station, a two-pumper, its cracked green dinosaur sign the last vestige of what once was. Gas and snacks had been replaced by a roadside stand where folks sold fruit, vegetables and boiled peanuts.

The old filling station took her back to when it had been a stop for a roving woodcarver up from Louisiana. He'd passed through selling his handmade art when she'd been in that curious slot between her fifteenth and sixteenth birthdays. She could still hear his creaking pickup pulling a trailer full of wooden gators, eagles, and bears he'd carved from cypress with chainsaws. He wasn't much older than her, maybe nineteen.

She'd spent two summers earning pocket money by sweeping wood chunks and sawdust for him. That allowed her to buy her first CD from the station's spinning display rack: Bonnie Raitt's *Longing in Their Hearts.*

She took to her own heart a yearning song called *Dimming of the Day.* She'd been so inspired by her new singing-poet hero that she saved enough to buy a buzzy acoustic guitar from the pawn shop and dreamed of seeing Miss Bonnie at the Grand Ole Opry in Nashville, though she knew that would never happen.

The woodcarver was a hero of sorts as well—she was awed by the creatures he could coax from a misshapen stub of tree, and that something as lethal as a chainsaw could express such hidden beauty.

But she was most intrigued by a beat up acoustic guitar he toted around. When he said he was a Delta blues man, she told him she wanted to be a blues musician like Miss Bonnie.

"Girl," he replied, "you gotta suffer to sing the blues." When she reminded him she was stuck in Mosely, he winced and said, sure enough, that would qualify.

One day he showed her how to carve a little bit, letting her handle his small Stihl with the sixteen-inch cutting bar. He had put his powerful arms around her from behind to show her how to grip and control the roaring saw, his husky voice in her ear.

That was when Boone Mosely, who may have been Officer Mosely's father or uncle for all she knew, had come racing across the neighboring field in a cloud of hay dust on his dirt bike while she was sweeping up.

Boone and his sandy blond hair, blown all wild. His renegade teen bluster drove the girls crazy—almost as much as his Brad Pitt chin scruff. Plus, his dad, Jackson Travis Mosely, owned the town and, for all practical purposes, owned Dad, who worked the Mosely Limestone Company pit.

With all their business entities and companies, the Moselys, under J.T. Mosely's watch, had created a tangled empire. Not even someone with the legal smarts of Atticus Finch could fathom the strands and cross-strands in such a huge web.

Straddling his motorcycle in tight Wranglers, legs splayed like the bike was an extension of his manhood, Boone pulled a can of beer from his boot and made a show of slugging off it.

Lennie caught him looking down her shirt while she was bent over sweeping. Next thing she knew, he was jawing about how the carver was just a bayou perv trying to get in her pants. Boone followed that up by bragging that he'd been voted best kisser by the girls in his Mosely High class, two years ahead of hers.

"I'll show you how to do it," he said with a wink. "Tongues an' all. Git you so hot you'll wanna give it all up to me."

She froze. She'd never kissed a boy before. Was it a slippery slope to the devil's playground? She stumbled over what to say. So she lied.

"You don't have to show me. I already know."

"What, that perv slippin' you the tongue?"

"He's not a perv. You're just jealous 'cause he can do something you can't, no matter how much money your daddy has."

Boone had guzzled his beer and smirked. "I don't need to run a chainsaw, girl. I'll run the guys who run the chainsaws."

Lennie's mental detour came to a screeching halt, just like her tires; she suddenly jammed the brakes to avoid slamming into the back of John's slowing Lincoln at the cemetery entrance.

A child's face, obscured by the inky window, looked at her from the rear hatch glass. The silhouetted head didn't have curls like the little girl she'd seen with John and his wife in church, so it had to be Stevie, his boy. He pressed his small hand against the glass and slowly waved it back and forth. Hello. Lennie found it adorable and gave him a little wave back.

She parked under giant oaks which she imagined had witnessed every burial here since before the Civil War.

She knew the cemetery well; she would walk to visit Mom's grave by herself when she was a kid, leaving behind fistfuls of roadside wildflowers and apologies for taking her life. Dad, too, used to visit the grave with little gifts. He always went on the anniversary of Mom's death before bringing home a bouquet of purple helium balloons for Lennie's birthday.

A wave of anxiety tightened her lips as she checked her makeup in the rearview. The church service hadn't invited conversation. But here, out in the open, questions could be asked, lives pried into. And she couldn't look like her face was melting off.

She reminded herself that she had every right to be here. No matter how long she'd been gone. No matter that John had shut her out of the arrangements. No matter the looks she got from those who counted themselves among the righteous.

She grabbed the balloons from the back seat and followed other mourners up a rise to the gravesite.

The sight of Mom's headstone near the head of Dad's plot distracted her from Pastor Fisk's prayer. Roselyn Delia Riley, Beloved Wife and Mother. Her gaze was drawn to the praying hands carved in relief over Mom's name.

Even though it seemed Lennie's prayers had long been forsaken, she'd gotten down on her knees at her shelter bed and prayed for a healing, heart-to-heart with Dad. His death felt like God's cruelest-ever rebuke.

She glanced at John, who stood stone-faced with his family on the other side of Dad's polished mahogany casket. Jowly men in dark suits surrounded her, along with women in their Sunday dresses, hair done up in intricate weaves that added a solemn weight to their faces.

She knew she looked as if she didn't belong, what with her flowy tunic dress of abstract orange and yellow, a clutch of purple balloons dancing over her like thought bubbles.

Raindrops hitting her face brought her back to the pastor's prayer: " ... and so, we ask you, Lord, to free Benjamin from his earthly shackles and allow him to join his precious Roselyn in your heavenly kingdom, until reunited with their beloved children, John and—" When he stopped, so did Lennie's heart. God's stand-in looked at her with uncertain eyes.

"Lennie," she said.

Pastor Fisk repeated her name to the mourners. "In Your name we pray."

Lennie turned her purple helium balloons loose, murmured "Amens" escorting them up into the drizzle.

She noticed Stevie watching their every move as gusts of wind took them this way and that. Others, too, seemed drawn to their flight. But John only gave her a withering stare. As she stared right back, she realized they were the last of their generation.

The rain had let up, but gusty winds rippled through the trees as Lennie walked with others making their way back to their cars. Aging men tugged at tie knots while the women cautiously worked their way down the slick grassy rise in their church shoes.

She saw John unlock his SUV at the bottom of the rise. He hurried to load his kids, then pulled open the driver door. Rushing to get to him, she became jarringly aware of how dry her mouth was.

"You did real nice with the eulogy at church," she said as she came up from behind.

Tugging his jacket off, he turned on her and flung it into the back seat. "It was his funeral, for God's sake. And you show up looking like some kind of ... what? Gypsy nomad? Farmers- market fashion and balloons? Really? Show some respect."

Lennie saw the girl in the back seat, oh so proper in her black funeral outfit. She looked to be about twelve, and her expression gave nothing away as she locked eyes with Lennie. The boy, Stevie, joined the watch party, craning his neck to see. He looked seven or eight, dressed like a little yachtsman in a navy suit, wheat-colored hair swept back with gel. His eyes crinkled when he gave her an impish grin.

"John," Lennie said, "if I could—"

"No. We're not doing this here."

Lennie lifted her hands, palms skyward, then dropped them. "What was I thinking? Hoping for some polite conversation. As in, 'Nice to see you, Lennie.' Or, hey, here's an oldie but goodie: 'How long's it been?'"

John slid behind the wheel, slammed the door and started the engine as the woman he was with suddenly made her way around the front of the vehicle. She was leggy, with country club curves and a cascade of blonde curls, undeniably gorgeous in her mourning attire.

Lennie wasn't expecting the woman's insistent hug. She stood stiffly in the embrace, arms pinned to her sides.

"I'm John's wife, Holly." She added an extra-friendly squeeze and pulled Lennie's face to her neck. "He's really not like that. He's just hurting."

Her amber fragrance was overwhelming. "Yeah, I hear that's going around."

Holly turned her loose but held onto her hands. John leaned on the horn, and his wife gave Lennie a mannered grin that communicated both pain and support. "You're coming to Dad's house, right? For the reception?"

Lennie regarded the impenetrable black window separating her from her brother. "Is that what's next on his program?" She hadn't meant to sound so snippy.

"He's a planner. It's how he copes with ... well, everything. Nothing to chance. You understand, right?"

"I know where the hang-ups are hung, if that's what you mean."

Holly looked at her for a long moment. "He won't admit it, but he needs you right now. Do you remember the way there? Do you want to follow us?"

"No."

"Please." Holly gave Lennie's hands a farewell squeeze and Lennie watched her join her family. Then John zoomed off, his kids gazing at her through the window. As the SUV receded among the rise and fall of the cemetery's rolling grounds, her vision clouded with a press of tears she held back.

"For your information, Daddy loved those purple balloons! You don't know every damn thing!"

She turned and walked toward her car, and her heart sank as a groundskeeper lowered Dad into the earth. And with him, her hope.

EIGHT

A Home Divided

It was the same scrappy neighborhood she remembered. Scattered 1960s houses built amid old-growth forest. Lennie parked among other cars angled willy-nilly along the street. She sat for a moment, a stone's throw from her childhood home. The house where Dad had lived. And died. In a way, the house where she had lived and died, too.

The cracked vinyl siding was patched with sun-dried caulk that had splintered like varicose veins. Not much else had seemed to age. She wondered if that was because everything had already looked so old to begin with.

The melodic tinkling of the wind chime on the back porch carried her back to her girlhood bedroom overlooking the porch and the backyard.

She could feel the soft single bed where she'd sit strumming her acoustic guitar as raindrops the size of silver dollars pounded the porch's tin roof outside. Could practically touch the sea of loose-leaf poetry that always surrounded her, scribbled pages spread on the patchwork quilt as she tried to twist her words and a few clangy chords into songs.

As she approached the house, her feet crunched the crushed-rock road that overlooked the railyard below. She passed the driveway basketball court where Dad had taught her and John to play as kids. The pavement rose toward an encroaching magnolia tree she had planted as a sapling.

The gate in the chain-link fence leading to the backyard squealed as she pushed through. In the yard, a curtain of kudzu vine descended from towering sweetgum and loblolly pine to form a giant elfin cap over Dad's beloved woodworking shop.

She pictured him standing amid shafts of sunlight that streamed through the windows of his "craftsman's chapel" as he called it, the light alive with fine sawdust from his stirrings. He'd spend hours in the shop, finally emerging at dusk with the fine, golden flakes etching the folds of his ruddy face, burnished by decades of limestone quarry work in winter freeze and summer heat.

Lennie had heard the story of how he'd traded his school-books for a shovel at thirteen to help support his mom. That was after his dad had died from tuberculosis contracted in the Mosely limestone pit. Like his father before him, Dad had worked his way up to shift foreman.

But the woodworking shop had been his heaven on earth. The aroma of freshly cut wood. The comforting layer of sawdust underfoot. Table saws, vintage planes, a tilt-top router to cut custom chamfers and angles. Lennie had never been interested in woodworking. The shop had been John's place for special time with Dad.

The wind chime drew her around back, and she entered the house through the porch door. It smelled a little musty, with a hint of aftershave she recognized as Dad's Aqua Velva. She forced herself to weave through the people who had gathered, mostly his friends, neighbors or former work buddies.

The afternoon of refreshments and remembrances passed pleasantly enough, although she and John didn't speak a word— he seemed to be working the room with polished three-minute conversation skills that conveyed warmth and sincerity, flashing that smile of his.

He certainly seemed to have it all. The family. The fancy suit. The money to afford enough roses for the church service to make the Kentucky Derby jealous. And he looked good, too. Healthy. Happy. She tried to be glad for him.

Lennie sipped sweet tea, hoping to find a measure of familiar comfort for herself and others in attendance as she circled the parlor; it felt safer to stick to the periphery now. When she stopped at Dad's old-fashioned armchair, she pictured him there with a newspaper or Bible on his lap.

A burgundy scrapbook wrapped in a clear dust cover lay within easy reach. She made out the title in small sticky-back mailbox letters: SPACE SHUTTLE TRIP. Lennie inhaled sharply, knowing what souvenirs the spiral-bound album likely held of their only family vacation.

Settling into Dad's time-worn impression in the chair, she carefully put down her cup and then slid the scrapbook toward her.

A faded Polaroid photograph appeared on the first page. In front of a Tennessee motel, all three of them smiled for the camera, her eight-year-old self in her best Sunday dress. She held her father's hand, her eyes alight with anticipation. It had been her first time out of town.

Lennie closed the album and returned it to the shelf. Maybe Dad had gone through it recently, reminiscing about the trip they had taken together. She had no desire to see more. Too many years and too much hardship loomed between then and now.

On her feet again, she gazed at some old photos on the fireplace mantel. Sprinkled among them were Dad's cherished model rockets, the result of his fascination with space flight. They had been proudly displayed above the fireplace for as long as she could remember.

A photo of toddler John caught her eye. He sat on the couch, hugging Lennie from behind when she was just an infant, a corrective leather shoe pressuring her right foot to turn outward, into proper alignment. That foot still pained her occasionally.

She remembered the day her brother had left for the University of Tennessee, which had set all his wheels to glory in motion. The memory had become tougher to swallow through the years as she came to realize that her hopes, her dreams, had been sacrificed to launch John's life.

He'd cashed in every last chip Dad had to secure a successful future for himself—from the favors Dad's boss, J.T. Mosely, called in to get John accepted at UT in the first place, to the savings Dad had emptied to help pay his way, to the money Mr. Mosely put up for John's schooling when Dad's ran out.

With a railroad and limestone mining dynasty seven generations in the making, the Moselys controlled virtually everything that made money, paid a wage, or exerted authority in the western midsection of the Smokies. Cross them, and folks had been known to be blacklisted from jobs, loans, the church council, even plots at the cemetery.

All the doors were opened for John and—

"You're Daddy's sister." Lennie startled and looked down to her left. John's daughter stood, one hand on her hip, the other holding a can of *Barq's* root beer. She wore a black dress with scalloped sleeves and matching hair ribbon, and her pixie hair, the color of fudge, framed cobalt blue eyes.

Lennie couldn't help but feel she was looking into John's eyes when he was a boy. She offered the girl a smile. "Did you figure that out all by yourself?"

"As if it was hard to," she replied in a tone that implied she was already bored with their conversation.

Lennie sipped her tea. *Girl's got some pluck.* "My name's Lennie. What's yours?"

"That's not a girl's name."

"It's short for Eleanor. Eleanor Grace. Your Grampa Riley nicknamed me Lennie."

"I see. But he wasn't Grampa. He was Pawpaw."

"Oh." Lennie was a stranger to her own family. Maybe she could change that. "Y'know, in a conversation, it's polite to tell the other person your name."

"Abbey. That's short for Abigail Delia Riley. I'm ten in age and thirteen in smart years, according to all the tests. Where have you been?"

"Excuse me?"

"Daddy said you've been gone a long time. Where did you go?"

Lennie began to grow irritated with the little darling's intrusive attitude, a spitting image of Johnny at that age. He'd always been smart and lorded it over anyone who would allow him to.

"Well, *Abbey,*" she informed the girl with a forced grin, "I've been back for a little bit. Let's just say that."

"We can say that, but you didn't answer my question."

"I went exploring."

"Why?" the miniature prosecutor in the satin mourning dress shot back quick as a bullet.

"To see what was there."

"There *where?*"

"What's the opposite of here?" Lennie watched a response come together on Abbey's face.

"There," the girl conceded with an inflection that suggested Lennie had done well in fending off her verbal parries.

Lennie held up her hand for a slap. "High-five. You just graduated to fourteen." Abbey didn't make a move, calculating eyes ping-ponging from Lennie's face to her raised palm.

The impasse was broken when Abbey's kid brother walked up, tugging uncomfortably at the little suit vest he still wore, the eight-year-old's lips ablaze with red fruit-juice stains.

"Hey!" he said, high-fiving Lennie's offered hand with a grin. It mattered not a stitch that the hand wasn't intended for him. "You're the balloon lady."

Abbey rolled her eyes. "Duh, Sherlock."

She studied Lennie's colorful tunic dress, accented with an embroidered trim of metal beads, and she seemed genuinely perplexed. Words suddenly burst from her like steam from a boiling kettle. "Daddy said his sister needed help dressing for Pawpaw's funeral."

Lennie nearly spat up the tea she was sipping.

The boy laughed. "Eww, cool!"

"Later he scolded you for the way you're dressed," Abbey said. "That's how I know you're his sister. It's called deductive reasoning."

Lennie cocked her head. Did she hear that right? "Your Daddy said I needed help *dressing*?"

"Repeatedly," Abbey affirmed, underscoring her certainty by pretending to press an answer button with her bossy index finger.

"Well," Lennie informed her, "a girl has the right to do things her own way."

John's daughter counted off the exceptions with her fingers: "Unless it involves running with scissors, jumping off a bridge because everybody else is doing it, or trying to bounce your friend off the trampoline."

"Or sticking junk up your nose," the little guy added.

"I think she gets the point," Abbey said. "Now, if you'll excuse me, I wish to refresh my root beer. Perhaps we'll chat again. We can discuss your wardrobe choices."

Before Lennie could say a word, Abbey spun on her glossy black patent leather heel and marched off, her funeral dress twitching across the backs of her knees.

"Gracious," Lennie said, feeling more amused than off-put. "That peach didn't fall far from the tree."

The boy gazed up at her. "You're kinda weird. I like it."

She extended her hand. "My name's Lennie."

"Stevie," he said and shook her hand.

"Whaddaya think, Stevie? She gonna be a lawyer?"

"Tell me about it." He let out a heavy sigh. "Nobody said eight was going to be like this. It's like I'm in hell, but without the flames."

She immediately fell in love with the little guy as he gazed up at Dad's model rockets. She lifted one down. "You like rockets?" He nodded and took it from her, and a thought jumped into her head.

"Will you do me a favor, Stevie?"

She retrieved Dad's scrapbook and handed it to him. "Give this to your father for me?" Maybe memories of that long-ago road trip would help John to deal with his loss.

"Is that *it*?" He sounded disappointed as he tucked the album under one arm while holding onto the model rocket.

"No." She took down another rocket and gave it to him. "I think Grampa, I mean, Pawpaw, would've wanted you to have these. To take care of."

Stevie's eyes lit up. He glanced back over his shoulder as if to ensure his sister wasn't within earshot. "I think the balloons were the coolest part all day."

"Thank you."

He gave her a little kid smile powerful enough to conquer the most profound grief, if only for a moment.

As the gathering wound down, Lennie recognized three older women helping to clean up: the church flower ladies from her childhood. Miss DeeDee, Miss Lydia, and Miss ... *What was her name?* ... Mary. Miss Mary.

She had named them the Jesus Jasmines when she was ten, a point in her life when she took to renaming things according to how she saw them. Now, time had bent the bodies of these elderly women like flowers deprived of rain.

In younger years, Lennie had often contemplated whether Mom would have been a Jesus Jasmine, had she survived. And Lennie had regularly dreamt of her. They'd always meet on the back porch. One night, Mom visited her dream world as one of the flower ladies, and they had gone to pretty-up the church together.

In the next night's dream, they sipped sweet tea from sweating porcelain cups after clearing up the supper dishes. Just the two of them. Talking. Laughing. Sharing secret hopes and dreams.

That dream, and those that followed, had seemed so real. Complete with fireflies and a humid twilight filled with the hum of a weary window air conditioner that dripped water into a rust-stained porch bowl. Everything was so vividly *there*.

Lennie would push off the porch slats with her feet, her toenails painted with her favorite purple polish, and she and Mom would totter in Dad's handmade spindle-back rockers.

Lennie took to calling these back-porch dream visits their *After Supper Club*. It was an exclusive membership: just the two of them. It was so very magical. Until she'd wake up and realize it wasn't true, no matter how much she wished or how hard she prayed.

At that point, she'd lay curled in her bed, listening to the trains and thinking about what it would be like to have a Mom like everybody else. What did they talk about? Or do together? Lennie promised herself at twelve that, one day, she and her daughter would talk all the time.

But she'd been forced to leave all that childish thinking behind as the years unfurled and had long ago stopped wondering what it would be like to hear the word "Mom" from a child's lips.

NINE

Slipping Away

D ad's bedroom. From next to the bed, John surveyed backyard trees that shaded this side of the house and created a
mottled darkness, weak sunlight filtering through the cur-
tains. He put the scrapbook Stevie had given him on the bed. For
a few moments, he just stood in the stillness, absorbing the eve-
ryday that Dad had left behind, half expecting to hear his voice
from down the hallway.

A stack of bills waiting to be paid sat on a small desk in the
corner. Empty slippers bedside. A Bible on his nightstand. A
half-empty glass of water. An unfinished birthday card for Stevie.

He clicked on the nightstand's lamp. The light bleached the
dusty green walls, washing over a framed newspaper article from
the *Mosely Times Weekly* on the wall.

He stepped closer for a better look at the photo in the yellow-
ing article: Lennie and him in baggy green and gold Mosely High
School basketball uniforms. Dad stood between them, arms
proudly draped over their shoulders. The headline read: "Historic

State First: Girl Lennie Riley Cracks Starting Lineup on Boys' High School Hoop Squad."

"Yep," he murmured. "Never saw that coming." The squeaking of basketball sneakers on the hardwood court in the Mosely High gym echoed in his mind as the bedroom's pinewood floor creaked underfoot on his approach to Dad's closet.

When he ventured into the enclosure, a small metal object bounced off his forehead and swung like a murky pendulum in the shadows. He tugged on the binder clip suspended from a string and a bare bulb flared overhead. Index cards dangled from hangers holding Dad's church slacks and shirts, each marked with the date he last wore the piece and when he had last laundered it.

John fingered through the hangers and checked the stringed cards for the dates of last use. He found a shirt Dad had worn the day before he died and pulled it to his nose. He closed his eyes and inhaled Dad's fading essence.

Looking down, he saw a stack of Johnny Cash albums in a box next to Dad's shoe rack. Everything so neat and orderly, just like his life. His throat tightened and his eyes began to sting as he fought like hell not to cry. He stepped out of the closet and pulled the door closed.

To fend off encroaching despair, he turned to the rickety vinyl scrapbook on the bed and studied the cover lettering: SPACE SHUTTLE TRIP. Happier times.

He turned the album over in his hands with a reverence typically reserved for a delicate archival classic. Thick pages crackled with age as he eased it open to the cover sheet. It was titled in block letters—

TENNESSEE.

Memories swarmed at the sight of Dad, Lennie and him in front of the mid-century Chattanooga Choo Choo Motel. Its brassy orange and sunbeam-yellow colors offered a splash of

1950s eye candy, although the lighted sign of a small-scale, 1850s steam locomotive was slightly out of focus.

John flashed to an image of the old man at the motel who had agreed to take that picture with the first camera John had ever owned. All these years later, he still remembered being crushed when the guy dropped his prized possession, breaking the film advance lever, along with his heart. It was the only photo they had of the entire trip.

On the next page were his and Lennie's crayon placemats from the Huddle House diner. He couldn't help noticing the contrast between his considered, ten-year-old approach to coloring barnyard cows and chickens and little Lennie's eruption of color and improvisation all over the place, regardless of the lines.

He turned the page to—

GEORGIA.

Taped there were three postcards from the rollicking "Six Flags Over Georgia" theme park, west of Atlanta. The topsy-turvy Mind Bender rollercoaster. The Dahlonega Mine Train, rip-roaring through the wilderness. The howls of family fun on the Log Jamboree water flume rattled his mind as he flipped to the following page—

FLORIDA.

Souvenir postcards from Cape Canaveral and the official NASA photo of the Space Shuttle came into view. The latter brought back the tightness in his chest which he had felt as the rocket rose on a column of smoke and fire. He gently closed the scrapbook, lost in the memory of the family's one and only vacation.

What had Dad been, early thirties? Mr. Mosely had just given him a raise at the quarry, so he bought a used Pontiac Bonneville Safari station wagon—big enough to haul kids *and* wood in the days before station wagons were replaced by the minivan.

Eager to put the car through its paces, Dad had announced a three-day weekend trek along the back roads of their Southern homeland. They were to stop along the way at a few tourist spots enroute to the grand finale: a Space Shuttle launch at Florida's Cape Canaveral.

John spied the bent corner of a piece of loose-leaf paper peeking from the back of the album. He pulled it out and unfolded a note Dad had penned. Seeing the handwriting somehow brought him closer.

As he read the letter, a disquieting feeling settled over him. He knew even less about the man who had meant so much to him than he thought he did.

TEN

Wooden Heart

Lennie ran her hands over the back of a spindle rocking chair Dad had made. The worn armrest reminded her of the countless hours she'd spent in it—the same rocker she sat in during her recurring *After Supper Club* dreams with Mom. She had never said all that much. It had taken Lennie a while to figure out Mom must have enjoyed hearing her little girl talk.

She breathed in the stillness of the back porch as dusk filtered through the canopy of hardwoods and pine. She peered through the trees at Dad's woodworking shop and frowned when she saw the door. He had harvested the wood from the Appalachians to build the shop himself, and he kept a lot of tools inside. He'd always locked it tighter than Fort Knox.

A time-trampled footpath through the trees led her to the shop. At a workbench that jutted from the wall, John stood with his back to her. As a boy, he'd spent a lot of time in here with Dad. She knew he felt at home with the simple order of well-maintained tools and organized bins that brimmed with dowels and hinges and clasps and nails.

John and Dad had formed a bond over precision measures, straight lines and true corners. She was certain Dad's emphasis on the importance of exactness had sparked John's interest in engineering.

John's starched white shirt and slate slacks, however, were a stark contrast to Dad's shop clothes: a worn leather apron over a Dickie's work shirt and trousers that ended at red high-top Converse All-Stars, his favorite basketball sneakers.

John surveyed precision chisels, wood clamps and an army of glue bottles lined in height order as if awaiting a call to duty. Behind him, she shifted on her feet, still weighed down by the funeral. *Jump in and say something.* Oddly, a stern scolding felt right.

"Either put the tools back where they belong ..."

He didn't even flinch when he finished her sentence: "Or keep outta the dadgum shop."

Lennie tucked her hair behind her ear as the rule Dad had drilled into them as kids flitted through her mind. Try as she might, though, she couldn't recall the sound of his voice.

She contemplated the remnants of his woodworking life. A child's rocking horse, half finished. A couple of cribs. A spindle rocker and matching bassinet. Kitchen crosses and angel figurines that had always been top sellers at the bookstore. The makings of a grandfather clock, the body cavity completed, its time-keeping soul still missing.

John half-turned toward her. "Sorry about earlier." He sounded exhausted.

"Don't worry about it." She gazed up at milled lengths of wood stored in the exposed rafters. "We're all kinda weirded out. Leastways, I am."

She waited for him to respond, maybe work through this together, but he seemed more interested in the row of supply bins he had moved to, inspecting them as if something meaningful were to be found.

She eyed a shuffle of sawdust footprints, and her gut told her they were some of Dad's last.

John cleared his throat. "Writing the eulogy was just ... I mean ... how do you capture a lifetime in eight-and-a-half minutes?"

"I don't know, Johnny. I figured maybe he shared some of that with you in the cards you might'a gotten from him through the years. Birthdays. Christmas. Holiday gatherings?"

"Those tailed off." He palmed a partially formed angel figurine and finally looked at her. "It's just been nothing but work. Or soccer with the kids. T-ball. All the ... stuff."

"They're beautiful children. Spirited."

"I should've been coming down here more instead."

She eased next to him as he grabbed a nail and began to dig into the workbench with it. "Maybe you should've written the eulogy," he said. "You were the poet, right?"

"But you always won the penmanship award."

He peered outside at the dying light in the trees. "They said it was an aneurysm."

She clenched her lips between her teeth and nodded as she ingested the cause of Dad's death. It couldn't have sounded any colder.

He hollowed out a hole with the nail. "Acute. Aortic. Aneurysmal. Rupture." He spoke the words as if they were burned into his memory. "And just like that, he's gone."

Gone. The gut punch of finality caught Lennie off guard. She exhaled sharply as if trying to expel the notion.

"Your being there at the end was surely a blessing to him," she said. "He was always so proud of you."

John stared straight ahead, silent in the light from a naked bulb overhead that illuminated fine specks of dust swirling the glow around him.

Something she'd wondered for years suddenly sprang into her mind. "Did he ever say anything about me?"

She thought she saw him shake his head. "He worried about you, but ... as time went on, and you stayed away, he didn't want to interfere. You had clearly gone your own way. You know Dad. He kept things to himself."

He stopped digging at the workbench and turned to face her. "He died in my arms."

A wisp of connection fluttered inside her as she held his gaze. "I'm so sorry." He barely nodded before he stepped around her and left.

She rubbed her eyes and breathed in deeply through her nose. As she dragged her hands down her cheeks, something caught her peripheral vision—a dark spot in an otherwise golden scattering of sawdust on the plank wood floor.

Over by the window, something lay half-buried in the floor's sawdust. She heard a basketball begin to bounce out on the driveway court as she moved closer for a better look. What she could see resembled a chocolate crescent moon. She dropped to her knees and gently cleared the tiny wood shavings away from the object, like the time she'd unearthed a Cherokee arrowhead from the bank of Chickamauga Lake.

A carved heart made of walnut emerged, about the size of a pocket watch. *Lennie* was wood-burned into it with cursive letter strokes she instantly recognized as Dad's.

Her face flushed with warmth as she fingered the fine wood grain, from the cleaved top where the opposing halves met, down the graceful sides that curved to a point at the bottom.

She gazed up at Dad's wood-burning tool in its coiled metal holder on the window ledge. Most likely one of the last things he ever touched.

Lost in the flow of the lettering scorched into the rich wood, she became aware of the basketball continuing to bounce out in the driveway.

With a sigh that seemed to evaporate into the stillness around her, she slipped Dad's heart into her pocket.

Fall 1988

Dear Momma,

I turned ten today. We went to the Walmart in Sweetwater and I got a Totally Me Beads & Baubles kit so I can make my own ankle bracelets. We marked how tall I was in the kitchen where Daddy's been measuring us. I am four feet, five inches. Johnny's mark at my age is four feet, eight. Big woop.

I asked Daddy to put eleven candles on my cake after he visited you. I told him and Johnny I'm naming the extra one my Momma Candle.

Daddy said no and got real quiet. But I told him I wasn't gonna make a wish and blow the candles out then. So he did it. I just wanted to remember what you did for me! Johnny looked at me all weird like I did something wrong. He does that a lot.

I know you're not supposed to say what you wish for, but I tell you everything. Why stop, now that I'm older? I wished that you are happy and have everything you need in heaven.

Here is my new poem ...

"Ankle Bracelet" by Lennie Riley, age 10

A colorful weave above my foot, my ugly shoe long gone.
My toes, how they hurt sometimes, but I walk on and on.
Thoughts of you, a missing joy, I'll hold you deep 4-ever.
And with this birthday poem for you, I'll forget you never.

Good night.
Luv,
Me

ELEVEN

Words Unspoken

Lennie watched the dusty orange basketball spin against the backdrop of a gray sky that was somehow illuminated by the retreating sun. Her shot caught the edge of the hoop on the driveway court and the ball bounced to John, who dribbled around, then tossed it up as the buzz of a distant dirt bike grated the air.

She'd found him out here after he left the workshop. The magnolia she had planted as a girl rose majestically behind the backboard, the broadleaf tree summoning a sense of déjà vu—she'd grown up on this court, her only real connection to John and Dad.

Their father would run them through drills from a coaching book he'd picked up with all the finer points of the game. She always competed as hard as she could against her brother; that was how she developed the skills to play with the boys at school.

She could still hear the boys on the other teams snicker when she took the court. But as soon as she blew by them with a crossover dribble, or hit a jumper, they stopped. From age seven to seventeen, a pebbled Spalding basketball gave her a solid link to Dad and John, who just now sank a free throw.

"You interested in his Johnny Cash albums?" he asked as Lennie grabbed the ball and spun it up into the basket.

"God, remember how he played those over and over and over?"

John dribbled away. "Every note."

"And every word," she added. "J-Cash could rock a story. I'd love to have 'em."

He flipped the ball out in front of himself with a backspin—it struck the driveway and zipped back to him. "So, what's going on in Lennie World these days?" It sounded like an obligatory afterthought.

She passed her fingers over the walnut heart in her pocket. "Don't ask if you don't want to know."

John stepped forward and back with his dribble as if he were about to bolt for the basket. "Just being polite."

"Strangers stuck on an elevator are polite. But you don't really want to know."

He raked her with his eyes. "Hey, don't get pissed at me. You're the one who took off."

Lennie waited a fraction of a second for his accusation to lose its sting. She had known he wouldn't understand her need to leave or why she stayed away. Not being able to explain had bothered her for a long time. Not that John had made it possible, being the way he was.

"And that matters to you *how?* Nothing ever seemed to faze you. You and Dad both. With both y'all bottled up, the three of us got tied in knots that cinched tighter the more we pulled at each other."

She couldn't help thinking about how the family ties that had bound her to them began to fray when she was thirteen and had pressed Dad at the supper table to tell her about Mom. It was Christmas Eve, the night of which kids dream.

To this day, she couldn't stand to eat what they'd had for supper that snowy night at the kitchen table: country-fried steak with instant brown gravy and canned corn she swirled into mashed potatoes.

She had mashed the spuds herself and made a pitcher of sweet tea. And not just any ol' sweet tea from Piggly Wiggly—this was Momma's sweet tea recipe from before she died, which Lennie had learned to make from an index card she'd found bent up in a kitchen drawer, under the utensil organizer.

Momma's secret blend, which Lennie instantly memorized, was to pour gently boiling water over a mound of Dixie Crystals sugar and six tea bags in a pitcher, lower into the steaming water mint leaves in a stainless steel tea ball infuser and let the brew gradually cool. This became the special tea she served Mom when she'd visit during her *After Supper Club* dreams.

Waking the next morning, she could often taste the mint in her mouth. That's how real Mom's visits were. She wasn't sure how that was possible, but kids at school talked about waking up from a scary dream with their hearts racing, so why couldn't she wake up from her joyful dreams with the taste of mint on her tongue?

She developed into a young teen who had questions about *everything*. And on that Yuletide night, Lennie had longed for more than the taste of Mom's sweet tea—she hoped this night that Dad would give her something extra special and precious to hold onto about Mom as a Christmas gift. She held off on her questions until he had a chance to eat some of his meal because he could be cranky when he was hungry.

The smell of pine from the Christmas tree mingled with Johnny Cash performing *Little Drummer Boy* on Dad's record player, his deep baritone somehow making the pine scent even sweeter as she waded in.

"Daddy? With it being Christmas an' all, I was hoping you'd tell us about Momma."

Her eyes flicked to Johnny. She had told him she was going to try to coax Dad into some answers. Her brother had promised to back her up—only, at the moment of truth, he folded like a busted popsicle stick and shot her a frantic head shake in an attempt to back her down.

Dad's lips pulled taut against his teeth as he sat there. He didn't even look up; folds of skin scrunched on his forehead as he positioned the cutlet on his plate.

"What have I told you about Momma?"

"That her passing was a part of God's mysterious plan and not my fault."

"And that you should try to trust in the ways of the Lord?"

"Yessir."

First, he wiped his mouth with one of the napkins she had insisted they use; it was printed with Santa and his reindeer sleigh arcing across the face of the moon.

He arranged his knife and fork on the edge of his plate. And then he gave her the *look*—the look that meant he was about to say something she didn't want to hear. *Please God, don't let him say what he always says. Not on baby Jesus' birthday.*

But it wasn't fated in the stars or the infant's stable to go her way. "We all have our burdens in life to bear, sweetie," Dad said. "And the Lord don't make our crosses so heavy we can't carry them just like Jesus did. So that's what *we* do, too. Looking back can be more hurtful than helpful."

"But *why* did God take her away? Doesn't he have enough people up in heaven?" She watched her brother nervously hollow out a crater in his potatoes.

"Eleanor Grace." Dad's voice was firm. "We can't always understand the ways of the Lord. I keep telling you and you refuse to—"

"But why did he take her?"

"Please pass the gravy," Johnny blurted, eyes drilling Lennie like carbon bits as she handed him the porcelain gravy boat and pivoted to her questions. "What was she *like*? Was her voice soft?"

The muscles at the corners of Dad's eyes twitched. "Your Mother was a fine, Godly woman," he said as he separated his cutlet, golden niblets and mashed potatoes into isolated islands with his utensils.

"Where did she come up to on you?" Lennie pressed. "Was she *this* tall?" She put a hand on his chest. "*This* tall?" She leaned closer and slid her hand up to his chin.

"This ain't somethin' we're gonna discuss." His tone ended the inquiry: case closed.

Lennie drowned in his steady gaze. Then she scrambled to her feet, stomped to her room and slammed the door on Christmas, the *pah rum pum pums* just beyond her door.

In a few breaths, she cracked it open and watched them sit in silence across the table from each other, forks moving food around their plates. Johnny asked to be excused. Dad nodded and sat alone, staring at his coffee cup. Then he rose and started to clean up.

She was clearly on her own, and the gulf grew between her and Johnny throughout their teens. Sure, the family home maintained a veneer of togetherness, the days and months blurring into years, but there was always something under the surface. A lingering resentment.

By clinging to the attention Dad gave her for her basketball prowess, she alienated Johnny, especially when she horned in on "his" Mosely High basketball squad. He would never admit it, though, whether it was male pride or because it was all she and Dad had in common, a bond that kept things from breaking apart like a flywheel spinning out of control.

Try as she might, she couldn't find her footing in the harsh foothills. Playing on the boys' squad made her unprecedented achievement a topic of high school hallway conversations. And because she stood out, she struggled to fit in. She was *different*.

She became more isolated, more uncertain of her place in the world, while Johnny grew more convinced of his, the proverbial favored son on whom Dad pinned his hopes and aspirations. She'd never been able to figure out what future might await her.

And now, on the driveway with John, she wasn't sure if anything *at all* awaited her. "Things got to the point the three of us couldn't untie the knots," she said. "It was plain as day."

He kissed a shot off the backboard. "He had standards. You just didn't try hard enough."

You have no idea how hard I tried. "At least I was genuine. I remember when you ran for student council. You were a hallway charmer who got by on a smile and a sound-bite of empty chit-chat."

"For your information, it's called situational resilience."

Lennie instantly recognized his condescension. "I call it situational *revulsion*." In a single motion, she grabbed the ball and launched a bullet pass he caught cheetah quick.

"It happens to be a very valuable skill in the business world." He smirked. "Kind of like reflexes."

"Good for you. I'm glad that's carried you on a fulfilling path where you've never had to look back."

John took a shot. She grabbed the rebound as he glanced at the woodworking shop. "You know the worst part?" he said.

"I think I do, but I know you'll tell me different."

"The questions I never posed. There was something I never knew because I didn't ask."

She spun the ball up into the basket. "Might'a not done any good. He wasn't big on giving answers." She regretted the resentment that tinged her statement of the cold hard fact.

John frowned. "There are still so many unknowns about his life. The pieces."

"Why do you have this need to break everything down to the nth damn degree?"

A cleft formed between his eyebrows. *"What?"*

"The nth degree. This constant need of yours to reduce things to the teensy-tiniest, little-bitty nit-nats of the whole. Why do you have to do that? Can't you just step back and admire the entirety of the thing you seem to want to reduce beyond recognition?

His voice tightened. "It's called engineering, Lennie. It's what I get *paid* for. That nth degree you see as some sort of shortcoming earns me a damn good living and provides for a wonderful family. You should try it sometime."

Holly appeared at the kitchen door. "John? We need to get going so we can get the kids to bed." His wife gave them a smile. "It's nice you two had a chance to talk."

John glanced at Lennie then headed for the door. "Just forget it."

"I specialize in that," she called after him.

TWELVE

Through the Glass

Lennie's breath fogged the observation window separating her from premature newborns in the neonatal intensive care unit at the Tri-County Hospital.

She'd tucked her hair into a scrub cap dotted with clowning cats and wore a hospital gown adorned with children's letter blocks. A surgical face mask dangled from her neck, just above the Volunteer Cuddler sun logo stitched on the gown above her heart.

She considered seven preemies in incubator cribs. Monitors beeped and tiny heartbeats jumped on ECG machines amid the hiss of respiratory devices. *Tubes and tech may surely keep you in this world, but only human touch can make you feel alive.*

Her thoughts drifted to Dad. She couldn't let go of her feeling that he had died bearing the family stain of her shameful pregnancy. *You thought you knew the whole story.* But there were layers she had kept to herself to protect him and John. Her failure to come completely clean reared its ugly head every time she watched a TV show where a witness swore to tell the truth, the whole truth and nothing but the truth.

"Sorry about that." Lennie startled at Maggie's voice. She was a twenty-something nurse with cute blonde hair, her toothy smile wrapped around a soft twang. "I had to take care of something. I swear, some doctors think they're God's gift."

"Hon, you don't have to tell *me*," Lennie said, chuckling.

"You all scrubbed in?"

Lennie lifted her hands like a surgeon. "Three-minute gel. Crystal clean."

"Awesome. You're with Noah today."

"Aww, I love that little guy."

"Poor little scooter's been colicky."

"Sounds like somebody needs some extra special love," Lennie said. "Don't worry."

The ICU nurse sighed. "You can't help but worry in here." They pulled sterile masks over their mouths and noses.

The infant's crib was surrounded by wires and tubes hooked to blinking machines. Maggie gently lifted Noah and eased him into Lennie's arms.

Lennie slipped into a rocking chair, snuggling close, caressing his head. His wrinkled eyes fluttered open, then closed. *He sees me.* She felt the edges of her mask tighten on her cheeks when she smiled.

"Fifteen minutes," the nurse said.

Lennie lightly rocked back and forth and glanced through the room's glass windows at the nurses' station before turning her attention to the baby.

"Hey there, little buddy," she whispered. She felt a slight pressure around her index finger. Noah's tiny hand, with its impossibly flawless fingernails, had found its way to hers. His grip strength surprised her.

"That's right," she murmured. "We'll hold on together." She began to hum as his sleepy eyes fixed on hers. A stab of silver-blue light played for an instant on his face and a surge of panic shot through her. *Something's wrong.* She twisted around to see the monitors, and everything looked the same as when she had entered.

Flustered, she gazed through the windows that cocooned her and the infant.

Dad.

In his woodworking clothes.

He stood gazing at her from outside the observation window, the nurses' station twenty feet behind him. A disorienting wave overtook her. She closed her eyes to still her heart. *Get a grip.* She pinched them tighter to vanquish the impossible, then let them flutter open and gazed down at Noah, whose head nuzzled her breast as he let loose a sleepy yawn.

Lennie stroked his cheek. "You and me both, big guy."

Her body relaxed into the chair, when a spark of light seized her attention. It reminded her of the time she'd seen the sun glint off a coin at the bottom of a babbling creek behind the Mosely rail depot. She'd reached directly for the coin but missed because of the optical illusion created by the water bending sunlight. She couldn't resist turning toward the glass again.

Dad.

Wrapped in his worn leather apron over his work shirt and britches. The unit's staff seemed completely unaware of his presence.

She felt oddly outside herself. Submerged in something she couldn't even fathom. The ridges on his forehead tensed, and he looked as if he had no idea where he was, or why. He took a step closer to the glass and seemed lost in her eyes. Her heart hammered her rib cage and she released a breath that warmed her face behind the sterile mask. She was afraid to keep looking. Afraid to look away.

Sawdust lined the folds of his face and powdered the spikes of his gray flat-top hair. Over gunmetal blue eyes, his silver brows drew together in furrowed consternation. She knew that look.

"Dad?" The word filled her mask with clammy moisture. All she heard was her own breathing. It quickened as she stared back at him. Noah's warmth next to her slipped back into her senses, and she rose from the rocker with the infant in her arms.

Confusion rippled Dad's face, as if he were trying to figure out if he knew her. She suddenly lost the need to breathe—felt only the urge to be *present* in this shared space between them.

She bit the inside of her cheek, the coppery taste of blood seeping into her mouth. Panic twisted in her stomach as he offered an uncertain half-grin. His eyes seemed to plead with her.

She eased nearer to the glass that separated them, mind scrambling. *This can't be real.* Still, he wasn't a wavering specter or a gauzy apparition like those in the ghost tales of Savannah or Charleston, which she had heard so many times as a child.

He seemed as physically present as she was in every way. Even his tear-rimmed eyes. He tried to say something, but she couldn't make it out behind the glass.

How was it possible to feel so afraid and so full of wonder at the same time? As he reached for her, she instinctively stepped back and pulled Noah closer.

She watched Dad's hand until his fingertips contacted the glass barrier between them—they alighted amid the smudged prints of others who had stood in the same spot to peer in at frail little lives fighting to go home with them.

His thick fingers strained to breach the boundary. A wave of confusion swamped her as the window resisted his effort to penetrate it. Still he tried, and the solid plate of glass slowly gave way, wrapping around his advancing hand like a translucent glove as he pushed through.

BEEP! BEEP! BEEP!

She jerked toward the screeching alarm behind her and realized she'd moved Noah too far from his crib, disconnecting a port from his torso. Frantic, she turned a half-circle, not knowing what to do, her untethered world a swirl of sensations as Nurse Maggie rushed in and reconnected the tube.

"I'm so sorry," Lennie sputtered. "Oh my God. I was just ... walking with him a little bit and I didn't realize—" She couldn't finish her thought, her gaze darting around the ICU.

"It's okay," Maggie said with an expression that looked as perturbed as it was reassuring. "They sometimes move in their cribs, and things can get disconnected. That's why we have the monitors."

"I'm so, so sorry." Even the remotest possibility that she could put a baby's life in danger was too much to bear. *What just happened?*

The nurse looked down at the infant. "He's all right. He must really miss you," Maggie said.

Lennie stared at her. *She didn't just see what I saw?* "*Who* must miss me?"

"Noah. You couldn't come in on Tuesday, and he seemed extra cranky. I think you're a natural."

It took a second for the compliment to sink in as Lennie's gaze drifted to the partition glass. Everything looked normal.

"Thanks," she finally managed to reply, shaking off a chill that gripped the back of her neck. "It's easy to love on 'em when they're so precious."

"Hey," Maggie said as she laid Noah back in his crib. "Did you ever get that book deal for your poetry?"

Lennie took a moment to still her galloping thoughts. "No ... No, they, um ... They said it wasn't what they're looking for." She peered beyond the glass one last time. Dad was gone.

John stared at the roadway rushing into his headlights. Night was turning on, just like the lighted billboards that touted who was *Appearing Now!* at Nashville's Grand Ole Opry.

As he drove back from an engineering survey of the Mississippi River bridge he'd won the contract to replace, he decided death wasn't about sweet release.

It was about Dad clinging to him on a hot driveway, his frightened eyes boring into him. It was about death certificates and insurance claims. Erasing a name from the mailing list of *Woodworker* magazine. The cruel, hard logistics it took to come out on the other side of a loved one leaving forever.

The pressure in his head fueled a hurricane in his mind. He couldn't stop thinking about how he had failed Dad in the eulogy. How writing the last formal words ever spoken of him had been a dismal bust because John had come along midway through his life—the man had lived an entire existence before children ever entered the picture.

What were his hopes and dreams as a boy? Did life work out the way he'd planned? *How could I really know him? I don't even know if he had a middle name, for God's sake.*

Dad deserved better. He'd sacrificed and worked his whole life at Mosely Limestone to support them. In fact, the only time Dad ever left town was the trip to Florida's Space Coast, an experience that apparently meant so much to him, he memorialized it in a scrapbook. *Dad had a scrapbook? Since when?*

Holly's voice sprang out of nowhere, reading from Dad's scrapbook note, "... so I loaded the kids into the Bonneville, and we took our first family vacation."

"The space trip," John said, his eyes locked dead ahead. "Turns out, it was our last. Four stops. The topper was a Space Shuttle launch."

"I don't know why," she continued reading, the scrapbook in her lap illuminated by a map light, "but watching that rising trail of fire disappear into the heavens forever changed me."

John glimpsed the Tennessee page with the family photograph and the souvenir postcard from the Chattanooga Choo Choo Motel.

Holly flipped through a few pages of the album and ran her fingers over the yellowed postcards. "Looks like fun."

"Forever changed him?" John murmured. "How come I never knew that?"

She rubbed his shoulder. "Honey, it's a little too close right now. You just need to give it some time."

Give it some time. "That's the thing, Hol. Time's the enemy. The longer he's gone, I'm afraid the more he'll fade."

His mind churned as he tried to figure a way to learn more about Dad, to understand him, in Lennie's words, to that *nth degree* that always led him to answers.

Ideas flashed and were discarded. By the time he pulled into the driveway of his country estate, his analysis had totally failed him. The best course of action was to get a good night's sleep and tackle it in the morning.

THIRTEEN

The Space Between

L ennie's dreams had stopped the night she struck out on her own from Mosely—not only in the sense of her longing for the life she'd hoped to live one day, but the actual ability to dream when she slept.

In younger years, her slumbering forays to faraway lands and high adventure had offered an emotional escape from the confines of Mosely, a desolate whistle-stop that squeezed the life out of people.

In one dream, she'd be a sky pilot in a streaking locomotive to the stars, while in others, she'd walk the depths of the ocean or master a piano that played to millions. And she would often dream of Mom.

This was different.

She realized she wasn't in her bed, though she clearly remembered laying down in the same room where she had grown up. Recalled seeing its pretty lavender walls before closing her eyes.

Dad must have repainted the room in the same shade in her absence, maybe in an effort to keep her memory alive.

Gradually she became aware of muted colors. A sense of motion. Sounds around her curiously slowed as if they were passing through a thin liquid. There was no time to question where she was or even be afraid as her surroundings took shape and form.

She was squeezed in the back seat of the family Bonneville wagon, next to her Kid Self. Her astonishment grew when something jabbed her in the arm, and she looked to her right. There sat Kid Johnny, ten years old and fidgeting with his camera in the glow of a flashlight clenched in his teeth. He elbowed that other version of herself to give him more room.

"I seriously doubt Princess Leia would let her honey-bun hairdo get as messy as yours." *Dad.* For the first time in more than twenty years, Lennie heard his familiar drawl. It was the voice of a young, strapping father who added a chuckle to his teasing comment.

"It ain't about the hairdo," her Kid Self replied next to her, shaking out the Leia locks Lennie recalled wearing after she saw *Return of the Jedi.*

"It *isn't* about the hairdo," Kid Johnny corrected her.

"That's what I said. It's not about the hair. It's about setting things right in the universe." She switched on a toy *Star Wars* lightsaber, bathing the interior in a blue glow as the car seemed to float along a stretch of night highway, Dad up front, behind the wheel.

Lennie pressed a hand to her breastbone to still the erratic beating of her heart. *Is this what it feels like when people awaken from a coma and nothing makes sense?*

Whisked along on a current of memory, she tried to piece things together. *I'm eight here?* That was her best guess because her child-self wore Princess Leia *Star Wars* pajamas, which she had had to toss out, broken hearted, when she was nine; they got ripped shoulder to shoulder on a back-porch nail.

Streaks of headlights raced past. A billboard flashed by too quickly to read. Dad looked in the rearview and seemed to meet her eyes. *A dream ... I know I'm dreaming.*

Kid Johnny reached for the headrest in front of him and his sister whacked him on the arm with her lightsaber. Lennie covered her mouth to muffle a laugh, but she couldn't stifle the long-forgotten joy of a simple family moment. "Cut it out, turd face!" Kid Johnny howled.

"Don't call her that, Johnny," Dad said.

He shielded his prized Nikon F3 like a football player protecting the ball. "She's gonna break my new camera!"

Dad glanced into the rearview again. "That's enough. Both of you. And watch your language, young man."

"But she's gonna break it!"

Although no one in the car acknowledged she was there, Lennie remembered this family feud and was miffed at John's reaction to her Kid Self—just as she'd been when she *had been* her younger self on the actual trip. "I'm not gonna break it," she muttered.

"I'm not gonna break it!" Kid Lennie said and bounced her lightsaber off the front seat.

The past crackled through Lennie's mind like fingers of lightning. *We're almost there.*

"Are we there yet?" Little Lennie said with a huff.

Her brother scoffed. "If you paid attention for once in your life, you'd see the sign."

Kid Lennie stretched her neck for a better look out the window, and Lennie followed her gaze to see an instantly recognizable landmark: the elevated sign in the shape of a train locomotive flashing bright yellow as they approached the Chattanooga Choo Choo Motel.

The brakes squeaked as the tires crunched over the gravel parking lot. They rolled to a stop in a wash of fluorescent light spilling through the registration office's picture window. The family piled out, but Lennie couldn't get herself to move.

The instant transformed itself, and she suddenly found herself standing with them in the parking lot of the squatty 1950s motel. Momentarily jarred, she scanned a row of motel room doors, but couldn't remember which one they had stayed in.

"Keep an eye on your sister," Dad instructed Kid Johnny.

"Why do *I* always have to watch her?" he whined, his shoulders drooping as if it were the worst chore in recorded history.

"Because that's what big brothers do," Dad replied.

"He doesn't have to watch me," Little Lennie insisted. "I'm grown."

Dad headed for the office. "Just you never mind."

Kid Lennie raised her blue-glow lightsaber; it hummed an ominous warning as she wagged it from side to side at her sibling. "Prepare to meet your doom, Vader."

A surge of bravado surged in Lennie as she witnessed a re-creation of the first time she had challenged her brother to a duel. Kid Johnny rolled his eyes the way he always did when Lennie knew he was feeling threatened in his lofty role as the oldest.

He half-heartedly turned on his glowing red lightsaber. "And why am *I* always the bad guy?"

Little Lennie's eyes widened in disbelief. "And you're supposed to be the *smart* one? Because I'm a princess warrior, that's why!"

The second Little Lennie's lightsaber cracked his, Lennie found herself inside the Choo Choo's registration office.

Dad walked in, the ding of the door's little brass bell announcing his arrival. Behind him, her sibling past continued to battle in the parking lot, lightsabers slicing the night with streaks of blue and red.

The desk clerk, a spindly stalk of a young man with carrot-colored whiskers, tossed aside a tattered magazine and sprang to his feet behind the counter, cheek bulging like a hamster at feeding time.

"Hey-hey, name's Pepper Dupay!" he said with enthusiasm. The husk of a sunflower seed escaped his mouth and stuck to his lower lip. "Welcome to the Choo Choo!" His frame was draped with old-timey train conductor overalls, a red kerchief in the pocket, a conductor's hat keeping carrot-colored hair snugged down tight.

"Hey there," Dad said. He shook Pepper's outstretched hand. "Boy, that sign out front sure makes it easy to find y'all. We're the Rileys, down from Mosely. I reserved a room. One night."

Lennie yearned to reach out and touch her father but resisted as Pepper flipped through a six-inch-thick register. "Riley, Riley, Riley," he mumbled as his finger traced down pages. "Yep, here we go. Room six."

He spun the register to Dad, who signed it before grabbing a postcard of the Choo Choo's landmark locomotive sign from a rack.

A disquieting mix of dread and hope overtook her. Not because she recognized she was dreaming, but because she was dreaming in the first place. How long had it been? Twenty-five years?

What seemed a lifetime ago, her fascination with dreaming had led her to research it in books she found at A Likely Story. She was particularly intrigued by lucid dreaming, in which a person became aware she was dreaming *while* dreaming and could explore the mystic realm like a sort of virtual reality.

I wonder if—

The Choo Choo's office door dinged behind her, and she had to clamp down on the sharp breath she drew when she saw John.

Not Kid Johnny, still engaged in a lightsaber battle outside. No, this was adult John. He stepped into the office. Into her dream. She stared at him and waited to see if he'd look her way. But his focus remained locked straight ahead, as if he were here for a purpose from which he couldn't be distracted.

How is it possible ... a shared dream space? Dad turned to look at him and the locomotive postcard he'd just bought slipped from his hand. It created a visual ripple as it twirled toward the floor like a broken bird's wing.

John snatched it mid-flight. He politely offered it back to Dad, and in the breath that existed between moments, her brother met her father's eyes. An expression of incredulity spread across his face.

She sensed what John was feeling—he was trying to grasp what he was seeing, the same as she was. The two men simply stared at each other for a moment before Dad took the card from his son.

"Keep an eye on your sister," Dad said, echoing what he'd told Kid Johnny in the parking lot. He turned with his postcard and stepped out into the night, the brass bell dinging in his wake.

She glanced at a perplexed John, then watched with him as Dad rejoined their childhood selves outside. "John," she said, reaching for him. The movement broke the dream's gossamer veil.

John's body spasmed with adrenaline as he convulsed awake. The dream had been surreal. His familiar surroundings doused some of his fears like sand thrown on a campfire. All the same, he checked Holly next to him; a soft snore gurgled in her throat. He tossed the covers.

The sound of his feet rushing down the hallway pounded in his ears. He swung Abbey's door wide, hall light flooding the room where she lay wrapped in a sheet.

Opening Stevie's door across the hall revealed his son sloppily sprawled in bed, one sock on, one sock off. His bubbling fish tank murmured like it always did in the semi-darkness.

He stood and listened to the quiet house for a long moment before he eased Stevie's door closed and backhanded the sweat off his forehead.

He silently padded to Abbey's door and watched her chest rise and fall in a reassuring rhythm, trying to slow his breathing to match hers. *Whatever dreams she has, they can't be half as crazy as mine.*

FOURTEEN

Reaching Out

Water surging skyward crumbles,
expires against the clouds' low rumble.
Wounded bird gravity fights,
Grasping sky to take its flight.

Lennie looked up from the verse she'd just recited to Yolanda from her notebook, her body tensing as she waited for a response. She hated being so nervous about reading some of her poetry out loud. But she couldn't help it: laying your heart out there was never easy.

"That's awesome," her friend said, eyes widening. Lennie thought the years they had been apart since she'd left had only enhanced Yolanda's natural beauty. The short raven hair really suited her, peach tips a perfect complement to her ebony complexion.

Lennie breathed a sigh of relief. "Really?"

"Yeah, girl! I love it!"

"You're just being nice."

"No, I'm not."

Lennie grinned. "It's about this fountain I saw in San Fran. Years back, when I was traveling. So beautiful against the sky."

They were on a break from taking inventory in A Likely Story's lovingly named Basement Bauble Room. The storage area was down a rugged set of stone steps and housed souvenir collectibles like Great Smoky Mountain refrigerator magnets, shot glasses, coffee mugs, snow globes and key chains.

A stack of handmade soaps leavened the musty air with the aroma of lavender and lemon myrtle. A dehumidifier rattled and hummed under lightweight steel shelving that ringed the stone-walled room.

Windows at ground level allowed just enough clarity for Lennie to notice the dust suspended in streams of light. She liked to think of it as breathable history, particles dating back to the former church's birth in 1789.

After she clipped her pen inside the notebook and closed the cover, she glanced at the last of Dad's hand-carved wooden angel figurines on a shelf. She picked up a little cherub with petite wings and a baby-blue choir gown. Head bowed. Hands clasped in prayer. A round sticker on the bottom read $9.95.

She cleaned off the dust with her finger and traced the small angel's swirl of black hair before placing it among its heavenly host.

"Honestly?" Yolanda said, picking up Lennie's notebook and skimming the pages. "I think you write some of the best poetry I've ever read."

"Have you read a lot?"

Her friend blinked at her and paused before she answered. "That's not the point. The point is, are you gonna put the fountain one to music if it doesn't find its way into a book like you set out?"

"Maybe. I don't know." Lennie hoped it would be her break-out poem, one that finally lifted her into the ranks of published poets. But she'd been disappointed so many times with the "unfortunately, the material doesn't meet our needs" rejection letters, she'd learned not to get too emotionally attached to the idea.

She had been flattened so many times by all the turndowns that she suddenly needed Yolanda's feedback to be genuine. "You really think it's *that* good?"

"Girl, please." Yolanda's voice jumped an octave. "All I've got to say is, 'Maya Angelou, move over.'"

Lennie couldn't stifle a sputtering laugh and fanned herself with her inventory clipboard. "You're an Easter egg short of a basket."

"I'm serious! After hearing you read, in that sweet voice, I'm ready to climb into that fountain and get unbound myself."

"Maya Angelou?" Lennie playfully popped Yolanda's shoulder with her clipboard. "I swear, her words were piped in straight from above. Every syllable."

She sat on a rolling step stool, tugged off her right boot, and kneaded the arch behind the ball of her foot.

Yolanda plopped down opposite her. "What's the matter? Cramp?"

"No. Childhood." She sighed. "I had to wear a dreadful corrective shoe as a little kid. Some kind of bone thing. But it did straighten my foot out. Now it flares up sometimes if I'm on it too long." She looked around the shelves, still massaging her foot. "Well, guess we best get back to it."

"I suppose." Yolanda got up to count snow globes. "You know," she said, jotting the number on her clipboard sheet, "Momma says they're never really gone."

Lennie pinched the tips of her toes. "Who's never really gone?"

Yolanda's lips moved as she silently tabulated dusty coffee cups. "The dearly departed," she finally said. "Can you believe that? Momma thinks God allows kin who've passed to reach back to the kids they've left behind. To help them with their earthly struggles, through what she calls guardakin angels."

"Guarda*what*?"

Her friend apparently couldn't spare a breath to answer her question because she had a few more thoughts on the subject. "Isn't that the craziest thing you ever heard? Momma told Aunt May about this guardakin angel, an old woman who put her in touch with her long-gone daddy. Well, you can guess what happened."

"What happened?"

Yolanda shook with a deep chuckle. "Aunt May passed straight out. We had to bust an ammonia stick to bring her 'round."

"Are you talking about *guardian* angels?"

"Nope. Those are different. There's folks who believe guardakins are a peculiar ilk unto themselves. Like, highly specialized angels. Their whole job is to connect parent and child kin."

"Whoever heard of a Special Forces branch of angels?" Everyone knew about the phonies who claimed to be able to link folks with the deceased for goodly sums of money.

Lennie chewed the end of her pencil. "Y'know, I once read about spiritual beings called divas." She pronounced the word DEEVuhs.

Yolanda tallied bear-claw keychains. "Mmm, but they're called DEVuhs, not DEEVuhs. We're not talkin' Beyoncé."

"I read where Hindus and Buddhists and such believe in them. Seems what they call divas, we call angels. God's messengers."

"All I know is, Momma believes parents who've passed can help their children through these guardakin angels."

Lennie looked off, eyes riffling tourist trinkets, not focused on anything in particular as her mind scuffled. *Tell 'er what you saw. No, don't! Just tell 'er!*

"I think maybe my Dad's trying to do that," she finally blurted out. She waited for Yolanda to tell her she was moonshine crazy, but her work-buddy was focused on counting T-shirts.

Lennie rapped her knuckles on a shelf. "You hear me?"

"Sorry. I lost you."

"I said, I think Daddy could be trying to help me with my earthly struggles." Her mind attempted to stop right there, but her mouth had other ideas. "I saw him at the hospital while I was cuddling. Earlier this week."

Yolanda stopped writing and cocked an eyebrow. "Your *dead* Daddy?"

"Yep." Over the last few days, it had also occurred to her that he might have had something to do with the lucid dream about her childhood vacation.

"You're telling me you saw your dead Daddy."

"Yes. He was there. Plain as the nose on my face."

Yolanda sighed. "Okay, Eleanor Grace. Dish. What's going on in that head of yours?"

Lennie locked on her deep brown eyes. *She thinks I've done lost it.* "I saw him four days after the funeral. At the hospital. In the preemie room."

A slow nod accompanied Yolanda's skeptical tone. "Do tell." She gazed at the ceiling, then back at Lennie and sniffed in a way that seemed to indicate she thought her friend was on the bullet train to crazy town. "And there were other people around? Nurses an' all?"

"Yes."

"And nobody else seemed to think anything was out of the ordinary?"

Lennie cleared her throat and stroked her earlobe with all the nonchalance she could muster. "It didn't seem ... I mean, nobody said anything like, 'Hey, you can't be in here dressed like that.'"

"Mmm-hmm. And how was he dressed? Like, in that nice casket suit he was in at the service?"

"No. Like he had just finished working in the shop. All sawdusty an' everything."

"And nobody else saw him because ..." Lennie suspected Yolanda was waiting for her to follow her line of thought to a practical conclusion, just like Miss Day used to do back in sixth grade.

"Because ... they weren't looking?" Lennie heard herself grasping at straws.

"Girl, let's cut out the ghost talk and pull the spooky spoon outta the soup you're settin' ta boil."

"I'm not settin' anything ta boil! Rascal's bubblin' all by itself."

"Lennie, I've known you since we were five. You may be a grown woman, but I can see it in your eyes, just like when we used to sit and listen to stories in the reading room. Your imagination runs plumb wild."

"But he was so ..." Lennie searched for the right word, rapidly tapping her middle fingers against their opposite thumbs like a jittery yoga instructor. "... present."

Yolanda shook her head. "Girl, I'm telling you right now: Momma's guardakin angel talk? You can just put it outta your mind. It's just old-timer crazy jaw."

Lennie rose from her stool and hobbled to Yolanda, one boot on, one boot off. "But why does it have to be crazy? I mean, what if he wants to make things right between us?"

"Okay, first off, I know you're hurting. That's why you needed time off. But you're starting to wig me out!" She took

Lennie's hands, her eyes melting to genuine concern. "What was wrong between you and your Daddy before he passed?"

"I wish I could tell you, but ... it's a long story that only he and I can resolve together."

"And he's dead, so there's *that* little hitch."

Lennie squeezed Yolanda's hands. "But what if he wants to help me with my earthly struggles? He reached out. I *know* he did. What happens if I reach back?"

Yolanda clenched her eyes and scratched the sides of her head, as if she could coax out something that would get through to her.

She took Lennie by the shoulders and gave her a little shake. "Look, my Momma is stuck in the old ways her Momma taught her, just like *her* Momma before that. This is the twenty-first century, not a magic, conjuring potion buried in a mason jar under the old oak tree."

Lennie dropped her gaze. She knew the possibility was one in a zillion. Absurd even.

"Look at me," Yolanda said. "Just because some folks choose to believe something, doesn't make it true. Dead kin reaching back across the *great divide* to help the children they left behind? That's all just dirt-old blibbity-blab from a corner of the Appalachians. Momma claims a little town in Georgia called Tallulah Falls. It makes about as much sense as high heels in a sack race."

Lennie held Yolanda's steady gaze. Absorbed her concern. Her certainty. Her *unproven* certainty. She knew what she'd seen sounded loony by any measure in the normal world. And then there was that other unexplainable experience: her lucid dream of their long-ago family vacation. Somehow, the two things were connected—she could feel it in her gut.

"Tallulah Falls." She tried the word on for size, her voice barely above a whisper. Then she kissed Yolanda's cheek. "Thank you." She grabbed her discarded boot from the floor and marched toward the stone steps.

She glanced back to see her friend's flabbergasted face. "Where you going?" Yolanda demanded.

Lennie pushed through a sense of being off kilter, herky-jerky hips riding up and down, the single boot she wore making that leg two inches taller than the other. "To let Daddy do right by me!"

She clambered up the steps, Yolanda's pleas growing fainter behind her. "But he's done passed."

Lennie unleashed a shot in the dark: "But maybe he hasn't passed *over* yet!"

"Can I have that yogurt you left in the fridge?" The shout of her co-conspirator was barely audible.

Lennie paused at the top of the steps, the cool dampness of the basement rushing up at her as she cupped her hands around her mouth. "It's all yours! And thank you, hon!"

FIFTEEN

Baggage

Lennie pulled a duffel bag from the closet in her old room and jammed in a few changes of clothes. Next she packed her makeup and Dad's carved wooden heart into a bookstore tote bag.

Staying at the old house since the funeral had brought her a measure of comfort. She liked knowing that only a short time ago, Dad had walked through the same rooms and passageways. Breathed in the same air.

The leather basketball he'd given her for her twelfth birthday caught her eye. Its surface worn to a pebbled luster, it sat in the corner, her name scrawled on it in fading magic marker. She spun the ball in her hands with a flick of her wrists, feeling somehow a little closer to Dad. It was coming with her.

She hurried out of the house with her duffel, moving so fast she nearly stumbled down the steps outside the kitchen door. *Chill out. It's only a few hours to Tallulah Falls.*

She'd gassed up on her way home from work and savored the trip with her Bonneville bestie. She had a thread of hope when it came to connecting with Dad. A thin one, but still a thread she'd follow until it broke.

As she pulled the station wagon's tailgate open and tossed her bag in, she began working on what she might say to an angel. *What's heaven like?* That seemed like a good place to start.

Her phone rang. She darted a glance at it and saw No Caller ID. *Another robocaller.* She tapped the ignore icon and slipped the phone in her shorts pocket as she swung the tailgate closed. It rang again as she dropped behind the wheel. She dug it out once more. The same mystery number. *That's weird.*

After she terminated the repeat call, she saw the two more missed calls. She'd turned the ringer off at work this morning so she wouldn't be interrupted while she took inventory and hadn't seen the first attempt until later. Someone was trying to reach her.

It rang a third time. Maybe Captain Ahldren in Alaska got a new phone. The crab boat skipper loved his gadgets. She tapped the answer icon.

"Hello?"

"It's me," a male voice said. Her spine stiffened. *Oh my God.* Her wretched ex had changed his number? Her hand tightened on the steering wheel. "Yeah?"

She heard a tiresome *tch* and recognized it instantly. John. *Thank God.* His timing, though, couldn't have been worse.

"How'd you get my cell?"

"I need the car," he said.

"Excuse me?"

"The Bonneville."

John sat on a swivel stool at a granite kitchen island the size of Texas. He had bought the elegant estate home after seeing it on the cover of *Southern Living* magazine, a story he didn't mind repeating.

Bathed in sunlight streaming through two-story windows, a Bluetooth earbud in his ear, he unfurled a road map in front of him and carefully smoothed out the creases.

Dad's scrapbook lay open on his right. To his left was the printed spreadsheet he had prepared earlier—each destination, length of stay and travel time between stops calculated.

"I need the car," he repeated. A feeling of relief washed over him at finally getting in touch with her. She could have taken off with the vehicle and gone somewhere on a whim. A detail this important wasn't something he would ordinarily leave to the last minute, but he'd come up with the idea only this morning.

"Yeah, I heard you. I do, too. It's *my* car."

Using a yellow highlighter, he traced a small, secondary road heading south from Knoxville on the map. *This is going to be perfect.* "I'll give you five thousand dollars."

"I really don't have time to play Let's Make a Deal right now, Johnny."

"Fine. We're all busy. Let's skip the jabs and get right to the punch. Six thousand."

He waited for her counter-offer. He understood how the game was played, and he knew how to win. Everybody had a price.

"Six thousand. *Dollars?*" she said after a long pause. "It doesn't even have AC. Why would you pay that?"

"Cash."

"Why?"

"You wouldn't understand."

"Try me."

He ran his hand around the curve of his chin and down his neck, trying to banish every bead of tension. "I don't think so."

"Can't you trust me with *anything? Why* do you need the car?"

He groaned to himself at the soft inflection in her voice. So genial. So transparent. She was going to try to talk him out of it.

"I'm gonna hang up," she said.

He dismounted the pewter bar stool and strode out to the pool deck. "Okay," he said as he dipped his toe in the crystal blue water, "if you must know, I'm re-creating the space trip we took."

He heard her exhale, then the nickering sound a cowboy uses guide his horse. *The money's got her thinking.*

"The space trip," she said.

"That's right. To the letter. The Choo Choo Motel, Rock City, Six Flags Over Georgia, Cape Canaveral. I'm going to drive the exact route Dad drove and hit the same stops he did, including a space launch. It follows that I need the car Dad drove to get everything right. A faithful reboot, down to the last detail."

"Wow. You gonna leave anything to chance, or just script the thing to within an inch of its life?"

He marched back inside to the kitchen. "Yeah, see, I figured you wouldn't understand." His attention went to Dad's scrapbook postcards on the counter top—

—the Chattanooga Choo Choo Motel.

—Rock City in Lookout Mountain, Georgia.

—the death-defying roller coaster from the Six Flags Over Georgia theme park.

—a Space Shuttle launch at Cape Canaveral.

John leaned over the map he'd begun marking up and traced a tiny back road from eastern Tennessee into north Georgia and down to Florida's Atlantic coast.

Any reliance on GPS mapping was out of the question because that wasn't a part of Dad's experience.

"It's a lot of money, Lennie. I don't know anything about your living situation, but I suspect it could help."

Her *living situation*. Cell phone pressed to her ear, Lennie considered her cracked dashboard. It *was* a ton of money. Visions of fixing up the Bonneville danced in her head. But there were other things that carried more weight. Things that weren't *things* at all.

The space trip. She'd been replaying her dream over and over in her head, and her heart quickened at the thought of returning to that place where Dad had seemed so near. So real. *Could this be ... is this call Dad's doing? Him pulling some strings up there?*

"Maybe I'm taking a trip too," she said. "That ever cross your mind?" She grabbed a tattered Rand McNally Road Atlas from under the seat and finger-traced a southbound road out of Mosely, south of Knoxville where John was, toward Georgia.

"Let me guess," he said into her ear. "More aimless wandering."

"It's not aimless. I need to clear my head."

"Will seven grand clear it then? I'll rent the car from you for the weekend. Seven thousand dollars, easy money."

Lennie pulled herself close to the steering wheel and rolled the stress out of her shoulders. "Why would you pay seven grand for a weekend car that'd be lucky to fetch seven hundred to own outright?"

"Okay, I'll buy it then."

"She's not for sale."

"Damn it, Lennie. Something happened for Dad on that trip."

She sat back and stared at Dad's workshop through the trees. The events of the past week had left a trail of unanswered questions. She needed clues. "What happened?"

"It's ... the scrapbook. The one you wanted me to have."

"Right. You're welcome."

"Did you *look* at it?"

It's hard looking back. She lifted each leg in turn to peel the backs of her thighs from the vinyl seat and rubbed under her nose. "A glance."

"Well, it obviously meant a lot to him. I'd like to know why. Just to understand him better, okay?"

She glanced through the neighbor's trees at a junked car, wheeless and abandoned on cinder blocks.

"Hello?" John said, jarring her thoughts.

"I'm here."

"So, we have a deal or not? I've got to get going to make a dawn launch on Monday."

Lennie's mind churned. "How about—" She hesitated, knowing that what she was about to say would sound almost as crazy as stalking guardakin angels: she could barely spend three minutes with John before sparks flew, let alone three days.

"I'm thinking maybe you go with me," she finally said. "You want the car? I'm heading south. I'll work your route in."

"That's not what I had in mind."

A wave of disbelief swamped her goodwill gesture. She was doing him a favor! "Well, guess what, Johnny? You want an exact re-creation? I was there. Remember *that* little detail? So that's the deal. You want the car? You get me. I'll be at the church."

She hung up, tossed the phone and cranked the engine.

SIXTEEN

Shaky Start

The parking lot of the old family church on Highway D, the First Baptist Church of Deliverance, was empty and quiet, unlike the last time Lennie had been here for Dad's funeral. She and Johnny had gone here as kids, just like Dad before them. Second pew from the front, on the left. Mom and Dad had been married here, just like their parents before them.

Versace soft-side suitcase in his hand, John stared at the station wagon. Saggy rear. Three hub caps gone. Sun-eaten paint mixed with rust marked its surface with bubbles of automobile acne. "You think she'll make it?"

She fixed him with a stare and pointed at the Bonneville. "Hey, we've kicked the Rockies' patoot a half-dozen times, so don't you worry about her making it. She may not have big fancy wheels like yours, but she knows how to roll."

He peered inside the rear cargo area. Steering clear of a greasy box of motor oil next to her road-worn duffel, he set his hoity-toity luggage inside. The elegant crimson suitcase looked as out of place in there as Lennie imagined he felt standing outside her beater car.

She watched him dig a piece of paper from the pocket of his pressed Bermuda shorts and study it. *Oh, please, no.*

He checked his watch. She snuck a closer look at what he was up to and saw *Rolex* on the timepiece's face. It was encircled with diamond chips that sparkled when he moved his hand.

"All right," he announced, tapping the crystal face, "we need wheels rolling in three minutes to stay on schedule."

"Oh. My. God," Lennie mumbled to the overcast sky.

He pressed a knob on the side of the Rolex casing. With a *click,* the stopwatch engaged.

She let out an exasperated sigh. "Please tell me you're not gonna do this the whole trip."

"What, ensure success? I've reverse-engineered everything to keep us on point."

He showed her his paper, a color-coded spreadsheet that indexed their four stops: Chattanooga's Choo Choo Motel; Rock City, just across the state line in Lookout Mountain, Georgia; Six Flags Over Georgia, west of Atlanta; and Cape Canaveral.

Columns marked departure times, arrival times, and flex travel time for what he called unforeseen contingencies.

"All synched right here." He gestured to his wrist.

"Okay, that's it." She raised her hand, like a soccer referee issuing an ejection. "I'm officially declaring A.O.A.R."

He drew back with a bewildered look. "A.O.A.R.?"

"Adult Onset Anal Retentiveness."

"Hey, just because I plan doesn't mean I'm anal retentive. It's not about control."

"It's *all* about control."

"I've devised a buttoned-up approach to re-create one of the key moments of Dad's life so I can experience it for myself. That doesn't make me anal retentive."

"No, more like a life plagiarizer."

John waved her off. "Whatever. There's something from that trip I have to *live*. Have to surround myself with. I need to focus and process to find closure."

"Pray tell, where are you going to find closure?"

"Nineteen eighty-six. That's what this is all about. And to be honest, you were not a part of my methodology for this do-over."

Lennie found it hard to believe they'd laughed and played together as kids. John had always been a little rigid and tended to overanalyze things, but nothing like this.

She put her hands on her hips and cocked her head. "*Methodology? Seriously?*"

"Let me finish. You weren't originally a part of my plan but, upon further consideration, I realized the car was key." He turned to face the Pontiac wagon.

"And we're a package deal, so you had no choice."

"No. I came to the conclusion I could live with you wedging in because—"

"Thank you *sooo* much," she said. "*Wedging in* means the world to me."

"I figured you were an annoyance on the initial trip, just like you'd undoubtedly be again if you held true to form. Obviously, I was right, so I'm completely confident it'll all work out."

This dude needs his own Netflix reality show. "You always did know just what to say." She thought she'd weathered the brunt of his *nth degreeness*, but she couldn't have been more wrong.

"No cell phones, texting, Facebook, tweets, Instagram, GPS. Nothing digital in the car."

"*What?*" she shot back.

"It didn't exist back then. Hand over your phone."

She could hardly contain a burst of incredulous laughter. "I'm not giving you my phone."

"You're going to jeopardize the schedule if you fight me every step of the way." She stared at him in silence.

John eyed the Rolex. "See? This is what I'm talking about. The annoyance factor. Thirty seconds to departure." He stuck out his hand.

Lennie wondered if they'd survive the weekend.

"Twenty-five seconds."

Friday to Monday. Three days stuck in a car with this?

He shifted on his feet, hand outstretched, gesturing "give it" with his fingers. "Twenty seconds."

Well, time to find out if there was anything left to salvage. Trapped in a car for seventy-two hours should do the trick. She dug out her phone.

"You seeing anybody about that OCD?" she said as she slapped it into his outstretched hand. "There. Unwired. Disconnected from the world, except our own."

"Scary as that sounds," he replied, "I'll do my thing and you do yours. Parallel paths."

He pulled a drawstring bag from his pocket, dropped their cell phones inside and locked it inside his Lincoln. He hustled back to the Bonneville. "I'm driving."

She tried to scorch him with her glare, but he just beelined for the driver door. Refusing to let him bull her over crossed her mind, but then she reconsidered. No point in causing a conniption before they even got started.

She pulled open the passenger door and gazed at him over the roof. "Y'know, I'm the only one who's driven this beauty in the last two hundred seventy-eight thousand miles." She tossed him the keys. "Try not to turn left. Louise gets a little clunky."

"*Louise?*" His face seemed to corkscrew around his nose. "You *named* the car?"

"Thelma'n'Louise. Cool movie. They did it *their* way."

"Yeah, and they died at the end."

Inside the church, she peered through a leaded glass window at Lennie as she tossed her keys to John over the roof of the station wagon.

The two of them loaded in and a plume of coal-black smoke shot from the exhaust pipe at the same time the engine fired up with a rumble; it stirred misgivings in her along with infinitesimal ripples in the baptismal water that had been sleeping in the font next to her. The quivering surface momentarily distracted her, but her attention snapped back to the car outside when it clunked across an uneven patch of parking lot, its shocks groaning.

She watched the station wagon lumber off on Highway D. *What's Johnny doing here?* It wasn't at all like him to cotton to Lennie or her fanciful notions. And where were they headed? Far enough to need luggage. None of it made sense.

Her troubled thoughts were disrupted by the sacred baptismal water as it resettled smooth as glass. She leaned over the surface and willed her eyes to see her reflection.

An image of vulnerable youthfulness stared back at her. Why had she feared looking old? Just as she remembered, ash brown hair fell in a side-braid that brushed her shoulder, setting off her green eyes. She gave herself a tentative smile and smoothed the ivory lace collar of her simple blue church dress, the nicest piece of gussied-up clothing she had ever possessed.

A moment later, her likeness fretted at her, even though she wasn't supposed to worry. Not here. Not where the uncertain and the weary found refuge. But she couldn't help it—given the old car's condition, she was afraid it wouldn't deliver them safely.

This too shall pass. She tried to reassure herself with that morsel of hand-me-down wisdom.

It only partly worked, and the regret that stalked her attempted to steal her resolve. She managed to tamp it down but couldn't fully escape her disquiet when she realized she was where she had to be, but not where she belonged.

SEVENTEEN

Trashed Heart

The flare of sunlight that had reflected off the car keys Lennie tossed to John back in the parking lot stirred a memory of when Dad had chucked a set of glinting Jeep keys to her brother.

He had been in college at the time, and she was sixteen, at the start of her senior year at Mosely High. They'd stood on the basketball court driveway.

By then, Johnny was spending all his time in Knoxville, where he attended the University of Tennessee. The only reason he came back was to claim the vehicle Dad's boss, Mr. Mosely, had bought him in recognition of making the Dean's List.

Lennie cradled her basketball under her arm and watched him hop into his automotive *'atta boy*. She couldn't blame him for bailing on Mosely: most could only dream of getting out.

Dad's face glowed with pride. "Give a ring when you get to campus. And let's nail those grades again!"

Johnny cranked the Jeep. "No problem!"

He shot Lennie a look. On top of the world, he had still tried to offer her encouragement. And why not? He'd made it out, and she'd never be a bother again. Or maybe he'd noted her slumped shoulders and pitied her. "I've got my study abroad year, so I won't be around for a while. You know what you need to do, right?"

He had no idea what that was, but he was going to tell her anyway. "You need to keep your head in the game and work hard so you'll be ready to perform at hoops camp in Watkinsville."

She forced a half-grin as he backed out, and he left her with a final piece of advice loud enough for the whole street to hear. "And lose some weight, lead bottom! You're looking a little porky!" With that, he drove off, and she trudged back to the house.

His flung criticism only made her more despondent. The weight she'd put on was obvious even in the droopy basketball jersey and shorts. It didn't help that the sagging uniform was blaze green and accessorized with a goofy headband and green and gold tube socks.

So many things had changed for her since Johnny left. The whole direction of her life became painfully clear. She would always live in the shadow of her brother's success, her only future the one that her father mapped out for her.

Months passed, surviving the emotional minefields of high school. She had somehow managed to keep up her basketball practice. It shocked her, though, how little she now cared for the game she used to love. She couldn't even stomach the thought of basketball camp anymore.

Then the day she'd been dreading came. She sat on her bed crying, hiding behind her buzzy acoustic guitar amid scribbled pages of her poetry. She'd spent the morning trying to feel her way through one she could wrangle into a song, but nothing had worked, and hopelessness swamped her.

She took refuge in the tune that had inspired her to take up the guitar, softly strumming Bonnie Raitt's *Dimming of the Day*. She had always been self-conscious about her voice, so she mouthed the words she heard Miss Bonnie singing so beautifully in her head—

> *This old house is falling down around my ears.*
> *I'm drowning in a river of my tears.*
> *When all my will is gone, you hold me sway,*
> *and I need you at the dimming of the day.*
> *You pulled me like the moon pulls on the tide.*
> *You know just where I keep my better side.*

She stopped playing when Dad appeared in the doorway. He glanced at her packed suitcase. "We need to get a move-on if we're gonna get you checked in up there."

She cleared the tears from her eyes with the back of her wrists. "I don't wanna go."

His lips pulled tight and he slowly inhaled. "Eleanor Grace, we've been over this. It's all about you keepin' your shot at college. Right?" He wasn't asking. He was telling.

"Please don't make me."

He sat on the edge of the bed. "Look at Johnny." His voice softened. "Look how well he's doin'. On his way to somethin' better. Colleges are offerin' more basketball scholarships for girls these days. And we need to make sure you got your best shot. Keep you on track to somethin' more."

Lennie looked down at her poems. At her suddenly meaningless feelings, cradled in her stupid words. "I know, but—"

"I've been down the road without a proper education to open doors." He patted her leg. "That's hurt what I been able to do for you two. I just want you to do better'n I done. That's all."

She sniffed and rested her chin on the swept shoulder of her guitar. *Maybe if I threw up.* "If Momma was here, she wouldn't make me."

"Lennie." His shoulders sank until his elbows reached his knees; he stared at the floor.

She sensed a ripple of weakness in his resolve and leaned on Momma's memory to try to break it. "Well, she wouldn't. She'd be on *my* side."

She couldn't wrap her mind around his way of thinking. He had never remarried because he believed the Almighty had seen fit to "call Momma home" for reasons beyond his understanding and the Lord was testing him with the burden of carrying his life's load alone.

As she clutched her guitar, her mind battled upstream against a river of confusion. His reasoning may have strengthened his personal faith, but what about *her?* There was no one to understand her at times like these.

She set her acoustic aside and ripped up her pages of poetry, letting the shreds fall like ashes to the bed.

Feeling his weight lift from the creaky mattress, she watched him move to the door and pull a purple helium balloon into the room from the hallway. Shiny yellow words on its surface spelled out *I Love You.* The balloon was ribboned to a hand-carved walnut heart just the right size for her palm.

"Maybe you can take this with you." He held out the wooden heart to her. When she glanced at it, she saw her name woodburned into it with his fancy cursive lettering and turned away. He placed it on her bed, the purple balloon floating above her.

His nose whistled low as he took a deep breath. "One day, I hope you'll understand."

She refused to look at him. Or his bogus heart. She could feel him standing over her in a tortured silence for the longest time, as if she would talk with him. *As if.* A tear tracked her cheek as he left the room, and she wasn't sure if it was for the way he was treating her or the way she was treating him.

She picked up the carved heart. Still warm from his hands. She held it and tried to *feel* something. Anything. But there was nothing. She tossed it into her metal sunflower trash can, numb to the clanking echo she heard when it hit bottom.

EIGHTEEN

Driving Past

Lennie gazed at the hazy peaks of the Smokies in the passenger-door mirror and remembered the hurt in Dad's voice that long-ago day. She realized that the heart she'd found in his shop, the one tucked away in her duffel, might've been a second chance. Was it asking too much for a third?

She and John traveled a divided highway intermittently crossed by a country road that was marked by a blinking yellow light.

Endless pastureland rolled past her window, sprinkled with stately trees providing shade for cattle. She could see white egrets scrambling in the heat after bugs which the lumbering herd stirred from the grasses whenever they moved.

"How did I miss it?"

John's question jarred her, and she looked over at him. "Huh?"

He was behind the wheel, elbow resting on the door frame. He had placed Dad's scrapbook next to him; it leaned against the back of the seat as if it were a person.

"I thought I knew Dad pretty well," he said. "How could I not be aware that one of the most important moments in his life was on this trip?"

"We can't know everything."

"I even had a dream about it."

A tingle shot through her. "About this trip?"

"Not *this* one. The one back as kids."

"When?"

"I don't know. Wednesday night, I guess it was."

Same as mine. Goosebumps sprinkled her legs, and she tapped her foot on the floor mat. "Are you sure it was Wednesday? The night before last?"

"Yeah," he replied. "Now it's stuck in my mind, like one of those songs that won't stop playing in your head."

He couldn't get past the dream. *Our dream.* She turned her attention to the road and tried to connect the peculiar dots. A tractor idled at an approaching intersection, waiting to cross. *Should I tell him?*

"He talked to you," she blurted.

"Who?"

"Dad. In your dream."

He paused. "You know, I think he might have. But, really, it was all ... just disjointed images."

"You were at the Choo Choo Motel." Although not intentional, her words sounded to her like a leading statement made by the attorneys on *Law & Order.*

John slowly nodded. "Yeah ... come to think of it, I was. Only, I wasn't there. I was in bed."

Her mind churned as she uncapped a bottle of water and took a glug. *Do NOT tell him.* She took another swig and swished it in her mouth before swallowing. *Don't you dare say it, he'll—*

"We shared a dream. I was there. You looked dead at me."

"You were *where?*" he said.

"In your dream." She rummaged around the glove box, grabbed four tortoise shell hair claws and dropped them on the seat between them.

"You came into the registration office." She slid one of the hair claws close to two others. "Dad and I were already there. He was in front of you, with his back to you at first, and I was to your right. There was a guy behind the counter."

Lennie pressed the fourth hair grabber into the seat with enough force to leave a divot in the upholstery.

"Remember the sunflower seeds? You looked at me and—" She felt her speech pick up speed, words tumbling off her tongue. "I rode with us. I mean, the kid versions of us. We were there in the dream with our lightsabers. I laid a lick on you, and you whined to Dad about your camera. He told you to keep an eye on me, and you whined about that, too."

John sopped his forehead with his sleeve. "It's like a sauna in here. How can you stand it?" He stuck his hand out the window and used it to direct air toward him.

"I saw us in the parking lot. We had those Star Wars lightsabers. Remember the streaks of light?"

He fiddled with the staticky dash radio. "I don't remember any lights."

"Mine was blue, yours was red."

"I told you, Lennie: it was a jumble. Flashes. Shards of stuff that went nowhere. It doesn't mean anything."

"Yes, it *does*." She heard her voice rise and knew he'd tune her out if he thought she was getting carried away. She chose her words deliberately. "I was *there*. With *you*. You were there. With *me*. It could mean *everything,* because I think Dad is—" She stopped.

John shot her a glance. "Dad is *what?*"

She averted her eyes and shook her head. "Nothing. He was *there*. Both of us were, too, as adults. I was aware and present.

Inside the dream." She grabbed the scrapbook and fanned her face. "The three of us shared the same dream, Johnny."

He dismissed her with a flick of his hand. "That's ridiculous. How could we be in the same dream?"

"We don't have to know how."

"We're *mourning*," he said, emphasizing their state of mind, "and just because—"

"Something's going on, Johnny. Something bigger."

He glanced up at the droopy roof liner and chuckled. "Oh, for God's sake. Your thinking is absurd. It's called a coincidence. You had a dream. I had a dream. People dream. We're both processing Dad's loss with vivid memory receptors."

"Dreaming at the exact same time, about the exact same place and circumstance? There was a postcard!" She opened the scrapbook and jabbed the Choo Choo Motel postcard with her finger. "This one! He dropped it, you caught it and gave it *back* to him. You call *that* coincidence?!"

He stifled a smirk. "Nooo. I call it a shared childhood memory. Like millions of other siblings have." She couldn't stand his parental tone, like he was informing a child that life wasn't all rainbows and unicorns.

Lennie fluffed some air on her neck with her ponytail. She needed time to think through what their unexplainable dream could mean—like reading between the lines of a poem. *Let it sneak up on you when you're not expecting it.*

She eyed the "See Rock City!" postcard in the album. "Rock City." She grinned to herself as she recalled the chilly dampness of the network of underground caverns. "Like going down a rabbit hole."

John nodded. "And, pardon me, boys, is that the Chattanooga Choo Choo?"

She scanned the route he had highlighted on his map, then noted a sign for Dollywood approaching and made a radio-squawk sound.

"*Skrrrch!* This is your conductor," she said in a raspy tone, pretending to talk into a hand-held microphone. "Next stop, Dollywood."

"We're not going to Dollywood."

"C'mon, Johnny. Why not?"

"We're doing Dad's route. And that wasn't on it."

Lennie saw country music legend Dolly Parton, in all her beaming, big-haired, buxom glory, draw closer on a billboard that could probably be seen from outer space. "Where's your sense of adventure? We can shoot over to Pigeon Forge and see what's what."

"We're on a schedule."

"Vacations aren't about schedules."

"This isn't a vacation."

"That's what it *was*. What's it now?"

"A personal-development project."

"Okay, here's a project for you: let's make a *new* memory. Just the two of us. Starting with Dollywood."

"Did you hear me? There was no Dollywood. Dad. Didn't. Go." A touch of irritation sharpened his voice. "If it's not on the map, we're not going."

Dolly whizzed by, her uplifted hand waving goodbye instead of hello. "He woulda gone if he coulda," she countered.

"How do *you* know what he would've done?"

"Ruben-esque women is how I know. I caught an exhibition in Santa Fe."

"Ah," he sniffed. "The artistic hotbed that *is* New Mexico."

"Seriously? Your boyhood hero, Ansel Adams, captured the heart of the world with his photography there." She let him chew on that, then realized he'd diverted her from the conversation she wanted to have.

"Dolly is a living Peter Paul Rubens portrait," she said as she swiped a sweat bead that drizzled the side of her neck. "Curvy women. Mr. Rubens liked a little junk in the trunk."

John gave her a patronizing smirk. "Junk in the trunk. That's your assessment of one of the greatest painters in history?"

"His artwork oozed yearning. Human expression." She flipped another page of the scrapbook. "Of course, you and your *methodology* wouldn't know a thing about that."

"Bull," he shot back. "I explored expression and the possibility of becoming a photographer when I was a kid, but—"

"You chickened out."

"Grew up is more like it."

Lennie eyed his old-school Nikon dangling by its strap from the rearview mirror. She removed it and toyed with the film-advance lever.

"Be careful with that part. It's been fixed, but I didn't get any pictures after that old guy at the motel broke it. I intend to right that wrong."

She couldn't believe he'd held onto it because it had to be a reminder of a calamitous childhood defeat. What happened back then had likely fueled her brother's later determination to win at whatever he took on.

At nine years old, he'd entered a photo contest sponsored by Thomasville Furniture, a Southern staple right up there with Piggly Wiggly.

The contest was called "Dress Up Your Drawers," and children ten and younger were encouraged to showcase how nicely they managed to store their clothes in Thomasville's line of kids' dressers, something sure to impress parents and spur sales. The winning photo would be featured in the company's full-page ad in *Southern Living* magazine.

John focused on his underwear drawer, certain his photograph would launch a career of fame and fortune. He'd saved enough leaf-raking money to buy a used 35mm Nikon F3 from the back of Dad's *Woodworker* magazine—a "real" camera with a fancy lens.

His entry featured his underwear rolled and packed tight as relay-race batons, accompanied by meticulously folded white t-shirts, and his beloved Tennessee Volunteer gym shorts with the orangest of UT orange.

Framed by the dresser's honey maple wood, the image truly dazzled. To create the perfect effect, he worked out an elaborate lighting scheme using every lamp in the house, plus the blue-glow mosquito bug zapper from the back porch for extra punch. As foolproof career launches go, he figured it was airtight.

Second place crushed him. There'd be no grand acclaim. Instead, that honor went to Penelope Parsons, whose uncle happened to be the vice president of marketing for the company. The contest people swore up and down it was a "blind" competition—nobody knew whose picture was whose.

Johnny, of course, didn't buy it. He just *knew* his pocket had been picked. It didn't help that Thomasville instituted the "Penelope Rule" after the deal had gone down, barring employees and their family members from participating in the future.

His consolation prize added insult to injury: what he considered an artistically laughable click-n-whir Polaroid Land Camera identical to the one the proclaimed "winner" had used to beat him.

There would be no launch of Johnny Riley's Smoky Mountain Photography, a name Lennie had helped him come up with for his can't-miss photos of "international renown" and she became convinced Penelope Parsons was the root of his control issues. Ever since that loss, John had tried to manage everything around him. Lock down every variable. Overcome every obstacle. And just win, baby.

All the same, she had to admit he'd done a thorough job of controlling and winning, given the level of comfort in his life. Except when it came to her, whom he had never been able to manage.

"And by the way," she said as she turned the camera back and forth in her raised hand, "you want to keep your photo hopes alive, you best update your gear, Ansel."

"Oh, really? You want to talk about keeping hope alive? What about *you?*"

"I'm a poet-in-waiting."

"Yeah, with no hope of making it." He moved to the left lane to pass a slow-moving tractor.

"I've got all the hope I need right here." She thumped her heart.

"That and six bucks will get you a Starbucks. We're following Dad's route. What he did is the whole point."

She tapped her fingers on the armrest. *This was the biggest mistake. He has as much bend in him as a railroad spike.* "That's the thing: *he* did it. It was *his* original. You can make your own way."

John kept his eyes on the road. "I'm not going to argue for the entire trip about where we go. If it's not on the map, we're not going. Period."

Lennie stewed in the silence, wind buffeting the open windows. "Except the Appalachians. That was the deal."

"What's with the Appalachians all of a sudden?"

She watched two passing farmhands repairing a fence. No way was she going to tell him her plan. He'd say it was only more of her aimless nonsense. "Just seems like an interesting place, is all."

"Dad's route cut south, through the middle of Georgia."

"Right. And the Appalachians run down to a little town called Tallulah Falls, east of where we crossed."

"Fine," he said, his voice edged with exasperation. "We're in, we're out, we're on our way."

Lennie took in the tapestry of countryside rushing past her window. She knew her words would be swallowed by the wind. "We'll see about that."

A peculiar shape caught her eye, a dancing shadow of sorts amid tree limbs in a windswept pasture. She squinted in an effort to get a clearer view as they sped past. The tree was suddenly shrinking in her passenger door mirror, leafy branches clasping what she could have sworn was a gaggle of nearly deflated purple helium balloons. *Could that be ...?* The balloons she'd released to the somber skies over Dad's grave floated back into her memory.

She twisted in her seat to double check what she had *thought* she'd seen, but the tree was too far behind them now.

NINETEEN

Now and Then

Lennie's eyes widened as they pulled up to their destination. Her recent dream, she realized, had re-created the Chattanooga Choo Choo Motel from her childhood memory; she tussled to reconcile those images with what now lay before them.

Walloped by the decades, the 1950s motor lodge looked like a B-rate scary movie. Rust stains crept down a faded concrete block exterior. Even the overhang that ran the length of a breezeway past a dozen doors sagged between steel supports.

"What the hell happened?" John said, looking as shocked as she felt. He raised his camera and snapped a shot.

She jumped out of the car, then hooked her thumbs in the pockets of her shorts as she searched for a hint of the past they had known here.

The neon yellow sign in the shape of a vintage steam locomotive, with its inverted funnel smokestack, still clung to its landmark status. It slowly rotated atop its eighteen-foot pole like it had so many years ago.

What looked like the same plastic wicker rocking chairs bracketed motel doors. The big window marking the office, though, was marred by two small crosses of orange duct tape. *Bullet holes?*

Time's relentless passage was bound to affect a place like this, stuck in the middle of nowhere on a two-lane country road.

Still, Lennie figured the Choo Choo had held fast to its territory with all the downtrodden dignity it could muster. "This is your basic four-star accommodation in some circles," she said. "You should see the Salmon Run Lodge in Alaska."

John ran his hand over his mouth. "At least I reserved our same room. Six."

"You remembered the room?"

"A screw was missing, so the six hung upside down and looked like a nine."

Speaking of missing screws. She headed for the office. When she pushed through the door, a spring-loaded bell announced her arrival.

She instantly recognized the proprietor from their childhood stop and, more recently, from her dream. His face was unforgettable—the left side swollen like a hamster hoarding sunflower seeds in its cheek. A seed husk stuck to his lower lip, where other men might clench a toothpick after supper. He was still decked in a conductor's cap, denim overalls, and railway boots, but his chin had been lost to gravity and the years had saddled him with a tangled gray beard and a gut so big it must have had its own zip code.

He closed his *Truck Trader* magazine and groaned when he stood up. "Hey-hoo! Welcome to the Choo Choo!"

She saw her smile reflected in a mirror behind him, his name still vivid from her dream. "Mr. Dupay?"

"Mister? Please, child. I *work* for a livin'. Call me Pepper." He grinned. There was a sense of wonder to him, like the children in her reading group.

The doorbell dinged and she turned to see John, who stepped up next to her. He offered Pepper a handshake. "How you doing?"

The frumpy stump of a guy dipped his head to look at John over reading glasses. "Well, I'll tell 'ya," he said, shaking John's hand, "I got more aches and pains than I got bugs disgracin' my windshield, but I'm still hangin' in there." He spat a seed husk into a wide-necked ceramic vase spittoon with practiced ease.

"What can I do for ya?"

"I'm John Riley. I called this morning and reserved the same room we stayed in thirty-four years ago."

Pepper straightened behind the counter. "Well, my goodness! Y'all the second-honeymooners?"

"No," Lennie blurted with a suddenness that surprised her.

The expression on the ancient proprietor's face changed to puzzled concern. "Hmm. Who might'cha be, then?"

"We stayed here as kids," John said. "Our dad had the Pontiac Bonneville Grand Safari wagon you liked, with the rear-facing, third-row seat you can fold down for cargo. You went out and looked in it. Sat behind the wheel." John's eyebrows lifted, as if they were key to jarring the old guy's memory.

Lennie studied Pepper's face, waiting for his gears to mesh. His head seemed to sink into his shoulders as the folds of his face deepened with thought. "Not ringin' a bell."

"You *sat* in the car and *raved* about the room for your deer decoys," John said with rising exasperation.

"Johnny, he's seen tons of people pass through here."

Pepper gathered his beard into his hand and gave it a little twist, eyes gazing sideways at a rack of postcards, like he hoped for some kind of clue there.

Postcards—the display still contained the locomotive sign variety Dad had in his scrapbook. Lennie considered them a moment, then leaned her elbows on the counter and squeezed the man's forearm.

"We were the kids who fought with those sticks of light. Right out there in the parking lot. I was the little princess swinging the blue one."

His face lit up. "Yes, yes, yes!" He pushed his conductor's cap back, then snugged it down again. "Them *Star Wars* dealies. My goodness. Look at y'all!"

John gave her a confounded gaze, as if he couldn't believe his attempt to jar Pepper's memory had failed where hers succeeded.

Duh. She lifted her hands. "Men are visually oriented. Labrador meet squirrel."

Pepper said, "You were the little girl who wailed the tar outta your brother with the *Star Wars* stick."

John scowled. "She didn't *wail* the tar out of me."

"I *did* open a big ol' can of whoop-ass, didn't I?" she said to Pepper with a chuckle.

Pepper belly laughed as he started to fill out their paperwork. "I don't know what you call a whoopin' where y'all come from, but around here, that would qualify."

John waved him off. "Whatever."

Lennie hid her smile. That was John-speak for *I didn't win.*

Her brother pulled out his wallet. "I talked with a woman this morning and booked room six."

"Lorraine?"

"Yes."

"You sure she said six?"

"Positive."

"Well, that'd be quite a feat." He spit another seed husk into his vase spittoon. "Man got killed in there goin' back about ten years now."

Lennie tensed. "Somebody was killed in our room?"

"Poor fella was gutted like a dadburn deer," Pepper said, marveling at the memory. "Word got around on the World Wide Internet and nobody wanted to stay in there, so we made it a storage room. Yep, ol' number six is as gone as gone kin get."

Uh-oh. She glanced at John, who tossed his hands. She knew staying in their old room was crucial for him, a part of his faithful re-creation.

"But I confirmed with this Lorraine lady not ten hours ago."

Apparently at a loss, Pepper rubbed his right cheek. "Well, Lorraine ... She's been havin' some issues with what the doc called her ... let's see ... her age-related cognition function."

John blinked at him. "Cognitive. Function." The words marched in lockstep, as if they somehow spoke to a conspiracy against his plan.

"Yeah, right. That's what it is. It clouds her thinkin' sometimes. You understand."

Lennie felt for both John and a stranger named Lorraine. "Tell you what," the old clerk said with a glint in his eyes, "I got a nine. You can have it for half-price. Save you a few nickels."

John turned away, then offered a small nod.

"I'll even throw in the towels at no additional cost."

A few minutes later, towels over their shoulders, Lennie led her brother past the row of pumpkin-orange doors.

She glanced at each number as it passed and knew John was doing the same, his wheeled luggage clunking over seams in the concrete breezeway: 1 ... 2 ... 3 ... 4 ... 5 ... Storage Room ... 7 ... 8 ... 9. Their room. Their *wrong* room.

"I can't believe that number six is the only one not available," his voice came from behind her.

"Keep on keepin' on, Johnny," she said over her shoulder, thinking how different their lives were. He was used to always getting his way, while nothing but disappointment had dogged her steps over the last twenty-odd years. When things didn't work out, she simply moved on.

But now, with her long-shot hope of connecting with Dad, there was a lot more at stake for her. She wondered how she'd cope if it didn't happen.

The clatter of John's rolling Versace stopped behind her. She dropped her duffel to the walkway at their room and looked back to see him staring at the door marked Storage Room. A cloud of misery hung over him.

"Hey," she said. "It's Happy Hour. And I'm buying."

TWENTY

The Big Still

Lennie had spotted the honky-tonk hunkered just a few hundred yards from the Choo Choo. As she approached the Big Still Lounge, she heard thumping country music tinged with crying steel guitar. Lighted beer signs in the windows washed out over muddy pickup trucks. Judging by the crammed parking lot, they had a full house tonight.

According to Pepper, the place prided itself on the fact that country music superstar Brad Paisley had stopped in one night and jammed with the house band. He described The Buckshots, the house band, as ragtag thrashers who melted eardrums with sheer volume.

She pulled the door open, instantly blasted by a wall of sound. The Friday night crowd took her back to Jake's Last Stand, a local watering hole where she liked to dance after a long day at the cannery on Kodiak Island. As she wound her way through the jam-packed room, a muggy wave of body heat enveloped her. Already in tune with the rhythm of the place, she looked back to see if John was keeping up.

She saw him work his bigger frame through the people walled along the edge of the dance floor. A dude in a black cowboy hat, whose barrel-chested laughter was dwarfed only by the size of his belt buckle, stumbled backwards. He bumped into John, sloshing some of his beer on him.

John shook off the sticky suds and kept pressing through the jostling throng. His aggravation mixed with an overwhelming feeling of disgust. *How did I let her talk me into this?*

He was certain Dad hadn't bellied up to any bars on their family vacation. *We're getting off-point.* The only reason he had agreed to walk down here was to get something to eat—Pepper had said it was the only place for miles. *Seriously? Bar food?* He'd hoped for something along the lines of a nice *filet mignon.* Medium rare. Paired with a robust Cabernet.

Less than a day in, and his vagabond sister seemed dead set on pulling him off track with her Dollywood antic. Then there was the motel that had decayed into a hot mess. Come to think of it, he could use a drink after all. He caught up with Lennie at the end of the U-shaped bar.

She was admiring the bar's polished pine surface when John took the stool on her left. A barmaid with a tumble of fiery red hair and a peek-a-view midriff shirt, tossed them two napkins and some cantankerous attitude.

"Talk to me," she hollered over the music as she flipped up the hinged lid of a garnish bin. Before Lennie could respond, the young woman took inventory, opening and whacking the bins shut.

Cherries. *Slam!* Olives. *Wham!* Limes. *Bam!*

"Limes!" she yelled over her shoulder. Then, she stared at them, an impatient hand on her hip.

Lennie figured she must've had a rough day. Or night. Or life. She could relate. She offered the barmaid a friendly grin. "Rum Runner, please. No lime is fine. Thank you."

Scooping ice into a glass, the server didn't even look at John. "How 'bout it, sport?" she shouted above the clamor. "You in?"

"Brandy Gump. Up."

She put her hand to her ear. *"What?"*

"Brandy Gump! Up!" he hollered over a wailing guitar.

She flicked a discarded lime peel down the bar like a pesky bug. "Brandy *who?"*

"Gump! With a P!" Lennie knew he was winding up like a spring ready to let go as he raised himself on his elbows to get closer to the barkeep. He spelled it out for her in no uncertain terms. "G-u-m-p! Gump!"

Her brother and the drink-slinger locked each other's eyes in a simmering starefest. *Irresistible force, meet immovable object.*

"Like Forrest!" he shouted. "That Alabama guy who led a charmed life through no effort of his own. Maybe you've heard of him in this fine establishment."

Easy, Big Hoss. She can put anything she wants in your drink. Dudes as thick as tree stumps yammered for beer down the bar. This could get ugly quick. For all she knew, a team of brass-knuckled bouncers was about to bust loose. *I wonder if I could outrun them?*

"If you'd be a hon," Lennie said with a grin, "chill a cocktail glass. Martini glass if you've got it. Two shots brandy, splash grenadine, splash lime. Shake over ice. Strain to serve."

The barmaid shifted her defiant gaze to Lennie. "I'm sure I *will*, sweetheart." She glowered at John then headed for the mixing station.

Lennie shot him a sideways glance. "Jeez, Johnny. Relax much?" He didn't look like he was in any mood to answer, so she swiveled her stool and checked the place out.

Not a square inch of space left on the dance floor, the usual suspects shooting pool in a corner of the room, and beer-drinking braggarts laughing as they surely lied about their exploits.

"I wouldn't have guessed you know brandy drinks," John said.

"Lots you don't know about me."

"Like what? You're tending bar?"

Lennie noticed a couple of guys in ball caps eyeing her from just around the corner of the bar. "Once upon a time," she said. "Out in Cali."

The band blistered a final guitar chord and announced a twenty-minute break, spurring dance couples to head for the jukebox. John regarded the musicians' instruments glinting under the stage lights.

When he turned back to the bar, a ragtag carpet of celebratory dollar bills mounted on the drop-down ceiling drew his attention. "You still playing that guitar of yours?"

Lennie scanned the cash snapshots in time. Birthdays. Engagements. Anniversaries. "I had to sell it to help pay for tires a long time ago."

"As much as it was by your side growing up? I thought you loved that thing."

"Yeah, well, sometimes life has a way of squeezing the love right out of you."

The barmaid delivered their drinks with icy speed and left just as quickly. Lennie lifted her glass for a toast.

"So ... " She waited for John to lift his drink, which he half-heartedly did. "To Dad," she said, trying to lighten his mood with a smile.

She clinked his wide-brimmed cocktail too hard, spilling some of his drink on his hand. "Sorry. Just eager to share a moment, I guess."

She sipped her cocktail as John cleaned up the splatter with a wad of napkins. Maybe some easy conversation might help soothe the wound inflicted by the unfortunate demise of his precious room six.

"You getting good vibes yet?" she asked. "Walking in his shoes?"

He drew a long sip, then set his drink squarely in the center of a fresh napkin. "Not a vibe I'm after. More like completion."

One of the guys who'd been checking her out stood up. He looked forties, well-fed but not well-balanced as he swayed with a coppery drink, whiskey she guessed. A soppy napkin dangled from the bottom of his glass. If he was trying for a Santa Claus beard, he'd nailed it, only it was as brown as dirt after a rain.

She realized John was explaining a feeling he once had. "It's like the time I found my old BB gun in Dad's shop," he was saying. "Like a piece of home." He looked at her. "You ever have that feeling there?"

Before she could answer, Santa slid onto a stool on her other side. "How you doin', sweet thing?"

Lennie turned to him and mustered a polite smile. "I'm sorry, but I'm with someone." Her knees clunked against the face of the bar when she swiveled back to John. "I never lived in the same house you did."

"What are you talking about?"

"Same roof over my head, but that's as close as it got. You were always his hero. We can say it out loud now."

"Hmm. Maybe we *didn't* grow up in the same house. Either that, or your memory is shot. Because, from what I recall, he tried to do the same for you as he did for me."

"Really? Is that how you see it?"

Santa tapped her shoulder and she ignored him, easing nearer to John. "Basketball? That's the shot he gave me?"

"Even arranged that camp in Watkinsville to position you for a scholarship."

Santa suddenly was in her ear. "What's your name, darlin'?"

She turned back to him and offered her most disarming smile. "Excuse me, but I'm trying to have a conversation over here and, despite your obvious charms, I'm afraid you're going to have an off-night with me. But it's not you. It's me."

She swiveled back to John. "You think I *liked* basketball? I played because *he* loved it. Turns out, that round ball was the one thing I could do to turn his head. We had nothing else. You got it all."

He scowled. "How can you say that? He paid hard-earned money to send you to that camp."

She smelled Santa's whiskey before she felt his moist breath on her neck. "I think I'm *on* tonight, sweetheart. *Big-time* on."

John came at her from the other side: "Turns out, you just weren't interested enough in college to work at it."

She recoiled in her seat when Santa caressed her arm, and John's expression flipped from accusatory to uneasy.

"What's wrong?" he said.

"Nothing." She heard the defiance in her voice. It was the same tender touch that at one time had persuaded her that her latest mistake didn't mean to hit her, the same crippling lie that had trapped her in past relationships. Dread roiled her thoughts, but she shook it off, reminding herself she was working to put all that behind her. What she *couldn't* put behind her was John's attempt to define her life.

"I had other things on my mind," she said, urgently needing to defend the path she'd been forced to choose as whiskey Santa pushed his finger into the back of her arm. "Things you know *nothing* about."

"Right." John gave her a dismissive nod. "So you left. And that's the way it's been. You run away."

She felt her chin quivering and fought to hold her own. "Hey, here's an idea: Let's not screw up our one meaningful moment in the last twenty years with a lecture. How about *that?*"

He lifted his hands as if she'd just charged him with a crime. "You always quit. Yes or no?"

Lennie stared at him for a moment. Could taste the bar's musky air as it rushed in and out of her lungs. A breath away from crying, she felt the impact of what she just knew was Santa's boot helping itself to the bottom bracket of her stool.

"You have no idea," she said to her brother. The hushed words barely made it out of her mouth before she pushed off her chair and sliced into the crowd.

John watched her work through the press of bodies. "See?" he yelled after her. "Just walk out and prove my point!"

He caught only a glimpse of her as she pulled the door open and hurried into the night. Looking down into his drink, he lightly shook his head. "Damn it."

He didn't *want* things to go this way. Why did she have to live in a dream world instead of facing facts? She had never even *tried* to live in the real world. That had always hurt her.

The barmaid arrived with a smirk. "Well, bless your heart. You're just a charmer all the way around, ain't'cha, sport? Actually repellin' people." She took Lennie's drink and walked away.

John stared at his reflection in the mirror behind the bar. *What the hell are you doing?* He took a long draw off his drink, the brandy concoction biting the back of his throat. He set the glass down and stared at the rust-colored liquid.

The glistening swirl stirred a grainy memory of Lennie as a preschooler. The doctor had just taken off the foot brace she was required to wear after her corrective shoe was removed, and she was running and laughing in the rain, through muddy puddles at the end of the driveway.

"Look, Johnny!" she hollered to him. "I can run!" It was then, in her excitement, that she tripped in a pothole obscured by the muddy water and tumbled face first to the gravel road.

He sprinted across the yard as she shrieked in pain, her face a mess of blood and dirty water. When he tried to pick her up, she screamed and pushed him off—she wanted to get up herself.

Afraid and helpless, he stood over his broken little sister as she lay there bleeding, and—

"Don't sweat it, man." The words were jarring. The guy who'd been sitting on the other side of Lennie had moved over to her stool, next to him. He gave John a slap on the shoulder. "You get the bitch in the sack, and she'd probably just lay there and make you do all the work."

Rocked from his memory, it took John a second for the heinous words to register. Then they speared him like a lance, and he felt his eyes tighten as his spine went rigid. "What did you just say?" He didn't recognize his own voice; it trembled with guttural menace.

The dude shot back his drink and gestured for another. Then he clamped John's shoulder. "I said the bitch—"

"I heard you, asshole!" John erupted to his feet, his barstool crashing back into the crush of people behind him. Fury fired every fiber in his body.

The guy swiveled with a sloppy grin as John's heart pounded his ribcage, nails digging into the palms of his clenched fists.

"Firstly, my name ain't asshole," the bearded hulk replied with a rasp that cut the ominous stillness that settled around them. "And B, you need to apologize for such a rude outburst."

The barmaid handed the local a whiskey glass filled to the rim and gave John a hostile smirk. The guy gulped down his drink and stood up. And up ... And up ... Two heads taller and three sizes heavier than John.

"I'm waitin' on your apology."

Coiled with adrenaline, John focused his rapid breathing, peripherally aware of guys forming a semi-circle behind him as a country love ballad dripped out of the jukebox. There was only one way out. He held up his hands in surrender.

Backed away.

Turned to leave and—

—spun back with a lightning fist at the guy's face, stopped by a hand the size of a catcher's mitt. The dude grinned for the briefest second, seemingly in appreciation for the attempt, and punched John square in the face.

John's vision went watery as the ceiling blurred past. He landed on his back, cracking a table as a clamor rose and frantic hands grabbed scattering drinks.

Cloudy faces converged over him. Hands yanked him to his feet. Shoved him toward his hazy foe, who landed a boot to his gut and forced the air from his body. Voices roared. And what felt like a concrete piling thudded his back.

Chaotic light, form and sound pummeled him. Lifted him. A riotous sea of bodies parted to reveal the door rushing at his face, blearily illuminated by neon.

He clenched his eyes, managed to loosely cross his arms over his head, and went weightless before crashing down in dusty clay that kicked up into his face.

Blaring music and laughter behind him faded away as he pushed up to his hands and knees. He wiped his watery eyes and saw blood dripping beneath him, drops hitting the absorbent clay in splotches.

He dragged the back of his hand over his mouth and winced at the searing pain. *Shit.* Crimson smeared his fingers, his wedding band bloodied. He pressed his tongue into the back of his teeth—nothing was loose.

He hauled himself to his feet, his polo shirt drenched with beer, tinged garnet by his leaking face, and blinked to focus on the amber light pulsating from the distant Choo Choo's locomotive sign. Pulling off his shirt, he pressed it to his face, applying pressure to stop the bleeding as he set off for the motel.

As his Gucci slip-ons scuffed along the darkened road, he wondered what had just happened. And so fast. Something had grabbed hold of him. *A fight? What the hell?* He hadn't thrown a punch since high school, when Tommy Poe had tried to muscle in on Kelli Ann Wilson.

He could've diffused the situation and walked away. *Why didn't I?* It had been beyond his control. A reaction to Lennie? It scared him.

With an iron grip, he held on to the sound of Dad's voice. Advice the old man would give him when he hadn't played up to his capabilities in a big basketball game. *Put it behind you, son, and get back on track tomorrow.*

TWENTY-ONE

Into Darkness

Lennie lay on a sunken mattress against the wall in Room Nine. Her single bed was separated from John's by a nightstand covered with cigarette burns.

She stared at the ceiling, trying to settle her mind. Should she tell John about why she'd bolted Mosely without a word? She'd been so close at the bar.

Or she could reveal her plan with an Appalachian guardakin angel. *Yeah, right.* A reputed go-between, so she could ... what? Reach across the Great Divide and connect with Dad? *Now that I hear it, it sounds flipped out, even to me.*

The window AC hummed in the darkness, the locomotive sign slowly throbbing outside, its amber light filtered through a threadbare curtain.

She was certain her brother already thought she was loosey-goosey. *If I told him about some next-of-kin angel, he'd* really *think I've gone off the deep end. Maybe I have.*

How did a person know if she'd gone nutty as a pecan pie anyway, because, well, she's nutso. She should've asked Yolanda. *Okay, no more lies.* She'd tell John everything. If she was going to rebuild their relationship, it started with trust, right? Why did she—

A key grated the deadbolt's tumblers, and she tightened her hand around a fistful of sheet. John entered, silhouetted against the curtain by the flashing sign outside. He'd removed his shirt. No wonder. It was hotter'n a two-dollar pistol at a turkey shoot.

He locked the deadbolt and stepped to his suitcase against the wall, at the foot of the beds. *Say something.*

He rummaged through his Versace, disappeared into the darkness of the bathroom, and closed the door with a soft click. *What's wrong with you? What did Emily say? You're hiding.*

Facing the sink mirror, John touched his busted lip and checked his left cheek, grimacing as he pressed the discolored skin below his swollen eye. He'd have to come up with something to explain it away. It was embarrassing, and it was important to move past the entire ugly event. He needed to stay focused on the task at hand.

He moved his jaw up and down, side to side—a little sore, but it wasn't broken. Bar pandemonium still ringing in his head, he gave himself a disappointed look, although part of him was proud of the way he'd taken a punch.

He turned on the shower, and water pounded the enclosure as he slid a plastic bag out of a small trash can. He rinsed his bloodied shirt, jammed it in the bottom of the receptacle, and put the bag back in on top. By the time housekeeping found it, he'd be long gone.

Was Lennie awake? Probably. Ready with a barrage of talk? No doubt. He only wanted to get down to Rock City at Lookout Mountain in the morning, because that meant he'd be back on track.

He showered and pulled on a pair of gym shorts. Back in the room, he moved quietly to the door, unlocked it and stepped outside.

Stretching his arms overhead, he took a deep breath and exhaled. No pain. At least that boot hadn't landed squarely on his ribs. He'd weathered the impact, which he chalked up to his consistent core strength regimen at the gym.

He gripped the breezeway's steel support and stretched his shoulders. A thin layer of fog had settled in. The murky moon appeared, then slipped behind drifting clouds before peeking out again in the shifting skies.

Its hovering glow set his mind to wandering. Holly was probably reading in bed about now, and he'd missed the kids' bedtime ritual: Stevie saying goodnight to each of his aquarium fish by name, while Abbey's electric toothbrush hummed down the hallway.

He glanced back at the room's black aluminum "9," his aspirations for room six dead as a doornail. Like a pitcher shaking off a catcher's signal, he banished the negative thought and—*wait a second!* He grabbed the beam that ran between the overhang supports, pulled himself up and then dropped down to the walkway. *Yes, of course!*

Room Six could still be a win. Somebody's untimely death had stolen his childhood, but he could steal it back with a little engineering.

He shot a glance left and right. Not a soul around. A tiny nail between him and victory. Forcing his fingertips behind the "9," he exerted pressure until its rounded top eased away from the metal door. Careful to not bend the attachment nail, which he removed, the "9" swung upside down on its bottom tack and transformed into a "6."

He considered his handiwork. *Yessir.* It was all still in front of him, and it began right here. All he had to do was stick to the spreadsheet, which he had committed to memory—

Cell B19. Saturday morning, Rock City's renowned underground caves at Lookout Mountain, Georgia.

Cell B20. Saturday afternoon, Six Flags Over Georgia.

Cell B21. Sunday travel to Cape Canaveral.

Cell B22. Monday, dawn launch.

Dawn launch. Even the words were beautiful. Smoke and fire streaking the sky. Dad's moment, and the pinnacle where his answer awaited.

Back in the room, he locked the door and stretched out on the bed, across the nightstand from Lennie, trying to ignore the pulse of the locomotive sign as he settled into the pillow. Finally, he closed his eyes on the day.

Lennie had waited for him to come back in. "Everything okay?" She hung on for a handful of heartbeats.

"Yeah," he muttered. "Fine." She knew better.

"What were you doing out there?"

"Nothing. Just ... wishing things were right."

She pushed up on her elbow and turned toward him. "Got yourself a pretty tall wish there."

No reply. "What's right," she said, "has a way of shifting gears on you." Still no response. She lay back down and gazed at the ceiling as stucco swirls rose and receded with each throb of curtained amber light. She wondered if—

"It's called relativism," the darkness said.

Relativism. She died a little inside. *Yeah, Johnny. Go ahead and explain the world to me.*

The coarse pillowcase rustled in her ear as she shifted toward his shapeless form, barely an arm's length away. "Slap your fancy words all over it. The fact remains, things change."

No way he can argue with that. And he didn't. He said nothing, deadening her hope that they could find their way to a better place through these hurtful times.

She cleared her throat. "Dad ever tell you about my basketball camp while you were studying in Europe?"

"It's time to sleep, Lennie."

"*Did* he?"

"Just that your heart wasn't in it."

She batted his response around in her head and chose the easy way out. "Sounds about right." Separated from him by five feet of dingy carpet and twenty-five years of living, she turned away and stared into the mottled shadows.

Fall 1993

Dear Momma,

Blake asked me to Homecoming. Ghaaaa!!! What do I do??? He's nice and all that, but I think Axel Briscoe's gonna ask me. He was looking at me at the Pizza Palace and threw a pack of sugar at me. Becca says that means he wants MY sugar!

He rides a motorcycle. Daddy can't stand him. He gets all "devil's temptation" and how Axel will lead me down the wrong path. He says fifteen is too young for a school dance. Can you believe that???? He's ruining my life!

I don't even know you, but I miss you so much. How is that possible? To not even know someone, but to miss them so much it hurts? Am I weirded out? I hate not being able to miss you for real. Like you're away visiting someone but will be back. Don't forget to come see me at the After Supper Club!

I'm working on a new poem ...

"Rollin' with Axel"

Rain runs to nothing, the cold and hard.
I watch from the porch of my own back yard.
It's my life, but not my time,
It hurts to wait for you on the line.

God, that sucks. Never mind ...

TWENTY-TWO

Hung Up

"Closed? You can't close Rock City!" John paced the length of their room and glimpsed the bruise under his left eye in the bathroom mirror as rain hammered outside.

A crack of thunder made the nightstand lamp flicker. "How can you close a Southern institution?" He wound the phone cord around his fist, listening to an explanation he wasn't buying. "It's like cancelling Christmas!"

"I'm sorry, sir, but it's a weather decision," the man said. "The grounds are extremely slippery, which creates a safety hazard and—"

"Yes, I understand all that," John cut him off, eyeing his Rolex. He was relieved the watch hadn't been damaged during his fight. The valuable timepiece had remained on his wrist while he slept, reassuring him that all was well in spite of the rough night. It now read 8:03 a.m. They had to get moving or else.

"We have lots of families with children and—"

"I know. I have kids myself. But you don't understand. This is my *one* shot. I'm on a schedule." His eye ached, his swollen lip began to throb and, worst of all, his *second* stop was in jeopardy.

He'd been in plenty of high-pressure meetings before, had advised the governor, and presented in conference rooms brimming with officials. He could handle some backcountry phone boy who stood between him and his memorial itinerary. Time to swing the leverage hammer.

"I just lost my Dad," he said. "I'm here in memory of him." Tough to say no when death is in the mix. "Surely you can let me in on some type of bereavement accommodation."

"Sir, I'm so sorry for your loss. We anticipate reopening tomorrow."

"I can't come tomorrow. I've got an all-day drive to another stop. Don't you *listen?* My Dad is dead, and I'm on a schedule!"

"Sir, Rock City apologizes for the inconvenience. I wish there was something we could do, but it's a safety issue for all concerned."

John pulled his head back with a fistful of hair and slammed the phone. He stared at his spreadsheet itinerary on the nightstand, its efficiency mocking him. Yanking open the scarred furniture's drawer, he pushed aside a Gideon's Bible and snatched a sawed-off pencil. Then he scratched out his *See Rock City!* entry so hard, the pencil gouged the nightstand beneath it.

Lennie suddenly ripped open the door, soaked to the bone from the storm and bouncing her basketball on the covered walkway.

He spun away. *Great.* He'd slept a little later than her and had made a point of staying under the sheet so she wouldn't see his face.

"You finally get up?" she said behind him. "I found a cool court."

He had no choice but to face her. "They closed Rock City. Can you believe that?"

Actually, yeah, she *could* believe it. What she couldn't grasp was how he looked. "What happened here?" She swirled her hand around her face to indicate the area in question.

He shot her a dismissive wave. "Nothing. I slipped in the bathroom at the bar."

"And broke the fall with your face?"

John flopped back on his bed. "There was water all over the floor, and I caught the sink. Place was a real gem."

He got to his feet and gave his spreadsheet as disgusted a wave as he'd just given her. "I do all this planning, and what do I get?

"Tough to account for acts of God, Johnny. You know what they say about life and planning, right?"

"No. And, obviously, neither do you, so spare me."

She couldn't talk with him when he was like this. *So much for a chat to get everything out in the open.* Maybe the way to his heart was through his sneakers.

"C'mon. The court's behind the Choo Choo at this elementary school. Let's shoot around like we used to. It's even got a chain net. Remember those?"

John massaged the back of his neck and winced.

"Rock City is closed," she pressed. "We're gonna miss the underground caves, so roll with it. We'll shoot around and then take off for Georgia. You have another stop, right? Six Flags? Dad woulda shot around. Aren't you trying to do what *he* did?"

"Not in *this* weather he wouldn't have." It was like he couldn't even take in her suggestion, too caught up in his latest disappointment. "I can't believe they closed it," he muttered, repeating himself.

"You know what *I* can't believe?" she quipped with forced amazement. "That you're afraid *a girl* is gonna hoop-school your ass."

He couldn't have looked any more annoyed. "What are you, *eight?*"

"No, I'm a chicken." She dropped her ball and flapped her arms. "BAAK! BAAK! BAAK!"

"I'm *not* playing!"

TWENTY-THREE

Face-Off

A basketball court was where their lives had last touched. It wasn't where Lennie wanted the heart-to-heart talk with her brother, but she still lacked the courage to begin. Maybe this time together would create the connection they so badly needed. She could feel their shared past closing the distance between them with each thumping bounce of the ball.

She crouched face to face with John on the elementary school's cracked asphalt court, drenched in the downpour under a pressing sky of steel gray. Water pirouetted off her nose and streamed from her chin, just as it did his.

They were alone, the rumble of distant thunder a sign of the magnitude of the heavy summer storm that now soaked their half-court game.

"Make it, take it," Lennie said, slowly dribbling the ball, face gripped in concentration. "First one to ten."

John mopped the water off his forehead. "I cannot believe how stupid this is."

"It's not stupid, it's an adventure," she said.

With low-slung brick school buildings and the hazy outline of a distant chain-link fence barely visible through the rain, the place resembled the prison yards she'd seen in the movies. Even the shafts of muted pole lights piercing the gloom looked like those atop guard towers.

She, though, felt like a kid who had been let out to play. This was a good old-fashioned gully washer! She'd never realized until this instant how much she missed the intensity of Southern storms.

Saturated T-shirt and shorts sticking to her skin, she focused on his eyes, just as she'd done growing up on the driveway basketball court at home. Only this time, Dad wasn't there to shout instructions on a proper chest pass or offer encouragement after a pretty pick-and-roll play or a crossover dribble to throw an opponent off-balance.

The wet basketball felt familiar slapping and retreating from Lennie's hand as she dribbled facing the basket, rocking side to side just a touch, toes grabbing the bottoms of her soaked sneakers, ready to make a move. She felt downright giddy.

When she dribbled toward John, he widened his stance. His arms spread, his left one high to defend the quick jumper, the right one stretched out to cut off her path to the basket. She remembered all his moves.

Lennie had a knack for dribbling. She had no idea why. Maybe it was fluid hands. She'd even posed with the ball in the 1994 Tennessee Female Athlete of the Year photo when she was sixteen, the only girl in the state who had earned a starting roster spot on a boys' sports team. As team captain, John had resented it. Who wanted his little sister hanging around the guys?

The ball had been her only physical connection to Dad all her years away. An outdoor Spalding with well-earned scuffs and scrapes, her name in block letters barely visible in Sharpie.

Lennie faked to her right to test his reaction. He was ready, shuffle-stepping to block her. Her biggest competitive advantage had always been her quickness. That and a sheer grit born of a desperate need for Dad's attention. He'd been the one who helped her get good enough to compete with the boys.

At five feet five, she relied on that quickness and determination to make up for her lack of size against the bigger players, including John, at six feet.

She pivoted, backing into him with her dribble. John half-heartedly defended her as she spun away from him and took the ball to the basket for an easy layup. The ball splashed down and he grabbed it.

"Two-zip," she announced with a grin. "I thought you played this game before." She clapped her hands. "C'mon, let's go, slo-mo. Finding my rhythm."

He rolled his eyes, whipped her the ball. She dribbled at him, spun to keep her body between him and the ball.

John hip-bumped her, held his ground, using his weight to counter her attempt to move him back toward the basket. He swatted at the ball over her shoulder.

Dribbling with her right hand, she pushed him off with her left. He pushed back.

"Watch those knees, old man," she warned with a chuckle.

His facial muscles tightened. "More game, less gab." He swiped at the ball again.

She faked a move to her left, and he went for it like she knew he would, getting him off-balance.

She pulled up to hit a short jumper, the ball singing through the chain-link net like a waterlogged wind chime. "Oooh!" she yowled, tossing her shoulders from side to side. "She hits the J!"

John grabbed the ball. "Lucky shot."

Of course. It was always some sort of fluke when someone bested him. Just like Penelope Parsons of Thomasville Furniture.

It had all started there and just kind of snowballed his whole life. "Tough losing a step, huh?" she teased him. "Four-zip."

He slung the ball to her as the rain sliced through the court lights. "Fine," he said. "You really want to play?" He untucked his t-shirt, wind-milled his arms and waved her toward him. "Bring it."

She faked a move, then rose for a shot. John blocked it and snatched the ball.

Face coursing water, she hustled to guard him as he dribbled, and he pushed her away with his free hand.

She tried to hold her position but bounced off his bigger frame with a grunt, the impact driving the air from her lungs. Grimacing, she refused to back down.

She lunged for a steal.

He spun away.

Two quick dribbles, and he hit a jump shot. "Yeahhh!" He pumped his fists as he trotted around in a victory lap. "He hits the three!" he bellowed in a sing-song voice.

Lennie chased the ball down and threw it to him at the three-point arc, nearly twenty feet from the basket. She scrambled toward him, but before she got there, he nailed another three.

"Whoosh!" he yelled. "It's raining treys!" He cupped his hands around his mouth and imitated the sound of a roaring, adoring crowd. "You better grab some jelly," he said with a smirk, "because I'm toasting you, girl. What's that, six-four, mine?"

She grabbed the ball and gave him a forced grin. *Let him go. Just let John be John. It's just a game.* But she knew it wasn't just a game to him.

Try as she might, she couldn't subdue the bitterness that cracked through the determined composure she'd nurtured through the years as a buffer against the harshness the world had thrown at her. He was flogging her with his life. His superior life. His top-of-the-world, buddy-to-the-governor life.

Years of suppressed resentment rattled her core. John had gotten the best of everything. From Dad. From Mr. Mosely and his string-pulling at the university. From fate. All of it. And she'd gotten less than nothing.

As she stared at him, the rumbling netherworld seemed to envelop them. She almost felt like an apparition in a schoolyard of hazy light and shadow as she walked the ball to him in the mist, hand-delivering a dare. "But can you take me to the rim?"

"Please," he snipped. "Don't waste my time."

They hunkered down in stances ready for action, eye-to-eye like enemies in a sudden-death match, the storm pounding them. John backed into her with his dribble.

She shoved him.

Staggered him off-balance.

He spun past her.

Powered toward the basket.

She pursued him, a lifetime of lassoed wrath surging into an anger unlike any she had ever known, teeth gritting as she went up with him.

Her furious forearm hammered him in the face as the ball dropped through the chain net, and she stumbled into the mud behind the basket.

She turned to see blood oozing from his split lip. He grabbed the ball, started to dribble again, and gave her a dismissive smirk. "That the best you got, Eleanor Grace?"

Working to catch her breath, she pushed her sopping hair off her face and scowled at him. "You think that was on purpose?"

"Doesn't matter. You can't stop me."

She stood sucking air, hands on hips as he spun the ball on his fingertip, water spooling off the blur of orange.

She closed in on him. "Watch me stop you."

"Try." He bumped into her with his dribble.

She pushed him away.

He heaved back into her. "That what you're all about now?" he taunted. "Cheap shots? Cheating?"

Lennie shouldered him, determined to hold her position. But she was no match for his bigger frame, and he jostled her relentlessly toward the basket.

John scoffed. "You're out of your league, girl."

She shoved him again and again as he kept bulling her backward, and anguished tears filled her eyes as she tried to fight him off.

"You think you can stay with me? Huh, girl? You gonna stay with me?"

He pivoted, swept her aside like a pesky nuisance, and drove for the basket. She groaned as she bit her lip and gave everything she had to stay with him in the downpour.

As he rose for an easy layup, she could barely see through her tears when she sledgehammered him with a forearm to the head.

They crashed into the muck behind the basket, and she was up before John scrambled to his feet.

"What the hell was that!" he screamed, bull-rushing her.

"I had position!"

"Bullshit! The rules are for everybody but Lennie."

She popped him hard in the chest with her open hands. "Don't blame me if you can't even play a game without getting pissed if you lose!"

"Yeah, I like to win! And excuse the hell outta me for taking things more seriously than you!"

She swiped at the tears in her eyes. "I take things just as serious as you!"

Contempt oozed from him. "Oh, right! That's why you quit high school and wasted any shot of doing something with your life! You ran off on a ridiculous scheme to be some sort of bullshit coffee-house poet!"

"A spoken-word artist!"

Laughter sputtered from his mouth. "*Artist?* All the decisions you've made have led you to what? A dead-end job back in Mosely pushing throwaway paperbacks."

Her heart broke piece by piece. "I'm still working on my book!"

"Ooooh, that's right." His bottom lip curled in derision. "How could I forget? Lennie's book! Another childish delusion!"

She clenched her fists, fighting to keep her head above the rising waters of his damning ocean. "You'll never finish any book! You never finish *anything!* An education? A relationship? You've been aimlessly wandering a desert of your own making, and now you're bitter and alone!"

A quake began in her chest as every word ripped away another piece of her like a hurricane consuming the shore. "You couldn't even stick out a dinky high school basketball camp with a college scholarship on the line and a chance to do something with yourself! You've lied to yourself your entire life!"

Her body went taut, and she arched back then exploded forward, savagely head-butting him, the front of her skull burning as he staggered backward and tumbled into the mud.

She pounced on him, her knees straddled his chest, and she threw seething punches through her tears. "You don't know, Johnny!"

He covered his head against her eruption. "Lennie!"

She kept swinging as he writhed under the weight of her uncontrolled rage. "You don't know!"

Finally, he corralled her manic arms, twisted her off, and scrambled to his feet. She came at him again, frenzied fists flying.

"You don't know, Johnny!" she cried from the depths of her soul.

He reached out. "Lennie, stop it!—Lennie!"

"Nobody ever knew!"

His pinwheeling arms blocked her blows. "Lennie!" He managed to grab her, spin her away from him, and wrap his arms around her from behind. As she punched the rain, he hugged her back against his chest until her fists slowly gave up the fight.

"I can't—" Her sobbing words seized, dread welling from somewhere deep inside, a place she'd kept locked away. A crushing grief that had been suffocating her for more than twenty years. It took her by the throat and started to shake her head. *Nooo ...*

She twisted back to him, locked on his confused eyes. "Oh, God," she moaned as she felt her face contort in agony. "Watkinsville ... I didn't go for camp." Her voice quivered. "I didn't go for camp, Johnny. I went ... I went to have my baby."

Turmoil filled his eyes, as if he'd just taken a bullet that had screamed in from out of nowhere. *"What?"* he stammered, the word barely audible in the downpour.

She felt somehow bewildered. Like she was hearing the words for the first time herself. "My baby." The words tasted bitter on her lips. "Dad ... he made me give up my baby."

The pain was even more wrenching than it had been that desolate day at the women's clinic, the moment of delivering her child to the world. The bright light over her. The smell of disinfectant. Sweat stinging her eyes as she lay exhausted, legs splayed.

"They just kept encouraging me," she said in a distant voice, her vision obscured by water droplets dangling from her eyelashes. *Breathe, honey, breathe. Push ... that's it. You're doing fine.*

As the nurse's voice echoed down her memory's dark alley, she slumped forward, broken. She hid her face in her palms, and her spine withered until the backs of her hands rested on her muddy legs.

John took hold of her arms and muscled her up until she looked at him. "It's okay," he said.

Her eyes gripped his as her dreadful words kept coming. "I came home ... back for senior year. I thought I could push through and finish school." Her voice grew weaker. "They wouldn't tell me if I had a boy or a girl. I left there not knowing. I left my baby."

She turned away from him. "My baby, I—" The words died on her lips. Speaking to a memory hers alone, she felt a desperate need for absolution. For forgiveness.

"Listen to me," John said.

"My child is out there in the world somewhere. Abandoned."

"Lennie, no." He squeezed her shoulders. "It's important that you allow yourself—"

"Born to a nothin' momma."

"Stop it."

"A walk-away. The lowest of the low."

"This isn't—"

"Calls herself a poet." She laughed at herself through her tears. "A poet. Can you believe *that?*"

She crumpled into him, hiding from the then, the now, the future that threatened to crush her. She held on to her brother, trying to hold on to herself.

TWENTY-FOUR

The Lake House

Lennie sat hunched over in a plastic wicker chair outside their room, elbows on her knees. Even a Raggedy Ann had more spunk; she had never felt so winded. A thin motel towel draped over her head, she stared at the stained concrete between her bare feet. She had borne her burden alone for so long, it had become who she was. Who was she now? And what would she become?

The aroma of bacon, drifting from the motel's bare-bones breakfast bar down by the office, reminded her that there were lives enjoying simple pleasures. *Just to have one of those moments, free and clear.* She wasn't hungry. She felt sick to her stomach, knowing she had to somehow deal with the truths she had unearthed.

Amid a steady drizzle, lightning reflected off a pond that had overtaken the parking lot. She wasn't sure if the low rumble that followed was distant thunder or John clearing his throat in the chair next to her.

She leaned back until her head contacted the concrete wall behind her. The ceaseless rain summoned an image from the recesses of her mind. "I never felt so alone as when we were up at the Mosely lake house." She closed her eyes for a few seconds to let it come. "It was like we didn't belong in that world, and all those people knew it."

The covered breezeway kept her dry and the temperature still hovered in the muggy eighties, yet she couldn't suppress a shiver.

Opening her eyes, she raised her aching right foot so she could massage the arch while John silently rolled her basketball between his feet.

The lulling motion reminded her of a desktop novelty at the Mosely's multi-million-dollar shorefront estate—those clacking steel balls suspended on nylon strings that would remain in perpetual motion and were supposed to induce calm. Mr. Mosely had told her the gadget was based on one of Newton's Laws. He'd been proud of it.

The Mosely estate was on Fort Loudoun Lake in one of those exclusive communities where the homeowners' association provided each property owner with a fancy golf cart, so they could get around without having to worry about pine tree sap getting on their luxury cars.

Dad, one of Mr. Mosely's most loyal and seasoned laborers, had put in a ton of extra hours to complete an important excavation at the limestone quarry. Dad had explained that he wouldn't get paid for going the extra mile; instead, his boss had invited him, Lennie and Johnny up to his summer house for the holiday weekend. Lennie had always thought it was a raw deal.

"Boone paid me some attention," she said.

She saw the surprise in John's sideways glance. "Boone?"

"I know, right?" She let the towel slide to her shoulders and ran her fingers through her soppy hair. "What did he want with a girl like me?"

"That's not what I meant."

She gathered her hair into a ponytail and tried to wring out the last of the playground's dirty water. "C'mon, Johnny. He and I were from opposite sides of the tracks. No, check that: he actually owned the tracks. I just ... dreamed about riding them one day."

Boone Mosely. Eldest son of the family patriarch. Mosely High's number-one party boy. The only thing bigger than his glossy black Hummer H1 was his ego. Boone would raid his daddy's liquor cabinet to keep the party cranking for kids looking to numb the harshness of their hill-scrub lives. A gusher of whiskey that lubricated the single link between his entitled life and the school's working-class tribe.

"I'd never gotten much attention from the boys." Though she had long ago turned the page on high school days, memories of those echoing halls could still take her back to Friday night football games, the Pizza Palace afterwards and waiting for boys' phone calls that never came.

"Playing basketball as good as the boys did, I didn't make sense to them. So they made up stuff. The whispers? Dyke. Lezbo ... The whole girl-invading-their-world thing must'a blown their minds or something."

John stared at his feet and said nothing. Of course, he had been guilty of freezing her out on the team, too.

She slowly exhaled. "I felt like such a weirdo. But that night at the lake house? It felt nice, you know? To catch a boy's eye. And I thought maybe ... to feel special for just a minute. With a boy who could have had any girl he liked with his silver-platter life." She tried to fluff out her hair, but it collapsed to her shoulders. Why did nothing ever go the way she wanted it to?

A pickup pulling a horse trailer drove by, shocks clanking. As the rig trailed a spray of road mist, she followed it into the past. It had been a Fourth of July weekend up at the posh lake community, a time when the wealthy with summer retreats gathered at dusk for a barbecue Mr. Mosely hosted every year.

John steepled his fingers and rested his chin there. "You left the bonfire down by the lake. Cut out early and went up to the house."

She bit down on her bottom lip and stared into the drizzle. If only it were a curtain she could somehow pull back and reach into that time to change things. She didn't say anything for a long moment. Then she ran the towel up and down her face and wadded it into a ball in her lap. "I had to use the bathroom."

John nodded as he swung his gaze to her. "Right." She could see the pieces coming together on his face. "Yeah. Boone came down after a while. He'd been out hunting. He told everybody on the shore that you'd turned in. Something about you telling him the sun and heat you'd been out in all day had made you tired."

A tiny burst of air fled her nostrils. *Of course.* He always did have a way with spouting outright lies in the halls of Mosely High with such absolute certainty that kids believed him. She bottled up her revulsion and forced herself to relax into the chair.

The Mosely lake house had shadowed her, no matter how many miles or years she'd put between that grand residence and her pain.

Through the blur of time, she had learned to lock that night away, push it down somewhere so deep and unreachable that she could create the façade of a happy life, or at least of going through the motions.

Without fail, though, the smell of smoke had always unlocked her memory of that night. Whether she was sitting around a crackling fire with friends in the snowy wilderness of Alaska, or simply caught the scent of a distant wildfire. Didn't matter. The smell had always whisked her back to that house because Boone Mosely had smelled like campfire.

TWENTY-FIVE

Unexpected Heat

Lennie let her eyelids flutter closed, unable to chase away that night a lifetime ago at the Mosely's lake estate.

As she'd headed for the house, its soaring plantation columns and elegant friezes had filled her with a sense of awe. Nestled on ten acres of forest, with rolling lawn extending to the waterfront, the place also felt secluded. She'd seen photographs of similar houses in Charleston or Savannah, with the same type of breezy verandas wrapped around their first and second floors, but nothing this elaborate.

With everyone down at the lake, the house was silent as she entered. She paused a moment to take it all in, feeling so out of her element that she just wanted to use the bathroom and leave.

On her way down the hallway, she glanced at the mounted head of a wild boar with its fierce eyes and razor-sharp tusks, a trophy-kill Boone had brought back from the mountains last year. She felt sorry for the animal. It had never stood a chance, not with "hog reaper" dogs flushing it from cover into a hail of gunfire.

Boone often bragged in tones of conquest about how dangerous the Southern bloodsport was. The rush of adrenaline at surviving the charge by a thundering cannonball of an animal packing hundreds of pounds and a kill-or-be-killed attitude. How awesome it felt to drop it in its tracks with a .308 Winchester semi-automatic.

Mr. Mosely had told everybody hanging out at the water's edge that Boone was away on this year's hunt, and that his butchered hog would be roasted for supper at the community clubhouse the next day.

Stepping into the bathroom, Lennie closed the door and heard a rumble outside the house. She peered into the dusk through a curtained window and could make out Boone's Hummer pulling up to what looked like an equipment barn across a small pasture.

The mammoth 4x4 had been a gift from his dad for finishing high school. Word had been all over Mosely High that Mr. Mosely had also bought Boone's way into Fauntleroy, an elite college in Atlanta, with a donation large enough to fund the expansion of their athletics complex.

A couple of property hands she'd seen clearing underbrush earlier drove up to Boone's Hummer in a pickup truck. After exchanging a few words with him, they hauled a hulking boar from the Hummer's rear cargo hold and loaded it into their truck bed before driving off. Must've been the designated butchers.

Beginning with motocross racing, Mr. Mosely's only son had always had a fearless edge, something that Lennie found as unnerving as she did exciting because she fancied an edge of fearless grit in herself.

Though she tried to convince herself otherwise, she found Boone's dare-devil attitude intriguing, and his arrival at the lake house sent a tingle of anticipation down the backs of her legs. She hadn't seen him in a year.

As she sat on the toilet, she rubbernecked to maintain her view out the window. A light clicked on at an outdoor shower stall across the yard, where Boone hadn't bothered to close the wood-slat door as he peeled off his hunting camo.

Her eyes flitted away from him and then back again. She felt a pang of guilt for looking, but her curiosity paid no heed. What did it matter, when she could barely see in the twilight? Even with the hazy silhouette, though, she easily pictured his glistening six-two frame standing under the shower water.

She pulled back from the window and saw herself from the eyes up in the gilded sink mirror, like someone on the other side was peering over an edge at her.

She sat taller to see her full face and, suddenly self-conscious, awkwardly tucked her sable hair behind her ears. Sixteen, and Dad wouldn't let her wear makeup, which she secretly did anyway. She'd put it on in the school bathroom and clean it off at home before he got back from work.

She turned her head slightly to the right, then the left, catching different angles of her unadorned face in the mirror. The rise of her cheekbones. The sculpt of her chin. The glance of her eyes. Any chance of creating an alluring look like the models on TV? Ugh. No. More like gross chic.

She hung her head and tossed her hair with her fingers to let it curtain her eyes. To hear some of the girls talk at school, it was like everyone was sleeping around, even wearing color-coded jelly sex bracelets that the teachers had no clue signified how far they had gone.

And her? Not even close to being with a boy. What did it even mean to *be with* a boy? She didn't have anyone to talk with about it. How to catch a boy's eye. What they liked. What to do. And not do.

The other girls rolled their eyes when they blabbed about the advice their moms had given them. Lennie often wondered what Momma might have shared with her.

She hurried to finish peeing and was pulling up her bathing suit bottom when she heard "Achy Breaky Heart" start to play in the great room beyond the door.

In the days before things went "viral," that song had taken the world by storm—boot-scooting dancers in honky-tonks from Texas to Timbuktu were line dancing to Miley Cyrus' dad, dreamboat Billy Ray, with his mullet haircut.

She'd never been a fan. Of Billy Ray or of line dancing. Everybody moving around the floor in lockstep didn't make much sense to her. Dance was meant to be self-expressive.

She came out of the bathroom, her lavender two-piece visible under a thigh-length eyelet cover-up. And there stood Boone, pouring whiskey over ice and adding a splash of ginger ale at a polished bar between the gourmet kitchen and the hardwood great room.

Shirtless in camo pants, with his dirty blond hair wet-slicked back, he seemed happy to see her. Even joked about her having grown up since the last time he'd seen her back in high school. *Really? It's only been, like, a year.*

She couldn't help but notice the solid cut of his body. He'd obviously been working out as much as, or more than, he'd been studying up at college; everybody knew he'd sail through no matter what because of his dad's big-bucks donation.

He raised his glass tumbler. "Want one?"

She hesitated. "I don't know if—"

"What, afraid Daddy'll find out?"

"No." She didn't mean her snap-back to sound so defensive, but she could see adulthood just around the corner, could taste it, with all the freedom it promised. "I'm not a little kid anymore."

Boone grinned, his eyes roaming her body. "Nooo, maaa'am." He exaggerated each word, his drawl dragging them out. "You sure as hell ain't *that.*"

No guy had ever looked at her the way he was, ever used that tone with her, and a warmth rushed her face. She tried to convince herself it was just the sunburn from a day at the lake. But, deep down, it felt exciting to be noticed for the first time.

He turned back to the bar, and she could see the muscles in his toned shoulders move as he fixed her a drink. As he reached up for another glass, she helplessly followed the fluidity of his motions and her mind began to churn. *Oh my god. Is this really about to happen? He's fixing me a drink.* An unfamiliar tension welled up inside.

She glanced through a massive picture window to the woods and the distant lake through the trees while nibbling on her bottom lip. She could barely make out the people on the shore.

She heard the ice tinkle into the glass. The bottle clink the rim of the tumbler. The fizz of ginger ale. Whiskey'n'ginger. She'd heard about it at school.

His back muscles rippled as he turned to her, swirling the russet-colored cocktail with his finger. She found it funny: even *she* knew you didn't put your finger in someone else's drink, or your own for that matter. *Guess money doesn't guarantee manners.*

Wiping his stir-finger on his pants, Boone handed the drink to her with a playful wink. "I won't tell if you don't."

He clinked his glass against hers. "Happy Fourth'a July. Here's to the fireworks."

He took a long, cool sip, gazing at her over the rim. His tongue traced along his glistening lips afterward. "Mmm. Tasty."

She could tell he was measuring her, his denim-blue eyes probing hers for a hint of her intentions, probably waiting to see if she was scared of the demon alcohol their First Baptist Church of Deliverance was always preaching about.

He didn't have long to wait.

She raised her drink and took a strong pull, felt the strange sizzle in her mouth, taste buds along the sides of her tongue coming alive. Her throat tightened slightly as the heat from the whiskey burrowed down the center of her chest. She managed to flash him a no-big-deal grin as the unfamiliar warmth suffused her senses.

"Guess you *are* all grown up," he said, then shot back the rest of his drink in one gulp.

Trying to appear confident, she slowly swirled her drink like she'd seen in the TV movies. "What about it?" She brought the tumbler to her lips and drained it. The sizzle seeped more deeply into her.

"Look at *you*." Boone nodded with obvious approval. "All slammin' like you a party girl."

"Maybe I am," she said. She felt the whiskey prickle her chest and slink into her arms and legs, like spidery fingers working their way through her blood vessels.

He filled their glasses nearly to the rims, skipping the ginger ale. "Daddy still not letting you wear makeup?"

She couldn't tell if the rising heat she felt was from the whiskey, or from his implying she'd yet to blossom into desirability and was still an immature little girl. The snappy come-back she attempted to muster eluded her, colliding with the emotions riffling through her mind.

Boone moved closer, and she glanced away, uncertain about whatever was coming next. When she felt his hand running through her hair, she turned and looked into his eyes.

"You don't need makeup. Some girls are natural pretty. And you're *some* girl."

His gaze lingered on hers, and she could feel the back of her neck flush under her hair. The room seemed to suddenly surge hot, despite the AC pumping cold air into the expansive space around her.

"Don't blush, girl," he said with a grin. His blue eyes dazzled her. "It's true. You lookin' fine."

Starting to feel a touch lightheaded, she watched him furtively eye the distant bonfire, which looked more like shoreline sparks dancing through the trees, the music and laughter barely audible.

She retreated a half step and forced herself to swallow. "I better be gettin' back to the lake."

"Aw'ight. You wanna hang with the little kids, go ahead." She didn't move as she peered down toward the lake gathering, then back at him.

"You need somebody to blow your nose, too?" he said.

She hesitated. *Maybe I—*

He took her glass and set it on the bar with his. Next came a mischievous smile as he started swaying to the beat of the music, slowly, suggestively, thrusting his hips.

"You ever ride a bull?" He curled his arm around her waist and pulled her tight. A guarded voice inside her head protested that things were moving too fast, but it was drowned out by her growing need to be wanted.

"Just tip it back," he said in a low, soothing tone.

A bolt of panic seemed to ignite the toasty whiskey in her because this was her maiden boy-dance and she wasn't sure what to do.

As she tried to follow his steps, she reminded herself of her skill moving her feet and staying balanced because of basketball. But that was on the court, where she was in control of her body. Not here in his arms. He wheeled her in a tight circle to the song's beat, tugging her into a few clumsy steps. She did her best to relax in his arms. Looking into his eyes, she found a bit of rhythm in her movements as the room spun around her.

In spite of the speed of it all, she couldn't help feeling special—not only was she partying with a college guy, it was Boone Mosely! None of the girls at school would ever believe her; they all wanted to be with him and go out in style.

She was nearly breathless when the song ended and felt so alive. So wanted. And he seemed to be just getting started. The songs and drinks ran one into the other. She scantly had time to wonder if this was how dancing worked: a hazy rush as the guy pulled the girl around in a whirling cyclone.

About the third, or was it the fourth, drink, she finally allowed herself to stop worrying about what the night, or anything else, meant. She let go in a way she never had before.

For at least this one night, everything that had gone wrong in her life—the secret blame she shouldered over Momma's death, the hardships and disappointments she felt trying to figure out where she fit in, the feelings of isolation under the roof of her own home—all of it broke away from her and faded into nothingness.

As she gave herself over to these new feelings of freedom and desire, she missed a few steps and almost lost her balance. But Boone didn't seem to notice. He just held her more closely, the moistness of his warm breath on her neck, the musky campfire scent of his hair filling her senses.

Suddenly, his mouth devoured hers with a deep kiss, and a fevered excitement passed through her like a relentless tide. At some point, her first kiss ended and the music died. That was when everything blurred.

She remembered following him upstairs and focusing on her feet because her toes were numb on the hardwood floor.

She might have chuckled at the odd feeling. He had said something about wanting to show her the stars from the roof outside the third-floor bedroom where she was staying. She thought she maybe had laughed when she called him a liar.

When she awoke in her bed that July morning, her memory a strobe of fragments, only two things were certain: an unfamiliar, throbbing pain in her pelvis, and the damp blood tangled in her pubic hair, staining the insides of her thighs and spotting the luxurious cotton sheets where she lay.

Thunder rumbled Lennie's chest as the rain turned angry and pounded the Choo Choo parking lot. "I wanted so much to be ... wanted, and it was nice to be paid attention to. It was all so new to me. He was being flirty, and I didn't ... I mean, things went sideways on me."

"Lennie," John said, his voice barely audible as he rubbed his hand over his mouth.

She stared down at her hands, clasped fingers intertwined. "The next morning, it was like ... I didn't know what to do. The next couple of days, I kind of pieced together what had happened. I was afraid to say anything because I thought maybe it was my fault, that maybe I—"

"No." Her brother heaved out of his chair. "You know what? You were sixteen years old. Still a minor, for God's sake!"

He slammed her basketball into the walkway, and it shot back into his hands. "He got you drunk and assaulted you. You need to get this whole thing out there. The #MeToo movement is shining a light on all this."

She could barely contain a snort. "Right. Call out the Moselys on Twitter. For what? In Mosely? Everybody's fate is tied to them one way or the other. Their jobs. The bank with their mortgages and car loans. Their entire lives. Nobody's gonna hold them accountable. They're too afraid."

"You're forgetting their business relationships. Hit them in the wallet. This kind of public exposure leads to lost contracts. That could bring a ton of pressure."

She had already hashed out in her mind his line of thinking. "You're overestimating the circles they run in. There's no such thing as pressure for the Moselys. They take on everything with brute force."

As they sat in silence, the sweetness of the drinks Boone had fixed Lennie seemed to creep into her mouth. "Why didn't I just get out of there and go back to the lake? I had ... there was this conversation I kept having with myself after. For days and days. Weeks."

She'd done her best to move beyond Boone Mosely years ago. Yet, here he was again. Maybe if she could've talked to Mom growing up, instead of flying blindly through her teens, she would've been better prepared that night. Would've been aware of the warning signs.

"Who would've ever believed me?" she said. "I thought about telling Dad, but ... I just ... I had to work up the courage. I figured I had gotten myself into it and I'd try to figure a way out, so I didn't say anything at first. I mean, this was the *Moselys*."

She emphasized the name in a way she knew John would understand; the family represented modern-day plantation masters, an aristocratic clan who dominated the flinching foothills. They took what they wanted, when they wanted, from whom they wanted.

John's shoulders slumped and he pinched the bridge of his nose. "Yeah. I know."

She tried to focus on something else. *Anything* else to take her mind off Boone.

Her eyes were drawn to a tiny bird feather that spun past her toes on a stream of rainwater rushing by. It got hung up on a stone, like an overmatched raft on a whitewater river. The current gradually, relentlessly, bent the feather to its will, spun it off the stone and whisked it away.

She closed her eyes against a surge of anguish. "Then ... it got worse."

TWENTY-SIX

Taking a Stand

Ten weeks after the night at the lake house, the husky voice of her homeroom teacher, Mrs. Forsyth, had come from the other side of the stall door in the girls' bathroom at Mosely High. "Lennie? You all right in there?" Hunched over a toilet on a blistering day, Lennie puked up her lunch, the heave reverberating in the green-tile bathroom.

Three quick raps on the stall door. "You okay, hon?"

Lennie flushed the question along with a viscous froth of stomach acid and three bites of the cafeteria's cream chip beef. *No, I'm NOT okay.*

"Yessum," she said a raw voice. Throat burning, she snatched a handful of toilet paper from the dispenser and swabbed the phlegm from her lips. She yanked another hunk and blew her nose. "I think it was the cafeteria," she said to Mrs. Forsyth's black flats, visible under the door. "You know how Miss Peggy tends to undercook."

Why did I eat? She should've known better: even the *smell* of food made her squeamish lately. She was exhausted, and her breasts were tender, bra cups like sandpaper.

She'd been nauseous for a week. And it wasn't because she had called Boone to tell him she'd missed her period and had seen the two pink lines on the pregnancy test strip. She'd had to swipe the test from the Mosely GasMart so the cashier, one of the gossipy flower ladies from church, wouldn't know. No way on God's green earth Lennie could *buy* one from her. That would be a dead giveaway and unleash the whispers at church.

Lennie was certain as sunrise that her moral failure would spread like a kerosene fire on a pond right to Dad, who would carry the stain of her immorality along with the blame for forsaking his duty to raise her up right.

In the teen storm of Lennie's mind, her life would become a local version of *The Scarlet Letter*, a book she'd found at A Likely Story in the mature readers section: she'd be cast as the foothills' very own tainted Hester Prynne. Good Lord, whispers would linger like the darkness, and truth would never see the light.

It had been nearly two days since she'd called Boone from a stifling phone booth at the Sinclair gas station after school. She'd left a frantic message on some kind of big-shot phone apparently installed in his Hummer, only God knew why. It sure as hell wasn't to answer *her* call. Or call her back. Her half-coherent rambling had boiled down to the two words that really mattered: "I'm pregnant."

Mercifully, she made it to the dismissal bell the day of her first morning sickness. Still feeling nauseous, she tried to hurry across the parking lot to get to a path that skirted the highway. From there, she'd cut up into the woods, a route she walked home every day from school.

Crossing the scorching pavement, she felt the heat through the bottom of her sneakers as a pearl-white Mercedes-Benz sedan appeared like a diamond in the sun. It had dirt-stained kick panels and opaque sun-film on all the glass. There was only one car like that in town. *Oh my God.*

The sedan stopped beside her. The driver's window powered down, releasing a cold blast of air conditioning as it revealed the tight-lipped smile of Mr. Jackson Travis Mosely.

"Hey there," he said, eyes hidden behind reflective Ray-Ban aviator sunglasses.

Shit! Boone called his dad? Her world flared brighter and hotter and she felt a roar in her ears, a wobble in her legs. She was going to pass out.

"How 'bout a ride?" he said in a burly drawl. She could barely make out her pale reflection in his caramel-colored lenses as she teetered on the edge of face-planting in the parking lot.

She grabbed his window frame to steady herself. "Owww! Shit." She snatched her hand away from metal that seared like a stove burner.

"Careful, that's hot," he said with a touch of annoyance. The sudden burn rocked her out of her wooziness. Trying to shake the heat out of her hand, she quickly scanned the school behind her and then the parking lot to see if anyone was watching.

Fortunately, scattering students seemed more interested in sparking smokes. And Jared McCaw's dirt-bomb Chevy was drawing a crowd because he always kept a cooler of beer in his trunk.

She could hear the hooting and hollering across the parking lot as she swung her uneasy gaze back to Mr. Mosely, then studied her shuffling feet. *Maybe he doesn't know. Chill out and say something normal.*

"Dad all right?" She squinted at him.

"I ain't here about your Daddy. I think you know that."

All the moisture suddenly fled her mouth, and she hesitated for a moment to fashion a suitable response. "Oh."

She'd never noticed before how ruddy his skin was, especially around his wide, flat nose, which looked like it might have been busted a few times. He was a thick man with powerful arms. The random flecks of silver-gray in his beard could've been mistaken for crumbs left over from lunch, while twisted whiskers crept down his mottled neck. He was old. In his forties at least.

He had the imperial bearing of Southern gentry, shot through with a strain of big-knuckled redneck. She had heard that his ancestors were cotton kings who literally owned people, the way he owned them now through the power of his signature on their paychecks—blacks, whites, reds or purples, it didn't matter. Everyone was a laboring cog that kept the big wheel of his family dynasty turning.

Apart from slave cotton, she knew branches of the Mosely family tree sprouted coal mining royalty, railroad barons, oil-well wildcatters and marble and limestone quarry commanders. When the Tennessee State Capitol was built in 1850, it was with Mosely limestone.

To the townsfolk beholden to him for their livelihoods, Jackson T. Mosely was right up there with God. God with a small "g" maybe, but a god nonetheless.

The job-shackled residents' Lord and Savior may have fed their souls, but Mr. Mosely fed their families. He knew it, and so did they. Maybe that was why he was so adept at exploiting people's fears and weaknesses with barely breaking a sweat.

"Y'know," he drawled, "it's a helluva lot hotter out there than it is in here. Why don't you climb in and we'll take a ride?"

Lennie knew he wasn't asking. She tried to swallow but couldn't because what felt like the rising flames of her own personal hell had completely dried out her mouth. *He totally knows!*

"Taking a ride sounds like something they say in the gangster movies, right before they whack somebody." She mustered a grin as weak as it was anguished. "You ain't gonna kill me, are you?"

He chuckled. "Boone was right: you're a firecracker. Everything's gonna be aw'ight, little lady," he said with a smile she read as a little too forced. "Trust me."

So, Lennie climbed in to see where trust would take her. The luxurious Mercedes was the quietest car she had ever been in. It was like floating above it all in a climate-controlled womb of mocha leather. There was even a built-in car phone, which convinced her he was way too rich. It also reminded her of Boone, who, in spite of his wild side, closely followed his father's lead.

He had already driven past the turn to her house, so she had no idea where they were going. *I wonder if anybody could hear me scream from outside? I mean, if he—*

"Boone called," Mr. Mosely said, his voice puncturing her thoughts, "and I just wanted to see how you were doing. Talk things through."

Staring straight ahead, she could feel him look from the road to her. A ramshackle house passed on the side of the rutted pavement, barefoot children playing in a plastic wading pool.

"You tell your Daddy?"

She curled her lips in over her teeth and squeezed down before shaking her head. When she glanced his way, she could swear his grip had relaxed on the steering wheel, the skin on his hands loosening around his rocky knuckles.

"Good," he replied. "The situation you got yourself into would put 'im in his grave sure as we're sittin' here."

Got myself into? What did Boone tell him?

"You know how your Daddy lives by Scripture. This would just turn his whole world upside down."

A tornado of thought roared in her head, shards of her life pulled into a funnel cloud. But what truly shook her was that she knew he was right about Dad. He turned left, up an inclined crushed-rock rural route. Bear country. Wherever he was taking her, he definitely knew the way. "I understand Johnny's doing well up at UT?"

She remained silent. *God, Daddy's gonna kill me.*

"Seems like he's on his way to good things."

Lennie realized he was talking to her. "What?"

"Your brother. Seems he's doing well at school. Settin' the table for the rest of his life. He's on his way."

She glanced away. "Johnny's *always* been on his way." She heard the defeat in her voice. "Is Boone gonna call me?"

She looked at him, then in the side-view mirror. Nothing behind them but roiling dust. "I need to talk to him."

"This ain't gonna go that way. I'm gonna handle things. For all concerned."

A shudder coursed through her—she'd heard the stories of how he "handled" things. Damage control was all in a day's work: a collapsed wall in the pit, an explosion or an unfortunate maiming of one of his conveyor operators.

But *this* damage control was going to be different. She could feel it. This was his family. His son. Heir to a family legacy that swept from Texas to the Mason-Dixon Line. There were even rumors the family business was looking to branch out into South American mining.

Mr. Mosely said Boone had told him the whole story. How she'd been waiting for him in the lake house when he got back from hunting, prancing around in her bathing suit.

Wait, what? Pranced around?

How she'd sweet-talked Boone into drinking with her. She realized the backs of her knees were sweating. "What are you saying?"

He just kept driving, apparently arranging his thoughts as the tires crunched beneath them. "I figure that, well ... it takes two to tango. So, let's say things will work out best for everybody involved in this unfortunate situation if a steady hand is on the wheel. That's why I'm steppin' in to take care of everything. Includin' you."

He eyed Lennie. "You have college plans?"

She caught a glimpse of herself in his sunglass lenses before he turned back to the ascending road. *College?* A future beyond these grim foothills invaded her thoughts, a lifeline suddenly appearing on the surface of a churning ocean drowning her. Maybe she should just shut up about the whole thing. Maybe somehow make it work. And find a way out of here.

"I'd hoped to go to college but, after Johnny, we don't have the money."

He offered a warm smile. "I'll see to it that you have everything you need. You thinkin' UT, like your brother? Y'know I've been floatin' his tab up there since your Daddy ran outta savings."

"I'm ... maybe art school?" she mumbled, practically thinking out loud, the impossible dangling as a possibility. "Stuff like poetry and jewelry design? There's an art school in Savannah." *Why does it sound like I'm begging?*

Mr. Mosely nodded. "Savannah's real nice. Beautiful old city. I'll cover tuition, room and board, even a monthly allowance so you can have some fun down there. Enjoy yourself."

Lennie rubbed her clammy palms on her legs. "You'd do that?"

"Absolutely. Once we get this deal straightened out. I only wanna do what's best for you."

She allowed herself to imagine it. Art school. Maybe play her guitar in a little coffee shop on weekends in the cute historic district. Watch the boats come in. It sounded heavenly.

"But sometimes," he added, "you gotta give somethin' to git somethin'. Your Daddy taught you that, right? Sometimes, a dream takes sacrifice."

Once we get this deal straightened out. His words suddenly boomeranged and clobbered her thoughts.

"There's a clinic," he said. "Over in Charlotte. I've arranged for you to go."

She didn't understand. *To have the baby?* "North Carolina?"

"That's right, sweetheart. It'll be more comfortable for you. And less of a to-do around here, for your Daddy an' all."

Lennie stared at the side of his face, his focus on the road. "But ..." she said, then rubbed under her nose to stall for time. "I'm gonna tell him. I know I gotta. I'm just workin' up how. I'm gonna start showing, and I can—"

"No."

"But I can have the baby right over at Tri-County Hospital."

He got real quiet as the muffled noise of tires pulverizing gravel mixed with the sound of the AC compressor kicking on.

She felt her legs begin to jiggle all on their own, as if taken by a muscle spasm. She watched the woods and stole a glance at him without turning his way. When she finally did, she could tell something had changed.

There was a tension in his face, his bottom jaw pushing forward to the point that it looked like he'd developed a spontaneous underbite.

"You gotta start thinkin' better," he said to the windshield in a simmering tone that set heart to thumping her ribs.

"But I gotta tell Daddy what happened," she insisted.

"Tell him what *happened?*" His voice was like a switchblade that had just flicked open. "That you *came on* to Boone?"

She tried to take in a breath, as a slow contortion of disbelief twisted inside her at the lies that continued to spew from his lips.

"That you pestered him for drinks, got drunk, hauled him into bed and spread those legs of yours? That you deliberately slutted yourself to get pregnant and trap him into marrying you into our family? Into the financial resources we've strived to build for seven generations now?"

"What?" Her voice trembled, like the rest of her. The jittering in her legs seemed to transfer to her hands. "That isn't what happened."

"Lemme tell you something, darlin'," he said, his right hand hanging over the top of the steering wheel, "I got lawyers that will prove that's *exactly* what happened." His manner implied she'd have to be dumb as a stump not to see that. "Boone could have any girl he wanted. Why would he pick *you?*"

"He kept making me drinks," she said, her voice taking on a rasp because she was suddenly short of breath. "I swear. He made me drinks."

He chuckled. "You think anybody's gonna believe that Boone had to get a girl drunk to bed 'er, especially a white-trash gold digger?"

Her racing pulse swamped his cruel slur. "That's exactly what he did! He got me drunk and—"

Mr. Mosely stomped the brakes and Lennie slung forward, the seatbelt strap cutting into her collarbone as she braced herself against the dashboard.

He ripped off his Ray-Bans, tossed them on the dash, and grabbed her upper arm with his meaty vise of a hand.

"Let's get one thing straight." She sank into the wrath of his predator's eyes. "Whatever crazy-ass story you concoct in that head of yours ain't gonna amount t'shit. This can be easy, or this can unleash a fury unlike anything you Rileys ever seen before, or will again. I guaran-damn-tee you that. Understand me?"

The ache of tears welled in her eyes. "Please. I didn't know what to do." She hated herself for retreating in the face of his rage, just like everybody always did. "I made a terrible mistake."

He pulled her to his face. "You damn sure did, and you're fixin' to make an even bigger one, you fight me on this. You and your family are gonna go on as you always have." His voice came from a place of absolute certainty. "There will be *no* baby."

Her tongue quivered against the back of her teeth.

"You will terminate this pregnancy in Charlotte at the clinic I've arranged," he instructed her in a tone he might use to order someone to step on a bug. "As for your Daddy? I'll tell him I'm sponsoring you to attend a weekend tour of a couple of colleges over there. *That's* the way this is gonna go."

She bit down on her tongue to control its trembling. The thought of ending the life inside her twisted deep down, as if he'd plunged a fence post into her chest and was standing on it with his full weight.

The image of Mom's picture hanging on Dad's bedroom wall flashed in her mind. She ripped her arm from his grip and back-handed her tears away, furious with herself that his onslaught had made her cry.

"*Terminate.*" She spat his word back at him, struggling to steady her voice.

"It's time to grow up, young lady." His tone was grating. "Set your sights on Savannah. School. On me. Full ride. A fresh start for you to pursue whatever it is you want for yourself."

"You want me to end my baby's life." The words were heinous in her ears.

He torqued his neck slightly sideways and his upper teeth raked up the whiskers that edged his lower lip. "I will *not* have a slut-born child degrading my family lineage."

White heat pushed through her veins. Radiated to her fingers. To her toes. She thought about the life Mom had given her. The life Mom had given up to do so. And something broke wide open inside her.

"No, sir." Lennie's fingernails dug into her palms. "This child. *My* child. Is gonna *live*."

A resolve unlike any she'd ever felt washed over her. She forced her eyes away from his and stared out at the tangled shadows of the trees. "And I'm gonna love him or her better'n any momma, ever."

He breathed heavily through his nostrils, his thick chest rising and falling under his seat belt. He retrieved his sunglasses from the dash like he was plucking a fragile flower from the ground. After slipping them back on, he eased the Mercedes forward.

They drove for another half-mile on the mountain road without speaking. Lennie's entire world was outside the window, a valley spreading below as they gained elevation. She wished her nausea would rear up so she could puke all over his car. Big, sticky, greasy chunks.

Her stomach gurgled as they came upon the high ridge of a great gash in the Tennessee hills: the Mosely limestone quarry. A quarter-mile deep. Eight miles around. Big enough for a squadron of airliners to fly through, below the surface.

She knew how massive the machinery at the bottom of the pit was: red earth-moving behemoths, colossal front-end loaders the color of school buses, with excavation buckets big enough to hold fifty upright men, dump trucks the size of two-story houses. But from up here, the machinery looked like miniature playthings.

On the far side of the ridge, a processing plant loomed like some apocalyptic industrial castle. A swarm of tiny white dots moved like ants below—the workers' hard hats. One orange speck among the white stood out.

"You know who you're lookin' at down there?" Mr. Mosely asked.

Lennie saw the orange fleck framed against the dusty earthen womb of the pit. It seemed to float as it moved, mite-size white hats keeping pace around it, like particles drawn to a center of gravity.

Dad.

She remembered the day six years ago when he had worn that foreman's orange hard hat home instead of his white one, the color the regular laborers wore. It was one of the proudest days of his life. A hard-earned recognition of his value in this world.

He had taken her and Johnny out to a celebration supper at Cattleman's Steakhouse, where she'd had sour cream and chives on her baked potato for the very first time.

"Your old man worked himself into that hat." Mr. Mosely lowered his windshield visor to block the scorching sun in the western sky. "Pulled himself up from shovel duty, back when he started working for *my* old man."

Lennie watched the speck that was Dad angle across the pit to a front-end loader. He was infinitesimal, like a star in a far-flung galaxy. Fuzzy distant. Something she ached to pull closer.

"You know he started here at thirteen, after he quit school to help support his Momma when his Daddy got sick?"

"Grampa died from tuberculosis from working here," she replied with an edge, trying to throw it back in his face.

Ever since she could remember, she had listened to the quarry whistle from her house at the end of the day, knowing Dad would soon be home to hose off outside, clearing a slurry of dirt and grime from his body before coming inside for supper.

He'd stand on a wood pallet amid the backyard pine, rinsing away the remnants of his day. That pallet had taken on a smoky slag stain over the years.

"Lung-sick is hard to pin down," Mr. Mosely said, shifting on his seat to adjust his khakis, the leather seat croaking under his weight. "From what I hear, your granddaddy smoked like a cheap outboard and drank even harder."

"Because he had to work *here*." She heard the flatness in her voice. Could feel herself shutting down. Drifting away. Her life wasn't hers anymore.

"A man makes choices, what he does in life. He don't like it? He can go find another job. Now, your Daddy there," he said, nodding over the edge of the pit, "earns one of the best wages around here. Believe me, I know, because one way or another, my signature's on pretty near every piece of monetary transaction that flows through this town. I've watched him work. He puts his back into it. Seems even more so since he lost your Momma on the day you were born."

The mention of Momma pierced Lennie like a needle. She refused to cry anymore. Tears meant nothing.

"Your Daddy's lookin' forward to the day he can retire to that backyard woodshop of his. Be a shame if anything threatened that. Like ... maybe it's found out he's been stealin' from the company."

It took a moment for his comment to register, the insinuation about one of the most honest, upright, and hard-working men she knew suddenly ripping through her mind.

She turned to him. "He's never stolen anything in his life, and you know it."

He faintly nodded, then froze her with his wolf eyes. "A few well-placed entries on an equipment log during his shift will say he did. And I'd have to fire him. Then make a few phone calls. You think he's gonna find another job anywhere around these parts after that? Guess he'd have to pick up stakes and move somewhere else to start over, wouldn't he?"

Lennie studied his hardened eyes, and her chest tightened as she fought the urge to lunge at him and wrap his seat belt around his neck.

"Worst part is," he said, sounding as if it would be the shame to end all shames, "the pension he's been settin' aside. Criminal conviction with a friendly judge? I'm thinkin' maybe Judge Abernathy or Judge Dampeer—someone I've helped with his campaign along the way—rules your Daddy's retirement fund null and void. Terrible thing. Just terrible. Wipes out his entire future."

Lennie forced herself to look out over the pit.

"Then too," he added, "I'd have to cut Johnny off the college funds. But, hell, maybe all wouldn't be lost. I might even let him take up a shovel like your Daddy did. Work in the mine."

With a flick of his finger, he removed a tiny wisp of red thread stuck to his white polo shirt. "So, yeah," he said, "you go ahead and birth that baby."

He started the Mercedes. "But you point a finger at *my* family? You utter one damn word to anybody—anybody at all— about Boone—" He shook his head slightly. "You best come up with somebody else to point that finger at, right quick."

He dropped the shifter into reverse. "Because I'll personally see to it that you Rileys end up lower than an ant's ass. Y'all will be lookin' *up* at the gutter. And you can take that to the bank."

Then he stomped his boot on the gas pedal. Lennie's head snapped forward as the car leapt backward, away from the pit's edge.

TWENTY-SEVEN

Someone to Watch Over

Lennie stared blankly at the steady rain, still seeing the speck of Dad in his orange hard hat move across the floor of the massive pit. A burgundy minivan chased the image away as it splashed through the waterlogged parking lot and pulled up to the Choo Choo's office. A boy and a girl who looked to be nine or ten pressed their faces against the vehicle's side window, clearly amazed by the lighted locomotive sign.

She picked at a strand of plastic wicker that stuck out from her armrest and glimpsed John leaning forward in his chair as he massaged his closed eyes.

"Oh my God, Lennie. That job was all Dad had. If he had lost that—" He straightened and glanced her way.

She nodded. "It would've totally crushed him." Not only would he have lost the job that was all he had left after Mom died, but his very identity as a man would have been shattered by accusations of stealing from the company.

"I was carrying a life," Lennie said, "and I know now it wasn't my fault, but back then, I thought ... did I lead him on? Maybe I was to blame, at least partly, and I couldn't—"

Her voice caught in her throat and a warm tear tracked her cheek. "I had to tell Daddy *something*, so I spun up a story about being with that Louisiana guy who passed through town a few summers during that time."

She saw a realization come together on John's face. "The woodcarver at the old Sinclair station. With the chainsaws."

Lennie nodded. "Dad was so deeply hurt and disappointed in me."

Through her tears, she watched the family unload from the minivan into the rain, mom and dad hustling into the registration office, while their barefoot children splashed in the nearest puddle.

"Bolivia," John said, every syllable thick with contempt.

"What?"

"Boone apparently moved down there a few years ago to head up the family's new silver-mining venture. Some kind of gringo cowboy with pistols on his hips."

"Sounds like him." She dropped her head and gathered herself as she listened to the children carrying on in the rain. "There was a complication with the pregnancy." She lifted her gaze to watch the kids chase each other around the car. A sorrow rose from her depths, a buried pain that had darkened her days no matter how much she ignored it. "I can't have any more children."

Letting out an exhausted sigh, she pressed her fingers against her eyes. "I'm sorry. I thought I'd gotten to a better place with all this."

"Lennie, this is ... " His words trailed off, deepening her anguish. He reached out haltingly and squeezed her shoulder.

She could tell the gesture felt foreign to him and knew how sad the smile she mustered for him must have looked. Turning away from him, she raised her heels to the edge of the chair, hugged her knees to her chin and slowly rocked forward and back. She couldn't ball up any tighter.

"Things just ... broke between Dad and me. I left school. Left town ... all of it. Just packed up. The longer I was away, the more I came to blame him ... To hate him. *Hate.*"

She winced at the mention of the emotion that had spread like a cancer deep inside her. "My own father. I was just a kid, and I had to protect *him* when he shoulda been protecting *me?*"

She shook her head, seeing now how warped her life had become, trying to deal on her own with overwhelming confusion and heartbreak at a time when she most needed adult guidance and understanding.

"I figured, if I wasn't worth protecting to my own father, then ... maybe I wasn't worth protecting at all."

She'd been within hours of going to see him. To talk with him. To forgive him for abandoning her in her need. And to seek forgiveness.

A small part of her held onto a thread of hope that it could still happen, a strand that stretched to the Appalachian Mountains. But if she stopped to think about it too long, really *think* about it, it scared her to death how far-fetched it all seemed.

John picked up her basketball and spun it between his hands. She found some peculiar comfort watching the ball blur between his fingers, a habit he had developed at a young age when he was thinking. She'd named it his *consideration rotation.*

"The worst thing?" she added. "Dad never knew what really happened. That's why I came back. To tell him."

An even stronger reason pushed up from the recesses of her mind, the one she hadn't dared to consider until the day in

Emily's office when she'd agreed to go see Dad. She chewed on her lower lip a moment.

"I also thought he might know what became of my baby. He handled everything with the adoption agency. I thought maybe he'd have some information I could use to find my child."

She looked past John, who was intently focused on the ball twirling between his hands, and again saw the two minivan kids playing in the rain.

Spring 1995

Dear Momma,

I left home in the middle of the night. The last weeks and months are just running to nothing now. I can't even look back.

I'm at the Blue Swallow Motel in Tucumcari, New Mexico. It's on this stretch called Route 66, which the desk guy told me is famous from an old book called On the Road. Jack somebody wrote it. You ever read that? Probably not. Who has time to read them all?

Anyways, the guy looked at me all weird, like, up and down, when I told him I was on my own. I bolted the door and shoved the dresser in front of it. Place is a dump, but so what? So is my life. I hope to make California tomorrow. It's supposed to be beautiful out there. I could use some beauty. I'm thinking maybe I'll head for Alaska. Get eaten by a bear.

I left because I can't live a lie. I can't stay in Mosely, in that house, and pretend that I didn't abandon my baby. A piece of me. A piece of you. I just can't. I set my child adrift. Do I deserve anything better than to live the same kinda life?

I've got to deal with my new life now. Guess I had to give up the life I was living for them—Dad, Johnny, and my baby. Like you did for me. I know you'd understand. I just want someone to understand! But how can anyone when I can't breathe a word?

Don't make any difference. My life is a hole with no bottom, so this is my last Quill and Testament. The last letter I'll write you. I know I've written all these years, but I just feel like I need a clean break. From everything. All the old ways. Because whatever I've done to this point isn't working worth a damn. Maybe these letters to nowhere are part of my problem.

"Dust and Bones" by Lennie Riley

Stone man works the pit,
ground down in a life that quits.
Wolf man prowls the walls of rust,
all before him crushed to dust.
Bone-raw man in the clay,
lungs all caked with hopeless days.
Above is the man on the hill,
a lynching rope cinches his world still.

Please watch over me ... I'll love you always ...
Lennie

TWENTY-EIGHT

Here and Gone

Rubbing concealer under tear-puffy eyes at the bathroom sink mirror, Lennie heard the thin sound of a Johnny Cash number coming from the cheap nightstand radio John must have just turned on, behind her in the room. She recognized it immediately and stopped doing her makeup. One of Dad's favorites, *Hey Porter.*

"Remember this one he played all the time?" John called from the room.

Remember? She couldn't forget it, even if she wanted to. It had been coming from Dad's cassette player in the kitchen that night.

She could still feel the lukewarm dishwater through the shirt stretched across her belly as she washed supper dishes, scooched up to the sink.

Dad was drying and putting the plates away. "I was over at the church a while back, measurin' for the new lectern I made for Pastor Fisk."

Lennie groaned inside. She couldn't stand the way people sat ramrod straight and righteous, all pious in the pews on Sunday, and then resumed their wrongdoings on Monday. Not everybody—but lots of certain somebodies.

"Amelia Tucker was there decoratin'," he said. "She has that little boy, special needs they say he has? He goes to that school over in Richland?"

His questioning tone suggested he needed to jar Lennie's memory, as if she'd been away from church *that* long. She didn't need to be reminded. Amelia was one of the flower ladies, the Jesus Jasmines, on the beautification committee. They dressed the church for services; it was probably a pleasant diversion from her job putting lipstick on the pigs that passed for vehicles at the used car lot Mr. Mosely owned.

"She said she'd noticed you weren't comin' to church anymore."

Of course she did. Lennie had stopped going in December, when she was five months pregnant. *What was I supposed to do? Show up with my belly out to here and shame you at Christmas?*

He told Lennie there had been rumors among the congregation about her being pregnant, and Amelia wanted to help. She knew how hard it was to be a single mom living paycheck to paycheck—especially with a little one like hers.

"Amelia has a sister who works for a Christian adoption agency over in Watkinsville," Dad said. "They place babies in good, Christian homes. Families with the means to raise 'em right. Amelia even offered to arrange a confidential call."

Lennie stared at the dirty dishwater as she pushed a scrubber sponge round and round the night's crusted casserole dish. She'd felt a conversation like this coming for months as they danced around the subject of her delivery, and she'd practiced her response.

"I'm keeping my baby."

Out of the corner of her eye, she saw Dad stop wiping the counter. "Lennie—"

"Daddy, no. *Please.*"

"We have to do the right thing here. For you and the baby. I've been weighin' things in my head, trying to figure another way, but ... do you have any idea how expensive raisin' a child is? Food? Clothing? Doctor bills?"

"But—"

"And, the Good Lord forbid, but what if there's a problem? What if the child needs special services, like hers? Maybe its whole life?"

Lennie stopped scrubbing—she could barely see the dish's baked-on mess through the blur of tears.

Dad touched her arm. "It's okay, honey. I know it's a lot to deal with. We'll let it go for now."

A week went by, then another. Lennie started to relax, assuming the matter had been dropped. Then, at supper one Sunday after church, Dad turned to her at the kitchen table with unflinching eyes. "I spoke to Amelia again. She's been in touch with her sister." He paused for a moment as Lennie leaned away from him in her chair. "There's this family that can give the child whatever it needs."

This family? Dread simmering, she stared past him at the wall. "I thought you told her I was going to keep my child."

In the leaden silence, a drip from the faucet dinged the metal sink. Finally, he said, "They can give the child everything."

"No. They. Can't." Her voice trembled.

"Lennie, I prayed on it harder'n I've ever prayed since Momma passed. I wish there was another way, but we can't—" She slammed her fists on the table, the impact rattling their half-filled plates and knocking their iced tea glasses over.

As she labored to work her swollen body away from the table and out of her chair, Momma's sweet mint tea spilled over the edge and drenched her belly like a torrent of tears.

"They can't give it *my* love! I don't care what you say. They can't give it a *real* momma's love!"

A sharp rap on the doorframe behind her chased the anguished memory away.

"I asked if you wanted me to take your duffel out to the car," John said. It took her a moment to respond as reality crashed in, and she considered his reflection in the mirror.

"You okay?" he said.

She dropped the masking cream into her makeup tote. "I've learned to be." She pulled out plum eyeliner.

She had realized ages ago that the past was too overwhelming to fixate on—sometimes she had to divert her focus to something else just to push through the day. Like right now. She needed to find her emotional footing amid the aftershocks of her former life.

He cleared his throat. "Why didn't you ... I mean, I can't believe you and Dad never told me about the baby."

I can't do this right now. But she had to try. "You were off at college. He wanted you to focus on school, not get sidetracked by me."

"Sidetracked?"

"We had completely different experiences as kids, Johnny. Different relationships with Dad. It was you two in that house, and then there was me, inside and outside at the same time."

She fingered the corner of her eyelashes to free the upper from the lower. "It was always about what *you* two thought was best. Not what *I* wanted. Then, you were gone. You'd made it out of Mosely. On your way. Dad always said there was something grand in your future."

She leaned closer to the mirror to check her eyeliner application. "He thought it was proper to have the baby and, of course, the church folks knew I was pregnant. Everybody knew."

"Of course they did."

"Even out of wedlock, having it was a ton better than an abortion in his estimation. And I *wanted* the baby. With my whole heart and soul. I thought it would be mine ... to love. Someone just for me. But ... he just wanted to put the shame behind him as fast as possible."

She caught a glimpse of John mulling things over. *Here it comes. His solution to everything.*

"The child is obviously an adult now," he said. Lennie silently capped her eyeliner, dropped it in her tote bag, and opened a small container of glinting copper eyeshadow.

"Have you ever tried to locate—"

"Whispering Pines Women's Clinic," she said, cutting him off as she tried to brush some warmth around her hazel eyes. "Watkinsville. Closed a long time ago."

"What about the web?" he pressed. "Social media? You hear all kinds of stories about moms reuniting with kids they gave up for adoption. Or kids finding their moms."

In the quiet just before sleep, at her most unguarded, Lennie had often thought about what it would be like to one day learn her child was looking for her.

"Maybe he or she didn't want to find me. I combed the web with this Amazon guy out in Seattle. A regular at a coffee shop where I worked before heading for Alaska. He helped me search. Facebook. Twitter. Adoption information sites. He even did one of those algorithm search things. There was nothing."

"But there have to be records *somewhere*," John said. "Granted, it was before computerized record-keeping became the norm, especially in Watkinsville. I mean, the place still doesn't have a traffic light. But there has to be a paper trail."

Lennie snapped her eyeshadow case closed, dropped it in her tote bag, and moved to mascara, her face coming together before her. "I tried, Johnny. Believe me, I tried."

"Maybe your child attempted to find you, but you've always moved around a lot, so—"

"You mean quit and ran away, right?" she said, her eyes locking with his in the mirror.

"What I'm saying is, he or she might welcome you in their life. I was thinking that—"

"That *what?* That you're gonna explain things to me? How it all works with the world? What to do? How to handle it? Well, don't."

Aggravation rising, she flicked the mascara brush along her lashes. "It's *my* life. I'm handling it *my* way." She realized the rigid makeup wand was precariously close to her eye and turned to face him only after taking a calming breath.

"Look ... what happened on the court? That ... meltdown, or whatever. Everything just ... piled up on me and I lost it for a second, okay? Now I'm maintained." She laid a hand over her heart. "I've got a little place where I keep him. His own little spot. And life keeps coming. I know my limits, Johnny. Really. I've topped out. And I'm okay with that."

He faintly shook his head. "But, you don't have to *settle* for things, Lennie. If you would just—"

"Don't ... say any more. *Stop*." She pivoted away and considered her reflection in the mirror. She decided it was the best she could do under the circumstances. Then she grabbed her makeup bag and tried to brush past him in the doorway, but he reached out for her arm.

"So, we good?"

She held his gaze. "I don't know. *Are* we?"

"If you want to stop, just head back home," John said, "we can do that."

Her irritation spiked again. "Contrary to popular opinion? There's no quit here." She pulled away, zipped her makeup tote into her duffel and carried it outside.

John pulled back the gauzy room curtain and watched her pick up the basketball near the chair. Then she tossed her belongings into the station wagon's cargo area as a light drizzle fell.

He wondered how many times she had done that in her life. Reappearing from behind the car with a can of motor oil, she popped the hood and began to add the lubricant to the engine.

He heard a rhythmic *clunk-clunk—clunk-clunk* as he stepped out onto the covered walkway with his suitcase and camera.

Old Mr. Pepper, a few doors down, pushed a rickety maintenance cart toward him; the sound came from the steel wheels as they crossed the concrete seams.

"Couldn't take 'no' for an answer, huh?" he said as he drew close.

John was momentarily confused. *He talking to me?* He looked down the walkway in the opposite direction, but there was no one else.

Mr. Pepper stopped at their door, a tiny nail dangling from the corner of his lip. "I come by a tad earlier and saw y'took to adjustin' my door number." He pulled a hammer from his cart, genial hospitality gone gruff.

John didn't need to see the door behind him to remember what he had done. "Oh, right."

He opened his mouth to explain, but before he could utter a word, the ornery proprietor snatched the nail from his mouth as his eyes narrowed.

"Ever since the killin', we don't brook no trouble 'round here." He pointed the hammer at John's face. "First, she's a black eye, then she's a gun."

John shook his head and held up his palms. "N-n-no. I slipped in the bathroom."

Mr. Pepper spat out a sunflower seed husk and took a closer gander at John's shiner. "Well, we cain't be held responsible. Says so in the room agreement."

"That's fine," John assured him with a wave of his hand. "And I'm sorry about the door number. I can explain."

He turned back to look at the door number, and the funny thing was, he *couldn't* explain. The number had been repaired back to a nine. "Oh," he said. "You already fixed it."

"No. I was fixin' to fix it, but pret'near as I can tell, you beat me to it." And with that, the old man shuffled back to the office, pulling his clattering cart behind him.

Lennie tossed her empty oil can into a nearby trash can as John pondered the door. How could that be? He hadn't touched the number since he'd re-engineered it.

"Did you fix the door number?" he said as she walked back toward the car.

She didn't turn around. "What was wrong with it?"

John scrutinized the metal number, then considered Mr. Pepper retreating into his office.

He smirked to himself as the only logical explanation hit home. The old fart must have forgotten he'd fixed it. "Maybe Lorraine isn't the only one with cognitive issues around here," he mumbled.

He perched his Nikon on the room's window ledge. "I want a picture of our first stop." He set the auto-timer and stepped out into the drizzle to stand next to the station wagon. Lennie joined him, her expression dull as dishwater.

The camera's flash ignited a memory Lennie had tried to drive away long ago: the corridor in the Whispering Pines Women's Clinic—ablaze with fluorescent overheads that ran along the length of terrazzo floor and gleaming tile walls.

She had wandered the empty hallway in a baggy hospital gown, fighting her exhaustion as chilled air cooled the vaginal discharge tracing down her leg.

The nurse had told her to stay in bed. Had given her a pill which Lennie hid under her tongue and then spit out when the nurse left.

Night had fallen by the time she made her way to the newborns' nursery. Her breath fogged the glass as she stared at the sleeping infants, overcome by a sense of wonder. She spied the name Riley on a blanketed, stainless steel crib. The baby was squirming a bit and had kicked its feet free of the swaddling blanket.

An unfathomable current of joy moved through her as she gawked at its plump little feet, toes curled into chicklets of flesh. *His toes? Her toes?*

She focused on its wrinkled right foot, curved outward as hers had been at birth, the one that had later been corrected by the special orthopedic shoe.

She let her eyes stray to her newborn's chubby left hand that reached out between safety bars. Palm up. Fingers flexing and clutching at something that she could only imagine existed in its blossoming awareness of itself in a strange new world.

She could hardly control her quivering hand when she reached for the nursery door handle. She twisted it and pulled, but it was locked.

"Miss Riley." Startled, Lennie turned to see her stout pediatric nurse, whose chunky fingers were suddenly digging into her upper arm. "You can't be in here, sweetie."

A surge of panic overtook Lennie, and she tried to find comfort or assurance in the nurse's gaze. "I need to hold my baby," she said, pointing, heart racing. "Riley. Right there. That's my baby. They didn't let me hold him or ... her? I just want to hold my baby. *Please.*"

The nurse offered Lennie a tight grin that looked more sad than understanding as she attempted to move Lennie away. "There were complications," she said. "Rest will help."

Lennie's panic gave way to fear. "Complications?"

The nurse averted her eyes with the same look Mosely High girls would get when they revealed to Lennie something someone had said about her, mistakenly thinking she'd already heard about it.

"The doctor will discuss it with you."

Lennie gripped the nurse's wrist. "What's the matter with my baby?"

"You need to calm down. Nothing's the matter with the baby."

"Not *the* baby." Lennie felt the sting of tears in her eyes as she pressed her palm to her breast. "*My* baby." It was the most important thing in the universe that this old lady understand the new life behind the glass was part of her.

But the woman merely regarded her in silence and calmly removed Lennie's hand from her wrist. "You need some rest now."

The nurse attempted to steer her away from the nursery, but she braced her foot in the doorframe. "No." She became terribly aware that her child was all alone in there. "Just let me hold my baby for a little while. *Please?*"

The nurse's grip tightened on Lennie's elbow and she tried to more forcibly move her.

"No!" Lennie cried. "My baby's in there!"

The woman forced her a clumsy step away from the nursery. "We need to get you back to your room. You've been through a lot. You need to get some rest."

"They wouldn't tell me the gender. Can you at least tell me that?" Lennie pleaded as her vision went blurry with tears.

When the nurse propelled her forward instead, a blast of heat suddenly filled every pore in Lennie's body, and she ripped her arm away. "Just tell me!"

"Assistance!" The nurse's call echoed the hard hallway. "Assistance, please!"

Sobbing, Lennie clung to the frame of the viewing window as two orderlies converged on her, and she futilely resisted as they maneuvered her onto a gurney under the nurse's watchful eye. "I don't need rest! I need my baby!"

The men restrained her while the nurse immobilized her with gurney straps.

All she could make out through her tears was the woman's name badge hovering over her face: Carol Prescott, snuggled by baby footprints. Lennie heaved beneath the nurse's pressing weight, every muscle burning as the corner of the name badge jabbed her face.

As they rolled her away, she twisted her head to look back until her neck cords strained. Somehow, she managed to fix her sight on the infant's tiny hand. Miraculous little fingers were still grasping air. Reaching out to the world. Reaching out to her.

The staff rolled her farther and farther away from the nursery, and a vibrating clang shot through her body when the gurney slammed through blue swinging doors as they cut her off from the only life that mattered to her.

TWENTY-NINE

Outside the Lines

Behind the wheel of the station wagon, Lennie felt the tightness in her chest begin to ease as they drove southeast from Chattanooga. Too much of the past had surfaced during their stay at the Choo Choo Motel, and she needed to clear her head.

She felt at home on the road. Something about the hum of tires and the gentle rocking she found comforting. She knew parents took fussy babies for car rides to calm them down. Maybe babies know something we don't.

The car that loomed ahead forced her to slow down; it pulled a ramshackle trailer. Clinging to its frame, a wind-whipped blue tarp sprayed a wall of mist into the air. The blast of color was jarringly familiar, recalling the heavy clinic doors that had forever closed her off from her baby. She did her best to sweep the memory aside, like the windshield wipers that now batted away rain that seemed to just keep coming.

In the passenger seat, John watched a sign marking the intersection of a county road, located it on his map and gave it a check. *He's too busy cataloging the trip to even see it.*

She left him to his task and soaked in the passing countryside. Glimpsed through the runny windows, the distorted view was like a surrealist painting come to life.

Between the water clouds spewed by tractor trailers, she saw distant tractors in farm fields. Closer to the road, prison workers in blaze orange jumpsuits swung scythes in overgrown drainage ditches while guards in ponchos kept watch from under wide-brimmed hats.

She glanced across the divided four-lane highway. A freight train ran parallel to the roadway on the left, heading in her direction. Norfolk Southern. She couldn't hear it, but she could *feel* it. Deep down inside.

She'd always connected with the steel thunderballs from her days growing up on the ridge over the Mosely railyard. She used to daydream about jumping on one and riding it to the end of the line. Freedom rail.

She steadily overtook the train. Its receding headlight splintered in the watery swirls of her side-view mirror as she glimpsed John jotting something in his spreadsheet. "What're you doing?"

"Just noting our mileage to Six Flags." He jiggled his Rolex wrist, checked the time and made another entry.

"Your detour to the North Georgia slice of the Appalachians will put us ninety miles northeast of the park, where we'll have roughly two hours to experience it through Dad's eyes."

"*Roughly* two hours? That's as close as you can get with all your calculations?" She hoped her sarcasm would help him see how ridiculous he was being, but it blew right by him.

"I'll know more the closer we get." He folded his spreadsheet inside his map and slipped the paper sandwich inside Dad's vacation scrapbook, like Russian nesting dolls. Mister Buttoned-up. Then he crossed his arms and tipped his head against the window. "Let me know when you want me to drive."

It was worse than she thought it would be.

John dozed on and off for an hour and then stared at the dreary low-lying clouds that hovered over an expanse of pastureland.

He was struck by how similar the sky looked to the ones Abbey used to color in preschool—the realization of the resemblance made him uneasy. *Why weren't her skies ever blue?* Wait. Maybe he should be more worried about Stevie, whose coloring-book skies were more like rainbow snow-cone explosions.

He couldn't help but notice how comfortable Lennie seemed behind the wheel. A wanderer's soul, he supposed, surprised to feel a stab of envy.

He wasn't interested in trading in the life and family he'd built, nothing like that. But the thought of chasing a childhood dream, like her poetry, held a certain allure. Of course, her chances of getting anywhere had been extremely slim as a teen dropout from the dirt-smudge of a town whose entire population could practically fit inside the corporate tower that housed his engineering firm.

It boggled his mind that she had mustered the guts to travel thousands of miles to the farthest reaches of Alaska and pursue a pie-in-the-sky poet's dream. *How small was the eye of THAT needle?* He gazed out over drenched farm fields whizzing by, wondering about odds.

"When I mentioned I considered photography as a kid?" he said. "I really wanted that once."

His words surprised him. It was the first time he'd ever admitted that to anyone. Even his wife. "More than anything. To be a photographer in one of those oversized coffee table books. Crazy, huh?" Lennie glanced at him, then turned back to the road.

"But I never tried," he said. "At least you gave it a shot. Your poetry? I remember you as a kid. Writing in your notebooks. You jumped out there with it. More than most can say." He gave that some thought, the sound of sizzling wet tires filling their silence.

She tossed him a look with a glint in her eyes that he knew only too well. As a kid, she'd turned to him like that every time she tried to talk him into something, to stray outside some line or other he didn't want to cross.

When she *did* manage to persuade him to follow a course of action that dunked them into a bucket of trouble, she would play the innocent little sister. *I'm just a little squirt, Daddy! Johnny shoulda known better.*

"Even Ansel Adams started with a signature shot," she said, nodding at a billboard that proclaimed, Welcome to Georgia, The Peach State. He grabbed his Nikon and snapped its picture as it zipped by.

Lennie grinned. Past the state greeting was another. "Don't forget this one," she said, pointing at an exit sign—Tallulah Falls Gorge. Appalachian Range Access.

He shot the photo as she veered off the highway. Then he held up Dad's vacation scrapbook. "We get in, we get out, we move on," he proclaimed in what she knew was his most authoritative tone.

Did she just smirk? "I'm not kidding Lennie. Don't screw this up."

Rascal dimples came out to play on her cheeks.

THIRTY

Over the Edge

Lennie looked past her toes with their chipped plum polish as they gripped the edge of a granite cliff. The waters of the Appalachian Raven Gorge awaited a dizzying sixty feet below while she teetered in a pair of cuffed shorts and a faded lavender tie-dyed T-shirt.

She forced herself to lean forward ever so slightly for a breathless peek down. *Wow.* Straightening, she slowly inhaled, heart hammering her rib cage. *What are you doing?*

She tried to calm herself by taking in the slanting sunlight on nearby peaks. The rain had passed, and a mountain breeze stirred through her hair, blowing a few strands in front of her eyes as she took in the gorge's immense size and beauty.

A roaring waterfall, fifty feet to her right, climbed another hundred above her, detonating into a pool of frenzied water below. Three other waterfalls cut distant silvery ribbons down sheer rock faces. She felt like a mere speck in the mountainous old-growth forest that stood guard over the gorge as if it were a great mythical fortress.

She glanced over her left shoulder and spied John with his camera, thirty feet away on a massive slope of rock, the station wagon parked beside him.

He eyed his Rolex and frowned. "We've already lost forty miles!" he yelled over the roaring waterfall.

"Seriously?" She gazed up at the mass of white water surging hell-bent over the fall's edge. Momentarily disoriented by the commanding scale, she wobbled and wheeled her arms to keep her balance, toes holding on for dear life.

"This is about the shot!" she hollered. "The only thing great shooters worry about. Capturing that *one* moment! I'm out here on the edge a' crazy giving you the shot of a lifetime!"

John inched his way down the slanted rock until he stood twenty feet below her; from there, he could track her fall from her launch point six stories high. "You're screwing up the schedule is what you're doing!"

"This is a one-shot deal!" she shouted. "So you better get it!" She took gulp of air. "In case I up'n kill myself," she mumbled to the wind.

John widened his stance, braced himself against the granite incline with its streaks of slick green moss. He looked up at her and raised his camera to his eye, hand cupping the bottom of the camera body, finger poised on the shutter button. "Okay, I'm ready!"

"You sure you got the angle?"

"Yes! You'll fall right past me."

"I'll go on three." She crouched. "Ready?!"

"Go already!"

Lennie steeled herself and took a last look over the edge, feeling like someone who was deathly afraid of snakes and peering over the lip of a basket full of them.

She needed to gauge the distance. Any daredevil jumping off a bridge knew that. Her pulse pounded in her ears. *Stay vertical. Feet down. Just like the YouTube videos.*

"One!" She sucked in a lungful of clear mountain air. *Focus.*

"Two!" She bent her knees as the world around her collapsed into a tunnel vision right in front of her. *Breathe.*

"Threeee!" She jumped with a full-throat battle cry.

Wind-milling her arms kept her toes pointed toward the water as rugged slices of terrain flashed before her eyes, blurred by a headwind approaching terminal velocity

Fear threatened to squeeze the life out of her—until something she sensed but couldn't explain tripped inside, and a primal rush of living to the fullest took over.

She glanced down the length of her body at the roiling water racing at her.

Fixed on the white churn.

Flexed feet downward.

SPLOOSH!

With eyes clenched against the impact as she speared the water, she was engulfed by an explosion of entry bubbles, and her descent slowed as the frigid depths took hold.

She opened her eyes in the womb of a liquid underworld, the fractured light spears from above illuminating her swarming bubble cocoon as it dissipated.

Dad.

He floated about ten feet in front of her in his workshop clothes, leather shop apron undulating around him like rippling taffy the color of smoke. Her astonishment left no room for fear as the water compressed her chest, hair streaming from her head like sea grass.

He looked at her with pleading eyes as he hovered in the shifting light from above. Unblinking, she treaded water, holding her position in the depths opposite him.

When he attempted to speak, all she could make out through the distortion of water was a warbling lament. A rising panic dissolved her sense of wonder and a single air bubble tickled her nostril as it fled her nose, rushing toward the surface. *Wake up! Get out!*

She held Dad's gaze, the water stinging her unwavering eyes. *Breathe!*

She clawed for the surface, feet kicking, lungs on fire. She could see sunlight needling through the water above; every fiber burned as she swam toward it.

She exploded topside into a frothing maelstrom, sucking air, coughing, head twisting left, right, then left again. Disoriented. The sound of water roared all around, relentless tons pounding the pool from the waterfall.

She spun in the roiled water as a man's voice, barely discernible above the liquid thunder, seemed to call out to her.

Dad?

She looked up the face of the cliff to see John excitedly yelling to her, but she couldn't make out what he was saying. She swam to calmer water and scrambled out, spooking a dragonfly that took wing from the swaying water reeds.

Her mind scrambled to keep up with her racing heart as she breathlessly scaled the pitched rock face. It took her several minutes to reach John, her imagination in overdrive the entire way.

It was him! Underwater! He tried to say something! His eyes had pleaded with her the same way in the hospital preemie ward.

Reaching the rock outcropping, she rushed toward her brother. "Did—"

"Man, you nailed that jump!" He was busy changing film behind the car, the camera resting on the roof.

"Did you—" Her body heaved, so out of breath she could only speak in small bursts. "—see him?"

"Him who?"

"Dad!" She bent over, hands on her knees, trying to slow her breathing and her runaway mind. "I just ... I just ... saw him ... In the ... In the water."

John wound the film spindle. "Yeah, I've seen him, too," he said, snapping the back of the camera closed.

Lennie straightened with a spike of amazement. "You have!"

"Yeah. In the dream I told you about."

She stared at the rock under her feet, giving her lungs a chance to slow. "I'm not talking about a dream. He was under the water. Right down there, in the bubbles."

John forwarded the film with the advance lever. "Like seeing a lion in the clouds."

"No, *not* like seeing a lion in the clouds." She grabbed his arm. "Listen to me. He was right in front of my eyes. He looked right at me."

"Lennie," he finally said in a parental tone adults take with over-imaginative kids, "memories are hard-wired into our brains. So powerful we may think they're real. We see someone who re-sembles the person we lost. Maybe out of the corner of our eye, or with a quick glance at a stranger who walks like him."

She looked away and scanned the gorge. The distant cliffs. The waterfalls. The forest.

"It's completely natural," he assured her, setting the Nikon back on the car roof.

She ran her fingers through her hair, trying to clear her mind. "But—"

"No, no buts." He grasped her by the shoulders until she fixed on his unwavering eyes. "You have to come to terms with an im-mutable fact: Dad is dead. And gone."

Without warning, the Bonneville emitted a groan and began to creep down the sloping rock. Heading for the cliff.

"Noooo!" Lennie screamed as she and John grabbed the top of the tailgate to try and stop the moving mass.

She arched back with teeth-grit exertion, arms burning like they were a tendon away from being pulled from their sockets.

She sank lower and lower onto her haunches, desperate to save Louise. The world flared bright and tingly as she wrenched her head sideways to look at John.

Moving in what seemed like slow motion, they transferred their grips to the bumper, butts dragging the rock as they tried to stop the two-ton family wagon's forward momentum.

But Louise picked up speed, dragging them, their feet lifting and planting, lifting and planting, overmatched by gravity.

"Emergency brake!" John screamed. His neck cords bulged as four thousand pounds of rolling steel pulled him toward the edge.

Lennie scrambled to the driver's door. Fumbled with the handle. Front tires inched toward the precipice like a roller-coaster car about to hit a death-defying drop.

Then it came: the sickening, crunchy scrape of rock on metal as the wheels chunked over the cliff's lip. Louise was a goner. Lennie jumped back, and John sprung up to snatch his Nikon off the roof as the front end broke over the edge and nose-dived down ...

down ...

down ...

down ...

SPLOOSH!

The windshield exploded into history as the Pontiac Bonneville Grand Safari from their childhood torpedoed the water.

The surface absorbed the impact, then recoiled and pushed Louise back on a surge of froth. She bobbed to a stop, her grille angled down. A sinking ship. Hissing and steaming.

Billowing horror clamped Lennie's chest as she peered over the edge, then she looked at John next to her, his face locked in blank silence.

THIRTY-ONE

Miles from Nowhere

Two hours later, Lennie pressed her hands to her chest as she watched an old tow truck drag Louise from the water. The bulbous truck could have doubled for the vintage junkyard vehicle in the old TV series *Sanford and Son*. Probably from the 1950s.

It must've been fiery red in its glory days, but that had to be a few transmissions ago. Now it was more of a watermelon color with splotchy rust.

Swooping front fenders converged at the wide grille where two horizontal bars reminded her of dinosaur bones encasing bug-eyed headlights. A cable-lift on a hydraulic boom-arm reassured her somewhat in the resemblance to its modern counterpart.

They were marooned in the middle of nowhere. All her hopes hung on this wreck of a tow truck, as did cherished Louise.

She shot John a glance. With the Nikon strapped around his neck, sweat beaded his face in the slanting afternoon sun. *He's thinking this is my fault.* But it wasn't. She had definitely put on the parking brake.

The rock ledge had been sloped, but not *that* much. Having explored mountainous areas of Alaska, she was cautious about parking in the wilds—she would never put Louise in danger.

Something had gone wrong. Or, maybe *right?* Everything happened for a reason, didn't it? She waded in cautiously. "Just so you know, the parking brake was on."

Faintly shaking his head, John stared at the accident scene and fended her off with his palm. He didn't want to hear it.

"Where'd you find that guy?" she said, determined to break the ice.

His jaw muscles tightened as he framed a response, which he delivered with dagger eyes. "I walked." A ventriloquist with a dummy would've moved her lips more. "Six. Point. Two. Miles."

He lifted his camera and snapped a photo of the family wagon, water pouring from the doors as the truck power-winched it to the bank.

She saw the stocky tow truck operator remove his ball cap, wipe his face with a forearm and toss dripping chest waders into the winch bed.

John pulled an ivory JTR-monogrammed handkerchief from his back pocket and mopped the sweat from his face. He jiggled his wrist then checked his Rolex. "So much for Six Flags."

She gasped. "Six Flags! In case you haven't been payin' attention to current events, my car's a friggin' aquarium!"

"*Your* car?" He stared at the waterlogged Pontiac hanging off the tow truck, where the operator appeared to be waving them over.

"Ready to roll?" the driver called out in a Spanish accent.

John spun on Lennie. "*That* car is a family heirloom!"

"Which I've been nursing for just south of a quarter century!"

His eyes nearly exploded out of their sockets. "You call *that* nursing! It hardly turns left! You ever heard of maintenance!"

"Hello?" The driver waved his arms over his head. "All set?"

Lennie poked her brother in the chest. "Louise has seen things you can only *dream* of!"

"Got driving to do!" the truck operator yelled. "*Vamos!* Let's go!" He opened the door and climbed in.

John got in Lennie's face. "Spoiler alert! You drove her into the ground!"

The driver started the tow truck and leaned on the horn, which weakly oscillated like a strangled duck. "Not getting any younger over here."

John stomped off toward the truck, leaving her no choice but to follow.

Lennie was wedged between the husky driver and John as the dinosaur of a tow truck rattled along a potholed mountain road. The rhythm of conga, maracas, and brassy music filled the cab from a cassette deck mounted under the dash.

She'd scoped out the driver when she climbed in. In his seventies at least, he wore frayed mechanic overalls and scuffed work boots. Speckled gray hair framed a lined face with skin the color of cocoa. His eyes were alert and capped by prominent eyebrows that seemed a perfect match for the bushy mustache. Although his mouth seemed a muscle twitch away from a smile, he didn't say a word.

Maybe he's mad we put him behind schedule with our arguing.

Even with the windows open, the cab smelled of working-man odor and axle grease. She could hear the clanging safety chains securing Louise behind them, the vehicle's shocks groaning when they hit road ruts.

She fretted as she looked back at Louise. They'd been through some rough spots before, but never like this—she'd been submerged!

She sensed John stewing next to her as he silently stared out the window. A skinny guardrail was the only thing between them and the gorge they skirted on the right, a five-hundred-foot drop into outcroppings of granite and dense trees.

Strings of green, gold and purple Mardi Gras beads dangling from the rearview *jinglejangled,* catching her attention, and the digital numbers on a clock affixed to the steel dash glowed red, showing 4:08. It felt later, though. The sun always seemed to bow out early in the mountains.

Stuck on the dashboard radio's face, an ancient *I Love Lucy* commemorative stamp featured Lucille Ball, cheek-to-cheek with her dashing Cuban husband, Desi Arnaz. The bottom corner of the stamp was starting to peel.

She reached out and tried to press it back down, but the heat had cooked all the sticky out of it.

"Best show ever," the driver said with a grin. "I used to watch it in Cooba as a boy. You probably don't remember, you being a kid. But it's on the web now."

Lennie smiled at both his charming pronunciation of Cuba and him thinking of her as a kid. "I've seen the YouTube reruns with Lucy and her friend."

"Ethel." His eyes lit up.

His enthusiasm was contagious. She slightly shifted to face him more directly, her voice rising. "Remember them getting a job on a candy assembly line?"

"Wrapping chocolates!" he exclaimed, his eyes ping-ponging from the road to Lennie.

"Yes! And they're stuffing them in their mouths. Like *this!*" She grabbed her puffed-out cheeks, eyes bulging, tipping her head back and forth as the truck rattled along. "It was hilarious!"

"Luuuuciiie!" the driver said with a laugh, imitating Ricky Ricardo, the husband Desi Arnaz played on the show.

"Would you mind staying focused on the road?" John snapped. "I'm over here on the edge of this drop and would prefer that my wife not have to tell our kids that daddy was killed by Lucille Ball."

Lennie rolled her eyes at the driver and made a sour-puss face to imitate John. The old-timer leaned forward and looked past her. "*No problema,*" he assured John. "I've driven these roads a million times. Since 1961. After the *revolución.*"

"And you couldn't have picked a nicer place," Lennie said, extending a hand. "Lennie."

He smiled, touched the brim of his cap and shook her hand. "Hector."

She noticed the scraped knuckles on his hands, which seemed permanently mottled by a patina of grease that he probably couldn't get off at this point.

"My travel buddy here," she said, nodding sideways, "is Mr. Sunshine. But we call him John."

John shot her a look that suggested she didn't understand how dire the situation was. "The whole damn trip's in the ditch."

"We can fix the car, John." She looked at the driver. "Right?" She thought she saw him wince when he didn't answer. What if Louise couldn't be repaired? The possibility made her stomach lurch.

"Do the math, Lennie," John said. "It's late Saturday afternoon. Fixing the car, if it's even fixable, is going to eat up most of tomorrow, Sunday, and we're still a good six hundred miles shy of the dawn launch on Monday. That's got to be, what? A ten-hour drive?"

"Twelve," Hector said.

He braked, and they descended on a long, sweeping curve to the left. The shift in direction forced them to lean to the right in their seats. Lennie's shoulder pressed into John's, compressing him against the passenger door. He drove the lock down with the butt of his clenched fist.

The truck eased onto a straighter stretch of road in the opposite direction and Lennie returned to her position in the middle, where she glimpsed her troubled eyes in the rearview mirror. *Yeah, this was a dumb idea.*

They traveled in silence along winding roads barely wide enough for two vehicles to pass. After a while, they emerged from a forest to an open vista overlooking a valley rich with verdant farms and homes tucked into corners.

Lennie noted a homespun road sign that proclaimed, "World Famous Main Street," with an arrow and some stenciled scroll work to give it the appearance of a genuine state historic site marker. *Charming.*

A bigger sign made her sit up straighter. It was higher and on her left—Town of Tallulah Falls.

The name of her original destination and purpose for her trip smacked her in the face, along with the realization that Dad's appearance at the gorge could have been an indication that she was on track.

John hadn't wanted to stop here and now they were stuck for at least a day. Maybe the mishap with the car was no coincidence. She just might get to stay longer in the land of guardakin angels than John's spreadsheet had allowed.

She didn't know if she believed the angel legend, and she had no idea how to find one. She knew, though, that things weren't always clear—sometimes you needed to feel your way for a while, trusting senses we may not even be aware of.

It was something she'd learned through her travels, and it had helped her find new jobs and make friends along the way. And now, she had the sense of being in the right spot at the right time.

Crisp mountain air swept through John's open window, and she drew it deep into her lungs, knowing that she only had to stay open to whatever happened next.

THIRTY-TWO

Roadside Relics

The tow truck creaked into a dirt-patch gas station situated on the side of Raven Gorge Mountain. Lennie spied a faded wooden sign mounted on the front that simply read: *Hector's Place.* Two old pumps and a single mechanic's bay big enough for one car.

It looked like the squat concrete block structure had sprung from the very ground on which it sat. Broadleaf kudzu vines climbed its walls and stiff grass rose knee-high on the sides.

"Home sweet home." Hector's mustache twitched as he smiled.

She hopped out of the truck and looked around. A basketball goal with a mildewed Atlanta Hawks logo on the backboard clung to the side of the garage. A free-throw lane had been roughed in with what looked like highway-stripe yellow paint.

"I put up the basket for my grandkids. Keeps them out of trouble when they visit," Hector said.

A small gravel lot separated the garage from a clapboard house that blended a simple Appalachian design with vibrant Caribbean colors of tangerine, lime, and deep-ocean blue.

After helping unhook her car from Hector's tow truck, Lennie peeked around the corner at a barn-red workshop made from the same clapboard siding as the house.

She marveled at how the little homestead was shoehorned onto maybe an acre of flat ground carved out of a mountain slope. The place overlooked the valley farmland, while scruffy peaks encircled everything like mossy agate.

"Do these things even work?" John's voice drew her attention. He and Hector stood in front of the red gas pumps, both topped by lighted glass globes with winged horse designs. Strips of orange duct tape patched the globes, but Lennie imagined they'd been pretty once.

"Like a charm," Hector said, running his hand over one of the pump handles. "Guess you could say 1953 was a good year."

He rolled up the bay door, then glanced back at the salvaged station wagon. "You're definitely looking at a night's stay."

"We'll find a place in town," John said.

Hector chuckled. "You're *in* town. I've got room if you're interested." He nodded toward the house. "It's not much, but you're welcome."

John waved him off. "You don't have to do that."

Hector wiped his hands on his overalls. "Folks get in a pinch 'round here, we help each other out."

"Thank you," Lennie said. "That's really sweet of you."

"Besides," he added with a wink, "I think you two could use some adult supervision."

While he stored various tow chains and straps in the bed of his truck, Lennie and John walked into the garage. With hands on hips, her brother surveyed the space. Granted, it wasn't much to look at, but it sure seemed to have everything a mechanic might need.

"This is never going to work," he said.

"Whaddaya mean?"

Irritation sharpened his voice. "Look around."

She already had. Tire racks ringed the bay. Various hoses and belts dangled from a crude, but effective, array of clotheslines and shirt hangers secured to beams in the ceiling. A scarred tool chest six drawers tall hunkered next to a chunky workbench that might have been built from reclaimed railroad ties.

Shelved next to the workbench was a D.I.Y. "entertainment center": a wire chicken coop rigged to hold a gargantuan boom box radio with a World's Best Grampa sticker plastered on it, and a bulky TV.

"Where are the diagnostic machines?" he said. "How's he going to analyze anything?"

"He's got a lot of experience. Maybe that counts more when it comes to fixin' Louise."

She wandered past pegboard-mounted tools to a colorful grid of Georgia license plates. The old steel plates were Velcro-mounted to strips on the wall. She liked the look of them. Dating to the 1960s, they were affixed in a pattern, five down and four across, forming a checkerboard of twenty rectangles. Mustard yellow. Peach. White. Green. Black.

Hector entered as Lennie checked out the plates. Each had three letters, followed by three numbers. "I mix and match the numbers to play the lotto over at Mineral Bluff every week," he said.

She grinned. "Luck been a lady?"

The old guy shrugged and gestured around the garage. "Who needs luck when you have all *this?*"

Lennie knew John was already counting down the minutes until they continued on their way to Cape Canaveral. He was zero-for-three on this trip so far, and she couldn't imagine a future in which he wasn't at that launch. At best, she had twenty-four hours in these mountains. These supposed *angel* mountains.

She wasn't sure if luck was a lady who smiled on the few, or if lady luck was even what she needed, but she would welcome her with open arms if she came along.

THIRTY-THREE

Off Track

Lennie stepped out of the tiny second bedroom that Hector had offered her for the night. She had showered and, as suggested, tossed her wet clothes into the washing machine. The grandfatherly mechanic had even loaned her one of his freshly laundered T-shirts and a pair of mechanic overalls to wear in the meantime. The overalls smelled faintly of transmission fluid and lye soap, and she had cuffed them because they were much too large, but she was grateful for his thoughtfulness.

Afterwards, he had rushed off for an auto parts junkyard down in the valley to catch it before it closed.

Where was his wife? He'd talked about grandkids but never mentioned her. And she'd seen only one coffee cup in the dish drainer. She never appreciated people nosing into her business, so she didn't want to nose into his if he didn't offer.

She wandered over to the matchbox-sized front room. The confined space, like the rest of his home, struck her with its sense of order. A couch and recliner shared a woven oval rug with a couple of side tables.

Lennie recognized the "shotgun shack" style of the house, common for those of little means in the South from the end of the Civil War through the 1920s.

The name came from the fact that a shotgun slug fired from the front door could exit the back without striking a wall because the interior doors were aligned. Southerners have always had to contend with oppressive summer months; and designs like this allowed for cross breezes to help keep things cool.

As dusk settled, she stepped onto the slightly-bowed front porch to see mountainous knuckles framed against a fireball sky. Dad's scrapbook, page inserts and postcards were precisely clothes-pinned to dry on a cord strung between porch supports. She smirked to herself. John. *He's a piece a' work.*

Across the gravel lot that separated the house from the gas station garage, John shot baskets at Hector's weathered back-board with a gangly African American boy who looked to be eight or nine years old.

"Looks like Hector's grandson found a playmate." Lennie turned with a start to see an elderly African American woman sitting in a porch rocker at the far end. "I suwannee, that boy makes friends wherever he goes," she said with a grin.

It took Lennie a moment to fully take in her whimsical outfit. The woman's painter smock was a riot of colors above her leop-ard-print sneakers with mustard-yellow ankle socks. When she moved her head, jet-black ringlets of hair rattled with affixed beads fashioned from miniature children's letter blocks. To com-plete her look, a mauve cloche hat had velvet flowers affixed on the side.

Either she was the queen bee of thrift stores, or she was like one of the woodsy folk artists Lennie had come to know in the Pacific Northwest.

The woman stood and came over to her. She was slight, had to be pushing eighty, and was a touch stooped. She offered Lennie a handshake and a welcoming smile. "Joella Johnson."

Shaking the woman's soft hand sent her whimsical bangle bracelets *clinking*. "Lennie Riley."

The smile remained on Joella's face as she placed her other hand on top of Lennie's and gave it a squeeze while still shaking it. *Maybe she's starved for company.*

Lennie started to feel uneasy. She looked over at John and the boy shooting baskets. "Johnny's, um ... just missing Stevie. About the same age as that little guy."

"That's Andre." Joella stopped pumping Lennie's hand but continued to hold it. "How many young'uns for you two?"

"What?" The question caught Lennie unawares. "Oh, no-no-no. We're not ... he's my brother. Stevie is his son. He has two kids. I don't have any."

"Mmm." Joella finally released Lennie's hand and curiously eyed the drip-drying postcards and scrapbook strung across the porch.

"Those are John's. He can be a little weird. Not *weird* weird. More like fussbudget weird. Although this time-travel kick he's on has me wondering."

Over at the makeshift basketball court, her brother was talking to the boy, probably giving him some pointers.

Joella's eyebrows arched. "Time travel?"

"Retracing a trip our dad took us on as kids. He just passed."

"I'm sorry." Joella descended three concrete steps that fronted the porch, and Lennie was taken by how sturdy she seemed, given her age. *Am I supposed to follow?* Seemed rude not to. But so was walking away. She trailed the woman over to Hector's garage bay, where the station wagon awaited his return.

"How's your Momma holding up?" Joella said.

"Beg pardon?"

"Your Momma. How's she handling things? Always tough on the trailing spouse."

Trailing spouse. Interesting way to put it. "She, um ... went first. Before Dad."

"I'm so sorry. Both of 'em gone on over."

"The garage looks like it has a lot of history," Lennie said, eager to change the subject as they stepped inside.

"Hector took it over from his daddy back in seventy-two. After splittin' time 'tween workin' cars and workin' the sawmill over in Umpka. Y'all stop here, back then on your trip?"

"Not exactly. I got us a little off track."

"Mmm." Joella drummed her fingers on the mechanic's workbench as she studied Hector's wall of license plates. "Men," she mumbled and tugged a yellow one off a Velcro strip. "It's a rare one that's got an eye."

Lennie watched her remove the plate. *What's she doing?* Given the old woman's appearance, she obviously had an inventive bone. Maybe she didn't like the color arrangement.

Joella studied the matrix of plates a moment longer, then tugged off another one. And another. Five, six, seven plates she removed and stacked on the workbench.

Lennie nibbled the inside of her cheek, uncomfortable at seeing her tinker with Hector's things while he was away trying to help them, and she felt a sudden urge to protect him.

"Um, are you and Hector together, or—"

"Lots of folks together with Hector."

"What're you doing?"

"These are statement pieces."

"I don't think you should be messing with them."

"I just think they could say more, don't you?" Joella returned her attention to the empty wall and reconfigured the grid, shifting the positions of license plates into a new color pattern. Then she stepped back and eyed the new arrangement.

"Don't fess up I did it. He'll notice in due time. It's a little game we play to keep ourselves occupied. Keep our minds sharp. You'll ruin it if you say anything."

That made sense, seniors staying sharp with fun little brain teasers, and she couldn't see any harm in playing along. At the thought of the woman engaging Hector in a golden-oldies game of wits, her shoulders relaxed slightly under the overalls.

"What're you looking for?" Joella said, browsing the plates.

Lennie was puzzled by the question. "Excuse me?"

Seemingly satisfied with the arrangement, Joella turned to Lennie. "You said you got you and your brother off track. There was a track. You got off it. Must be looking for something."

Not waiting for an answer, the woman walked back to the house. Lennie felt a tingle race down her spine at the intrusive insight as she watched her.

Yolanda had said Appalachian guardakin angels were just old-timer crazy talk. Yes, she was in the Appalachians. Barely. And Joella was old-timey. But just because she'd uttered something profound that *might* be a reference to Lennie's search didn't make her an angel. She could just as well be a busybody. They were everywhere. Angels weren't.

Lennie scratched her chin and drew in a slow breath. *Tap the brakes, girl.* She didn't want to get ahead of herself. Joella was peculiar. And kinda pushy. Whoever heard of a pushy angel?

She stepped outside where crickets now serenaded darting fireflies. Joella had again lowered herself into a rocker on the porch. Lennie realized she'd never see the woman again. *What's the harm in letting my freaked-out flag fly?*

Returning to the porch, Lennie sat in silence opposite Joella in a companion rocker. *At her age, she's probably heard it all anyway.* Gazing across the darkened valley, Lennie let her eyes catch the golden flashes of fireflies. In her mind, she was back in her girlhood dreams, rocking with Momma in the porch rockers. Their *After Supper Club*.

"There's this ... Or, *was* this thing between me and my Dad." She waited for a reply but heard only the rhythmic chirping of the crickets. *What am I looking for?* The elderly woman had asked a good question.

"It was a long time ago. I don't know if he ever wanted to try to figure things out. And now, I feel like he might be—" She searched for the right words. "He might be trying to reach me. To help me or—"

She caught herself, shocked to think she'd become so desperate that she would reveal something so deeply and painfully personal to someone she didn't even know. "I'm sorry. I mean, I don't know why I'm telling you all this."

Lennie glanced at Joella, afraid to see the expression on her face. But what she saw were rich brown eyes that reached across the few feet between them and held her close.

"Maybe you're tellin' me 'cause you just found what you're lookin' for."

THIRTY-FOUR

Suspended

After supper, John joined Hector in the garage, where the car was raised on a hydraulic lift, a good five feet off the oil-stained concrete floor. Box fans were propped in the driver door and the rear passenger door to speed up the drying, and water seeped from the foam-stuffed seats onto soppy towels.

Hector worked beneath the elevated car, reading glasses perched on this nose and attached around his neck with what appeared to be a strip of a discarded windshield wiper rubber. Engine oil drained into a receptacle as he disconnected a grimy severed cable and stepped out from under the vehicle.

"Yeah, it snapped all right," he said. "Explains why your brake didn't work." Hector frowned as he regarded the damaged vehicle. He muttered something beneath his breath in Spanish, then cleared his throat. "You really should have your cables and belts and such inspected regularly."

John rose on his toes to release the tension in his legs. He wasn't going to be thought of as uninformed on Lennie's account or get pinned with the blame for the accident. "It's my *sister's* car."

"Oh. Well, she might want to think about a maintenance schedule."

"Yeah, see, that's the problem: She *doesn't* think about things like that. If she had an organized thought, it'd die of loneliness."

The mechanic's eyes narrowed and he lowered his chin to gaze over the top of his glasses, looking perplexed. John followed his line of vision to the colorful grid of license plates on the wall over his workbench.

Whatever had caught the old-timer's attention could wait. John had places to go and very little time to get there. "We need to be at Cape Canaveral by six-thirty Monday morning."

Hector scratched the top of his head with the bill of his ball cap and turned to John with raised eyebrows. "You gonna drive six hundred miles after a Bonneville belly-whopper like *that?*"

"Between you and me? She's put this car through hell." He contemplated the station wagon, tracing the roof line from front to back with his eyes, as if he were taking the measure of an old horse. "I'm just hoping she still has a little fight left in her."

Hector chuckled and wiped his hands with a shop rag from his back pocket. "Man upstairs parted the waters. He didn't take none outta no combustion engine."

John grabbed a utility light and bent down to examine the undercarriage. "So, what are we looking at, part-wise and time-wise?"

Hector hunkered under the car and lifted the oil drain pan off a shop stand. John followed him as he carried it to his workbench.

Fingering his mustache, Hector stared at the layer of water floating on top of the murky engine oil in the pan.

"Flush and filters. Fluids, for sure. Fuel pump, carburetor, and electrical's gonna be tricky. It's a job. I'll know more when I get under the hood and get my hands dirty. Lucky for you, I have a secret weapon."

John's gears turned as he tried to assess what kind of ace Hector could have up his sleeve for the dilapidated station wagon.

"I've got an extra two hundred bucks for you if it's a tech certification from General Motors."

"Better." Hector pointed to his head. "Castro."

"*What?*" How did Cuba's dead president figure into this?

"You know those old American cars they always show driving around Havana in the news clips?"

John nodded. "Yeah, they're fossils. Tough to work on when you can't get parts." *Ah, wait a minute!*

"Who do you think kept those fossils rolling with duct tape and bailing wire?" Hector said, flashing a proud grin. "I worked on those beauties since I was a boy, nine years old. With my *Papá* before he brought us here, fleeing the regime. *El genios de la Habana,* they called us. The wizards of Havana. We could get *anything* running."

A bolt of optimism surged through John, but he fought the urge to let his hopes get too high—he was still dealing with a boondocks mechanic who, if he was any good, would surely have worked his way up to a more lucrative market, like Atlanta.

"Are you telling me you can get this running by five or six o'clock tomorrow afternoon?" he said. This project needed a *can-do* guy, not a *might-do* guy—those were the ones who dropped the ball and made everybody look bad.

"Can't say for sure, tomorrow being Sunday."

John's confidence took a nosedive. "Can you say *anything* that's for sure?"

"*Si.* I'm sure we won't be able to get any parts we may need 'til after church tomorrow. Nothing's opened."

Great. John lifted his hands and let them drop to his sides. Another wrench thrown in his carefully laid plans made it official: the space launch, the crowning moment of his tribute to Dad, was officially in peril. The man had given John *everything,* and he couldn't even give back this *one* thing.

His gut tightened at the thought of Lennie and her frivolous detour. Catering to her whims had cost him dearly. And if they didn't make the launch on Monday, it was one hundred percent her fault.

THIRTY-FIVE

Chasing Echoes

Moonlight sliced through an open window to where Lennie lay on a lumpy mattress, watching a ceiling fan spin over the bed. Two wooden knobs on the fan's pull-chains randomly collided and bounced off each other, seeming to reflect the inexplicable events in her life since Dad died, and her unsettled feelings as she tried to cope.

Cupping the wood-burned heart she'd found in Dad's shop, she absently ran her thumb back and forth over her scorched name.

In the silence, the conversation she'd had with Joella replayed itself inside her head. Why in heaven's name had she opened up to the brash old lady, a complete stranger? She should have picked up on her fussbudget ways when she'd asked about Mom from the get-go.

Disquieting thoughts rippled her mind. Hector's porch. The rockers. The chat. The fireflies. It was all *so* déjà vu—her brief time with Joella echoed her *After Supper Club* dream visits from Mom.

Could it be that …? Don't be ridiculous, Eleanor Grace. She shooed away the notion that the woman was some sort of earthly vessel of Mom. That was hot-mess crazy, plain and simple.

Still, she just couldn't get a handle on this Joella woman. *The way her eyes felt, like she wasn't looking* at *me as much as* inside *me.*

Shifting on the mattress, she curled up on her side. Maybe she *was* a guardakin angel or knew one around these parts. "Get real," she murmured to herself. Her thoughts were going in circles. How could she ever get a grip on the situation if all she did was argue with herself?

She's just an eccentric old lady with a dash of Meddling Mavis. Too worked up to sleep, she shoved all her wild running aside, got out of bed and turned on a double-jointed brass desk lamp perched on a clawfoot dresser straight out of Antiques "R" Us.

The dresser's bumps and bruises bore the years it had seen. Two sets of initials were carved into the face of the top drawer, alongside the shadows of what looked like a squad of kooky flower stickers from someone's hippie years. She couldn't picture Hector as a hippie. They had to be from a previous owner's life.

She wasn't a busy-body, but … she eased the top drawer open and scooted the lamp closer to the dresser's front to get a look inside. It was empty except for a tri-folded piece of paper. Maybe a bill of sale. When did Hector buy it?

She delicately unfolded the paper and discovered it wasn't a receipt at all. It was a letter, with petite handwriting. Short and sweet, only a few lines.

Dearest One,

*I know you've traveled far, but no matter the distance
that separates us, you'll always be close in my heart.
You were and still are a part of me. And if you're running from what happened, stop. You don't know how
I've longed to hold you in my arms.*

A wistful grin tugged at her cheeks. *How precious.* A love letter. Guilt tossed a seed of hesitation her way. Such shared
intimacies should remain in the private garden of those who
planted them. But she couldn't help digging a little deeper. There
were only a few more lines anyway.

*I don't understand why you've shut yourself away
from me all these years. I miss your letters. Why did
you stop writing me? Why, why, why your last Quill
and Testament?*

Her eyes stopped reading almost as quick as her heart stopped
beating. *Last Quill and Testament!* Those weren't the nameless
writer's words. They were hers! From the last letter she'd ever
written to Mom, on notepaper she'd found in her room at the
Blue Swallow Motel in New Mexico after she fled Mosely
twenty-five years ago! Her breaths came in rapid spurts as she
read the last line.

*I truly hope you'll keep an open heart, a song in your
soul, and your arms held wide to love.*

A sound as soothing as a soft rain filled her senses. *What in
the Sam Hill?* The room seemed to blur as she stared at a swirling
knot in the wooden dresser. She reminded herself to breathe,

then placed the letter in the drawer and eased it closed, fighting her instinct to flee.

She didn't realize she was backing away from the dresser until the backs of her knees hit the bed mattress and she sat down, as if an unseen hostess had escorted her to her designated seat.

She reeled in her labored breathing and willed the splintered sensations in her head to condense into a single thought: Mom. *Was it possible she ... ?* She pressed her palms into her eyes. *No, it's not possible! Y'know what's possible? That your noggin's worn crazy as all get out!*

She lowered her hands. "This has gotta stop," she scolded herself. *But what if that nosy Joella woman—*

A metal *clank* outside the window broke her lunatic fever and she instinctively spun like a jittery deer, peeked through a checkerboard curtain, and saw what looked like Joella's shadowy figure enter the workshop behind the house. A light flicked on inside.

Lennie sprang from the bed and moved to the spindled footboard for a better angle through the shop's slightly open door. But it pulled closed before she could glimpse anything inside.

Had Hector or John heard the noise? She eased her bedroom door open an inch. All was clear. Stepping out, she padded barefoot across the floor. She slipped past John, asleep on the couch in the front room, and heard faint snoring through Hector's bedroom door.

Onto the porch and into the night, she noticed John's postcards were missing from where he'd strung them up. She frowned. *Did that woman just take Dad's postcards?*

She made her way around the back of the house and arrived at Hector's shop, glancing back to see whether anyone had stirred. Nope.

She cracked the door open. Peering through a narrow gap, she spied Joella from behind. At a workbench against the far wall, she stood under a glowing light bulb, one of a handful that created oases of illumination in an otherwise darkened workspace.

There were murky storage areas holding hodgepodge lengths of wood. Another stall held what appeared to be works-in-progress toy boxes and chairs.

"Gonna let the moths in, you keep that door open," Joella said, startling her. The dodgy doyenne never turned around, but Lennie heard the reprimand in her voice. She stepped inside and closed the door.

Joella was hunched over the workbench, shifting her weight to her hands as she leaned over the bench and then back on her feet in a rocking motion. She seemed to be rolling out pie dough.

Lennie edged closer and could see her ebony hands working on Dad's yellowed postcards. "These will wrinkle like ol' ribbon candy if you leave 'em to dry on their own," Joella said, flattening a card with a kitchen trivet. "Thought I'd press 'em on out."

"At two in the morning?" Lennie didn't mean for it to sound as mistrustful as it did.

Joella moved to the next postcard with her trivet and began to pancake it. "I've always found it best to work when inspiration grabs a'holt."

Charging headlong into first things first, Lennie had to get to the bottom of the astonishing letter she'd found. "How well do you know Hector?"

"Oh, child, we go back a looooong ways."

"Mm-hmm. And he has you over to the house?"

Joella chuckled. "Oh, now. A lady never tells."

"Totally. Did you put a letter in the bedroom dresser?"

"You a snoop?"

"Just answer the question." Lennie winced at her short tone with the elderly woman. She was raised better.

Joella gave her a sideways look and a barely perceptible grin. "A lady is particularly protective of boudoir goings-on."

Lennie decided to let her interrogation rest for now. She'd catch Joella by surprise at some point and get a straight answer. Besides, Hector's shop had proved a powerful draw, and she was captivated by the shadowy realm.

There were two more workbenches to her right. A lathe. A sanding table. Bins of clasps, hinges and dowels. It felt like a piece of home, as if Dad's shop had hiked up its britches and traipsed on down to join her and Johnny's childhood do-over.

This can't be real. Lennie recalled the lucid dream she had of the Choo Choo Motel, with younger versions of herself and John and—holy fried green tomatoes! This had to be another of those dreams!

Hadn't she just been in bed? Her body was probably still there, lost in a deep sleep. She pinched herself to see if she could wake herself up. *Ouch!* Harder. *Double ouch!*

Joella didn't pay Lennie any mind as she continued tending to the postcards. "Your father worked with his hands."

Doesn't everybody? Lennie kept the thought to herself as she scuffed along the wood-plank floor. The velvety sawdust under her bare feet felt as it had years ago. A porch rocker, kids' rocking horses and a baby crib all waited to be stained as particles floated in cones of light that spilled from the overhead bulbs.

Lennie glimpsed Joella mopping her forehead with her sleeve and looking her way. "These are the closest you can get to your father now. Like an echo of him."

This place sure as heck *felt* like Dad's workshop, just like her conversation with Joella in the porch rockers had the feel of *After Supper Club* dream-talking with Mom.

Absurd as it seemed, could she be chasing the echoes of those she loved, after they were gone? The possibility hovered over her for an instant before she brushed it aside.

What she needed was a diversion to get Joella to lower her guard and fess up to the letter. With a couple of steps, Lennie joined her at the workbench.

At close range, she noticed Joella's porcelain trivet was etched with a young girl in a flowing sundress who held a delicate flower to her nose.

Lennie's heart fluttered—the design was exactly the same as the one on a bookmark she sold at A Likely Story back in Mosely. Another piece in the patchwork quilt of her life stared back at her.

Joella got back to work pressing out the postcards. "You ever think there's somethin' beyond us? Somethin' that has a hand in what we consider happenstance?"

Sifting through the woman's words, Lennie leaned her hands on the rough-hewn workbench. "If you're talking about the car, we had an accident. Otherwise, we'd be three hundred miles down the pike, and I'd have a less ornery brother."

"Your car face-planted from a cliff," Joella said with the raised brows of a wise old owl questioning a blind bat. "That seem a bit outta the ordinary to you?"

"Okay," Lennie said with a shrug, "maybe it's not high on your DMV probable causes. So?"

"So, maybe somethin' else is at work." Joella's steadfast eyes held Lennie's gaze as dust flitted around them in the bulb's golden light, like a billion seeking souls.

Lennie cleared her throat. "I ... don't know what you're talking about."

The woman went back to work salvaging the postcards. "Or some*one*."

"Someone *what?*"

With a little grunt, Joella applied pressure to the Cape Canaveral postcard. "Else at work."

"Yeah, right." Lennie's feet seemed to have a mind of their own as they backed her up. "Look, I don't know what you're tryin' to pull with your night-owl antics and all this oogity-boogity with the postcards, but I'm not some bumpkin you can hook like a catfish."

Joella turned, a glimmer of a smile on her face. "Why did you come out here?"

Lennie crossed her arms and gave her a sassy hip. "I've been around, okay? Includin' the pueblos of New Mexico and the Bering Sea. You ever stood night-watch on a trawler? I've seen plenty, and I'm not buyin' whatever it is you're sellin'."

"Sellin'?" Sadness clouded the aged woman's eyes as she regarded Lennie a moment. Then she gave herself a little nod, seemingly coming to terms with Lennie. "Okay." Leaving the postcards behind, she strode toward the door.

Lennie felt awful for her ungracious manner—Joella had been nothing but kind trying to restore Dad's prized postcards.

She hadn't claimed to be a guardakin *anything*. Lennie had made her into that in her own mind, and she realized maybe she'd looked at Joella through glasses fogged with the heartache of unbearable loss and a growing sense of desperation she couldn't shake.

"Wait," Lennie said.

Joella stopped and looked back. "You should drop by my studio on Main. Just a visit. Look for the circles that never stop turnin'." She stepped outside and closed the door.

It was quiet. Too quiet. Lennie felt her pulse in her ears and scuffed across the sawdusty floor just to create some sort of a sound. Lowering herself into an unstained rocker, she pushed back with her toes, rocking to still her heart. *Okay, girl ... either go all in, or get all out.*

THIRTY-SIX

Out of the Mist

It was his slumbering mind that first roused to the rhythmic bounce of a basketball on the edge of his senses as he slept on Hector's living room couch. Stirring, John opened his eyes and lifted his head from the pillow. The sound grew more distinct. *Thump, thump, thump.* It came from outside.

He swung his feet to the floor, not so much puzzled by the sound as preoccupied by the long-forgotten memory it triggered. A newspaper photographer had come to the house to take Lennie's picture for the story about her earning a starting spot on the boys' team at Mosely High.

John had watched from the kitchen door as his sister bounced her basketball on their driveway court and Dad looked on with a smile, gesturing for her to crouch lower, as if she were poised to make a break for the basket.

Lennie and her basketball. Rubbing his face, he traipsed to the door in his Bermuda shorts and went outside. He followed the sound of the steady beat through a dense fog that permeated the mountains like silvery, gossamer cotton.

The high-pitched *zing-zing-zing* of compressed air inside the ball colliding with asphalt reverberated off the shrouded walls of the house behind him.

In a sleepy haze, he let the noise lead him forward, barely aware of the moonlight that managed to infuse the mist and light his way.

He rounded the corner of Hector's garage, where the scruffy basketball goal was mounted and slowed at what met his eyes.

Dad.

In his leather shop apron and red Converse hi-top sneakers, he stood bouncing Lennie's basketball.

John stopped barely ten yards away from him, grasping to make sense of what he saw.

A flash of fear drove him a step back, then a voice seemed to whisper in his head, a voice he'd never heard, from a depth he'd never tapped. The murmur was indistinguishable, but its reassuring tone overcame his instinct to flee, locked him where he stood, toeing an inconceivable line between being and beyond.

A single word escaped his lips. "Dad?"

Lennie shifted in the workshop's rocking chair as she surfaced from an infinite realm where the divine held a solitary vigil. Something tickled the boundaries of her consciousness, where a familiar voice framed a question in a stunned tone. It seemed to float up to her.

Dad?

Dad?

Dad?

John's voice. The rising sound of a basketball bouncing outside sparked her awareness, and her eyes snapped open to the waking world. The workbench. Light bulbs dangling from the rafters. Sawdust. Her aching tailbone, bearing all her weight against the rocker's wooden seat.

She tousled her hair. *What time is it?* Standing, she pressed her hands into the small of her back and arched to stretch her muscles. *I was talking with that woman. She was—wait. There's a basketball outside?*

The beckoning sound drew her as she stepped out of the workshop and made her way toward it. Dewy moisture caressed her face, and she was fairly certain she was heading in the general direction of the garage, but the fog was so thick she couldn't be sure. Visibility was that of a picture-perfect Halloween graveyard.

Thump, thump, thump. The reverberations were so close, they seemed to move right through her. A spike of panic slowed her steps. She was right on top of the thumping, but she still couldn't see a thing. She extended her hand, suddenly scared she might walk into something. Or someone. *What if it's not John?*

She drew a sharp breath as two human forms suddenly materialized in the dense soup.

Dad and John.

She thought the thumping was her ball Dad was bouncing, but it was her heart as she joined them, doubt and wonder battling inside her. Dad looked at her and stopped dribbling. Then his attention drifted to John. So did hers.

Her brother stared at Dad, transfixed, a look on his face she'd never seen before. She didn't want to move a muscle, afraid she'd awaken from whatever this glorious moment was.

She caught Dad's smirk out of the corner of her eye, a twitch of amusement that preceded whatever practical joke he was about to pull.

Spinning the basketball between his hands, he leveled his gaze at John. "Stop looking the wrong way, Johnny."

Lennie's breath caught in her throat. He'd never been able to make himself heard in their encounters, though she was certain as sunrise he'd tried.

John's expression was baffled, nearly blank. *Yes, Johnny. Yes!* He seemed to be experiencing exactly what she'd been trying to explain to him.

Her bare feet tingled on the dank asphalt, and Dad glanced at her in a way she vaguely understood, just like when she was a girl taking an unspoken cue on the driveway court

She never saw his hands move as he blasted a two-handed chest pass at Johnny. The world seemed to slow as the ball hurtled through the mist of time, droplets of moisture swirling in its wake like the tail of a comet, until it clobbered John square in the face and dropped him as if he'd been hit by the world heavyweight champ.

She rushed toward him. "Johnny!" Dropping to her knees, she leaned over her fallen brother and slapped his cheeks. "Johnny!—Johnny!"

Relief shot through her when his eyes flickered open. "That's it," she said with an urgency fueled by excitement. "C'mon, Johnny. It's me. I'm right here." As his dazed eyes blinked, her words slipped and slid all over each other. "That was incredible! You see? You *see!* That's what I've been talkin' about!"

"Whaaa ...?" he murmured. "What happened?"

Lennie helped him sit up. "What *happened?* Daddy nailed you smack dab in the face with a gorgeous chest pass!"

John winced and rolled his neck, clenching and unclenching his eyes. "Oh my God. I can't believe it."

"I know, right?" She allowed her eyes to sweep the area, unable to see anything in the dense fog. "I didn't believe it either, at first. But there he was. Again. I mean, he just keeps comin'. Oh yeah, he's definitely reachin' out."

She gave him a hand in getting to his feet. "John Thomas, nobody's ever gonna believe us." She hoped the formal inclusion of his middle name would lend extra weight to her declaration.

His body crimped over, and he braced himself with his hands on his knees as he pulled in a few settling breaths. "I haven't done that since my master's thesis."

Lennie's mind raced. *A witness!* "They'll have to believe us now!"

He straightened and scanned the murky garage court as he massaged the back of his neck. "I remember laying down on the couch, and the next thing I know, I have this vision. Then there's a head. Hazy. With this ... bright light around it."

"That was me! I was kneeling over you."

He seemed to be piecing together what had just happened. No doubt it would all rush back to him in the next couple of minutes. Her jackrabbit mind could hardly wait for his tortoise realization.

"No. Before I saw you," he said. "I don't know ... something just hammered in." He brushed his hair back as an expression of bewilderment spread across his face. "This hasn't happened to me since college."

"What hasn't? Seeing *visions?*"

He looked around. "Sleepwalking."

"Sleepwalking?" she shot back. "What're you talking about? Daddy was just here!"

She'd been so torn up inside ever since Dad appeared at the hospital, she'd had to talk herself off the freaked-out fence once a day, and twice on Sundays, fretting she might be going looney tunes

"You're not listening," he said. "I sleepwalked while studying for my boards. Went through a couple nightly routines, and I had no clue until I woke up and Holly told me."

There was no way Lennie was going to deny she'd shared such an extraordinary experience with John, someone who'd seen what she saw and heard what she heard. A sickening feeling twisted inside as his words sank in—her corroborating witness was selling her out.

She could barely muster a response. "*What?*"

"It's often stress-induced."

"It's not sleepwalking!" she shouted. "Dad was just here. It was the three of us!"

John stared at her, and for an instant she thought a sliver of uncertainty stabbed his eyes. But just as quickly, she recognized she was up against his hardwired logic-rocket. And she was powerless to stop him from igniting it.

"It's called somnambulism," he explained, running his hands over his face. "That's the medical term. A sleep disorder belonging to the parasomnia category."

Lennie poked him in the chest. "You're refusing to consider the possibility of something going on beyond your understanding because you're scared."

Working his jaw back and forth, he seemed more interested in assuring himself with his explanation than in anything she said. "It's super common among high achievers."

"He was here, Johnny. Or—" She pressed her teeth into her bottom lip as she tried to figure it out. "Or, we were where he is. Or it was ... a crossing of some sort."

He scoffed. "That's ridiculous, Lennie. And I'm beginning to have some serious concerns about you."

"Well, it was *something!*" she yelled.

"Keep your voice down," he hissed. "It wasn't *something*."

"He talked to you! Just like in our dream at the Choo Choo."

"Oh, for God's sake. Really?" John scrubbed his hair with his fingers, as if he could shampoo away the entire episode. "What did he say? Huh? What pearl of heavenly wisdom did he impart?"

"He told you to stop looking the wrong way."

He let loose a burst of laughter. "That's it? He comes across *alllll* eternity to give me some sort of traffic tip?"

His dismissive grin stirred her swirling confusion to a fever pitch. "I don't know!"

"Well, let me tell you what *I* know!"

KABOOM!

A jarring blast drove them into defensive crouches as its echo dissolved into the fog-bound mountains.

"*¡Dios mio!*" In his bathrobe, Hector stood in the glow of the porch light, smoke snaking from the barrel of a shotgun.

"Us old people need sleep, or we get disoriented and can't be held responsible for our actions!" He pumped another shell into the chamber. "*¿Comprende?* Now go to sleep!"

He slung the firearm to his shoulder like a soldier walking guard duty, spun, and stomped back into the house.

They straightened, and Lennie looked at John, who closed his eyes, took a deep breath and slowly exhaled.

"Johnny—"

"Our minds are playing tricks, Lennie. We're both tired, and our dreams are getting weird, okay? You can't expect me to believe anything I may or may not have seen while I was sleepwalking."

"But I *swear*," she said in an urgent whisper.

The slight smile he gave her held a trace of compassion. "Scooby Doo isn't going to roll up with the gang and spin out some Saturday morning mystery here."

Even if it meant pleading, she had to make him understand. "But I'm seeing clear as day, Johnny."

"The only thing I'm seeing?" he replied, "is a super-long day driving tomorrow. Making that launch is everything to me, okay? It's *everything*. Please. Just ... can we do that? Can we make the launch?"

He clasped his hands and pumped them as if he were shaking dice. "The Choo Choo was a bust. Rock City? Bust. Six Flags? Bust. Right now, the entire trip is one big whiff. The launch is all I have left. Dad wrote that it changed his life. I need to somehow know that feeling. It's all I ask."

He mumbled something under his breath as he turned and walked back toward the house.

THIRTY-SEVEN

Surefire Proof

L ennie hadn't been able to hear exactly what John said as he walked away, but his tone indicated it wasn't a vote of confidence in her. Now alone in the ghostly gray, she let her eyes roam the murk. Was she losing touch? Or worse, already *touched?*

The letter!

She spun and raced headlong through the mist, heart slamming her ribcage. Yes, it was a smidge eerie, but the letter was surefire proof of contact from the beyond. From Mom, no less. *That'll show him!*

It couldn't have been more than twenty yards to the house, but it didn't appear, didn't appear, didn't appear—until, finally, the porch's murky form materialized.

She hurdled the three steps in a single stride and burst into the living room.

She barely made out John's form on the couch as she beelined for the bedroom. Turning on the dresser light, she yanked open the letter drawer.

It was empty.

A dizzying shiver overtook her, and the earlier buzz of the ceiling fan now swelled loud as a swarm of cicadas. *Why is this happening?* Had the letter ever really been there?

For reasons she could never hope to understand, a child piano prodigy she'd seen years ago in Seattle flashed from her wayfarer's chest of memories.

She clung to the thought of that little girl in the burgundy jumper to fight off throwing up into a dried out five-gallon paint can in the corner. The wonder-child had done the impossible: perform a virtuoso piece that was mind-boggling in its complexity. How had it been coming from those little hands?

The phenom had even stood upright to work the pedals because her feet couldn't reach them from the bench, her nose barely at key level, eyes peeking over the ivories, fingers unleashed as if seized by some unforeseen conductor.

Lennie stilled the chaos in her mind and allowed the captivation she'd felt in that moment to blossom into the rapturous enjoyment of being back there. Of sharing in an unbelievable, unexplainable experience.

Maybe she was wrapped up in something akin to that child and had slipped into some curious dimension where her virtuosity was being able to perceive things others couldn't. A perception prodigy. Was that a thing? It made about as much sense as anything else that had happened over the past few weeks.

The jarring possibility sent a tremor through her, and she eased into bed, the ceiling fan lightly buzzing over her once more as she curled on her side facing the window. She closed her eyes but couldn't keep them shut. She searched the mist outside, trying to see more than it would allow.

The first light of dawn had always been Lennie's favorite time, ripe with the possibility that each day would be better than the last.

This Sunday morning, shadows lay long across the valley as the sun sliced through lush mountain passes. A pearly sunrise invited her to steady her tossed mind.

She pulled away from Hector's in his tow truck. Wind rushed through the cab, rustling her hair and her thoughts. She needed to think. And she'd always done her best pondering when she was in motion.

A couple of narrow ridgeline roads later, she was on a gravel trail bordered by an upland pasture where ghostly horses stood watch in the fog.

She was determined to break down what was happening into discernable pieces, to make it more manageable. She was too rattled to care that it was exactly the way John would approach it. She needed answers.

First, there was Dad. Right in front of her face. Three times now. And what about Momma? A gentler touch with a handwritten letter, just like the ones Lennie had penned to her in vain all those years ago.

She couldn't wrangle her turbulent thoughts. Was this a family intervention across some kind of ethereal no-fly-zone that barricaded the *here* from the *hereafter?*

Her deliberation was jarred by the sight of a small family farm approaching on the passenger side. There were a few fenced cows, and a weathered barn rose behind a rambling house.

Drawing closer, she saw a girl with impossibly curly hair in a plain summer dress, tending flowers in a patch of land dotted with headstones—generations of kin, Lennie guessed, wagering they dated to the Civil War, like the Mosely cemetery back home.

The truck's creaking shocks must have announced Lennie's arrival because the girl suddenly stood, glanced her way and offered a friendly smile, waving a hand dirtied by the rich earth.

She seemed about twelve, an age when Lennie had regularly visited Mom's grave, needing to touch the headstone—proof that the woman who brought her into the world had once lived and breathed for real. With every wildflower she'd planted on that sacred soil, Lennie had felt a connection.

Chugging slowly past, Lennie waved back at the girl, so peaceful in the plot of eternal rest, framed by mountains that had existed long before either of them had and would carry on long after they were gone.

The girl in her rearview, she gripped the steering wheel tighter as a possibility deepened her uneasiness about what was happening to her. Her anxiety was chased away by the rumble of a train from somewhere nearby.

The road dipped and she was suddenly paralleling the track where the train rolled along. Familiar warning bells rang out. Rounding a bend, she braked to a stop at a railroad crossing, safety gates down, bells clanging as the train's passing vibrated the cab.

She watched rusty freight cars clank by, until the last finally cleared the crossing to reveal a white wooden church, just up on the next rise. The crossing bell stopped and the safety gates lifted as she pondered the hillside house of prayer from the idling truck.

She eased the wrecker over the tracks and drove to the church. A scrolled sign out front announced the sanctuary as the Ebenezer Missionary Baptist Church. The lot was full, so she parked alongside the road and sat for a moment. *Do you even remember how to pray?* She figured she had nothing to lose. She sure wasn't having much luck figuring things out on her own.

THIRTY-EIGHT

A Mess of Maybe

Ambling toward the church, Lennie heard a commanding voice coming from inside. She pulled the door open by its wrought-iron cross handle and immediately became the focus of attention for a packed congregation of African Americans who turned back to see who had the gumption to walk in late. Heat rushed her face as she stood paralyzed by the multitude of inquisitive faces.

"For the Lord tells us each and every day we must look for the way!" the preacher up front thundered.

The church echoed with spirited responses: "Keep them eyes open! Praise Jesus! Yes, Lawd!"

"Follow his call, and come out of the darkness!" the preacher bellowed.

Lennie let her eyes dart left, then right among the congregants in their Sunday finest. She hadn't been to church in years, but memories of Dad lecturing her about "proper church attire" welled up. She could still hear him scolding her over her sleeve-less blouse, comfy drawstring shorts, and strapless Walmart sandals with big plastic daisy buds that seemed to sprout from her toes.

She was a heartbeat away from fleeing when she heard, "Psst!" It was John's pint-sized basketball buddy, Andre. Back pew on the right. He smiled and scooched over, motioning her to squeeze in. Too late. The preacher had already spotted her.

"It seems the Almighty's delivered us a weary traveler this glo-rious morn," he said with open arms.

She looked up the center aisle at his welcoming smile, and he gestured for her to come forward. "Welcome, sister. There's al-ways a place right up front at the Lord's table."

When she looked to Andre for help, the boy gave her big eyes and a bigger church whisper. "Reverend Lewis says come, you best go!" He gestured with a flick of his wrist. "Tell'im Andre Porter sent you."

Lennie swallowed and slowly scuffed up the aisle. Her sandals clapped her heels with every step as the hushed faithful watched her make her way.

Women in their church dresses and hats regarded her ap-proach to the Reverend in pin-drop quiet, cooling themselves with wicker fans or church bulletins. Gentlemen in suits nodded graciously, dabbing their glistening foreheads with handkerchiefs as she arrived front and center and offered the Reverend a trem-bling smile.

"She's lost!" Andre's voice filled the rafters from behind her, and she turned to find him straining in his pew to see her up front, weaving and bobbing to get a better view between ladies' hats. The congregation tittered, and Andre gave her the widest smile in history.

"Well, Andre," Reverend Lewis said, "sometimes we all get a little lost."

"But she's a whole lot lost!" the boy informed him and the rest of the flock. A clamor of whispers and chuckles followed.

"I think he means I'm not from around here," Lennie said.

The Reverend pulled a handkerchief from his back pocket, wiping the sweat from his brow. "By what glorious blessing, then, are you among us?"

She blinked a moment in the quiet and gave the question some thought. "I—"

"Her Daddy's dead!" Andre yelled. She looked back at the boy, and they held each other's gaze. A little piece of her embraced his childish take on honesty, an unfiltered recognition of the world as it was. Still, the unforgiving finality of his pronouncement in this holy space tightened in her chest.

A burning sensation rippled her eyes as she turned back to the Reverend, keeping her tears at bay with a pained half-smile.

"My Dad just passed. And I, um ... I don't know. I've been—" Searching for the right words, she shook her head and clasped her hands together. "Experiencing his presence, I guess you'd say."

The Reverend's response was for her, but his wide-armed gesture seemed to include the rapt congregation. "Only the vessel returns to dust."

"Praise Jesus!" came the response from somewhere in the sea of congregants. Other responses followed, swift and sure. "Rise on up!" "Feel the glory!"

She'd never felt so exhausted as she stood alone in the aisle, trying to put faces to the voices that sought to assure her.

What struck her was the churchgoers' bedrock of belief, and their steadfastness laid bare a hard truth: her own faith, in God and in herself, had long ago been destroyed by the Mosely's emotional arson. How could the merciful Almighty she'd learned of as a child have looked the other way and allowed to happen what she endured?

Her vision grew speckled, and the church flared more radiant by the second. She was going to faint. A soft hand took hers, and the touch of downy skin calmed her sweaty flush. She looked into the milky eyes of an elderly woman whose wrinkled fingers were crimped by arthritis, her face deeply creviced. She squeezed Lennie's hand, her voice as gentle as her grip. "The spirit carries on, child."

Lennie felt a tear track her cheek, her words barely a whisper. "Yessum. I'm trying to believe."

The Reverend patted his chest with both hands like a satiated soul who had just feasted on a heavenly meal. "The soul never dies!"

Consumed by his unshakeable certainty, Lennie withdrew her hand from the woman's. The congregants had their faith to shore them up. She had only a brother who thought she was wacko. How could they possibly understand?

Her mind ricocheted between doubt and anxiety. She couldn't explain what she was feeling, but she had to try.

"Yes!" Lennie exclaimed to the Reverend, then spun to face the congregation like a misunderstood candidate in a town hall debate. "The soul never dies. I get that whole line of thinking from back in my—" She winced. "Church-going era."

She frantically searched rattled faces. "What I'm saying is, I've been seeing my Dad while I'm *awake*."

The Reverend swept his hand toward the rafters, voice booming. "Brothers and sisters, how many have had a loved one raised up by the righteousness of the Lord? Lift those hands unto Him!"

Every hand shot up with resounding cries of Amen!

Lennie grabbed fistfuls of her hair and looked up into the rafters. "Yes, yes, yes! But that's *not* what I'm saying. Listen to me!"

That seemed unlikely because the Reverend wasn't ready to relinquish his bid on God's glory as his voice steamrolled on.

"And how many here have visited with that glorious soul?"

Hands in every pew reached heavenward as the organist launched into an exalting spiritual, wicker fans waving in the congregation like flowers in a mighty wind.

"Hold it, hold it, hold it!" Lennie shouted and signaled the organist to pipe down. She pivoted to the congregation as the last note faded out up above, suddenly realizing that she of little faith was fighting for her spiritual life smack dab in the middle of God's house.

"Brothers and sisters," she cried out as she fluffed her blouse to cool herself and gestured for a show of hands. "Has anybody, right here, right now, played basketball with their deceased Daddy?"

The murmurs came fast and furious: *Say what now? Basketball? Deceased daddy?*

Mumbling whispers gave way to a profound silence she hadn't heard since John's walk back to the pew after delivering Dad's eulogy.

Hands dropped one by one as she confronted a sea of bewildered looks. Still, she kept her hand held high as she clung to a sliver of hope.

Her desperate gaze swept the church, looking for somebody, *anybody*, to raise their hand with her. To stand with her. But there were no hands. She was alone. The only one who had pressed up against the barrier to the beyond.

She turned a slow circle, her world collapsing in the midst of hushed strangers as she silently begged them to affirm that anything was possible with God, just like she'd always been told

Her gaze found Reverend Lewis, placid hands folded at his waist. Someone coughed somewhere. There was no bottom to her hopelessness. *I shoulda known I don't deserve a blessing.* She fixed on an angular divot in the hardwood floor that looked for all the world like some poor soul had dropped the corner of a casket.

"I'll go then." Her voice was barely audible, and she wasn't sure if anyone heard her, but it didn't matter. Nothing mattered.

She turned to the back of the church, the light of morning in the four-square windows. She gazed at Andre and saw the struggle to understand in his eyes.

She instantly felt worse for him than for herself, knowing that someone would have to explain to him about that zany white lady at church, tell him that sometimes people who've lost their way fall into despair and create a pretend world where things worked as they wish they would.

As she headed for the door, she picked up speed, sandals smacking dead air.

"Miss?" It was Reverend Lewis's voice, behind her. "Miss, wait."

It wasn't his words that stopped her as she rushed toward her escape. It was a sound she recognized from her childhood church: the crack of wood in the hush—clear as a gunshot creasing a mountain pass. Someone had shifted in a pew.

She turned to see a quivering hand rise. With the entire congregation, she stared at a gentleman in a blue suit who looked as old as the ages, his corded neck wrapped in a starched white collar, his tie neatly knotted. He didn't seem to be in any particular hurry as he grasped the back of the pew in front of him and pulled himself to his feet.

His furrowed expression suggested he was gathering his thoughts as he took an extra second or two to make sure his tie hung straight. Then he secured the top button on his jacket and smoothed it against his lanky frame.

He spoke a few words, but his voice rasped, making them unintelligible. Sensing he might be nervous, Lennie felt for him and took a few steps closer. "I'm sorry, sir. I couldn't hear you."

He cleared his throat. "I said, does croquet count?"

She barely recognized the word she repeated: "Croquet?"

"I, um ... a time or two. I have ... with my Pappy. He's been gone a spell, but he'll visit sometimes and we play." Murmured comments about *poor Zeke's mind* rose, and she glimpsed a few shaking heads.

A tug of her hand drew her eyes down to Andre. "That's Mr. Reynolds. He tells me he talks with Jesus sometimes."

She refocused on Mr. Reynolds and realized her jaw had dropped slightly open as he gave her an assured nod that seemed to say *you're welcome.* Then he graciously unbuttoned his jacket and eased himself back into his seat with the same measured manner as when he had stood.

She couldn't take her eyes off him as the hush closed in and her thoughts suddenly rushed in every direction at once. *Maybe...* Something flickered deep down inside. *Maybe I'm not alone.*

A longing swamped her like a tsunami that overwhelms all. She wanted with all her heart to believe in possibilities. Why couldn't Mr. Reynolds have spoken with Jesus? Hope sparked from a dying ember to a wildfire in an instant. And her soul stirred, a soul that had been laid waste by a life of heartache.

Before she knew the words were escaping her lips, she heard herself shout out, "Son of a bi—"

The multitude gasped as one, and she clamped her hands over her mouth, lopping off a cuss word she was certain Ebenezer Missionary Baptist Church had never heard uttered in this hallowed space.

"I'm not the only one," she mumbled, feeling her smile stretch into a grin behind her hands.

THIRTY-NINE

Take Wing

Tires rumbled beneath Lennie as she crossed back over the train tracks down the road from the church. Adding to the commotion in her head, Hector's rearview Mardi Gras beads filled the cab with a constant clatter.

Her thoughts cycloned, but instead of corkscrewing down from above, hers spiraled up. Elderly Mr. Reynolds had affirmed the possibility of rekindling a departed-kin hook-up. Another old-timer guardakin angel connection. Maybe.

The adorable old man said he'd whacked croquet balls around the lawn with his deceased dad. But the churchgoers said he wasn't playing with a full deck. So? Who were *they* to say? Maybe God was dealing him a hand they'd never been dealt.

Her forearms ached from her iron grip on the wheel as she steered the lumbering wrecker up a twisting road.

The sun reflected off the rump of Hector's chrome bulldog hood ornament, and a solar flare stabbed her eyes as she swung the Ford through the arc of a turn—one more maneuver in a life that had always twisted in ways she'd never expected.

She glanced at the digital clock stuck to the dash. She'd been gone for nearly two hours. John would be all in a tizzy if he woke up and learned she'd simply taken off. But after the way he'd upped and walked away last night, she felt no obligation to clear her schedule with him.

What was she supposed to do? They were stuck, waiting until after church for parts they'd need to try and salvage Louise. Why just sit around doing nothing when you could venture out and get the lay of the land? Besides, Hector had said she could use the truck if she wanted.

Topping a crest, she saw the World Famous Main Street sign they'd passed hauling Louise from the gorge. She slowed. Joella had mentioned her studio on Main last night. Her hands seized control before her head had a chance to weigh in on the decision, steering the truck in the direction the sign pointed.

The rutted blacktop narrowed as it wound through sidewinding turns bordered by woods and massive granite outcroppings. The rough surface ended in a gravel trail, and she rolled up to a gathering of old buildings that lined a cobblestone street. She idled past a sign: "Welcome to Tallulah Falls' World Famous Main Street, Est. 1885."

She thought the place could've been the inspiration for Mayberry, the tiny fictional town she'd seen in reruns of *The Andy Griffith Show* while holed up in Alaskan winters.

Only a few folks were out and about on this sleepy Sunday morning. The biggest storefront sign belonged to Lester's Hardware, which was squeezed between Kuts'n'Kurls Beauty Parlor and Big Dawg Diner.

At the far end of the street stood a railroad crossing gate and a regal building that looked like it might have once been a courthouse. A clock face high on its facade lacked hands.

She couldn't remember the name of the Nervous Ned guy who ran the Mayberry barbershop, but she instantly recognized a barber pole on a brick exterior about halfway down the street, blue and red bands twirling the illusion of a perpetual upward spiral.

Lennie shifted on the creaky seat when Joella's words from last night floated back into her mind: *Look for circles that never stop spinning.* She eased the truck past the barber shop and saw a sign over the spinning pole, fanciful peach letters on a sky-blue background: Joella's Take Wing Studio.

She parked down the street and mulled the studio from a distance. Over pale window silhouettes of a straight razor crossed with scissors and a comb, she could make out the remnants of old-timey whitewash lettering: *Haircuts & Shaves. Whiskers Not Refunded.*

She drummed her fingers on the steering wheel. What if Joella had been the one who got Mr. Reynolds and his dad together over croquet mallets? For a long moment, she allowed for the possibility before shaking off the notion. Too far-fetched.

Everything pointed to the local artist being an eccentric with her own quirky style, not some kind of spiritual go-between. But Joella *had* invited her to the studio, and she was curious about Joella's creations. She didn't need to buy anything. She could just window shop.

She got out and shuffled along the storefront sidewalk toward the barber shop studio. She couldn't fathom why she felt uneasy as she glanced back over her shoulder at the mostly empty street.

Once at the display window, she could barely see inside because of the sun's glare. Leaning close, she cupped her hands to the sides of her face like parentheses and pressed her hands against the glass, instantly intrigued by a shrine to the divine.

Strings of tiny white lights crisscrossed the ceiling, echoing a starry night. Little angel collectibles spread their wings in the display window, some dainty antiques praying, their more modern relatives frozen in choir poses. She considered a chipped porcelain angel surrounded by tiny children's letter blocks similar to those she'd seen in Joella's hair. It was missing an eye, worn away by time.

She strained against the glass to peer deeper into the shop and spied hefty cherub garden statues hunkered in three leather-and-chrome barber chairs, as if waiting for a trim.

Beyond the alabaster trio, elegantly curved pieces of wrought-iron leaned like question marks against a wall, and there appeared to be a back room separated from the main studio by a beaded curtain. *Maybe she works back there.*

Lennie noticed a wall-to-wall ceiling fresco through the canopy of string lights. It depicted an angel winging headlong into a raging storm, trumpet blaring. The image sent a little shiver up her neck because she knew from childhood Bible school it had to be Angel Gabriel heralding the resurrection.

All the same, she felt the need to go inside and see what other treasures might await. So many angels. What did it mean?

The thought drew her eyes heavenward, and a memory twinkled in the ceiling lights, pulling her closer to Dad than she'd felt since she was a little girl. It was a ritual she had performed when he came home from work—washing his feet with the hose in the driveway, cleaning off the gritty mine slurry that had slithered inside his work boots.

She took a few steps to the door's recessed entryway. Because of the early morning angle of the sun, the building's jutting brick façade created a shaded oasis there.

Within the sheltered alcove, a bulbous pitcher of ice-cold tea sat on a wrought-iron flower-pot stand, the capped glass sweating in the mugginess. A handwritten sign over a stack of red Solo cups read: Free! Take one! She caught a wistful grin in her reflection in the glass door. A little Southern hospitality. *How sweet.*

According to the business hours posted on the door, Take Wing didn't open until noon on Sundays. She tugged the handle. *Clank.* The deadbolt cracked against the frame.

Her shoulders slumped in resignation and she backed away. It was then she heard a frail *crack*. A piece of ice must have splintered inside the pitcher.

Her eyes were drawn to the complimentary iced tea. She was parched from the ride. Backhanding sweat from her cheek, she glanced around. The street was practically deserted. Be a shame to let perfectly good, and perfectly cold, tea go to waste on a sweltering day.

She snagged a cup and filled it halfway with the copper-colored liquid. Lifting it to her nose, she knew the lively aroma in an instant: sweet tea with a hint of mint. Just like her *After Supper Club* sweet-tea dreams of Mom. She took a sip. It tasted exactly like Mom's brew, which she'd had been drinking her whole life! A blade of turmoil sliced through her as she held fast to this cupful of her childhood.

Her legs went wobbly as she retreated from the alcove and twirled a circle, her jaw clenching. She placed the cup on the sidewalk and backed away from it. As she spun for the wrecker, she fought a rising wave of panic.

From atop Big Dawg Diner, Roselyn watched her daughter race off in the truck, resisting the tug of dancing shadows created by wind whirling around a weathervane. *No, no, no!*

She wasn't ready to leave this world. But the inevitable call of the afterlife had weakened the strength she needed to remain in this realm, and she'd depleted almost all her energy when she solidified from its ethereal state the pitcher of their *After Supper Club* tea. Clinging to her bodily vessel was becoming more and more difficult.

To keep the speeding wrecker in sight, she shifted location to the top of the water tower near the railroad crossing where Lennie would pass. Lingering there, Roselyn struggled with a realization she had tried to deny: her allotted window to reach back to Lennie was quickly closing.

She'd felt her essence dwindling ever since the night a few weeks back, when she'd approached Lennie as she sheltered in her car, tapping the glass with a pebble to reach her before earthly law had barged in. Even the letter she'd left for her daughter had succumbed to impermanence, expiring like a temporary visa to a mysterious province.

Roselyn sensed Lennie was again slipping away from her, and she recalled the instant she first understood there were precarious moments between breaths, when a heart might never beat again. The memory floated in on distant voices and sensations on the edge of her senses that day.

"Stay with us, Mrs. Riley!"

"We don't have a pulse."

"Begin compressions."

Her chest rocked by a rhythmic force.

"Keep talking to her."

"It's a girl, Mrs. Riley. You have a baby girl!"

"Code blue, delivery room two."

A piercing screeeech ... voices frantic in the delivery room.

"We've cut the cord!"

"V-fib." *Screeeee ...*

Her crying infant ...

"Paddles charged. Two-hundred joules."

"Stay with me, Roselyn!"

"Clear."

A jolt lifts her ragdoll body as she squeezes someone's hand...

She had never held her daughter, never touched her face or soothed her nicks and bruises and fears.

She'd given Lennie life while her own released, and there had been no way to get back what fate had denied them. Only a deep concern for Lennie had convinced her to stay in this ethereal state for so long. Now, never was forever, and her soul grieved at the prospect of forsaking her daughter to this world.

Little time remained for her here, and Roselyn could only pray she was not too late to make her presence felt.

FORTY

Caution to the Wind

Her mind racing, Lennie nibbled her bottom lip, wondering if she should interrupt Hector. His legs stuck out from under the car, the rest of him concealed under the vehicle on a rolling mechanic's creeper. She didn't want to break his concentration. Still, it was difficult to hold back when your entire world came down to one question.

"You ever heard of guardakin angels?" she said.

The *clang* of a wrench hitting the concrete floor rang out. "What?" His reply was muffled. She knew she had to be quick about this, before John came around.

"Guardakin angels," she said, louder.

"That you, Lennie?"

"Yes. You ever heard of 'em around here?"

He muttered something, then banged on whatever it was that was refusing to cooperate under there. "Guardakin angels?" he grunted. "Where'd you get a *loco* notion like that?"

"A friend of mine back home, someone in the know, said they might be around here."

"Uh-huh." She'd heard a lot of skeptical replies in her life, and Hector's was in the top three. She hoped for more information but met only silence.

"My friend said these guardakin angels can help deceased parents reach back to the children they've left behind."

Hector rolled out from under the car and looked up from under the brim of his grease-smudged cap. "I've heard jibber-jabber. But you ask me? It's those PR people down in Atlanta trying to hook tourists."

He rolled back under the car. "Y'know, Savannah's made lots'a money on ghost tours and such. It's a thing. They been ridin' that horse for a long time." A wrench's chatter seemed to signal he had to keep working if he was going to hit John's deadline for leaving.

"Okay, thanks," she said with a sigh.

Wandering outside, she spotted John down the sloping road, taking pictures. She couldn't stop thinking about the funky barber shop studio with its host of angels and the memory of Dad that had come rushing back.

When she left Main Street, she'd reconsidered the possibility that Joella could be just the person she had been hoping to run into in Tallulah Falls. Something fluttered inside when she thought of the time she'd spent with her in Hector's workshop. Well, why not play detective and return to the scene for a look around in the light of day?

Sunlight streamed through the workshop's dusty windows as she scuffed amid in-progress woodworking projects—cribs, rockers, kids' rocking horses. She let her eyes roam scattered footprints on the sawdust floor.

Her heart instantly thudded in her chest when she noticed a little girl's bedroom nameplate on a router table, her name burned into it in Dad's familiar script lettering, and she dug from her pocket his wood-burned Lennie heart.

The heart's scorched lettering perfectly matched the name-plate's. *What the—?* Her thoughts careened in a million directions at once as—

"My postcards."

"GAAAH!" she yelled as she stumbled away from the bench and spun to see John behind her, arms crossed.

"Good Lord, Johnny! Don't do that to a person! You about gimme a coronary!"

"I hung them on the porch, and now they're gone."

Her head in a tizzy, she grabbed the nameplate and held it to his nose. "Look at this."

He brushed the nameplate aside with a look of annoyance. "Hector told me you asked him about some local angel-spirit messenger nonsense."

She lifted the sign to his eye level. "Would you just look, please?"

John glanced at it and sighed. She knew exactly what that meant: whatever was going on with her paled in comparison to his situation. "It's a sign." His voice was so flat, he might as well have said *so what?*

"Yes, it is!" She held up Dad's carved wooden heart for his inspection. "I found this after the funeral. We were in Dad's shop. Look at the letter work on it, then look at the nameplate letters. It's him!"

John gave the heart a quick look and rolled his eyes. "Or someone with a letter template available at any hardware store on the planet."

Lennie closed her eyes to choke her frustration. No use—when she opened them a second later, utter exasperation had taken hold. "Y'know, Johnny, you must be in a constant state of exhaustion, what with knowing everything about everything all the time. How do you do it?"

"Please don't tell me you're going to try to connect with Dad through some bogus angel. He's dead, you know." His haughty air was thick as blackberries in July.

"Excuse me?" she shot back, arms spread. "That's exactly what *you're* doing with your whole obsession retracing his life."

She couldn't tell him about Mom. Good Lord, no. He had completely blown her off when she'd told him about Dad at the gorge. Just her mind playing tricks. That was his take. He'd measure her for a funny-farm suit for sure if she added Mom to her mystifying claim.

"I'm not trying to reconnect literally, for God's sake," he said. "In *my* world there's no ghost whisperer."

"Can't you even allow for the possibility that—"

"That *what?* That a boondocks charlatan can be your interface with death's realm, like some kind of killer app?"

Drowning in his eyes, she saw a realization come together on his face. "Oh my God," he said. "You think you've actually *found* one. For real. A celestial interloper who—"

"She's not an interloper."

"An interloper, who can reach departed family in some other... beyond?" Disbelief twisted his face. "This is why you diverted me here?"

"Whoa-whoa-whoa." Her indignation shot up, along with her palms, like a cop stopping wrong-way traffic. "*You* diverted *me* with your insane spreadsheet. Let's not forget that. *You're* just along for the ride. This is *my* trip, and I think Dad's trying to help me find *my* baby. He led me here and—"

"*Led* you?" he sputtered. "You've got to be kidding me."

"He knows what happened now." The urgency in her voice was only eclipsed by her racing pulse. "Don't you see? He knows about Boone and the baby. And he knows I protected him by leaving. Knows the forced adoption broke us. He wants to make us right again."

John's head lolled back, and he let out a laugh. "Do you hear yourself? How does he know what happened!"

She grabbed his shoulders. "Because—"

"He's dead!"

When Lennie tried to shake him, John's body remained rigid—a steel pole had more give. "And now he's reaching out! To both of us. How is it that we've been in shared dreams with him? Dreams, *plural*. Not once, but twice." Okay, so she'd been fully awake the second time, but when it came to the possibility of a miracle, who had time to split hairs?

John grabbed her wrists and removed her grip from his shoulders. "First of all, that's *your* belief. Not mine. It's impossible! And repeating it over and over and over isn't going to make it any truer. The synapses of our brains are firing with memories. It's purely physiological. Like my sleepwalking."

"You *are* sleepwalking. Right through all of this."

He raked his fingers through his hair. "They're powerful memories, Lennie. That's all *any* of this is."

She met the certainty in his eyes for a tortuous moment. As a hollow feeling spread through her, she suddenly felt spent. "Just hear me out. Let me—"

"Lennie—"

Tears rimmed her eyes. "Can't you listen to me? For *once*?" His answer was an exasperated scowl.

"Dad has ... gone beyond," she said, *so* deeply needing him to understand. "He sees ... people who pass know all that ever was. They become *that*. And they can ... They watch over us. Intercede with God on our worst of days to help us."

"By what stretch of the wildest imagination—"

"Dad's got the whole picture, Johnny." A tear tracked her cheek. "He's got—" She labored to put into words what she was trying to believe. And then a path presented itself, a way to draw a parallel with something the photographer in him might understand. "He's got the wide-angle view on our lives. Mom, too."

John shook his head and looked away with a trace of sorrow in his smile. "*This* is what it's come to for you?"

"It hasn't *come* to this." Her voice welled with sadness over his refusal to allow her any credence whatsoever. "It *is* this."

His expression softened. "Lennie ... I'm sorry about what happened. What you went through. But please don't make everything worse or jeopardize your future by hanging your hopes on this absurdity—that some angel, or whatever, is going to help you find your child. Once you allow this huckster into your life, where does it end? You're going to be devastated all over again."

She couldn't look at him anymore. "Your postcards are on the bench."

John stepped away, moving through a shaft of sunlight alive with darting dust and into a shadow that draped the workbench. Picking up the postcards, he turned back. "You have to let him go. Let *this* go."

She pondered him in the dim light. Maybe it was the ensuing silence between them that calmed her. *It's just the way it has to be.* Maybe it was knowing that she *had* to find out if Joella was in any way the answer to her prayer. Whatever it was, she was afraid it had broken her and John apart forever. She'd have to live with that.

He looked at his Rolex. "You do your thing. I'm leaving for the launch in five hours, twelve minutes. If Hector can't fix the car in time, I'll go in a rental."

She swallowed and tried to still her trembling voice. "I wish you everything, Johnny."

"Yeah." He shuffled the postcards. "You can stay here and do whatever you think is right. Or you can finish with me. If this is it for the trip ... then it's the end of the road for us, too."

Walking toward the door, he stopped and turned back. "I hope you find whatever it is you're looking for. You deserve to be happy." The glare of daylight swallowed him as he stepped outside, leaving her to find her own way through the encroaching shadows.

FORTY-ONE

Down to the Wire

His camera clicked as John snapped a picture of the farmland valley Hector's place overlooked, struck by the shadows carved into the terrain by the afternoon sun. Lowering his Nikon, he realized his situation with Lennie was beyond his control, and he wrestled with a sense of pressure that had built up inside until it was ready to burst. Shooting photos was all he could do to stop himself from hovering over Hector's shoulder every passing second while he worked on the car.

Why had disaster stalked his entire trip? What were the odds of so much going so wrong so quickly? Now, to top it all off, Lennie seemed ready to plunge into a preposterous rabbit hole. He barely believed in leaps of faith. Leaps of folly? Never.

All that remained to go astray was missing the launch, the event that had touched Dad so deeply. Surely, he could make one—just one—of his stops. The most important of them all.

He checked his Rolex. 2:37. Departing by dusk was going to come down to the wire. Marching into the garage, he found

Hector bent over the Bonneville's grille, at work under the hood. "How we looking for departure?"

The old guy straightened and stretched his back. "Staying on it, chief."

The TV over Hector's workbench caught John's eye. An Atlas 5 Rocket sat on a launch pad behind a reporter, who said, "Preparations for the launch of the Orion satellite, which will probe the farthest reaches of the galaxy, are running smoothly, with liftoff on the Space Coast on schedule for six thirty-six tomorrow morning." *Great. The one time I could use a delay snafu and things are running like clockwork.*

Stepping outside, he paced behind the old gas pumps and checked his watch again. 2:40. It didn't take a rocket scientist to run the numbers: Hector had said it was a twelve-hour drive, which meant he absolutely had to leave by six-thirty. T-minus three hours, fifty minutes.

He didn't relish the prospect of driving all night on his own. Lennie, though, seemed hell-bent on her absurd search in Tallulah Falls, and he wasn't going to beg her to reconsider. What choice did he have but to leave her behind?

Somehow, he'd pull through—he'd always excelled in difficult situations, hadn't he? Especially at crunch time. Still, the likelihood of going zero-for-four on his memorial trek taunted him. *Not gonna happen.* He wouldn't allow it. No way was he going to flop on the crowning moment from Dad's trip.

He marched back into the garage. "Any way we can step up the pace? I'll gladly pay for expedited service."

Hector emerged from under the hood with a grease-smudged face. "There's a right way to do things and a wrong way to do things. The distributor package should be here shortly. That's the next part we need."

"And then she'll start, right?"

"Hard to say 'til we turn the key. I'm sure hoping."

"That's your professional estimation? Cross our fingers and *hope?*"

The mechanic tipped his cap back and pondered the engine. "Understand, electrical's a fickle lady. You gotta treat 'er right."

John scratched his beard-stubbled neck, debating another question he wasn't sure he should ask. He was certain, though, that the answer would prove him right. "Did you make a sign for a little girl's bedroom in the shop?"

Hector soaked up the sweat from his forehead with his sleeve. "I don't do signs. Cribs, rocking chairs, coffins. *Eso es todo.* Beginning, middle, end. That's your steady business."

John didn't put much stock in his answer. He'd probably forgotten. Given the slipshod organization in his shop, how could the old guy keep track of anything?

A vehicle horn blared. Groaning at the interruption, John followed Hector outside. The mechanic grinned at an arriving van, Ebenezer Missionary Baptist Church emblazoned on the sides.

The driver parked and got out. Hector wiped his palms on his britches before offering his hand. "Hey, Reverend Lewis. *¿Cómo estás?*"

"Buenos dias," the Reverend replied with a wide smile.

"Actually, it's *tardes,*" Hector said. "Good *afternoon.* But hey," he added with a shrug, "what's a few hours among friends?"

"You make it to Mass over at Sacred Heart this morning?"

Hector grinned. "I woulda, but my calling was *here.*" He nodded sideways at John. "I'm like the Good Samaritan, helping weary travelers. I figured the Lord would understand."

"Fair to say there's nothing He *doesn't,*" the Reverend said with a chuckle.

"What brings you by?"

"The van needs some new wipers. The Lord helps me to see the light, but I think it's up to me to keep the windshield clear."

"I hear ya, padre. Fix you right up. Just put in a good word with the Big Boss upstairs for me." He headed for the garage, a half-hitch in his gait.

"I'm on a deadline here," John shouted after him.

"Waiting on that part," he called back.

"Hector's a good man," the Reverend said. "I'm sure he'll get you on your way."

John took a measure of the man of the cloth. He'd never admit it, but he was suspicious of anyone who believed in anything without tangible proof. Lennie, though, held no such reservations and had willingly taken the bait. If he could get the Reverend to admit it was utter nonsense, maybe she'd change her mind about her foolish scheme.

"Your town here has me wondering about angels," John said.

"Me too." The Reverend smiled. "If you figure it out, would you clue me in?"

John knew an evasive answer when he heard one. "Would seem to me, there's really nothing to figure out. An angel is just a mythological construct to provide answers where there are none. Mostly a comfort to grasping minds."

"Mmm." The Reverend tapped his lips as he weighed John's theory. "Yet they're found in one form or another in every corner of the world. Nearly every religion. Every culture. Would seem people believe."

"In folklore. Myth."

"JoJo *is* hard to explain, I'll give you that."

"Who?"

"Joella Johnson. Our local angel." He offered John a friendly grin. "As the kids like to say, that's the way we roll around here."

John felt a stab of disappointment. It was the kind of gibberish Lennie had likely swallowed hook, line, and sinker. He searched for an honest response that wouldn't sound offensive.

"Hard way for a rational man to roll."

Slowly nodding, the Reverend pursed his lips before answering. "Things might roll easier if you realize we aren't human vessels trying to make our way on a *spiritual* sea. We're spiritual vessels trying to make our way on a *human* sea. We tend to focus on the surface. What we can see. There's a lot more below than there is above. Currents and such. Tough to roll on water like that."

John offered a tight-lipped smirk. The guy's bread and butter depended on thinking like that, and he saw no point in arguing. He shifted his attention to the garage. The only wheels he wanted to get rolling were sitting in that bay.

FORTY-TWO

Heaven's Door

Lennie eased the tow truck to the curb in front of Joella's Take Wing Studio and killed the engine. Perspiration tacked her sleeveless blouse to her back in the scorching cab. Shimmering condensation rimmed the display window, hinting at the air conditioning inside. But even the prospect of relief from the heat couldn't coax her out of the truck.

What awaited inside the peculiar little studio could be everything she hoped for: Joella was a guardakin angel. Or, the perplexing golden-ager might be what she most dreaded, as John had warned. A charlatan. Hadn't Yolanda told her in no uncertain terms that any talk of guardakin angels was merely the dirt-old blibbity-blab of a bygone generation? Her stomach churned.

As she gathered her hair into a ponytail and secured it with a dangling rubber band she snatched from the gear shift, a wisp of air brushed her neck and the barber pole's stripes drew her gaze. She hadn't noticed their dinky wobble before. It seemed they were either warped by time or simply growing weary from constantly going round and round and round.

In the display window, a few angel figurines with outstretched arms seemed to plead with her to decide. Or was that a heavenly invitation to come right in? She nibbled on a cuticle. *Just go in and see how it feels. You don't have to ask her.*

The sudden blare of a locomotive horn snapped her attention to the railroad crossing at the end of the street. Her days hanging around the Mosely railyard as a girl rushed back, a time she'd read up on what the various horn patterns meant, akin to the dots and dashes of Morse Code; she had learned to "speak train."

The thunderous iron horse was still out of sight when its horn screamed again: two long blasts, a short burst and a lingering howl—the sequence that warned it was approaching a public crossing. The safety gates lowered across Main Street, triggering clanging bells and flashing red warning lights.

The rearview's Mardi Gras beads rattled as a Norfolk Southern locomotive clamored through the intersection, triggering a familiar tingle in her skin as clanking cars streaked with grit followed behind. She found a quiet comfort in the unexpected visit of a friend from a simpler time, just when she needed a dose of moral support.

She shouldered the cab door open, marched to the studio and pulled the door open.

Brriiiiinng!

Lennie's hands flew to her chest as a metal comb atop the door raked across the strings of a mandolin mounted over the entry, setting her heart on a mad dash. She knew the musical chord instantly, her teen heartstring, the opening strum of *Dimming of the Day*. Her memory conjured her idol, Bonnie Raitt, singing a verse from long ago.

What days have come to keep us far apart?

A broken promise or a broken heart?
Now all the bonnie birds have wheeled away.
And I need you at the dimming of the day.

Trying to keep her heaving lungs mouse-quiet, she fluffed her blouse to get some cool air moving and let her gaze drift. She was the only lookie-loo in the place. String-lights twinkled above, and the three garden cherubs in the pump-handle chairs now each wore a vintage hat. Sea captain. Pillbox. Newsboy.

The beaded curtain in the opening to a back room remained still, even though the mandolin she'd set off could probably be heard two doors away. *Old people take naps. Maybe that's what she's doing.*

As she surveyed the display window bay, she wiped a fine layer of dust off the little porcelain angel who was missing an eye.

She turned to soak in what she hadn't been able to see from outside. Origami dove and butterfly mobiles dangled in front of a wall-length mirror behind the barber chair trio.

Adorable crosses made from tiny children's letter blocks mingled with folksy keepsake boxes on a waist-high shelf beneath the mirror. *Should I say something? Call hello?*

Was that a hint of aftershave? *Wait a minute. Is that Dad's Aqua Velva?* An airy clattering spun her toward the beaded curtain as Joella suddenly entered the studio space from the back room.

She was draped in a painter's smock two sizes too big for her slight frame, and her arms were folded on top of each other across her stomach, chock full of arts and crafts supplies. Coils of picture wire, packets of tacks, fabric glue, beaded jewelry items, and a collection of colorful children's letter blocks.

"Hey there," the woman said with an offbeat smile. "I surely am happy to see you. Thank'ya kindly for droppin' by." The skin on her face looked splotchy in this light. *What kind of angel has age spots? Isn't heaven perfect?*

It wasn't until Lennie tried to swallow that she became aware of how dry her mouth was. *Don't say anything. Let her do the talking.* That may have been a laudable plan, but her need to know the truth steamrolled right over it, and she blurted, "You're a guardakin angel."

Joella cocked her head with a puzzled smile. "A *who* now?"

"A guardakin angel."

"Lawd, child, whoever told you that?"

"So you've heard of 'em." She fought the urge to do the neighborly thing and help the old timer with her armload. "Are you?" Her feet clutched the soles of her sandals until her toes curled away from the straps.

Joella drew closer, edging between the barber chairs. "Names are just names."

Lennie distanced herself, darting to a water fountain in the corner, where she drank like a desert disaster survivor. *She's not gonna answer. Pin 'er down.*

Coolness bubbling on her lips, she had a moment to think. Joella was like Big Jake, the wily bass at Chickamauga Lake that used to escape her hook by tangling her line on sunken logs when she was little.

She straightened and dabbed the corners of her mouth with her collar. "Then, you *are*."

Joella shifted the art supplies in her arms. "If that's what you need to believe."

Thoughts simmering, Lennie kept a wary eye on her and wandered the shop's sacred knickknacks, feeling her way toward something she hoped she'd recognize once she found it.

She ran her hand over the arm of the sea captain cherub. "What I need to believe is that folks who've tried to lead a good life, do the best they can with the hand God dealt 'em, are rewarded a place in His skybox."

Joella's eyes widened. "The Almighty has a skybox?"

Lennie stopped wandering. "A room on high. Heaven, if you please. Whatever is beyond what we know. Like you say, names are just names, like streams that flow to the same ocean."

"I see." The woman waited for her to go on.

Lennie sucked in a deep breath before plunging ahead. "I need to believe my Dad's up there, with a view unlike anything we could ever know or understand. Trying to help me find my baby, because he now knows and understands. And I need to believe my Mom's right there with him because she does too."

Joella's mouth tightened. "You told me you didn't have any children."

Lennie averted her eyes, settling on the plastic daisies on her sandals, blurry yellow from the sting of tears. "I lied."

Joella met her upward gaze. "The darkness takes comfort in a lie."

Lennie backhanded her tears away, the defensive move she'd shown the world for more than half her life giving way to Joella's regard. "I've been lying for a long time. To myself and everybody else ... even those I love."

Shame rose like the bubble of a long-held breath from her innermost depths. "But—" Her throat tightened, choking off her words.

"Mistakes don't define us," Joella assured her. "They point us in a new direction."

Lennie pressed her trembling hand to her breastbone. "If my child just *knew* me ... knew how sorry I was ... how *terribly* sorry, I could make him or her love me ... I *know* I could. If I just had a chance. That's all I'm asking ... a chance."

Joella's face softened. "Your father *is* there for you." The words fluttered through Lennie as she absorbed an extraordinary moment that passed like fleeting light.

"And he's so very proud of you. For the burden you bore for his sake. And for your brother. For the life of givin' and goodness you've tried to make for yourself and others in the face of it all."

Lennie had endured the last twenty-odd years with her chin up, trying to look forward and put on a brave face for a world that seemed to throw perpetual punches her way. To have her personal struggles acknowledged—*seen*—by what was on the far side of heaven's door took her breath away.

She lowered her head as emotion gushed through her like a hurricane rain breaking over a levee. A tear slipped her cheek, bathing her big toe. When she lifted her gaze, her focus became the jumble in Joella's arms.

She let her eyes rest on something she hadn't noticed before. How could she have missed it? It was right there. Or maybe it was simply her need to believe playing tricks on her—she had no way of knowing if this backwoods woman was God's touch. But even if it all turned out to be a sham, she had to know what it *felt* like to believe, if just for a flitting instant.

Cradled in Joella's arms, amid the hodgepodge of art supplies. Eight children's blocks of light wood. Two inches square. Each carved with a letter, their outlines in red, blue, yellow, green. And they spelled a name. A gorgeous girl's name.

M I C H E L L E

Goosebumps raced from Lennie's toes to her fingertips as she absorbed each letter, sounded them out in her head. *Michelle ...* Finally, she lifted her gaze to meet Joella's.

"He wants you to know you have a beautiful daughter."

She moved her mouth to respond, but her jaw went slack, cool air gliding into her chest as she breathed in the notion.

"Michelle." Her voice was barely a whisper as her innermost desire tried the name on for size. *Michelle. My child.*

Then her past faintly shook her head. The setbacks, sorrows, heartbreaks suddenly threatened her resolve to fully commit to her belief. Something stronger, though, quickly banished it, and she refused to be ruled by the fear of giving herself up to her longing.

"Where ...?" she heard herself utter. "Does he know where? Where I can *find* her?"

"Your brother will help you."

What? She choked back a scoff. Had she heard Joella right? "John?"

Joella nodded and let the items in her arms slip into the lap of the seated cherub wearing the pillbox hat, Michelle's name tumbling into a random jumble of wooden squares.

No! He would never help her. They were done with each other. She surrendered to a single chuckle of disbelief to keep from sobbing, and her shoulders slumped under the crushing weight of the cruelest fate of all: she'd foolishly given in, had allowed herself to taste her dream.

Starved of it for more than half her life, she'd feasted in a moment of gluttony, a moment she'd consumed and been consumed by. And now her hopes hung on John? Her disbelieving, show-me brother? That was even more far-fetched than trusting Joella.

She saw her devastated reflection in the mirror behind it, uttering disconnected thoughts as if it was the only one there. "He doesn't ... I mean he won't—"

"He will."

"No, you don't understand. The two of us. We're *over.*"

"*Are* you?"

Their conversation seemed so real, but so had her long-perished *After Supper Club* dream visits with Mom. Devastation gave way to anger, and Lennie backed away from the stranger who was suddenly, inexplicably, inside her pillaged life.

Joella offered her hands. "You don't have to run anymore." But a sudden urge to do just that welled up, and Lennie rushed to the door, grabbed the handle and—

"Eleanor Grace." Lennie froze. The voice had come from behind her, different from Joella's. Her chest tightened. *She doesn't know my full name.*

Turning around, she was gripped by a disorienting sight, and she leaned on the door for support as her legs trembled. It took a few accelerating heartbeats to fathom what her eyes were telling her, and she stared, unblinking, at the woman she knew only from the faded photo on Dad's bedroom wall.

Mom.

She stood fiddling with the ivory lace collar of a blue dress, a side-braid of hair gracing her shoulder. Her eyes held Lennie's with a tenderness she'd never known, and Lennie drew a tremulous breath as she involuntarily covered her mouth with her hand, unable to form a single word.

She could only gaze over her fingertips at the startling vision she had once beckoned as a child sipping sweet mint tea in a dream forgery, their *After Supper Club.* The memory whose headstone had rested beside Dad's at his burial. Roselyn Delia.

The name echoed in her head, and Lennie became terribly aware of how lost her life had become as she saw herself in Mom's face. Same tawny hair. Apple-green eyes. Graceful cheekbones. She looked to be about twenty, the age Lennie knew she'd been when she died in the delivery room.

"Eleanor Grace." Mom's soft Southern lilt had the kind of warm, welcoming tone that had surely put folks at ease all the years of her life. "Stop your runnin'."

Lennie's scattershot panic somehow shifted to a sense of wonder as she watched Mom fidget with her dainty collar.

"When I slipped away," Mom said, "I knew you were safe. I could hear them assure me of that." She lowered her hand from her collar and pressed it to her chest. "It was a blessin'... givin' my life for yours. It wasn't your fault. You understand?"

The memory of Michelle's perilous birth brought Lennie a swift understanding and a feeling of agonizing kinship with her mother. She struggled to find words to fill the silence.

With a trace of sorrow in her eyes, Mom stepped toward Lennie, sturdy church shoes crossing noiselessly across the terrazzo underfoot. "You've gotta turn that blame loose ... turn *me* loose. You know those balloons you set skyward at Daddy's funeral?"

A forlorn smile swept Mom's face and was gone just as quickly. Then she tipped her head a'piece, like someone does when she wants to drive a point home. "Was my time. That's all it was. Now's *your* time. And you gotta make the most of it."

Her heart beating fast as a hummingbird's, Lennie took a deep breath to rein in her emotions.

"The dresser letter?" she whispered.

Drawing close, Mom nodded and lifted a hand toward Lennie's face, and she resisted the urge to pull away from the unfathomable.

"Momma?" She heard herself plead from a smothered depth as Mom touched her face for the very first time. Lennie drowned in Mom's eyes as her thumbs traced the contours of her cheekbones and glided up to her eyebrows.

Giving herself over to the divine, she allowed her eyes to close as Mom's touch came to rest on her temples and then lifted from her face.

Lennie quivered when she next felt two fingertips skim her parched lips, a profoundly intimate moment, as if Mom were a blind person meeting a stranger.

Then, a playful whisper at her ear. "You need some sweet mint tea to wet your whistle."

She opened her eyes to see her entire world reflected in Mom's gaze. No one had ever looked as deeply into her. "You are so beautiful."

Mom slipped her fingers into Lennie's hair, her expression one of heartache as she winced and brushed past a knot of scar tissue above Lennie's ear. It was as if she were absorbing the pain of Lennie's past and the enraged fist of a destructive relationship that had left her disfigured in body, mind and spirit.

"Your days needn't be so dim, hon." Her voice was a tender whisper.

Lennie slowly exhaled as a subtle feeling settled in. A soothing, as if all the rough edges of her life had somehow been smoothed over through Mom's loving touch. How could that be?

Struggling to understand, she landed on her childhood Bible School. *The laying on of hands. The healing.* She'd never been able to fully embrace that belief. But, maybe—

Mom slid her palms down Lennie's neck and then gently squeezed her shoulders. "I miss our *After Supper Club.*"

"The back porch," Lennie said as if she were back there once more, her desire to hold onto this moment as long as possible sharpening her memory. "Water dripping into that cracked porcelain bowl."

Mom nodded, her cheeks reshaping into a grin. Only vaguely aware of the thudding pulse in her neck, Lennie was overcome with the sensation of reaching for something she didn't understand but found irresistible, like a curious child discovering a new world. She no longer cared if the moment was real—it merely *was.* She tasted a salty tear in the corner of her mouth.

"I love you, Momma."

Mom's eyes misted over as she caressed Lennie's face. "And I've always loved you. Deep as a tap-root." Tears moistened the crescent folds of skin under her eyes before sliding down her cheeks.

In her reflection in the barber mirror behind Mom, Lennie glimpsed herself nodding, a teary smile on her face.

Mom tucked Lennie's hair behind her ear. "I miss you so. Daddy does, too. He wishes things hadn't ended the way they did."

Lennie's throat clenched as she struggled to reply. Finally, she took refuge in a simple politeness, her voice trembling. "Yessum. I miss having you both in my life."

Mom leaned closer, as if she were about to share the biggest secret ever told. "You don't have to miss us." She rubbed Lennie's arm. "The *After Supper Club* is always open. Dream of us, and we'll be there."

Lennie nodded, her vision shrouded with tears. Mom thumbed them away. "Now, you g'won. Johnny's waitin'. You tell 'im I said he's to help you find Michelle."

Lennie nodded, although she didn't fully understand how that could ever happen, not with everything that had torn them apart. She spent a last moment in Mom's eyes before making her way to the door.

As she pushed it open, she paused to look back and saw Joella standing with her. And she felt the bright heat outside take her as she charged straight through the auto-strummed mandolin's remembrance of *Dimming of the Day.*

The truck's creaking shocks on the mountain road rattled her back to the fact that she was returning to Hector's with extraordinary news. *Mom. Michelle. Oh my God!* Fighting back tears of unspeakable joy, she gripped the wheel with one hand and palmed a tremulous grin she couldn't contain.

Michelle. The name played like music over and over in her head. She felt like dancing, hands waving free. She didn't want to slow her racing heart. No, she wanted to bottle it for safekeeping, make these feelings last forever. What she must have been missing all her life—joy, elation, release—all strung together now like charms on a bracelet. She felt *alive* for the very first time.

She had one piece of the puzzle. All she needed was the other: where was her daughter? She was gonna find out! Joella had said Johnny would help her with that. Momma said, too—she and Daddy were in cahoots! But how should she break the news about Michelle to her brother?

Hands drumming on the steering wheel, she shook her head, hair whisking back and forth in front of her eyes. Her happy dance. *Momma said you gotta help me, Johnny. How unbelievable is that?*

Immensely. To the *nth* degree, in fact. A harsh reality gripped her: the unlikely prospect of convincing John to trust what she had just experienced and to help her find Michelle. Whatever had been left of their relationship had shattered in Hector's workshop. *We're hardly even family anymore.*

But she had no other choice—this was about something bigger than either of them now. This was about her child. She tightened her sweaty grip on the wheel and sped up, careening down the mountain.

FORTY-THREE

A Dose of Real

Despite her best intentions to maintain her cool, Lennie couldn't contain herself. She paced the garage like a claustrophobic goldfish swimming circles in a cup. "She did it!"

Breathless, she pinballed between John at the rear of the car and Hector at the front as words jetted from her with the force of a fire hydrant. "I was there! And they were there! Both of them!"

"Slow down," John said, hands held out as she headed his way.

"First," she exclaimed, "Dad reached out to me through her! She's the real deal, Johnny."

She heard Hector clear his throat, and when she pivoted to face him, she caught his confused look. "Didn't he just pass?" he said. "I mean, that's why you're here and—" He startled when Lennie jabbed her hands into the air.

"Yes! He's now ... up *there!*" How could she say *dead* when he was still so alive to her? Pushing beyond the barriers of feeble form to make contact. "Dad reached back to me. And then. And then—"

"Who is *her?*" John demanded. As she spun back toward him, the question hovered in the air. His earlier dismissal of what he assumed was a huckster pulling a con warned her not to answer him. Not yet.

She walked slowly toward her brother. Clasping her hands in front of her in a gesture of calmness, she leaned into his face to underscore her next nugget.

"And then, Johnny," she said before hesitating to make sure her words were carefully measured, "she let me talk to Mom."

She stepped back, watching for his reaction. He quietly considered her, giving nothing away. Until, around the corners of his mouth, she saw the hint of a smirk.

Realizing she needed more to convince him, she played the biggest honesty card she knew. She raised her right hand and placed her left palm down, parallel to the floor.

"The truth, the whole truth, and nothing but the truth. So help me, God." She pointed at her left hand. "Stack a' Bibles." She didn't want to leave him any room for doubt about her solemn vow.

He nodded the way a parent does when a kid speaks with utter conviction based on her naive understanding of how things *really* work.

"Let's start at the beginning." His condescending tone ticked her off. "Who is this *she* you're talking about?"

Lennie looked beyond him, to Hector's tool pegboard above his workbench and his multicolored grid of Georgia license plates affixed there.

She sensed John still stringing words together, somewhere outside her focus, like the distant drone of an airplane. Something about a hocus-pocus swindler.

But his words didn't matter. The only thing that mattered was Hector's collection of car plates on the wall. The last time she'd noticed the grid of worn steel rectangles, Joella was rearranging them into a different pattern. What had she called them? Something peculiar. *Statement pieces.*

She swallowed, her pulse throbbing her neck as she swept John aside with her arm. She walked away from him, past Hector's rack of tires. Past dangling auto belts and hoses. Irresistibly drawn to the 5x5 matrix of steel plates on the wall, like the gravitational pull of a collapsing star.

Arriving at the wall, she let her eyes roam the checkerboard of rectangles. Green. Peach. Mustard. Black. Joella's explanation of what she was doing messing around with them drifted back to her. *I just think they could say more, don't you?*

The colors blurred away, leaving only the plates' letters and numbers. And there it was. Top to bottom. The succession of the first letters on each of the five plates in the first column.

She silently mouthed each letter. *M ... I ... A ... M ... I.* "Miami," she whispered to herself in a voice gravelly with emotion. She repeated it louder and stronger. "Miami." It tasted so sweet on her tongue. She spun and grabbed John, ready to burst. "She's in Miami!"

John clamped his hands on her shoulders. "This is *not* going to happen!" He checked his Rolex. "We've got three hours to hit the road. If you think I'm going to spin off on another one of your wild-ass goose chases—"

"Michelle." she said, cutting him off. "I asked her to get Dad to help me find my child. Her name's Michelle, and she's in Miami." She pointed to the license plates, her clinching evidence. "It's right *there!*"

Groaning, John released her and pinched the bridge of his nose. "Just answer the damn question! Who is this woman you've been talking to!"

Lennie caught Hector's gaze as it darted back and forth between her and infuriated John. She offered him an uncomfortable grin, and he returned to his work under the car hood with an awkwardly whistling nonchalance.

"Who is the *her* you asked to help you!" John demanded.

"Joella."

Hector skittered from under the hood like a busted spring as he and John blurted in unison: "Joella *Johnson?*"

"Yes!"

The mechanic's expression darkened as he absorbed the impact of her response. She waited for the interminable silence to give way as he wrapped his shop rag around his hand.

"But," he stammered, "Joella died two years ago."

"What?" Lennie steadied herself on the workbench as a disorienting wave washed over her, and she lowered herself onto a shop stool, spasms of denial and dread making her nauseous.

"Lennie." John's voice came from somewhere in her collapsing world.

She, though, was back in Joella's eyes, the letter blocks in her arms, Michelle on her own lips. Her daughter was out there. A daughter who needed to know her mother. Needed to know there was one person in all creation who loved her unlike any other.

She turned to John and searched his eyes.

"Lennie, this isn't ... What you're experiencing has taken a whole new turn. It's got you off-balance."

Off-balance? She didn't have time for any stinking off-balance. She only had time for Michelle.

"I'll show you." She headed for the bay door.

FORTY-FOUR

Collision Course

Lennie stared in disbelief at what had been Joella's Take Wing Studio. The display window, less than an hour ago chock-full of angel figurines, was now empty and dimmed by dust. Gritty moisture clung to the motionless barber pole's cracked glass cylinder.

A blade of panic stabbed her as she squinted through the window. The hatless garden cherubs were sprawled every which way behind the pump-up chairs. Dead ceiling lights drooped over peeling paint and bare shelves. Even mighty Angel Gabriel on the ceiling had lost his former glory, nothing more than a faded shadow of what once was.

John and Hector moved to the window on either side of her to take a peek. Hector turned his ball cap backward and pressed his face to the glass. "She used to do a pretty good business during the Fall festivals," he said.

Lennie's mind drifted, retracing her steps. "I don't understand," she said in a hollow voice. "I was just here."

Hector pulled on the door handle and a deadbolt clanked. "Place has been closed up tight for two years."

Lennie stepped back. With the studio's interior only dimly visible through her reflection, her mirrored expression of despair burrowed into her soul. She had let go and put her trust in angels. And this was her everlasting reward?

With tangible proof, especially the letter blocks—the eight of them spelling her daughter's name—at least she'd have a foot to stand on. *Something* that could help convince John to work with her in finding Michelle. Instead, this desolate scene made a mockery of her words and beliefs.

Unwilling to accept what appeared to be a lie, or maybe some kind of vanishing act, she cleared her throat. "Joella was here," she said. "I spoke to her."

John glanced at Hector. "You knew this Joella?"

"*Sí.* Everybody knew JoJo."

"Yeah, that's what the Reverend called her."

Lennie grabbed her brother's arm. "Reverend?"

John gazed around. "He came to Hector's garage for new wipers."

"The choir van," Hector added. "Ebenezer—"

"—Missionary Baptist Church," Lennie said.

John shot her a look. "How'd you know that?"

What does it matter? She couldn't fathom a reason to answer as she pondered the decaying Take Wing Studio sign.

"Okay," John said, clearing the sweat from his eyes with his shirt sleeve, "so, here's the deal."

What he meant was he was rendering his *verdict.* She needed to strike first. "Johnny, I swear. It happened just like I—"

"There's more going on here than you can understand," he said, shutting her down. "The trauma of Dad's death. Re-experiencing the loss of a child. Feelings of desperation. The kind that make you susceptible to manipulation and grabbing at straws, ready to bargain for any deal."

She shook her head. Of *course* he'd dismiss all possible explanations except for the most obvious which, of course, were always his.

She refused to back down. "Did it ever occur to you that maybe there's more going on here than *any* of us can understand?"

The old mechanic scratched his head with the brim of his ball cap. "She's kinda gotta point there."

"Thank you, Hector." She *did* have a point. And she was going to prove it, whether John wanted to face it or not. Grabbing his wrist, she snatched a glance at his Rolex, then marched toward the tow truck at the curb.

"Lennie," he said in her wake. "Wait."

Quickening her steps, she waved him off, rushing toward something she refused to let go but couldn't fully understand.

"Lennie!"

Reaching the truck, she ripped open the door. She scrambled in behind the wheel and cranked the engine, ignoring his voice behind her.

"Lennie, stop!"

She was already backing up when John jerked the passenger door open and hoisted himself into the cab.

"Where're you going?"

"To meet an old friend." She raced down Main Street.

"Slow down," he barked.

She lurched to a stop at the raised railroad crossing gates.

"Listen to me," he said, pointing at her as if he could plug a dam break with his finger. "You're running off half-cocked, without a plan."

"Wrong again." She wrenched the wheel to the right. Stomped on the gas. The truck heaved onto the tracks, the shuddering Ford jackhammered over crossties, and the tow-arm straps in the rearview swung wildly.

John grabbed the rattling door frame, panic in his eyes. "What the hell are you doing!"

Her jaw throbbed from clenching her teeth as the cab shook like a spacecraft re-entering the atmosphere.

She'd waited so long, had tried so hard to find her child. An hour ago, she'd stood at the threshold of a fresh beginning. Her daughter had been *right there*, in Miami. All because she'd allowed herself to believe in miracles.

Now, faith had been swept away by a raging current of grief intent on ripping Michelle's hand from hers. All she could picture was her daughter's tiny outstretched palm in the clinic's nursery, reaching for her through the bars of her crib as they were torn apart. *Don't let go.*

"I've seen Dad! I talked to Momma!" She accelerated, the steering wheel in a death grip. "As sure as it's three-fifteen, I have!"

She shot him a sideways glance through a shroud of tears. As he gripped the dashboard, he seemed a vibration in the convulsions beneath them.

He grabbed her wrist in the deafening clamor. "Get off the tracks!"

The cab's tremors shook the tears from her face and sprinkled her arms with tiny drops. "Admit it's *possible!*" she howled.

John's grip dug into her wrist. "Get off the tracks!"

Ripping her hand away, she fought to keep the truck between the steel rails that bellowed below as tracks raced at her in wavering lines.

"I've seen him! He's trying to help me find Michelle! Momma's with him!"

"Stop the truck! *Now!*"

A freight train appeared around the bend up ahead, just like she knew it would. The three-fifteen run from Copperhill.

"Lennie!"

The locomotive's warning horn screamed.

Adrenaline coursed through her as she locked on the closing steel beast. Silver and green. A Southern Railway freighter.

"*Lennie!*" Fighting her in a death match for control, he wedged his arm between her and the steering wheel.

She blocked him with her body, but the movement caused her foot to stomp the gas. "I saw him at the hospital!" she yelled as his elbow cracked her chin.

Tasting blood, she forced her body weight against his, holding him off. "The gorge!"

"Get off the tracks!"

"I talked with Momma at Joella's!" Her hands cramped on the wheel.

The pressure of his shoulder in her rib cage eased as he stiffened at the sight of the closing locomotive and her vision compressed, the peripheral world giving way to a close-up of the massive thunderball barreling toward her.

"We both saw him last night!" The locomotive howled like a wounded animal. "Admit it's possible!"

She could no longer see John, could only sense him. "Admit it!"

"It's possible!" His voice pierced the bedlam.

She yanked the steering wheel left, lurched sideways into John as they crashed against his passenger door, and spun out in a cyclone of rusty dust that engulfed them.

The locomotive thundered past, just beyond the bulldog hood ornament. A blur of brown-yellow-red-black-yellow-brown-black-red cars roared by for what seemed like forever. Clanking, screeching, grinding.

In the wake of the last car, the quaking cab settled into a quiet aftermath. Ears ringing, Lennie found herself tangled with John. Against his door. Her face inches from his.

Her hands tingled, heaving lungs maxed out as she gulped the dusty air that separated them. His frantic eyes were locked on hers.

FORTY-FIVE

Extreme Measures

Enough was enough. John had decided it was up to him to do something about Lennie as he glared down at the barrel-chested guy seated in front of him. His stern expression and the County Sheriff patch affixed to his shoulder spoke volumes. He was probably the only guy in this whole backwater sticks-town who wielded any real power, which John knew was best met with relentless intensity.

"She's out of control!" John slammed his hands on the man's desk and rattled Sheriff Doyle Wadsworth's nameplate.

"You might wanna take a gander in a mirror," the sheriff drawled. "I need you to calm down."

John wiped the sweat from his lip. "I *am* calm. I'm also *right*."

"Solitary *what*, again?"

John held his hands out the way a prosecutor conveys the reasonableness of his argument to a jury. "Confinement." Given

Lennie's nutso behavior, he thought it was the most prudent request in the world. "Just until I get back."

The sheriff's leather utility belt squawked like an overtaxed horse saddle when he rose from his swivel chair. Behind him, putty-colored filing cabinets supported stacks of binders on the edge of toppling, the Georgia State Seal embossed on their spines.

He looked to be in his fifties. Hair cut high and tight, with a firm, clean-shaven jaw. Probably ex-military. As Wadsworth came around his desk, John couldn't help but notice his seriously bountiful backside. Hell, he'd designed bridge struts under less duress than the seams of the sheriff's blue service slacks.

The lawman's eyes narrowed. "You want me to lock 'er up?"

John rubbed his jaw and realized he had some convincing to do to close the deal. He needed a shave. And he needed to quell the perfect storm roiling inside.

One, he had just escaped death-by-locomotive, leaving his nerves in ruins. Two, he was furious he'd allowed Lennie to detour him onto this unhinged highway in the first place. And three, the incessant launch countdown banged at the back of his brain.

"Lock her up," John finally said, "is such a harsh way to put it. Consider it more of a ... temporary detainment."

It sounded like an extreme measure, but there was no telling what Lennie might do next. He'd almost felt sorry for her when they got to that deserted studio and her self-delusions crumbled before her. No doubt that was what had set her off.

Wadsworth seemed to be mulling John's request as he crossed his arms and deposited his butt on the front of his desk. *Help him feel good about the decision.* "She's had a rough couple of days, okay?" John said with a hushed note of concern. "She just needs some space to, you know ... decompress. Catch her breath, if you will. You'd really be helping her out."

He caught his reflection in the glass of a shadowbox framing a collection of law enforcement patches. The image startled him, because he'd always prided himself on his appearance. As a deal maker, he certainly didn't inspire confidence with his darkened stubble and, thanks to Lennie, the blown-wild hair of a hurricane survivor.

The sheriff scratched his ear as he gave John a measured look. "She hit you?"

"What?"

Wadsworth dipped his chin to get a better angle on John's face. "Looks like maybe she clocked you one."

John stifled a defensive chuckle. "Can't a guy slip in the bathroom without everybody jumping all over his case?"

"Well, what'd she do then, to warrant temporary detainment?"

John's spine stiffened. "What'd she *do?* What *hasn't* she done is the question. She's hot-mess crazy!"

The lawman stroked his chin. "Aw'ight, let's explore that: hot-mess crazy. Because that right there's where I need you to be a little more specific."

"You're right. Okay." His ears were heating up, just like in client meetings when the topic of cost overruns brought his materials estimation into question. He eased down into a vinyl chair.

"Look, sheriff," he said with his best easy smile, "we're both reasonable men. I simply need you to hold her for twenty-four hours, and I'll pick her up on my way back. I have an appointment tomorrow in Florida. I'll pass back through on my return to Knoxville and get her."

"So, you want me to slap 'er in jail while you're gone?"

"I think that's a mischaracterization. Think of it as a reflection retreat."

The sheriff tugged the skin at the corner of his eye. "Nobody she can stay with?"

"She's not the type to stay in one place. She'd probably flee. But, like I said, it's just overnight." He fought the urge to check his watch. "Perhaps a cell with a mountain view."

"You're her brother."

"Correct."

"And you're tellin' me you want me to detain her based on your opinion that—"

"An *informed* opinion."

"Based on your observation that she's ... " He took a second to grab John's official complaint off his desk, and John seized the opening to make his closing statement.

"I aced two semesters of human psychology. It's a solidly grounded opinion."

"She's of unsound mind," the sheriff read from the statement.

When John gave him a precise nod, Wadsworth seemed to squelch a smirk. "Well, Mr. Riley, this here's Georgia in the U.S. of A. Not Russia."

John shot from his chair like a Little League dad who couldn't believe the umpire had just called strike three on his can't-miss kid. "She drove us at a train!"

The sheriff sat back, eyes widening. "That was you two idiots?"

"Yes! That was us two idiots!" John held his fists high like he'd just won an epic battle of wits. "And *that,* sheriff, is a confineable offense."

Wadsworth snatched his Smokey Bear hat and lumbered toward the door. "Take me to her."

FORTY-SIX

Full Disclosure

As Lennie curled in a ball on the damp carpet in the car's rear cargo area, the familiar confines gradually quelled her roiling mind.

That she was still alive and not smashed to smithereens by the train finally sank in. It didn't matter that Louise was perched on Hector's hydraulic lift five feet off the garage floor. They went back a long way, and this was still her safe haven.

In the stillness, she began to regroup her scattered thoughts. She didn't care who or what Joella was. Something undeniable had clicked inside when she found out about Michelle and saw the license plate letters spell Miami.

Before she could savor the wonder of what that meant, she heard the familiar rumble of the wrecker arrive outside. John. *Here we go.* He had left in the tow truck after they'd returned to Hector's in the wake of her ... okay, meltdown.

His coerced admission that her experiences were possible hadn't been her finest hour, and she wasn't proud of it. But what did he expect? She was in the depths of something extraordinary, and he wouldn't believe a word she said. The tailgate suddenly creaked open. A burly guy sporting a badge gazed at her through the widening crack.

"You doin' aw'ight, ma'am?" he said with a twang that reminded her of the football coach back at Mosely High.

A cop? She considered him a couple of breaths before answering. "Peachy." She gave Hector a disgruntled stare as he fidgeted with his bushy mustache, John looking on.

"I'm sorry," Hector said, shoulders lifting as he raised his palms. "You were so quiet up there. I was worried, so I told them where you were."

"It's okay," Lennie said. "Sorry to put you in the middle of this." She glared at her brother. "Who's our mystery guest, Johnny?"

The lawman removed his Smokey Bear hat. "Sheriff Doyle Wadsworth, ma'am."

John fixed Lennie with an icy gaze. "You can run but you can't hide from this."

"I'm not hiding. This is where I go to think." She gestured to the cargo area. "That against the law?"

"No, ma'am," the sheriff replied. "But I'd like to ask you a few questions, if I might."

Sighing, Lennie dropped down to the floor to face him. "Your brother here says you're havin' issues of the mental health variety." He sounded like a parent trying to gather both sides of a sibling spat.

"*Me?*" She glowered at John. "*You're* the one in denial."

"Not about me, Lennie." He gave Wadsworth a deferential nod, but he may as well have said, *please continue your interrogation.*

The lawman offered her a disarming grin. "He says you claim to be seein' dead people? Like in that movie with Bruce Willis and that little kid?"

"*The Sixth Sense*," Hector chimed in, seemingly pleased with his movie trivia smarts. "The kid was Haley Joel Osment. He played in *Home Alone*, too. No, wait. That was Macaulay Culkin."

The sheriff patted the mechanic's shoulder. "Much appreciated, Hector. But lemme handle this."

Lennie jabbed a finger at John. "He's seeing them, too. He just won't admit it."

John scoffed. "Children have imaginary friends, not rational adults. You're completely losing it. You should get help!"

"*Excuse me?*" Lennie snapped, getting in his face. "You're the mind tripper stuck inside your spreadsheet cells. You didn't tell him about seeing Daddy?"

The sheriff wedged his arms between the siblings and separated them. "Your brother asked me to hold you overnight, until he gets back from an appointment in Florida."

Hector seemed to sense a fuse had just been lit, and he moved back to his workbench to escape the line of fire.

Lennie scorched John with her eyes. "Hold me? In *jail?*"

"Just for twenty-four hours," John assured her matter-of-factly, as if she should see the wisdom of his action plan. "I'll pick you up on the way home." She tried to bulldoze her way into his face again, but the sheriff restrained her.

"Easy ma'am. Just somethin' to consider given that you chose to violate umpteen federal laws by introducin' a motor vehicle to a restricted railway. The FRA wouldn't take kindly to that."

"Federal Railroad Administration," John said with a nod.

"Thank you, Conductor Conrad," she snorted. "I'm familiar."

"It's for your own good," John said.

"Pray tell, in what friggin' world is jail *good?*"

The sheriff fingered the brim of his hat and glanced at Hector, whose nervous eyes darted between the family feud and the master brake cylinder in his hands.

"You close to gettin' these two on their way?"

"Working as fast as I can."

Wadsworth gave him a knowing nod. "I can see why." He frowned at Lennie, then John. "Y'all might wanna consider a dip in the deep end of the family counselin' pool." He snugged down his hat and walked out grumbling to himself.

Heat suddenly rushing to her face, Lennie followed him outside. She watched in silence as he drove off in a swirl of dust.

"Lennie," John called from behind her.

She wheeled on him. "You gotta be frickin' kiddin' me!" Three quick steps led her away from him before something made her freeze in mid-stride. *No. This is it.*

She spun back and closed in on him. "What is that? Huh, Johnny?" She pressed her nose nearly into his. "When family calls the cops on each other. What exactly is *that!*" John stared stone-faced at the cracked asphalt at his feet.

She leaned sideways, contorting herself to make him look her in the eyes. "You're the Chief Explanation Officer," she snapped. "Can you explain that? Because I'd damn sure like to understand *that* one."

He bent over and picked up an embattled bottle cap at the foot of one of the gas pumps. Buffing the cap's rusted face with his thumb, he looked off at the misty mountain peaks in the retreating light. "I'm sorry."

"No. Uh-uh." She moved in front of him. "Right here, Johnny." She poked her breastbone. "Talk to *me*, not some faraway nothing."

"You just—" he stammered, "you're out of control. I have kids, Lennie. A family. That train? That was off the deep end.

And I worry, okay? I worry about dying. Every. Day. What happens to *them*?"

"Johnny," she said, taking a calming breath to rein herself in, "I've had a lot of experience living close to the edge. A ton more than you. My life since seventeen has *been* an edge. I've been in plenty of nip'n'tuckers, and that train wasn't even in the top ten. But," she said, gazing out over the sprawling valley where a tractor tilled a field. "Okay."

She refocused on him. "You're right. I'm sorry. I apologize. I can understand it made you upset. But I have family, too. Even if we haven't met. And the fact that you won't acknowledge that makes *me* upset."

Keeping her eyes locked on his, she watched his jaw chew on a reply before he begrudgingly let it escape his mouth. "Michelle ... in Miami."

She lifted her hands in a gesture of gratitude. "Yes ... thank you. Michelle. In Miami."

He absently turned the bottle cap over and over in his fingers, like a magician trying to master a coin trick.

"And okay," she continued, "I told you I'd hit your stops, but I didn't get it done. I screwed up your entire spreadsheet. And for that, I'm sorry."

John leaned against a gas pump and backslid down the rusted steel to sit on the ground. "No, it was stupid to think I could gain any real insight by re-creating some long-ago weekend. It's just ... it's like my photographer dream. A kid's take on things. It's all just ... gone."

She sat on the pebbled asphalt next to him and clunked her head back against the second pump. "Maybe changed is all."

Her eyes soaked him in as he sat with his arms draped over his elevated knees. "Just tell me what you're thinking, Johnny. For once. Let me in."

He cleared his throat as he continued playing with the corroded bottle cap. She knew opening up wasn't easy for him, so she waited for him to get started, which he finally did. "I guess ... I guess I never knew Dad the way I wish I had."

A wrench *pinged* off the concrete floor in the garage behind them as she tousled her lifeless hair. She'd always believed everything was so complete between him and Dad.

"It's like ... like the years themselves," he said. "They got by me. So many missed chances to spend time with him passed in a flash. This trip was all about ... I just wanted a hint of understanding about something so meaningful to him that he memorialized it in a scrapbook. A *scrapbook*, Lennie. Dad didn't *do* scrapbooks. I thought this could help me *know* him better. Not just as a father. Not just that part of him."

He looked over at her. "He had a whole life before we came along. His own hopes and dreams as a boy, but I didn't think to ask about any of that. All I knew of him was as Dad. And *that?* Being a dad? That's just running scared. Believe me. Running scared every day. Trying to raise your kids right. Keep them safe."

She squinted into the late-day sun, its sinking edge nipping at the valley's distant westerly ridge. Looking back at him, she was drawn to the bottle cap in his fingers. The jagged teeth. The flinty snags time had left behind. The cork backing inside reduced to dusty flakes.

He said, "I thought maybe this trip would help me understand him as a man ... his *intentions* in this life."

Cocking his arm, he skipped the cap across the asphalt. She watched it twirl to a rest in the gravel. He leaned his head back against the pump and exhaled long and slow, as if revealing his emotional vulnerability had left him exhausted.

She had never known a silence as consuming as the one that descended upon them. During the hush, John's admission spurred her to dive into a deep well inside herself. One she'd boarded up long ago. Protected. So inaccessible she was taken off guard when she found its floodgates open, herself submerged.

She couldn't look at John. Could only stare at the space in front of her, caught between a life she wished was hers and the one she wouldn't wish on anybody.

"Does Michelle ever think of me?"

"Lennie …"

"I used to bounce back and forth when I imagined the birth. Sometimes a boy. Sometimes a girl. It like to kill me, not knowin'."

She pressed her fingers into the corners of her eyes and willed herself to trample a heaviness that rose in her chest. "That little life I carried was … restless. A kicker."

The past shook her head, as if it might one day leave her alone so she could find a new path to happiness. "I've always been afraid to find her … Ashamed. When I think of her now, I can scarcely take it in. I used to dream about her. She had these chubby … adorable little legs walking toward me. You know that baby chub you just wanna—"

She reached out and pinched a wisp of air. "She always had this great big smile leaping off her face as she came to me, all wobbly-legged … one of those God-awful corrective shoes on her foot, like I wore."

She studied the mist-shrouded mountains, felt the sun's last warmth on her skin. "Now? I don't even know her, and she scares me to death. Looking at me? With beautiful eyes? Wondering why. Wondering how her Momma could just up and walk away. Maybe I never really deserved her."

John breathed beside her, slow and steady, as dusk came on. "Maybe we should just call it. Head back."

Letting her eyes roam the shadowed valley, Lennie tried to find solace there. Instead the stillness only deepened her emptiness, and his suggestion seemed to make sense, when nothing else did.

"Yeah." The words pushed past the lump in her throat, dousing the smoldering remnants of her dream.

FORTY-SEVEN

Pressing On

"Tennessee or bust." John tugged his sheets off the couch in the front room. "Put all this behind us and get on with our lives."

Lennie stood beside her duffel, her arm trapping her basketball against her hip as she peered out the window at the garage. In the misty glow of the gas pumps' illuminated globes, Hector was refueling the family wagon. "Did you pay him?"

John balled up the sheets and dropped them on the couch. "Yeah. Plus a little extra for working the weekend."

"I'll pay you back."

"Don't worry about it. I got it."

She instantly heard Dad's voice inside, telling her she should carry her own weight. "No, you don't. I'll pay you back. How much was it?"

"I'm just saying I'm in a better position to—"

"I'm not a charity case, Johnny."

"We split the trip," John said, "so how about we split the bill?"

She flicked her basketball up in the air and it dropped back into her hand. "Deal."

"A thousand apiece." She did her best to casually nod and not look like her savings had just bottomed out.

John yanked up the handle on his Versace, the luggage not so much soft-sided anymore as it was side-sunken. "I think I can make home in time to tuck the kids in bed."

"Yeah, well, about that ... I'm not quitting."

She'd thought about it while she gathered her things—it felt like an eternity since she'd known the satisfaction of completion. She was tired of moving on before she finished anything or gave her life a chance to take root. Even if it was too late for her own dreams, what about Johnny's?

"You're on the right track, trying to understand," she said.

He shook his head slightly, lips tightening in what looked like resignation. "No. It's okay. I mean, you get too close to a memory, and it isn't the way you remember it."

"Please, Johnny. I don't know what's going on with everything. Truth is, I'm not sure about *anything* anymore. All I know is that we need to get you to the launch. For Dad. For you. That's something I can do. For us. I think we can make it if we press."

"Lennie, you don't have to prove anything."

"Yeah," she said, letting her eyes linger on his, "that's what I used to think, too." She headed for the porch with her stuff. Pushed the screen door open. Let it slam behind her.

John heard the determination in her receding footsteps as she trudged across the crushed-stone parking area that separated the house from the garage, and he couldn't contain an admiring smirk. *After everything she's been through, where does she get that grit?*

He checked his Rolex, and his affection melted into a grimace. Already after seven. They were supposed to have left fifty-six minutes ago to have a realistic shot at making the dawn launch. He hefted his Versace to the porch and followed Lennie into the descending darkness.

FORTY-EIGHT

One More Mountain

Lennie watched Hector return the fuel hose to its cradle. She smiled at him as she loaded her duffel into the cargo area, then tossed her basketball in the front seat of her station wagon. "I can't remember the last time somebody else filled my gas tank."

"My papa used to always say, '*Un trabajo bien hecho es un trabajo bien hecho.*' A well-done job is a job well done."

She nodded as John arrived with his suitcase.

"So, you're with me?"

He smirked. "Do I have a choice?"

While he stowed his luggage in the back, she took a moment to soak in the hazy lights of farmhouses sprinkled in the valley, the mountains' charcoal outline against the twilight sky.

The rear end of the creaky tow truck stuck out of the garage bay. She was going to miss the old Ford. It had taken her places she'd never been before.

A flutter went through her when she realized how close the train had come to sending it to that great junkyard in the sky as a bucket of bolts. The truck was a survivor, a kindred spirit.

The shutter clicks of John's camera drew her attention to him as he snapped photos of Louise in front of the pumps. Hector handed him Dad's reassembled scrapbook.

"You were busy packing, so I put this back together for you."

"Thanks. I appreciate that." John shook the crafty mechanic's hand. "And thanks for all your work on the car."

A grin creased Hector's face. "*No problema.*"

Lennie hugged him. "*Muchas gracias.* For everything. People 'round here know about the angel in overalls?"

Hector shrugged theatrically as he held up his hands with his best Ricky Ricardo impression from *I Love Lucy.* "Looocie, I been singin' that song for years and years, but I can't get anyone to join my band."

She chuckled. "We'll always have reruns."

John lifted his camera strap from around his neck. "I hate to break up the Lucy lovefest, but we've gotta get going."

"I'll drive first," she said. Opening the door, she sat low in the squishy seat, its foam core still wet. John got in the passenger side as Hector closed Lennie's door and leaned down to her eye level. "Go easy on the transmission."

"Okay, will do." She turned the key. The engine fired up and her spirits soared. *On the road again.*

Hector tapped the roof in a farewell gesture. "Godspeed. That's what they said to John Glenn when he lifted off to become the first American to orbit the earth."

"We're gonna need some speed, that's for sure." She pulled the headlight knob, and—

PHOOM! Flames erupted from under the hood. The smell of gas filling her nose, Lennie scrambled out, John doing the same on the other side.

Hector hustled to a fire extinguisher he kept by the pumps and rushed to the hood. He popped it open and blasted the motor with billowing suppressant, smothering the blaze.

Lennie waved the smoke away, rocked by the sizzling mess. The fuse box was a molten glob, the underside of the hood charred as coal. The distributor cap suddenly blew off like the top of a shaken bottle of Coke, making her jump back. Hector raked the engine compartment with the extinguisher again until it was completely coated.

The white froth reminded Lennie of a shroud. In the desolation that settled over them, she heard only one sound through her labored breathing. Crickets. Chirping like they always did, as if her world hadn't just exploded in front of her. Louise was dead.

Wincing, Hector set the extinguisher down and tipped his ball cap back. It took him a moment to form words. "Afraid that's our ball game. The electrical system's fried."

Lennie glanced at John. The only thing more vacant than his expression was the void she felt, absorbing the sight of her lifelong wingwoman, her smoldering hood yawed open like the smoking jaw of a dinosaur that perished in a meteor strike.

Hector ran a hand over his mustache. "I can, um ... junk 'er for you, if you want. Go to plan C."

A surge of nausea forced her to swallow. *Junk 'er.* The suggestion clanged in her brain. They were fightin' words. "Junk 'er," she muttered to herself.

She let her eyes drift to Hector. "Junk. Her." She hammered the coffin-nail words.

"Lennie," John said, trying to head her off at the pass.

"Junk. Louise."

Hector shot John a look. "*Who?*"

The words for Lennie just felt ... *wrong.*

"I know it's hard," John said, "but we don't have time to—"

"Junk 'er?" Her mind back-flipped over the years. The dire situations Louise had helped her escape. The countless times her travel companion had offered refuge.

Hector tapped the edge of a small pothole with his work boot. "Well, yeah. I'd scrap her for you. And I could, y'know, maybe get you a rental from over in Lakemont."

John cleared his throat. "That might be ... I mean if it's the only way, then—"

Lennie stomped her foot. "Junk 'er is not an option!" She refused to condemn Louise to such an inglorious fate. "Did they junk th-th-th-th-the *Mona Lisa* because she needed a little touch up?! Or the Sphinx because he needed a nose job? I don't think so, gentlemen!"

John's voice met hers decibel for decibel. "We don't have time for this!"

She pointed at Louise with the rising fever of someone making a grand proclamation for posterity's sake. "This vehicle is a classic piece of automotive history!"

Hector jumped into the fireworks. "Spoiler alert! Now it's a classic piece of automotive yard art!"

"We're *not* junking her, Hector!" As self-control gave way to an adrenaline rush, all she could think of was the second hand sweeping away time on John's expensive watch. A life of uncertainty dangled in front of her. A mysterious experience lay behind. Think, think, think ...

She had to regain the upper hand. Glancing around for something, *anything*, to bail her out, she sought a thread to pull, one that would unravel calamity's straitjacket.

Her focus bounced off the garage, the gas pumps, Hector, the house. She'd seen other women looking as frantic as she felt, mostly Christmas Eve moms on do-or-die mall missions for their kids.

She needed one more pair of dice to toss. Something to get all three of them to the launch. John glanced at his glinting Rolex. Of course he did. *Tick, tick, tick.*

Where he saw time, she saw possibility.

FORTY-NINE

Calamity's Straitjacket

"Barter," Lennie said. "It's when one person exchanges something for—"

"I know what barter is," John snipped, cutting her off. "You're forgetting we need two things of *equal* value." He jiggled the Rolex on his wrist. "This is a premier timepiece."

Lennie shot Hector a glance, then snatched John's wrist for a better look. "This is worth what? Ten, twelve grand?"

He scoffed, offended. "Try sixty-two." She had to swallow to keep from choking, and an amazed look twisted the mechanic's bristly eyebrows into question marks.

"*Thousand?*" he said. Turning his ball cap backward, he perched his reading glasses on his nose and leaned in to scrutinize the ritzy Rolex Lennie held for him at eye level.

She tightened her grip when John tried to tug his hand away. "If you think I'm going to give this up," he said, "you've got another thought coming. We're getting the rental."

"Give us a minute?" Lennie said to Hector.

After the mechanic retreated to the garage, she poked her brother in the chest. "Did you, or did you not, say you needed the car to faithfully re-create the trip?"

"Well, yeah, but—" He swatted away a moth the size of a finch that dive-bombed his face.

"Johnny, you know I'm right. We've gotta do this."

Looking off over the twinkling valley, he pursed his lips as if sipping sideways from a straw. "Damn it, Lennie."

"We have a solemn duty," she said with whispered urgency. "Like the Marines. The Few. The Brave."

He rubbed his face. "It's the few, the proud."

"The point is, we don't leave anybody behind." She swept her arms to include Louise. Charred engine still sizzling, the vehicle seemed to murmur as if awaiting its fate.

"She's a part of us," Lennie said in the kind of reverential hush usually reserved for burying a beloved family pet in the backyard.

"Remember the first time you drove 'er? Or the time you took Kelli Ann Wilson to the river? Or when we created that cool motion-blur for your moving shot of the night sky? You laid on the roof with your camera, shutter wide open, while I drove to the edge of town." She saw the memory tugging him back there.

"You were fourteen," he said.

"And everything was in front of us." Her long-ago drew her in as well. "We *lived* that night. We *walked* that line. Remember the photo you got of the stars? It was the most beautiful thing I'd ever seen."

A grin wavered on his face. "I still have that shot."

"Johnny," she said, locking her eyes with his. "This is *it*.". She needed him to turn that watch loose. To follow her outside-the-lines plan one last time, even if it was just for old time's sake.

"Think of that rocket rising on a column of fire, like Daddy wrote about." He hesitated with a groan deep in his chest. Then unsnapped the watchband's polished clasp.

She pumped her fist. "I smell hee-ro."

"How do I let you talk me into these things?"

"We've *got* this."

"We *better*."

Inside the garage, Hector had disappeared behind the tow truck. Lennie found him in the shadows at the far wall, an LED headlamp strapped on as he studied the license plates, his head cocked to one side. "Not how I had 'em."

There wasn't a moment to spare, and she had to move things along. "But they look nice, don't they?"

He rocked his noggin like a bobble-head doll. "Y'know, they kinda do."

"That's the spirit."

She knew they were already two hours late leaving for the launch. "We've gotta get a move-on. John's ready to make a deal if you are."

Back in front of the tow truck, John displayed his Rolex on a JTR-monogrammed handkerchief he'd spread like a jeweler's cloth on the wrecker's rust-red hood. The lustrous steel-and-gold band gleamed in Hector's headlamp beam.

"Sixty-two thousand," Hector mumbled as he examined the luxurious gold watch. "I shoulda been a, whatever it is *you* do."

"Actually, it's sixty-two thousand, eight hundred. I had it appraised three weeks ago for insurance."

They looked like boys in a treehouse, hunched over a priceless baseball card.

"Hector," Lennie said in her best conspiratorial tone, "it's got *diamonds*. What if you run this down to Atlanta and sell it? Imagine the rig you could score for sixty. Two. Thousand. Dollars."

"I'll write you a bill of sale," John said, "and send you the manufacturer's certificate of authenticity so you can verify it for whoever you sell it to. And remember, this isn't just a garden variety Rolex."

Lennie cupped her face with her hands—his highfalutin delusions of grandeur knew no bounds. "Oh, brother."

"This is a Cosmograph Daytona," John stressed, "with chronograph movement and para-magnetic hairspring."

Hector hummed as he nibbled a patch of wiry mustache that hung over his lip. "Sweet. The pepper-magnet care-spring," he said, mangling the specifications.

Minutes later, he was the proud owner of a Rolex, and Louise's front end was hooked behind his ex-truck, her grille angled to the sky.

Having insisted on driving first, John sat behind the wheel of the idling wrecker. Lennie rode shotgun as Hector snapped their picture.

He returned the camera to John with a warning. "Don't go playin' NASCAR and rip-roar the highway. Fifty or fifty-five is about all you should do pulling this weight. If the car gets squirrelly behind you, you gotta ease off."

"Got it," John said, hands fidgeting on the wheel.

Hector looked past him, to Lennie. "Sorry about the yard-art comment. Didn't mean any harm."

Lennie chuckled. "Hey, yard art can be beautiful." She wasn't sure about Louise's ultimate fate, but she couldn't let her become just another forgotten junkyard heap.

She removed the Mardi Gras beads from the rearview and carefully peeled Hector's *I Love Lucy* commemorative stamp from the face of the radio.

"Your new rig's gonna need these." She handed the mementos to him and they traded smiles. John dropped the wrecker into gear, and Lennie waved goodbye to the godsend mechanic as they rumbled off into the night.

FIFTY

Racing for the Light

Lennie leaned out the window as the tow truck slogged up a woodsy mountain road, the night air soothing her as the moon played hide'n'seek among the towering trees.

Looking over her shoulder, she could make out Louise's murky shape behind them. Two tons of dead weight. *Dead weight.* The very thought of it saddened her. Still, they were together, and she was grateful for that.

"This road has gotta be at least a twenty-percent grade," John said, his eyes focused on the stretch ahead.

She was thrilled that Johnny, the boy, the *let's jump off the river bridge* part of him, had come out to play. Sure, Mr. John Thomas Riley, the grown man who insisted on risk analysis and belts *and* suspenders as a failsafe, was still in there, but the inner kid he'd lost touch with now seemed to be in the driver's seat, at least for now.

She tried not to focus on the cold hard fact that the odds against making the launch were huge. They were going for it all the same. Together.

She snagged her ball off the bench seat and spun it in her hands to curb her nerves. "This is crazy, huh?"

He grinned. "Certifiable."

Four miles south of the garage, as Hector had suggested, she directed him to veer off the main road and onto a game trail the locals knew as a shortcut. All they had to worry about were bears.

It was a crushed-rock route that cut across the mountainside, instead of jockeying back and forth in a bunch of switchbacks that slowly worked down to the flatlands. They needed to whittle down the distance to Cape Canaveral as much as they could. It was their only chance to beat the clock.

Checking her road atlas, sodden pages clingy from its soaking, Lennie noted their next waypoint: Interstate 75, which ran through the middle of Georgia and into Florida. It would take them to the Florida Turnpike, north of Orlando. Cutting east from there, on State Road 528, would deliver them to the Cape.

When they hit the interstate nearly two hours later, she took over driving duties and kept a steady bead southbound as she navigated through Atlanta.

Four cups of coffee later, John was back at the wheel. He was keeping an eye on the oil pressure gauge, when the truck roared past the *Welcome to the Sunshine State* sign at the Florida-Georgia line.

The milestone made him consider waking Lennie, slumped against the passenger door, but he decided to let her sleep. He checked the stuck-on dashboard clock. Three a.m.

His mind spun up a rerun of what he'd seen on TV—on Florida's Atlantic coast, two hundred fifty-six miles away, an Atlas 5 rocket sat pointed to the heavens, bathed in glaring lights and venting vapor like a dragon. He could see the launch pad's digital counter : 03:28:01 ... 03:28:00 ... 03:27:59 ...

He glimpsed the jittery speedometer needle, sixty-five mph in the dimly lit instrument. *Damn it.* They were going to miss it by thirty-three minutes at this rate.

He put more pressure on the gas pedal, and the speedometer strained to sixty-eight. The steering wheel vibrated as he shifted in the seat and leaned on Lennie's basketball as an armrest.

He took his eyes off the road for just an instant to glance at Louise in the rearview and was suddenly blinded by the glare of enormous oncoming headlights.

Death paralyzed him with fear as he faced what could only be a tractor trailer's searing high beams—until his pending demise whipsawed into a different collision altogether.

Dad emerged from the searing radiance in his woodworker's apron and red sneakers, illuminated on the driveway court, Lennie's basketball in hand.

"Whaddaya want, Johnny, a written invitation?" He was fit to be tied. "Stop looking the wrong way. She's right in front of you, for heaven's sake!"

He fired a chest pass that rocketed at John's face, and John snapped up his hands to catch it. He must have dozed at the wheel because Lennie was suddenly shaking him as she steered from the passenger side.

"Johnny! Johnny! Pull over! You almost crashed off the road!"

His mind churning in that mysterious place between slumber and waking, John eased the truck to the shoulder and Lennie took over driving. The rumbling sway of the truck as they gathered speed again soon lulled him back to sleep.

FIFTY-ONE

The Long Way Home

"What time is it?" John said, groggy in the golden light of dawn that flooded the cab.

Lennie grinned. "Launch time."

John stretched in his seat, unsure how long he'd been asleep. He vaguely remembered Lennie taking over the wheel after ... wait a minute ... *Dad.* On the driveway court.

He must have been half-asleep when that semi seemed to barrel toward him. And while he couldn't clearly recall how the frightening incident had unfolded, he was certain of one thing. Dad's words. *Stop looking the wrong way.*

Lennie flipped on the turn signal as the wrecker slowed. "I think we're gonna make it," she said with a beaming smile.

It took him a few seconds to grasp her excitement. "As off-schedule as we were? How fast were you driving?"

"Fast enough to give us a fighting chance." She eased the tow truck into the Florida Turnpike exit lane, heading for an off-ramp marked State Road 528/Cape Canaveral.

A tremor shot through him—the ball, and the scolding, Dad had fired his way. "No!" he screamed.

Grabbing the steering wheel over Lennie's arm, he wrenched it left, slinging the truck back onto the interstate. Louise howled and fishtailed behind them, two tons of centrifugal force intent on pulling the entire rig over.

Crumpled coffee cups tumbled along the dash like pint-sized boulders and avalanched their feet as fear raked Lennie's face.

"What the hell're you doin! This is our exit!"

John felt her stiffen against his takeover as she leaned forward in an effort to get more leverage, and his internal warning bells clanged at such a reckless move, but something stronger had taken hold.

She tried to haul the tire-howling rig back toward the Cape's exit, but he strong-armed his way through her defense and managed to straighten the wheel.

"Pull over!" he yelled over the blaring engine.

"What?"

"I've been looking the wrong way!"

"What're you talking about!"

"Pull over. Please!" They held the wheel together, easing the slowing truck into the emergency lane until it came to a stop.

"I saw Dad," he said, breathless. His heart hadn't raced this fast since the birth of his children. "The day he died, we were shooting baskets with him at the house. Me and Stevie. I wasn't paying attention, drinking some Gatorade, and Dad smacked me in the head with a pass. He laughed that laugh of his and said I was looking the wrong way."

In the bewilderment on her face, he caught a glimpse of understanding. "That's what he said to you at Hector's last night," she mumbled.

"I can't say whether he did or didn't. All I know is that the launch is the wrong way."

A tractor trailer roared by, blowing sticky air into the cab as Lennie glanced at time ticking away on the dashboard clock. The passage wasn't his any longer. It was hers.

"But this is it, Johnny. The launch. It's *everything* now."

He shook his head ever so slightly. "At the gorge. You jumped. You *jumped*, Lennie."

She couldn't take her eyes off him as he reached out, placed the tip of his finger on her cheekbone, and nudged her head until her chin pointed toward the road's horizon.

"What's *that*?" he said.

That, *what*? The rising sun sparking off the bulldog hood ornament's butt?

"The *road*?" she murmured like a confused game-show contestant. Then she saw it, a smudge of reflective green framed by roadside trees. A sign just past their intended exit—Miami. 81 Miles.

Her world suddenly spun in a frightening new direction. "What're you *doing*?" Her voice barely escaped the crumbling walls of her defense.

"I. Don't. Know." The three words struck her as the most honest he had ever uttered to her. "You said you were giving me the shot of a lifetime at the gorge. *That's* Miami. It's *your* shot. *That's* the way I should be looking ... with you."

She twisted her hands on the steering wheel. "But, your spreadsheet. Your map." She couldn't avoid her pleading inflection. "Dad didn't go to Miami."

John laughed—a single, solitary burst. "It's not *about* the map." She saw him gaze out at the Florida wilderness before turning back to consider the road with her.

"It's about what he would've done if he were here with us. It's about his *intentions* in this life." The notion pinballed her mind. A raindrop hit the windshield.

Miami. The possibility there, which she had allowed herself to believe in and then abandoned, circled back. Everything about it wrapped around her at once: the despair, the joy, the anger, the renewed hope.

She reached up, turned on the cab light and peeked in the rearview. Eyes? Bagged and bloodshot. Face? Sweaty grime in the fine lines that had been creeping in around her eyes. Hair? A sop-frizzled disaster.

"Johnny?"

"Don't worry. We'll get you cleaned up."

"I need a shower."

"You sure do."

Shifting in her seat, she peered in the side-view mirror. Louise was right there, and the coast was clear. She pressed the gas pedal and got them back on the road.

She didn't want to make eye contact with him. Didn't want to tempt fate. She put on her poker face, as if she could bluff destiny. So many things could go wrong with this new game plan, but she couldn't let herself think about any of them.

A short time later, rolling past the turnpike's exit south of Orlando, she heard John say, "Godspeed." It came out of nowhere.

Glancing over, she saw him staring at something in his side-view mirror, totally engrossed. She looked into hers. A column of fire and smoke rose behind them into the awakening sky.

FIFTY-TWO

Unearthing the Past

As office chairs go, the seat John slumped in was a back-breaking junker. He tried to get comfortable in the lumpy seat inside a closet touted as the "Guest Business Center" of the Catalina Motor Lodge. The place was the best he could do on short notice: a 1950s art-deco throwback off Interstate 95 in Miami.

Not even the congas and claves of bouncy Cuban rumba music wafting in from the nearby lobby could put a dent in his road weariness.

He ran the numbers in his head: fifteen hours had covered eight hundred miles from Tallulah Falls to Miami. Average speed, fifty-four miles per hour.

Before pulling into the Catalina, he had suggested they stop at a beach shop so Lennie could grab a fresh outfit for her long-shot reunion with Michelle. The stop had given him a chance to call his corporate attorney, Kyle, in Knoxville to get him started with research into Lennie's past.

John had tried to persuade Lennie to take a day to catch her breath. After all these years, what was the rush? Why not let things settle for one sunrise before pressing on? She wouldn't have it.

She was now back in the room to shower and freshen up while he managed an information-retrieval campaign in front of the guest computer, printer and phone he'd spotted in this room just off the lobby.

A headache did nothing to slow his churning mind as he gazed at a faded tourist poster mounted on the wall above the table where he sat.

The promotional piece for *Gator Wonder Garden* featured a ripped guy in swampy camo shorts and snake boots who had his head jammed between an alligator's jaws, all those teeth and sinew held open with his bare hands. Somehow, John could relate—he could practically feel his head being crushed by the jowls of irrationality. But logic played no part in this last-minute derailment of their road trip. It was all about going the distance for Lennie.

An uneasy feeling simmered in his gut as he pressed the receiver of an ancient dial phone to his ear and spoke with Kyle, who had gone into their First Tennessee Plaza office this Monday morning at John's request.

John said, "Lennie told me the adoption facility closed years ago, so how did you get access to the archival info?" He knew a boondocks town like Watkinsville wasn't a place where businesses like the Whispering Pines Women's Clinic and its affiliated adoption agency would've had the kind of resources to deploy robust digital-records technology back in the mid-1990s.

"I did lawyer stuff," Kyle quipped in his ear. His words fought the rhythmic *wham–bam, wham–bam* of him slamming a racquetball off his office wall, something he always did when devising what he called "artful solutions."

John rolled his neck. "Could you stop with the ball?" The receiver went quiet. "Tell me it was legal, because I don't want another tangle like the time you—"

"It could be legal, if we need it to be."

"What's *that* supposed to mean?"

"Leverage, Johnny boy. A guy in DCS owed me big time."

John nodded to himself. Department of Children's Services. The perfect informational resource.

"If things get sticky," his attorney said, "we'll have your sister file a medical records request from DCS. We'll fudge the date. Trust me, my guy will work with us."

John raked his fingers through his hair. "I owe you."

"I'll take it in unmarked bills."

"Naturally. Just upload everything to Google Docs and I'll grab it here."

Hanging up, John dragged himself out to a vending machine in the lobby, bought a couple bottles of water, and pulled a heavy sun-blocking curtain aside to look at dead Louise hanging off the wrecker in the glare of the parking lot. Connected by the tow arm, the pair of road warriors looked oddly at home hunkered at the gritty motel. He also spotted a CVS drugstore down the street.

He'd insisted on no cell phones when they had set out, in keeping with his historically accurate reboot. Seemed perfect at the time. How could he have known he'd end up in a throwback Miami motel trying to help his sister catch lightning in a bottle? He needed supplies for Operation Lennie, and the CVS had a key item: a prepaid cell phone.

Lennie saw her mirrored reflection materialize from shower steam in the bathroom as she wiped away the condensation. She'd lost track of time and had no idea how long John had been gone. He'd left her in the room, saying something about research. Of course, he was using his ways of the world to help locate Michelle, and the thought of it rocked her to her core.

She spent a quiet moment with herself in the mirror, glimpsing a little bit of hope trying to keep a whole lot of scared in check. She was in free fall, and the Bonnie Raitt song that had captured her sorrows and given them a voice in her younger years spun up in her head.

> *This old house is falling down around my ears.*
> *I'm drowning in a river of my tears.*
> *When all my will is gone, you hold me sway,*
> *And I need you at the dimming of the day.*

No. She couldn't go back there anymore. Couldn't allow herself to be consumed by the past. Everything had been ripped away from her, starting with her child. She needed a new song— one she would write herself.

She grabbed a buzzy blow-dryer from the wall and went to work on her hair. Before long, she'd had it looking the way she wanted. Then, she finished her makeup and slipped into a beachy tangerine sundress from the shop they'd stopped at. And she did her nails in her favorite lavender polish. Fingers and toes.

The finishing touch was a plastic coral Hibiscus flower she'd picked up at the cute little shop, which she affixed behind her left ear. She was determined to see this through. Somehow. Some way.

She bent over to strap on new sandals when a document slid under the door at her feet. *STATE OF TENNESSEE.* A bolt shot through her and she straightened, her spine stiffening. She stared at the document, afraid to study it too closely, scared of what it might say—or *not* say.

"Lennie?" John called through the door.

"Gimme a minute." She closed her eyes and blindly slid her good foot—the one that hadn't required her dreadful corrective pediatric shoe—toward the document, as if slinking up on a robin she didn't want to spook. Gripping the page with her toes, she opened her eyes as she used her foot to bring it to her hand.

Certificate of Birth.

Hands quivering, she struggled to focus on information contained in boxes, her attention skittering over a torrent of words. She allowed her eyes to settle on a pair of adorable inky footprints at the very bottom. Ten nubby toes. To keep from weeping, she busied herself smoothing a wrinkle in the paper.

Birth Mother: Eleanor Grace Riley

Birth Child: Michelle Riley

Parent/Legal Guardian: Benjamin Roy Riley

With trembling fingers, she held Michelle's life in the palm of her hand.

"Lennie?" She yanked the door open and saw John through a blur of tears. He lifted his hands as if to slow her racing heart. "Let's stay cautiously optimist—"

She rocked him two steps back with a hug. His arms tightened around her as she quietly wept against his chest, his gentle hand on the back of her head. She felt a part of him again. A part of their family, as she pressed her face against him—it had been so long since she'd felt safe in anyone's arms.

After a moment, he stepped back and held her at arm's length. "There's something else." She could have sworn she saw distress in his eyes. Drawing a deep breath, she braced herself for whatever came next.

"I have an attorney at my firm. Kyle. He did some research," he said with the matter-of-fact tone of a doctor who had a devastating prognosis. She forced herself to swallow. *Something's wrong.*

"There were no computer records, but he was able to track down a paper trail." He lifted additional documents she hadn't noticed in her excitement, and she recognized the page on top from one of the worst days of her life.

"It's the placement request Daddy had to sign to bring the adoption agency into the picture," she said, not knowing why a knot of fear began to tighten around her chest.

"Right." He handed her another sheet of paper.

Notice of Referral.

She searched what looked like a form letter responding to individuals who referred expectant mothers. Addressed to Amelia Tucker, it thanked her for referring Benjamin and Eleanor Riley.

She lifted her gaze, jumbled fragments slowly fusing in her mind. "Dad and I ... we fought for months. He struggled with what to do. Whether he should allow me to keep the baby. He said he prayed on it. Amelia told him she'd heard a rumor that I'd gotten pregnant."

"Amelia Tucker, from church?"

"Yes. She said she had a sister, Elizabeth, who worked at an adoption agency. Whispering Pines, in Watkinsville, where I went for my delivery. Said what a wonderful thing it would be for the baby to go to a good home, to someone who could care for it proper and raise it right."

Those words from the past pierced her like a heart-seeking dart.

John's face creased with what looked like resignation. "I don't think Dad really had a choice when it came to the adoption."

"What do you mean?"

He handed her a third document.

Acknowledgement of Donation. Addressed to Mr. Jackson T. Mosely.

The back of Lennie's neck sizzled. She looked at John, then back at the document to make sure she'd read it correctly.

"Mr. Mosely gave them money?" The past avalanched her. *Boone at the lake house ... the swirling whiskey dance ... her helpless newborn reaching for her through the crib bars at the clinic.*

The thought of it nearly made her retch. The memory of the Mosely patriarch's threat on the rim of the pit as she watched Dad, small as an insect below, felt like his fists were wrapped around her throat.

John frowned at the papers in her hand. "Mosely was involved behind the scenes and bought his way to the top of the placement list. The adoption was fast-tracked for him."

She let her eyes soak up the letter. From the agency's director, it confirmed *the receipt of your very generous donation* and the expedited *placement of the child referred by Mrs. Tucker.* She bit down on her bottom lip to keep it from quivering as Mr. Mosely's secret involvement hit home.

"He wanted my baby out of town as quick as possible," Lennie murmured. "One way or the other, he was gonna get rid of my child. So, he used Amelia to coax Daddy into the adoption."

John's face was grim. "Yeah." He paced back and forth in their matchbox of a room. "I think there's more to it. Didn't Amelia have a special-needs boy?"

"Wyatt. It was just him and her after her husband left."

He studied the tile floor under his measured steps. "Amelia's husband was a Tucker. That was her married name. Do you know her maiden name?"

"Braswell."

He walked to the nightstand. "Braswell," he mumbled to himself. As he thumbed through a stack of papers, her stomach tightened as she recalled sinking into the leather seat in Mr. Mosely's Mercedes after he'd taken her from the school parking lot.

She drove the agonizing memory from her mind and concentrated on the crease that bridged John's nose as he swiped through the pages.

"What's all in there?" she said, digging her toes into the stiff soles of her new sandals.

"Everything that was preserved." He stopped flicking pages and focused on one that held his interest. "Whispering Pines was only open for seven years, 1990 to 1997." She heard in his voice the curiosity of someone tracing a family's past generations. He flipped through a few more pages, eyes scanning as he went. Finally, he looked at her.

"According to their corporate filings with the state, the agency was privately held and had the same eight staff members the entire time. There's no Elizabeth Braswell. Are you sure Amelia's sister was named Elizabeth?"

"Yes, but maybe she married and changed her name."

"There was no Elizabeth at all. Ever. Or Beth. Or Liz. Or Ellie. Or any kind of possible nickname variation."

Lennie clenched her hands, fingernails digging into her palms. "So, Amelia lied about having a sister there."

"Or was forced to."

Lennie had always thought Amelia was a nice person. Friendly. A hard worker. Quick with a smile. But there was a sadness about her, a beaten exhaustion beyond her years, especially after her husband left her and her little boy on their own.

John's eyes narrowed as he looked over his shoulder, as if an answer were sneaking up on him. "She worked as a clerk at that old Sinclair station on Barnett Shoals Road, right?"

"Yeah," she replied, the rusted relic she'd passed on the way to bury Dad flashing through her mind. A queasiness spread in her gut. "The church was always taking up collections to help her pay for the specialized care and education Wyatt needed."

"Specialized *and* expensive."

Her uneasiness surged to a bursting point. "You think she could afford the kind of health insurance Wyatt—?" The instant the words formed, she knew the answer. Mr. Mosely must have taken advantage of the little boy's crucial needs to force Amelia to do his bidding and push Dad into an adoption.

"Medical care for Wyatt," she said.

It fit with how Mr. Mosely was known to finagle all his dealings: pit someone's needs against something he wanted done, and emotionally extort them. *Mr. Mosely bought Amelia's cooperation with her son's very life.*

As the depth of his depravity struck home, she put her hand to her chest. And his vile words rushed at her again, this time carrying the full impact of his unveiled threat. *I will not have a slut-born child degrading my family lineage.*

From the look on John's face, he was connecting dark dots. "And don't think for a second," he said, "that Mosely wouldn't manipulate Dad into the adoption. Mosely floats some bogus claim about needing to cut costs? Tells Dad he may have to let him go? Dad could no longer provide for his family. How does he pay to help you raise a baby?"

Of course. That vicious man would have done *anything* to run her baby—her "shameful stain" on the reputation of his revered family—as far as possible out of town. And he would use his absolute power to bury anyone who got between him and his objective. Realizing Mr. Mosely had played Dad and her against each other, she sat on the bed, fumbling to grasp everything she had just discovered.

For the first time, she understood the kind of pressure Dad had been under to make sure her child would be provided for. She remembered how worried he'd looked during the last months of her pregnancy. The adoption must have felt like a godsend to him.

John lowered himself beside her, and his face pulled into a grave expression. "Even with all we've unearthed, we *don't* have any information on her adopted family. Their name. Address. It wasn't in the records."

Lennie's confusion melted into anguish. "*What?* How could the most important information *not* be in the records?"

"With Mosely involved, who knows? He was in a position to put stipulations on the donation."

Mr. Mosely's specter rose like a dark wind to extinguish the flame of hope she'd nurtured back to life. He could've arranged to have the information removed. *He'd walk through fire to keep me from finding the child he wanted as good as dead.*

"The bottom line is, our paper trail has dried up," John said. "Kyle needs the initial address of her adoptive life, or he can't get her current whereabouts traced. I asked him to keep trying, but let's temper our hopes."

Blink-blinka blonk-blonk. The sudden burst of a wooden xylophone was enough to jolt Lennie from the bed.

John dug into his pocket. "Sorry. I picked up a prepaid down the street so Kyle could follow up." As he pulled the ringing TracFone from his pocket, Lennie held her breath, hoping for a miracle.

FIFTY-THREE

Digging Deeper

Hands wrapped around a paper cup of coffee, Lennie sat at a wobbly garden cafe table in the Catalina's lobby and watched a thunderstorm pound the pavement through the rain streaked window, its fury barely drowned out by three blasting air conditioners that jutted from the seafoam green wall above her head.

She'd been certain John's lawyer would be able to pull that last rabbit out of his hat. But the magic, and the miracles, had run out. Without Michelle's adoptive family name and the address where she'd begun her life with them, Kyle had hit a brick wall.

"He said he didn't even need the specific street address," John said as he turned a packet of sugar round and round on the table. "Just the city."

Lightning cracked, flickering the overheads, and the AC units moaned right before the power died, leaving the room cloaked in a lifeless gray. The roaring deluge outside, now filled Lennie's ears.

She could scarcely make out the white remnants of powdered creamer floating in her coffee. *Just the city.* Kyle might as well have *just* needed a winning Mega Millions lottery ticket.

"With that piece of information," John continued, "he's got access to people who could digitally triangulate her current location, based on movement patterns, with ninety to ninety-five percent accuracy."

Distracted by a heated exchange in Spanish by the motel staff behind the reception counter, she had trouble focusing on what he was saying. Only one odd word stuck.

"Triangulate. What does that even *mean*?" She knew immediately she shouldn't have asked.

"Using data points to determine—"

"It doesn't matter what it means," she snapped. "We don't have it." She closed her aching eyes and lifted her hands. "Sorry. It's just ... too much."

Kicking off her sandal, she rested her ankle on her thigh and dug her thumbs into the arch of her troublesome foot. John leaned closer across the table. "Is there anything at all, no matter how seemingly insignificant, you can remember from the clinic that might help?"

"I've tried, Johnny." Her voice was cinched with a yearning she hadn't felt since she was torn away from her newborn. She'd spent the last quarter century battling to forget the Whispering Pines clinic. Forget the pain, the heartbreak. Forget having a piece of her soul ripped from her. "I've done nothing but try to remember since he called."

But it was no use. Maybe it was the pressure of knowing everything was on the line, and it came down to her plumbing the depths of the emotional hole she'd managed to climb out of to carve a life for herself. Her eyes began to sting, and she knew tears were close behind.

"I don't mean to press," he said, "but if you can just—"

"No. I can't. I've spent my entire life running from that time." Her voice trembled. "You can't understand unless you've survived it and ... come out the other side a completely different *you* ... a you that doesn't dare look back."

Her brother's expression told her he was doing his best to understand, but she knew *trying* was the closest he would ever come. She had to deal with this hurdle alone.

Welcoming a diversion, she watched staff hustle back and forth around the corner of the reception counter in their mango guayabera shirts.

She didn't have to understand Spanish to know an argument when she heard one—the raised voices and finger-pointing were a universal language. She figured it must be about the power outage.

Her chair skittered on the tile when she scooted away from the wrought-iron table. "Do you know where the bathrooms are?"

John nodded toward the reception. "Around the corner from grand central station over there."

Hurrying past the desk, she never actually saw the beefy guy until she veered into the hallway and collided with him. What she did see, big as life, was his name tag, *Miguel Ramirez*, just before it jabbed her in the face. The impact knocked her back two steps.

"*Perdón, perdón!* I'm sorry, *señora*," he said, looking aghast.

Momentarily stunned, she felt her cheek smarting from the plastic poke. At the same time, an image flickered in her memory, as if a barricaded door had been knocked off its hinges by the collision, and a sliver of light sliced into the impenetrable room behind it.

A tornado of confusion lashed her mind. In front of her, the motel clerk's lips continued to move with words she couldn't make out as she collapsed inside herself to a field of woven white that blocked out an overhead glare.

She felt the weight of it on her chest before other sensations swarmed her ... *floating face up amid echoing voices ... a chattering gurney ... a nurse's name badge jabbing her face.*

"Carol Prescott," she said to the clerk, who answered with a bewildered look. She grabbed his thick arms and gave him a shake. "Carol Prescott!"

"Lennie?" She turned around and saw the concern on John's face.

"My nurse's name was Carol Prescott."

"What's taking so long?" Pacing their room an hour after John had called Kyle with her nurse's name, Lennie stopped at the window. The thunderstorm had blown through and power had been restored. She stared at Louise through glass dripping with enough humidity to remove the creases from a pleated skirt.

"It's one *name*," she said. "Didn't you say there were only eight staffers there the entire time?" Spinning on her heel, she glared at John, sitting on the bed, back against the wall as he fiddled with his drugstore phone. "How can you just sit there playing with that?"

"I'm not playing with it. I'm tailoring it to my needs. I don't like the default ring-tone."

Arching backward, she shook her hands at the ceiling. "Gimme two words. A first and last name." He continued to tap his phone's screen. "Did you hear what I said?"

"First and last."

Forcing bursts of air between her clenched teeth like an old-school pressure cooker, she couldn't keep her eyes still. "I'm gonna clean something." She marched into the bathroom.

"Why?" John called from out in the room.

"Control my environment, just like you."

"I don't control my—"

Beep-beep-boop, bee-doo-bip. She spun toward the frantic digital whistles that *Star Wars'* R2-D2 made when the gang was trapped inside the Death Star trash crusher and nearly tripped as she rushed back into the room.

"He found her!" John was reading something on his phone screen.

"Michelle!" Her throat constricted and she stopped breathing.

"No. Your retired nurse."

Her heart sank momentarily because it wasn't Michelle, but Nurse Prescott was a step in the right direction.

"*And?*"

Eyes locked on his screen, he held up his hand as he read Kyle's message. "Just a second ... they spoke."

"Is she gonna help?" With a shiver, she recalled how heartless the woman had been with her.

"Kyle can charm the green off fresh-cut grass." He returned to his phone, relaying what he read. "You made an impression on her, and she remembers your case."

Case. She bristled at how her inability to choose the fate of her own flesh and blood, and all the pain and torment she'd endured for more than half her life, had been boiled down to a single icy word.

"Bottom line is, Kyle has Michelle's adoptive family name and the city she started out from. Jacksonville."

Lennie struggled to keep her mind from running wild as she realized John's legal eagle now had exactly what he needed to pull that rabbit out of the hat.

She grabbed her brother's arm. "Y'all are like to kill me with this drip-drip-drip."

"It's a process, Lennie. We're going to have to wait until he gets back with more." He patted her hand. "It'll probably be just a couple minutes."

John's minutes turned into a half-hour, then an hour. Then a lifetime.

She sat on the edge of the bed with her head buried in her hands as she watched an ant meander grooves in the tile floor, calypso music bleeding through the headboard wall from next door.

Shweet-beep-beep, bee-doo-bwoot.

Lennie spun to his tone. With a smile so big his cheeks must have hurt, John put the phone in her face. "Green, meet grass."

It was all she could do to breathe as she took the phone with shaky hands. "Oh my God, oh my God, oh my God." There it was. In glorious, trembling pixels. *5683 Suncoast Estates Blvd. Miami, FL., 14 miles SW your location. Kyle.*

She looked at John, then back at the screen. "How did he find her?"

"*Puh-lease,*" he replied as he stood and stretched. "He'll regale me with a bragathon of biblical proportions when I get back to Knoxville. Trust me, the details will *not* be in short supply. And I guess you were right."

She was so consumed reading and re-reading Kyle's staggering string of text messages that his words hardly registered. "Huh?"

"About Miami. You were right."

It sunk in that, although he'd traveled here with her, John still had serious doubts about her hunch. Grinning, she jumped up and handed him his phone. "Can you print me some directions?"

"Got it covered. We'll use the GPS on the phone."

Lennie faced him squarely. "Here's the thing, Johnny. This really isn't a *we* thing. As much as I appreciate the offer, this is something I need to do myself. Just me and her."

Indecision flitted in his eyes. He opened his mouth, only to close it again. Finally, he said, "Are you sure? I mean, I could be there in case … You know, if things get—"He hesitated as if he wanted to find just the right word. "Lennie loosey."

"Thanks. But after everything I've been through, I can handle this. Just be here when I get back, okay? That lawyer of yours isn't the only one who's gonna talk your ear off."

John hesitated for only a moment before heading for the door. "I'll get you the directions."

FIFTY-FOUR

Leap of a Lifetime

Fighting off an emotional hurricane as she waited for John to return from printing out the directions, Lennie took a deep breath and sat on the edge of the bed.

Could this really be happening? Could the life she'd dreamed about since seventeen be just fourteen miles away? Hundreds of thousands of miles in the rearview, the ruts and potholes and wrong turns. A handful to go.

John was right. This is my shot of a lifetime.

She had decided to follow her instincts—best to just show up on Michelle's doorstep. Let her see her mother's eyes, face-to-face. Heart on her sleeve. All she needed was some proof, a snapshot of their shared past.

Two steps brought her to the dresser where John had tossed the papers he'd printed out. The documents laid haphazardly, as scattered as her emotions.

She picked up the copy of Michelle's birth certificate, surely all the proof she'd need, and the closest thing she had to a family portrait, even if it was merely her daughter's baby footprints.

Birth mother: Eleanor Grace Riley.

Birth child: Michelle Riley.

Her eyes tracked over those two lines until they blurred into one. Lowering the document, she glimpsed herself in the dresser mirror. "Birth child," she whispered to her reflection, her chest tightening.

She'd missed half a lifetime that should have been overflowing with shared moments. First steps. First grade. First kiss. Instead, their separation felt like an immense chasm. And now that she was poised on the edge, ready to leap, she dared to glance down.

After years of holding onto a thread of hope that she might know the love of her child one day, she looked past the moment of meeting her, to what could happen next. And an unexpected storm struck without warning.

What if she rejects me? Wants nothing to do with me?

Dread spiked, ravaging her will to find out, the same way a lightning strike vaporizes a tree in a blink of destruction. She laid the birth certificate on the dresser. *I can't do this.*

She stepped back, edging away from the paper trail of her past, an ingrained sense of self-preservation fueling her need to run. She had to tell John she was calling the whole thing off. He would understand.

The movement of air when she pulled the door open flushed a document from the dresser, and it fluttered to her feet. She picked it up.

Acknowledgement of Donation—Mr. Jackson T. Mosely.

Who would think that one name rooted in unbridled power could be the source of so much heartache and pain. A brute who had threatened her and her child's life.

Resolve to right that wrong battled her impulse to retreat in the face of the agony he'd inflicted. She had been prepared to attempt to reclaim with her daughter all that she'd lost. If she turned away in defeat, that meant only one thing: the Moselys had won. She couldn't let that happen.

Both she and Dad had been snookered by master manipulators, Boone learning at the foot of his father and Lennie running from hers because of it. Her battle-worn spirit pushed through a thorny tangle of sorrow and fear to release the paper in her hand. It fluttered back to the floor, where she planted her good foot on it.

Then she picked up Michelle's birth certificate again, carefully folded it, and tucked it into her pocket. She had no idea how things would go, but she had to know if she had any shot at a future with her daughter.

Lennie refused to be one of the lives strewn in pieces behind Mr. Mosely. He had ruled their small town with a steel-toed boot heel for as long as she could remember, plundering people's vulnerabilities, leaving only broken shells behind. He'd certainly crushed her to bits at a point when she couldn't fight back.

Her dread was reborn as anger, and a surge of fury banished the panic and self-doubt that had once driven her to flee the life she might have had—the family, the fulfillment, the joy.

She was done with flight. It was time for fight. She would finally twist free of the Moselys with every ounce of strength she could muster—not only for herself, but for all the others whose lives they had poisoned.

She adjusted the Hibiscus knock-off in her hair as John stepped through the room door she'd left open.

"You look great."

"Thank you."

He handed her a printed Google map, her route to Suncoast Estates traced in yellow highlighter.

"I *got* this." She nodded to convince herself it was true.

"Yes. You do," he assured her.

The sudden thought of Michelle turned her mouth so dry, the insides of her cheeks stuck to her teeth. How her brother knew to pull a bottle of water from the pocket of his cargo shorts escaped her. He unscrewed the cap and handed it to her.

"For the ride."

She savored a couple of hearty glugs before studying the map as she walked into the scorching glare of Florida's August heat. "It's only fourteen miles?"

"There's an entry sign facing the road. The house is on the right side of a divided boulevard with palm trees." Just like John to study the Google satellite image for every last detail.

Rounding the wrecker and its precious cargo, she saw a sparkling purple rental and came to a halt.

"Purple's your color, right?" John said. "That's what I asked for."

Lennie raised a hand to shield her eyes from the blazing sun. "That's really sweet, but I think I'm gonna stick with the truck." She flashed a smile to soften her rejection.

His expression twisted, as if she'd picked a rickety ugly duckling over a beautiful swan. "You're going to show up in *that*?"

"Absolutely. Ricky's a part of things now."

"*Ricky*." he said, his eyebrows lifting.

"After Ricky Ricardo. In honor of Hector." She tapped the truck's fender. "In case you missed it, Ricky was kinda our thing."

John chuckled. "Right. *I Love Lucy*. Let's at least unhook the car." He reached for the truck's boom-arm lever, but she snatched his hand.

"Hold up there, Hoss. Don't go messin' with my wingwoman. Louise has been with me this far. No way she's not comin' with."

John shrugged and spread his arms theatrically. "Your call."

She searched his eyes, suddenly aware this was the instant for which he had sacrificed the crowning moment of his memorial trip. "Thank you, Johnny."

A grin tugged at his mouth. "Crazy as it sounds, I almost hate to see it end."

"What, our knock-down-drag-outs?"

"Hey, we're still standing."

She chuckled. "At least *I* am." She considered the fading bruise under his left eye. "About your fall in the bathroom. Wanna tell me about it?"

"Not much to tell." His gaze lingered for a moment on the traffic backed up at the intersection next to the parking lot before returning to her. "That drunk guy at the bar said something about you after you left, and it pissed me off."

"And you stood up for me?" She couldn't remember the last time someone had done that and was surprised at the warmth that rushed her face. He didn't answer. But he didn't have to.

"And you forgot to tell me?" she said.

"I'm telling you now."

"Man, he caught you a good one. What'd *he* look like after the fight?"

"Big."

Lennie took him by the ears and pulled him nose to nose. "I love you, John Thomas."

He grabbed her head like a melon. "I love you, too. Drive safely."

She clambered into the truck and cranked the engine. John closed the door. "You're going to *do* this, right? I mean, no last-minute Lennie conniptions."

"Who? *Moi?*" She dropped Ricky into gear and pulled Louise toward the motel's exit. Her last glimpse of him was in the sideview mirror as he receded behind her with his hand raised.

John watched her disappear into a steady stream of traffic. In spite of the brave face she'd put on, he saw the same scared girl he had walked to school her first day. The same nervous Nellie he'd prepped for her driver's license test, teaching her to parallel park in the rainy town square.

The memories teased a grin. How would he explain to Holly how he and his vagabond sister—Balloony, Stevie called her—had ended up in Miami on his highly scripted itinerary destined for a space launch?

Easy. *We'll blame each other.* Lennie's story would ring true, and he found something comfortingly amusing about that. For now, though, he was sure of one thing: whatever the outcome at the address she was hanging her hopes on, she—

Roy. The name rocketed into his mind. He looked back at the motel room. *The birth certificate. Parent/Legal Guardian.*

"Benjamin Roy Riley," he said aloud, his voice lingering on Dad's middle name. He would call the headstone company with the full name as soon as he got home.

"Roy!" His outburst surprised him as it reverberated off the motel's bubblegum-colored exterior. It was the first time he'd heard it aloud, and his mind played it over and over.

Roy ... Roy ... Roy. With each repetition, the distance he'd felt between him and Dad drew shorter and shorter, until it totally dissolved.

FIFTY-FIVE

A Breath Away

Fourteen miles seemed like four hundred to Lennie. Fanning herself with the map in the steamy truck cab, she couldn't remember a countryside this hot and flat since cutting across Texas a lifetime ago.

Working her way west from the interstate motel, she drank in the immenseness of South Florida's wild blue yonder. Unlike the mountains, there was sky in every direction, bottomed by pine scrub and palmetto as far as the eye could see.

She slowed as a sign came into view up ahead: Suncoast Estates, Where Paradise Awaits. If that was so, why had an increasing sense of dread crept over her with each passing mile?

Torrid sunshine slanted through the windshield and almost blinded her as she turned onto its namesake street, Suncoast Estates Boulevard. The sprawling neighborhood of squatty, concrete-block houses looked nothing like the country club McMansions the designation "estates" had conjured in her mind.

This seemed working-class. Not out of her league. She breathed a little easier, until she saw an alligator hunkered on the bank of a lake hugging the boulevard. Open-jawed, it seemed to be frozen in place as it sunned its teeth.

Easing along, she suddenly became aware of her pulse throbbing behind her knees, and she tried to relax her hands on the wheel. She took a moment to wonder how close she was to the Everglades, anything to avoid facing the harsh truth that her hopes and dreams would either live or die up around the bend.

The houses all looked similar. Dusty yellows, blues, and greens reminded her of faded Easter eggs. Scruffy lawns were well maintained and projected a pride of ownership. Full-sized dolphin mailboxes with hinged mouths for letters stood at the foot of all the driveways, as if doing synchronized tail-stands.

She slowed the truck to a crawl, foot poised over the brake as Michelle's address looped in her head. *5683 ... 5683 ...* Sweat beading her forehead, she watched the numbers on the passing dolphins, which sported their familiar grinning expressions, as if they knew the punchline to a secret joke. 5673 ... 5675.

A car horn blared behind her, kicking her heart into overdrive as she realized she was barely moving. She waved the driver around, and he sped past.

She did her best to soak up the sweat from her face with a wad of leftover Waffle House napkins and checked her makeup in the rearview. Wilting, but it would have to do. A rush of panic overtook her when she spotted the address up on the right. 5683. *Oh my God. Her house.*

Childish letters spelled Freddie on the graceful curve of the dolphin mailbox's body, which guarded a pale blue home with two windows facing the road. Like its neighbors, it had hurricane awnings, gray and braced open by narrow arms bolted into the cinder block exterior, ready to shut out angry weather at a moment's notice.

The past roared, a fractured chaos of memories that dissolved into white noise in her mind. *Doesn't matter how it happened. I abandoned her. I can't do this.* As she rolled past the house, the grinning dolphin drifted by her passenger window. She snapped her head forward.

The street was clear as far as she could see. *You found it. That's enough for today. You can come back tomorrow.* Something inside her pushed back against her desire to flee. Her foot was suddenly pressuring the brake pedal, and the tow truck rolled to a squeaky stop along the curb in front of the house.

A strand of hair was stuck to her cheek. Tucking it behind her ear, she closed her eyes and took a deep breath to calm her galloping heart, then peered at the house outside the passenger window.

A pair of kids' bikes were sprawled on the lawn, next to a plastic wading pool. *She has children?* Her already shaky core was instantly rocked by a thunderclap. *Grandkids?*

She caught her eyes staring at her from the rearview. *What're you doin'?*

She grabbed her bottle of water from the seat and swallowed the last of it, focusing on the bugs splattered on the windshield. When she flung the empty into the footwell, it seemed to clatter down the desolate hallway of her life.

Who the hell do you think you are?

All she had been rose up against her and yanked the stupid Hibiscus from her hair, as if it had somehow betrayed her. She threw the fake flower to the floorboard so hard it busted a petal off.

You abandoned your baby.

As she gathered her hair behind her head and strangled it into a ponytail with a rubber band she ripped from the gear shifter, a lifetime howl began to hound her.

You don't deserve love.

She white-knuckled the steering wheel.

Stop this foolishness.

She yanked up on the door handle.

Heartbreak city all over again!

Shouldered it open.

Where do you think you're goin'!

Hopped out of the truck.

Hey, Eleanor Graceless!

She marched up the cracked driveway toward the front door, heart beating as fast as her preying past.

Get back in the truck!

Sweat tacked her sundress to her back as she pressed the doorbell, suddenly aware that she had probably left the truck running.

You're gonna regret this for the rest of your life!

"Shut up," she mumbled through clenched teeth as her toes made little fists in her sandals and a young woman pulled the door open.

"Hi," the resident said with a friendly smile. She wore a Sunshine Paints team softball jersey and cuffed jean shorts.

Paralyzed by this stranger who looked to be in her mid-twenties, Lennie could now hear the tow truck chugging out on the street. *Say something.* She stood in an awkward silence. *Anything.*

"Can I help you?" the young woman said, uneasiness spreading across her face.

Lennie could only drink her in. Absorb every detail of her angular face, framed by the same chestnut hair she'd seen in her mirror all her life, eyes the deep brown of autumn's first acorns. A wisp of a hairline scar on the side of her chin did nothing to diminish her graceful cheekbones.

Miss Sunshine Paints' eyes flinched with a hint of panic, and she started to close the door. "I'm sorry, you must have the wrong address."

"I, um," Lennie stammered. *Breathe.* "No, please. Hi. I'm sorry." She pressed her palm against her chest as if she could still the raging storm that threatened to drive her to her knees.

"I ... first off, I'm not selling anything. Religious or otherwise." *You're rambling.*

She tried to force a smile, but it felt like a pained grimace. "I mean, I'm not one of those pyramid-scheme people." *Rambling Rose!*

She struggled to outrun her fear as the young woman's cautious face measured her through the door she held open just a crack.

"Please," Lennie said, "I just need to talk with you for a minute, if that would be okay. Ma'am."

When she warily eased out to glance at the street, alarm spiked her eyes. "Oh my God, was there an accident?"

Lennie followed her frightened gaze to the station wagon that hung off the back of the idling tow truck. "I told Tommy not to get that motorcycle!"

Lennie spun back to her and reached out. "N-n-no. There's no accident." She could see the panic on the young woman's face. "But if there ever is, I can help. Only if you want. Not that I'm some kind of crazy woman or anything. I mean, not someone who pushes herself into things or—"

She stopped short and brushed the sweat from her neck as the woman retreated behind her closing door. This wasn't going *at all* like the speech she'd practiced on the way.

Her heart pushed past her head and did the talking. "I'm sorry," Lennie said. "I'm really nervous. Have you ever been nervous? Could I possibly start over? *Please?*"

She clung to the sight of the young woman through the sliver of open door.

"I know this may sound strange. Crazy even, but ... please. I know you from a long time ago. You were born in Watkinsville,

Tennessee." She swallowed and wiggled her jaw to loosen what she felt was a tense smile. "And you may have had to wear a corrective shoe when you were a kid. Just a little girl."

With a quizzical look, Miss Sunshine Paints let her tongue peek out to wet the corner of her mouth. "How ... did you know that?" She pulled the door open a little wider.

Tell her. A calm she could never hope to understand pushed Lennie's hand into her pocket. She pulled out the birth certificate and handed it to her. Then she watched the rising confusion on the young woman's face as she scanned it with increasing urgency. Her eyes lifted from the document to meet Lennie's.

"Mothers just know," Lennie said in a thin voice, fighting tears as her deepest hopes collided with the despair she'd borne so long.

The woman's face twisted in anguish. "Are you friggin' kiddin' me?" she said, backing away as if from some awful nightmare that had suddenly come to life on her doorstep. "No—"

Lennie pushed a desperate hand out to her. "No, please, I just ... Michelle."

Her daughter recoiled. "How dare you." Her voice barely escaped her clamped teeth. "You don't just—"

"Mommy?" A little girl appeared behind Michelle. Lennie gazed at the shoeless child in the open doorway, and her heart stopped. *My grandbaby.*

Dressed in a kid's soccer uniform, the child had impossibly cinnamon-colored hair and eyes the color of green grapes. Probably about seven.

"Get your brother," Michelle said with parental firmness. "We have to go."

The girl offered Lennie a curious smile, a front tooth missing. "Hi." She pirouetted on one heel.

Eyes beginning to ache with tears, Lennie grasped her dress to keep her hands from trembling. "Hello."

Michelle reached down and moved the girl away from the door as if Lennie posed a danger. "Hannah Lynn, we have to meet Daddy for the game. Put your shoes on and get your brother. Now, please."

Hannah's lips drew into a pout before she scampered off. Michelle stepped out and closed the door behind her as Lennie spotted a little boy watching her from the front window.

"A boy and a girl?" she murmured.

Michelle shook her head, eyes blistering Lennie. "This isn't gonna happen."

"Please, I know this is—"

"You're not gonna just walk up to this house. This family. My life. And settle into whatever you think this should be." Her voice was like hardened steel.

The life drained out of Lennie faster than she could speak, and she struggled to string words together. "No, please. It wasn't what I wanted ... There were things I couldn't ... I mean, I was just a girl. Scared."

"So was I," Michelle shot back, voice rising. "With Hannah. I get it." She leaned toward Lennie with a hint of aggression. "You find a way."

Tears overtook Lennie, her world crumbling as her daughter unleashed. "Do you know what it's like to grow up not knowing who your biological mother is? Do you have *any* idea?"

"Yes." A silent prayer filled Lennie's head. *Please, give me a chance.*

Confusion flickered on Michelle's face and she stepped back, as if some fathomless reservoir had momentarily breached the dam restraining it.

Lennie melted into hopelessness, words pouring out. "I'm so terribly sorry. And I know what it's like to grow up not knowing who your child is. Or where she is. If she's safe. Or in trouble. Or needs help. If she's happy."

Anger wiped away Michelle's teary expression of confusion. "What was I? An *inconvenience*? You had other *plans*?" Her voice dripped with disdain.

"It wasn't my choosing," Lennie said. "I was—"

"It *was* your choosing if you just walked away!" Her daughter stood with clenched fists. "We *all* make choices. And I'm *not* doing this. I have a mom and dad who love me. Who took care of me. I have my own family. I have my own life. And it has *nothing* to do with you."

Michelle backhanded her tears away. When she shoved the birth certificate at her, Lennie stepped back as if accepting it meant certain death.

"I'm happy, okay?" Michelle said, her voice edged with scorn. "So, you can just turn around, go back to your life and feel good. I'm. *Happy.*"

She dropped the document at Lennie's feet and spent a last moment in her eyes before rushing inside and slamming the door.

Looking out from the window, Hannah was a blur through Lennie's tears as she knelt to retrieve the paper. Her dying dream somehow pulled her to her feet, and she wiped her eyes with her dress as Hannah stared at her with a look of compassion only a child can express.

Lennie couldn't remember walking back to the street. She merely found herself sitting on the wrecker's scorching vinyl seat, Michelle's birth certificate pressed to her chest, the official document of her hollowed soul.

She tried to find something to focus on through the smeary windshield, but there was nothing on the strip of boulevard except a shimmering heat curtain that wavered like an unreachable mirage.

FIFTY-SIX

Root of it All

Lennie tromped over the crusty snowpack that cloaked Mosely Cemetery. Footprints wandered everywhere amid gravesites lovingly decorated for Christmas in lively reds and silvers. She looked back at her parked *Lennie's Towing* rig to get her bearings.

In the four months since she had decided to stay in Miami to be as close to Michelle as possible, supporting herself with a one-woman wrecker operation, she'd barely started to acclimate to the subtropical heat. Now, back in the December winter of the Smokies, she longed for the sun's warmth.

A red poinsettia in her gloved hands, she looked up through the icy fingers of tree branches stripped bare by winter, the slate gray sky shrouding her mood. It wasn't that she wouldn't be spending Christmas this year with her daughter and her family—a vision she'd allowed herself to imagine on the drive to Michelle's house—it was that she wouldn't be spending *any* Christmases with them. Ever.

Living in the same zip code would be as close as she would ever get to her daughter and grandchildren. *Grandchildren.* She'd heard the girl's name. Hannah. But she didn't know her own grandson's name.

Engulfed by this frozen stretch of land where generations of hopes and dreams had died with those who harbored them, she drew bracing air into her lungs.

The shimmering snowfall reminded her of a holiday snow globe she'd shaken while visiting A Likely Story—she had almost been able to muster a smile at the cute reindeer antlers Yolanda wore.

When her childhood friend asked if she ever planned on coming back, explaining *never* had been too difficult. Besides, this was supposed to be a joyous time of year, and she didn't want to drag down Yolanda's holiday spirit.

Lennie buried any homecoming talk by explaining that she was just in town to visit Mom and Dad's graves and spend Christmas with John and his family up in Knoxville. She was grateful he'd invited her to be with his family—she couldn't bear the thought of spending another Christmas alone.

Had it only been a handful of months since she'd last seen him in South Florida? It seemed like the moon had tracked across the heavens a zillion times since then—and she had cried as many tears.

Still, she'd found some relief in nurturing the seed of a new song she was writing about how many tears someone could shed in a lifetime before numbness milked the last of them.

Making her way amid the frosted headstones, Lennie considered something that was as true about Mosely now as it had been when she was growing up: the place was always good for gossip.

Yolanda had caught her up, telling her an odd sort of mourning had taken hold in the wake of a noted death. It was partly genuine grieving, but it was mostly nothing more than proper manners to show respect for the dearly departed, even if he was generally disliked. Despised even. Boone Mosely had died in Bolivia, shortly after Thanksgiving.

Her former co-worker had heard he'd been caught in a dynamite explosion while leading the Mosely Silver Corporation's team of dirt-poor laborers, some of them just boys, on a daring mountain excavation. The tale had sounded downright heroic. Only Yolanda had heard wrong.

John's lawyer had discovered Boone had been killed by his own workers for attempting to force some wives and even daughters into sexual servitude to secure their husbands' and boyfriends' jobs in the mines.

Lennie had told Yolanda the real reason for Boone's death because the town needed to know. Surely it was time for the truth about the Moselys to come out, and she figured it might as well start with her.

Wishing she'd remembered her earmuffs, she pulled her fringed winter coat tighter as she walked among holiday-decorated grave sites dating back more than two centuries. Wreaths. Ornaments strung on garland. Tiny Christmas trees. Comforting, in a sad kind of way.

Before her, a familiar expanse of rolling hills and swales fanned out like frozen ocean waves. She crested the next rise and came to Mom and Dad's eternal resting places.

Benjamin Roy Riley. Roselyn Delia Riley. Side by side forever now. Her breath fogged the frosty air, and a somber silence filled her ears.

Placing the poinsettia between their headstones, Lennie was heartened to see John had been able to include Dad's middle name. Roy. Tears warmed her eyes. "I wish we'd all had a chance together." She pressed a tissue to her face. "We coulda had a time."

She let her eyes roam their etched names. "Thank you. I know you tried to help. I *know* you did. But my baby girl, she ..." The words trailed off in the frosty air, but she couldn't escape them in her mind. *She hates me.*

She imagined Mom's hand holding hers, until it slipped her fingers when her cell phone rang. Quickly tugging off a glove, embarrassed someone may have heard her phone's crass invasion of these hallowed grounds, she reached into her coat pocket and pulled out the offending device, its digital screech slicing the solitude.

"Hello, Lennie's Towing," she answered in a church-hush tone.

"Hello? Can you hear me?" The roar of background traffic battled a guy's voice in her ear.

She raised her voice to a whisper-yell. "Yes, hi. This is Lennie's Towing."

"Do you work the Kendall area?"

The name of the Miami suburb stopped her. Michelle lived out that way. "I do, but unfortunately, I'm out of town."

It took a full minute of his fighting off the din of passing vehicles on the other end of the call before he got her referral to Tropic Towing, run by an easygoing guy named Jeff she'd met at an accident scene.

It hadn't escaped her that they were both in the rescue business, dragging mangled messes to junkyards and fender-benders to repair shops for new leases on life. He'd even called her and asked if she'd like to get a cup of coffee or something. Although she wasn't ready for that yet, she had asked him to keep asking her.

She listened to the hush once again. What would life be like, now that Michelle was gone forever? Lennie's child had always been out there in the world, a distant flicker of light she might reach one day. A span of empty years stretched before her now. Where did she go from here?

She was distracted by what sounded like the lone bark of a distant dog. Or maybe it was a gravelly cough. As she heard it again, she realized it wasn't a dog, or coughing. It was sobbing. The kind that convulses the life out of you. Her heart went out to whoever was in that terrible place. She knew that place and wouldn't wish it on anyone. There was too much sorrow in the world.

She spied him through the shimmering veil of snow, halfway down the slope to the cemetery's access road. He was on his knees, shoulders heaving amid the skeleton trees.

Her heart hurt for him. She looked away. She'd learned from watching Dad that pain seemed to be a mostly private matter for men, best held close. Bowing her head, she closed her eyes and said a little prayer for loved ones gone and those they'd left behind.

She tried to keep her distance from the grieving guy as she made her way back to the wrecker, but the snowy slope forced her to brush closer to his shuddering form than she felt comfortable.

As she drew near, she caught a glimpse of the side of his face. A gray beard framed a wind-burned complexion. He must have heard her boots crunching through the snow as she approached, because his crying suddenly seized up and he seemed to hunker more tightly into himself.

Looking shaky, he grabbed the headstone and pulled himself to his feet. When she passed below him on the slope, time seemed to stand still as she met his eyes. Knew them instantly. They held a hardened wariness, even in this most vulnerable of human moments.

Mr. Mosely.

Her core stiffened. For the briefest instant, his sixty-some years had him wavering where he stood, clinging to the headstone. Snowflakes rimmed the letters that she could see spelled out Boone's name.

As he turned away, she stood stock still in the crystal flakes and fought off a nauseous flood of panic. All the years in her rearview. All the faces. Places. Heartbreak.

And, at the beginning of it all, Boone's smile astride his motorcycle in the dust of the hayfield by the old Sinclair station ... the whiskey's bite in her throat ... Mr. Mosely's bared teeth, cloaked by his lunch-crumbled beard as they sat on the rim of the limestone quarry.

The fire the Mosely men had set to her life seared every fiber. Craved a reckoning. A part of her suddenly leapt for joy that a power more commanding than even *them* had rendered judgment, had taken Mr. Mosely's first born. Just as he had taken hers.

Maybe their wickedness had branded her with a lust for vengeance—she wanted him back on his knees. Wanted to hear his sobs. His utter ruin.

Her lightly chattering teeth pulsated a white noise in her head as the sight of him cut through the desolation of the day. She couldn't take her eyes off the man whose viciousness had stalked her since she was a teen. *Does he know who I am?*

"I found her," she said to his back.

He turned around, eyes puffed up from crying, and held her gaze as confusion tightened his face. She squeezed her gloved hands into fists.

"You tore her from me. No doubt did your best to hide her adopted family, too. But you couldn't hide *her*." His mouth twitched as he considered her with an expression of quiet hostility.

"And I know what you did, cornerin' Dad into the adoption."

No denial. No response at all. Facing him in the snowfall, she realized how utterly broken he was. Not just because he had lost his son, but because he'd *always* been broken.

She relaxed her fists. And a bubble of understanding wobbled up from somewhere she never knew existed—Boone had sprung from feral roots, just as Mr. Mosely had, and Mr. Mosely's father had before him, and before him. All born of poisonous soil.

"I'm sorry," she said. His eyes were lifeless. "For your loss ... And for the roots that sprung you. Made you what you are."

Ignoring her, he shouldered his coat tighter against a surge of snowfall and turned his back on her. He touched Boone's headstone again.

Her lips tightened against her teeth. "You must be colder inside than even this place." She took a step up the rise, closer to him. "Been said that generations inherit the sins of their fathers. Check the Good Book you use against people. You heard that one?"

She didn't wait for an answer she knew would never come. "But I think generations also inherit the saving graces of their fathers. And mothers. I'm just glad I was blessed on the side of those. You and Boone weren't so lucky. That's what took 'im."

He began to walk away, toward a ruby-red Mercedes sedan that sparkled against the snowscape. She let her eyes linger on Boone's headstone before returning her gaze to his withdrawing father.

"I'll never forget!" she called after him. "Ever! ... But I *will* work like hell to *forgive*. Because I got a soul needs tendin'!" A great stillness answered her.

"You hear me! Forgive you and free myself!"

He kept trudging toward his car, his coat flapping in a gust as if to shake off her words.

The threat to her family, warning her not to breathe the truth to anyone about her baby, echoed in her head. *I'll personally see to it that you Rileys end up lower than an ant's ass. And you can take that to the bank.*

"You don't own me anymore! Take *that* to your bank!"

He ducked into the Mercedes and pulled away, and she watched the ruby car disappear and reappear on the rolling ground of desolate trees like a drop of toxic blood coursing through the pristine veins of the snowy cemetery.

Her heart was beating like a bird in flight as a brightening sky drove out some of the gray. After letting the muffled quiet wash over her for a solitary moment, she gathered fresh snow with both hands, flung it heavenward and watched it vanish.

FIFTY-SEVEN

Season of Hope

The snowbound country road on the way to John's reminded Lennie of driving to Seward, Alaska, a lifetime ago.

Shoehorned between glacial mountains and Resurrection Bay, the tiny waterfront town was where she'd had to pawn her cherished acoustic guitar that had helped her emotionally navigate her 'tween and teen years. She needed the money for a new set of tires for Louise as they started their lives in *The Last Frontier* state.

All these years later, as she returned to writing song-poems as a way to release her feelings and deal with the devastation of Michelle's rejection, she realized how much she missed that old guitar. Sure, it had been a little beat up, but it had earned every little chip and scuff and kept playing. Just the feel of it in her hands, her fingers pressing steel strings into chords, had always helped her through the toughest of times.

Maybe she'd never understand Mom and Dad's divine intervention to guide her to Michelle. As grateful as she was, there was one thing they couldn't do. *Make her love me.*

A jarring pothole diverted her from dwelling on that agonizing truth; although, thankfully, Ricky moaned less than Louise had on Seward's roads, especially that washboard route she'd taken to check out nearby Exit Glacier.

How the majesty of that icy mountain had withstood the test of time had inspired her. As she glanced at the GPS map on her dash-mounted phone, it struck her that she shared a curious kinship with that natural wonder—she didn't recognize it at the time, but when they had crossed paths, both she and the glacier had been receding. Melting away. And they still were. *Stop it, Eleanor Grace. Get your mind right.*

Squinting into the snow-glare night through wipers that batted away exploding flakes, she decided to do everything she could to prevent her heart from growing cold. Like accepting John's invitation to spend Christmas with his family. *Maybe the kids will even put out milk and cookies for Santa.* Life could simply be about the little moments now.

She slowed when her headlights reflected in the pinpoint eyes of a deer in the roadside thicket. It spun and darted back into the woods as a familiar Christmas tune on the radio caught her attention. She turned up *Have Yourself a Merry Little Christmas.*

Swallowing the lump in her throat, she elbowed her way past crying and nudged into the season to be jolly. *I'm gonna have myself a merry little Christmas if it kills me.*

She'd been dipping her toe into the Christmas carol pool over the past few weeks to get ready for this visit, even though it was a slippery slope to Sobville.

Still, she had made herself listen as she worked her road calls. To form a callous on her heart and fortify her emotional defenses—if there was one thing she absolutely did not want to do at John's, it was cry. Not in front of the kids at Christmas. Nevertheless, she knew her limits. The carols would be all she could handle—*Auld Lang Syne* would definitely be mothballed until next year. Maybe forever.

She had begun missing Louise the moment she'd perished in what she planned memorializing as The Great Tallulah Falls Fire. So, in Miami, after downloading the trip photos John had uploaded to the web, she'd found one she particularly liked and affixed it to the dashboard: A timer-shot he'd taken of the three of them at Raven Gorge. It had become a conversation piece with motorists who rode with her when she towed their vehicles.

The GPS flag icon that marked John's house peeked onto her phone screen. She was close. Set back forty yards from the road on both sides, grand homes with holiday lights twinkled through the trees like oases of joy. *Dang, Johnny. How big* are *the houses in your neck of the woods?*

She turned right off the road and idled along a forested drive that wound past a pair of small lakes, the lighted grounds a winter wonderland that played peekaboo between naked hardwoods and snow-frosted pine. Knowing Johnny, the summer grass would be as manicured as a golf course.

Braking to a squeaky stop at the top of the drive, she let her eyes take in the stately brick home. Fancy columns supported a soaring, domed portico over the entryway. The windows glowed like golden candles, and a life-sized Santa Claus waved as he rotated at the waist, next to wreath-hung double doors that had to be eight feet high.

As she stepped out of the cab, her turquoise-leather boho boots crunched into the snow, and she pulled on a calf-length coat she'd bought especially for the occasion from the melting pot of Miami thrift stores. It was vivid plum with embroidered flower appliqués and, her favorite part, ornamental shoulder epaulettes for a touch of fringed whimsy. She topped off the look with a smushed velvet hat Mary Poppins would've fought her for.

She grabbed a cheery Christmas gift bag, red and green tissue paper flowering out the top, and headed for the house. It reminded her of a gracious French country home she'd seen at one time or another on HGTV, and she practically expected a provincial prince to greet her.

But as she approached the residence, the welcoming party was even better—Stevie burst out, bear-hugging an acoustic guitar, a huge red ribbon wrapped around its curvy body.

"Look what Santa brought you, Aunt Balloony!" His eyes were as big as tree ornaments. "He delivered it here!"

It wasn't a Christmas carol that brought a tear to her eye. It was John's third-grader, delivering a relief valve for her heart. He handed her the guitar and hugged her waist.

"Don't ask me how he knew you were coming, but he did. Are you gonna play Christmas songs for us?"

Lennie dabbed at her eyes and gave Stevie a squeeze. "Only if you'll sing."

John buttoned a coat as he stepped out under the domed entryway. "Stevie, I think Santa meant that as a surprise for under the tree."

Stevie grabbed Lennie's hand and tugged her up the steps to the spacious portico. "I can't wait for you to be my aunt. They give presents all the time, right?" He pointed at the gift bag she held. "Is that for me?"

"Young man," John said with a parental frown, "that's not polite."

Abbey appeared in the doorway in a smocked green corduroy dress with candy cane embroidery on the collar. She could've been a proper little darling going to the theater for a viewing of *The Nutcracker*.

Lennie grinned. "Hey there, counsel. You look festive."

The little girl scrunched up her face and faintly shook her head as she scrutinized Lennie's look. "Yes. And I can help you with *this* holiday disaster as well." Her prissy finger pointed up and down Lennie's length.

Spreading her arms, Lennie turned a circle to give her the full view, guitar in one hand, gift bag in the other. "We can trade fashion tips."

John reached for the instrument. "Let me take that. Stevie kind of jumped the gun." Lennie could practically hear the favorite tunes she looked forward to playing again. "Thank you so much."

"I know your guitar had always been important to you, so when you had to sell it ... "

She let her eyes soak in the six-string. "It means more than you could know."

"What?" Stevie said, looking confused. "It isn't from Daddy. It's from Santa."

"But Daddy had to make the arrangements to help Santa get it here," Lennie said.

John wrapped his arms around her. "It's so great to see you." "You too."

Holly came out and hugged Lennie. "I'm so glad you could be with us. Waiting for you, John's been as much of a kid as the kids."

"Thank you for having me."

"Okay," John said with a sharp clap of his hands. "Who wants hot chocolate?"

"I do!" Stevie shouted.

Abbey shrugged. "I suppose that's appropriate on a cold winter's night."

Taking the guitar from John, Holly steered the kids back into the house. Lennie stood with her brother and watched the snow fall on the bulbous tow truck. Deceased Louise was strapped behind.

"Thanks for bringing her home," John said.

Lennie managed to chuckle. "You said you wanted to restore her, so I hope you're ready to get your hands dirty. She could use a little love."

"I'll get her running again. Mark my word."

"I have no doubt."

"How long can you stay?"

She rubbed the tip of her nose. "A few days."

"How was the trip up?"

Lennie sighed. "Long."

The visit to Mom and Dad's graves and the unexpected encounter with Mr. Mosely flashed through her mind. No point in going there now. This was a time meant for good cheer.

"But you know what?" she said. "It's behind me. I'm all about looking forward, starting right now." She offered him the gift bag. "For you."

John smiled. "You didn't have to."

"Oh, I had to all right. Most definitely." It took everything she had to hide her excitement.

He pulled out the crinkly tissue paper and peered inside. A puzzled expression washed his face as he removed an oversized, hardcover book wrapped in a dust jacket. The kind that adorn coffee tables. He stared at the title. *Chasing Echoes.*

Lennie had imagined this moment—giving him the gift that captured what Joella had said the two of them were doing by retracing their childhood. But she wasn't prepared for how lost he seemed. How unsure he was about what he was holding. He looked at her, uncertainty in his eyes.

"A little something for your coffee table," she said with a little chin nod.

"Lennie ..." His voice was barely audible in the hush as he ran his hand over the cover photo: his rich black-and-white shot of her mid-air as she leapt off the cliff at Tallulah Falls Gorge. A breathtaking moment frozen in time that would have made Ansel Adams proud.

Plum-colored words were centered under the book title: Poetry by Lennie Riley. Photography by John Riley. When he finally looked up from the book, his glistening eyes seemed to ask for an answer.

"*Whaaaat?*" she said with a playful smirk. "You think I had you send me copies of your pictures to stick in some scrapbook? That was *Dad's* thing. This is *your* thing." She poked him in the ribs. "Don't look now, but somebody's a photographer in a fancy coffee table book."

She set to fretting when he didn't say anything for the longest time. He just stared at it. Maybe the printing wasn't up to his standards? Then, a tear tracked his cheek. She had never seen him cry before.

He stammered, "This is ... You got published?"

"We. *We* got published." She offered a tentative grin. "A little book operation in Key West. Took us both a while, but there she is, in black and white ... Hope you like it."

"*Like* it?" He ran his fingers over their names. "I ... I don't know what to say."

She laughed. "Well, *there's* a first." He thumbed his tears away and then flipped through a few pages designed with her poetry and his trip photos. Lennie moved closer and looked with him.

In the rain with the car after their stormy court fight at the Choo Choo Motel. The *Welcome to Georgia* sign he snapped from the moving car.

John's lips pulled into a tight smile when he saw his photo of Hector pulling Louise from the gorge water. Then a shot of him and Lennie, ready to leave Hector's in the dead of night, their charred childhood strapped behind the wrecker.

She leaned against him and flipped to a dedication page. "I wrote something for the opening." When he stared at the words in silence, she gave him a little elbow. "Can you read it out loud? I've never heard it in any voice but mine."

He moved his mouth as if to try, but he couldn't seem to make it happen. She lent hers, reciting from memory. "These pages capture the spirit of a mighty trek across three states and as many generations—"

Her voice caught. *Damn it.* She had promised herself she'd get through this without crying. She took a quiet breath and soaked in the subdued wonder on his face as he slowly flipped through pages of poetry and photographs.

Her voice only quivered a little when she resumed speaking. "It is dedicated to our parents, Benjamin Roy and Roselyn Delia, who crafted one of those generations; my brother, Johnny, who chased the other; and my baby girl, Michelle, who inspired its telling."

A warmth washed through Lennie as her brother shook his head and tried to chuckle through the emotions that gripped his face.

"Thank you," he finally said. "It's amazing."

"You're welcome." She nodded and smiled. *At least one of our dreams came true.*

He held the book to his chest, hunched his shoulders, then let them fall as he gazed at the snowfall.

"This is ... I mean, I've been thinking about this for months now, trying to figure out how this Joella woman, and Mom and Dad ... the way we found the nurse and Michelle. Just ... all of it. It's ..." He seemed to run out of words.

"Lots to take in, yeah."

Wrinkles creased the corners of his eyes. "The things you say you saw."

"*Did* see."

"Okay ... *Experienced.* How that could all happen. I mean ... there's no—" His thought rode the vanishing vapor of his breath, and she saw him struggle for an answer to something that maybe would always remain a mystery.

"When you lose someone," she said, "the way you see things changes. You said it yourself. Whether it's a glimpse of someone who looks similar, or the sound of a voice."

"Yeah, I know, but I'm trying to figure out where the line is between seeing things and, you know ... *seeing* things."

"I don't know, Johnny. Maybe God opened ... a blind on something that was there, unseen before. Loved ones, when they're right there in your mind, in your heart, they may be gone, but they're still kinda here, y'know? We can hope, which, to my way of thinking, means leaving room for something bigger than ourselves to move in. A little of that magic. Make the unknowable a little more known. Or, at least ... felt."

Uncertainty etching his face, John tucked the book under his arm and pushed his hands into his coat pockets. "So, is ... Dad or Mom still looking out on things? Any of that ... *stuff,* going on now?"

She let her gaze wander to the snow-dusted truck and faintly shook her head. "No. It kinda ... it seems like I'm on my own now."

She couldn't stop the trickle of tears that moistened her cheeks. "I used to be able to dream Michelle could love me. At least I had that to hold on to. Now ... " She glanced at him, then looked away.

He pulled her into a hug as she closed her eyes against the hurt. "You'll always be family," he said in a voice as soft as it was reassuring.

Family. She knew the word as an explorer knew the tip of an iceberg—there was so much more to it than she would ever fathom. All she could do now was find a new place in life where she could be happy at some level. Where she could get to a point where she was at peace with never having known her child's love.

FIFTY-EIGHT

Questions Unanswered

Michelle wiped her damp forehead on her T-shirt sleeve and considered her bedroom closet, a space not much wider than her shoulders.

Cleaning it out was the last task on her agenda this Saturday, and she could almost taste completion. And okay, yes, she was the first to admit she got *way* too much enjoyment from completing a to-do list.

April had always been her time for spring cleaning, and it never ceased to amaze her how much stuff her three-bed, two-bath rambler could hold. Typical of 1950s tract houses, with its concrete block construction, terrazzo floors and glass block accents, it was what she and other locals called Old Florida style.

She'd come to think of the annual purging as life's very own shampoo-and-conditioner routine: it helped her wash out the family's unused, or outgrown, items which could benefit others through a charitable donation, and it gave her a chance to shore up her overall life-balance with an emotional line in the sand that separated what lay behind from what lay ahead.

She really needed such certainty now. Even though it had been eight months since her crippling past had shown up at her door last summer, it had taken that full stretch of time to put the encounter behind her, to move beyond the flesh-and-blood reminder of not being loved enough to be kept around.

She'd managed to mentally pack all that away in its own hardened emotional bunker because she was scared the sorrow from the first part of her life would somehow infect the happy life she'd worked so hard to build since then.

With a stack of boxes out in the garage ready to be hauled to the Goodwill truck at the mall, the closet was the only thing that stood between her and to-do-list victory.

Inserting her arms between a curtain of clothes, she spread the hangers apart to get a better view of the floor at the back wall. A mound of shoes that could definitely find feet elsewhere met her gaze, as well as her husband Tommy's knee-high snake boots.

She couldn't help but shake her head at the well-worn clodhoppers. As grungy as they looked, they were money-makers. Tommy had killed a twelve-foot Burmese python in the Everglades—the invasive snakes were causing all sorts of havoc for the native wildlife. He'd earned two hundred and fifty bucks from the state of Florida as a licensed "python removal agent." *More like a bounty hunter paid by the scaly foot.*

Looking up, she scanned the top shelf where Tommy kept a clear plastic storage container of ball caps he'd refused for years to thin out, no matter how old they'd become, all the while continuing to collect new ones.

That's it, Tommy boy. Time to move on. She decided to declare a one-in, one-out house rule: a hat comes in, a hat goes out. She'd just have to convince her pack-ratty husband there comes a time to let go.

On tippy toes, she reached up and grabbed the container's handle. As she tugged on it, the container angled down and launched a heart-shaped wicker box stacked on top toward her face. She raised her free hand to protect her head as she ducked, flinching as the bombarding box glanced off her arm.

"Jeez Louise," she gasped. Tommy had stubbornly declared his prized hat-locker a no-giveaway zone for so long, she'd forgotten she had stored her old keepsake box on top of it at the closet's highest point. She kept it up there both because she never really needed access to it, and the height was her best chance of protecting it from a potential hurricane storm surge without exposing it to the ungodly heat in the attic.

The impact dislodged the wicker top and hurled the contents to the floor. She gazed down at the memories lying at her feet—her first lock of baby hair, vacuum-sealed in a plastic sleeve among birthday and anniversary cards; her eighth-grade class picture; her wedding cake topper; and dried flowers from her bouquet.

Kneeling down to gather the contents for repacking, she couldn't resist peeling open a folded piece of notebook paper she could never forget—the first love note she'd ever received. Bernard Holt had secretly passed it to her in seventh grade.

She grinned. Sweet Bernard and his coke bottle glasses. A flood of wistfulness engulfed her—until a small manila envelope bound with a string tugged her emotions in a different direction.

She picked it up and read what she'd written on it long ago: *Only Open in Case of Emergency.* She groaned to herself. *Wasn't I clever?* The day she'd sealed the bundle of handwritten notes inside, her innermost thoughts penned on fancy monogrammed stationery her adoptive mother had given her for her thirteenth birthday, awakened in her mind.

She recalled inserting the notes in the envelope one by one on the night before her wedding eight years ago, the day she'd thought of as the beginning of a new life at seventeen, a fresh start with Tommy on a path they would travel together.

Crowned by a graceful "M" and bordered by her long-ago doodles, the pages formed a diary of her young teen years as her life had spun down into difficult depths. But, despite the anguish mothballed on the private pages she now squeezed with her hands, she'd held onto them for times she needed to remind herself of her inner strength, resilience and how far she'd come.

Together, she and Tommy had provided a good living for the kids, Hannah and little brother Josh. The family wasn't rich by any means, but they had each other and enough to go 'round. What more was there?

She enjoyed her work at their Dancing Dolphin Pool Service, building relationships with customers, keeping the books and coordinating service calls to keep Tommy busy in the field. Life was simple, and simple was good—a far cry from her arduous journey to 5683 Suncoast Estates Boulevard.

Still, lingering grief clawed its way into the ordinariness of this moment as she considered the envelope and what it contained.

It had been her therapist's suggestion that she write down her teenage feelings of being abandoned as a child. The words hadn't alleviated her pain, but they had somehow captured her struggle to understand why her mother couldn't love her enough to want her.

The woman who had intruded into her life barged once more into her mind—the sadness in her nervous eyes as she'd fumbled for words. Her tears. The way she'd pleaded, clutching Michelle's birth certificate pressed with her baby footprints in one hand and her sundress with the other. There the outsider had stood, the source of all the heartache Michelle had navigated to become the strong, loving young woman others often described her as.

Angling her face toward the ceiling's air conditioning vent to take a moment in the welcome coolness, she wanted to get her chore wrapped up by the time Tommy and Josh got home from pee wee T-ball. But the lure of the envelope held her; it had been eight years since the notes in that paper-thin fortress had seen the light of day.

You've moved past all of that. Past her. Running her fingertip along the envelope's edge, she pulled on the string until the knotted bow around her neatly packaged past released.

"No," she whispered to herself. *That was then.* It was time to move on, once and for all. But she couldn't simply toss into the trash the burden of being left behind on the day she was born. No, she needed to free herself from the scars it had left carved on her heart.

Taking the envelope to the backyard, she lifted the cover off the propane fire pit her family enjoyed gathering around with friends during the cooler winter months.

She pushed past her quickening pulse that seemed to fuel the sweat in her palms, convincing herself it was just the midday heat.

Opening the access panel to the enclosed tank, she twisted the squeaky valve to the open position and clicked the igniter switch. Flames knifed up through the lava rocks.

She stood back for a moment and took a quick breath before gazing at the envelope, absorbing for one last time what it represented: crushing heartache. Not only for having been left behind, but for the fruitless searches for her mother that had always dead-ended. She'd gotten to the point where she could no longer even watch the videos of mothers and their children joyously reunited through social media.

She inserted the corner of the envelope into one of the dancing flames and—

"Mommy?"

Startled, Michelle jerked the burning envelope from the fire, flapping it like a matador's cape to extinguish the flame licking up the corner before spinning back to her daughter.

Hannah wore a puzzled look and the neon green soccer uniform she insisted on dressing in all the time, even if there wasn't a game.

Heart clobbering her breastbone, Michelle took a gulp of air as she caught sight of the item her eight-year-old hugged to her body—the sturdy coffee-table book titled *Chasing Echoes* that had arrived last Christmas.

"Whaddaya think you're doing?" Hannah said with an edge of "Mom" attitude that Michelle recognized as the same she used with her and Josh when they weren't making good decisions with their behavior. "You don't have the water bucket."

Michelle couldn't decide whether to scold her third-grader for her smart-alecky tone or praise her for noticing the absence of the bucket of safety water they always had on hand at the fire pit, just in case.

"I'm just ... getting rid of some old papers."

"Why?"

"Well ..." Michelle wiped a stinging drop of sweat from her eye as she fumbled for an explanation Hannah would understand.

"Um ... you know how you outgrew your soccer uniform last summer?"

"Uh-huh."

"It's like that," she said, lifting the envelope. "Mommy outgrew these papers."

Michelle watched her daughter take a perplexed moment, tapping her finger on the book as she puckered her lips. Finally, she stopped tapping.

"How do you outgrow paper if you don't wear it?"

Michelle forced a grin. "You don't have to wear something to outgrow it, sweetie."

Realizing the fire-pit flames behind her were baking her backside, she turned to it with as much calm as she could muster and twisted the propane dial to the off position. The flames disappeared. She wished this moment would, too.

"The lady who came to our door," Hannah said from behind her. "She left in the big truck, crying. I remember. Last summer when I got my uniform." She pointed to the book's cover. "That's her. She's jumping."

Michelle ran her fingers through her hair and gave a weak nod. Of all the discarded items her little girl could have picked up, she had to choose *that* one?

She closed her eyes, wishing she could find in the filtered sunlight that penetrated her eyelids answers to the inevitable tangle of questions she wasn't ready to face.

A trickle of sweat worked its way along her scalp, opening her eyes to the glare of reality, and she realized she had the envelope pinched between her thumb and finger next to her leg, wrist-flicking it forward and back.

It was time to call on the courage she'd built up surviving the chronicled journey clenched in her hand. She set the singed envelope on a patio chair and looked at her daughter.

"Your name is in it," Hannah said.

What? Michelle had never even opened the book. The gift-wrapped box it had come in was adorned with a lovely handmade bow and had been left on her doorstep last Christmas Eve day. She'd assumed it was from Caitlin and Eric, the parents of a girl on Hannah's soccer team with whom she and Tommy had become friends.

At that time, she had opened the parcel and caught a glimpse, through festive tissue paper, of a black-and-white photo on the cover of a hefty book. She'd been instantly drawn to the shot of a woman leaping from a height amid a gorgeous forest and a waterfall.

At first glance, she thought it was Caitlin, an outdoorsy sort into bungie-jumping. And then she recognized the gutsy jumper on the cover. Her biological mom, the woman who had triggered the emotional pain of her past by crashing into her life the previous summer.

It was then she noticed an object buried beneath the book, between the sheets of tissue paper. A carved wooden heart. The name Lennie wood-burned into it. And, secured to it by a simple cloth ribbon was a business card for Lennie's Towing, Miami, FL, along with, oddly enough, a hand-written recipe for sweet iced tea with mint and a note that read: *This was your grandmother's. I'd love to make you a batch sometime.*

The sight of the recipe and the casual invite triggered an instant surge of anger. It was like the sender had assumed the last twenty-five years could be swept away with a homespun gesture of goodwill. Seriously? And she'd even used a family recipe to try to bridge the chasm between them. How dare she!

Michelle had immediately re-boxed everything, as if its mere presence in the house would somehow contaminate her life. She stashed it in a container for donations she'd begun to collect in the garage. And there the banned box had remained, awaiting an unknown destiny, just like all the other things in her life she was getting rid of.

Now, in the rising heat, the glare seemed to intensify in her squinting eyes. She thought she was going to pass out and gripped the back of a lawn chair for support.

The sound of Hannah's voice rescued her with intermittent words that whizzed through her awareness. "These pages ... a mighty trek ... my baby girl, Michelle ... "

Michelle wiped her hand across her forehead, as much to buy a few seconds to gather her thoughts as to mop the sweat away.

Then her gaze found Hannah's inquisitive eyes as she closed the book and extended it to her.

"You're getting rid of this?"

It took her a second to absorb the question. "Yes."

"Why?"

Michelle pulled the lawn chair she was leaning on into the shade of the patio and sat down to collect herself. "I just ... don't think I need it."

"Is that you she's talking about? Her baby girl?"

Michelle lifted her hands, then let them wearily drop to her legs, surrendering to a past whose expanding fault lines now threatened to swallow her present.

"Who is she?" Hannah said.

Deep down, she always knew this moment would come—a time when the children would be curious about Mom and Dad's past. Where were they born? Where had they lived when they were little? What did they do as kids?

It wasn't that she didn't want to share the details of her life with Hannah and Josh, she just thought she'd be able to have the conversation on her own terms, in her own time.

Hannah tilted her head, as if trying to get a better angle on a mystery. "She wasn't crying at first. Then she was, after she talked to you. Did you make her cry?"

Michelle had never lied to her children. Yes, she'd told them small necessary fibs to protect them from things they weren't quite ready to grasp. But this innocent question, seeking merely to understand, found its way to the very blood coursing through her, just as it spoke to the heart of who her children were.

She reached out and stroked Hannah's hair. "Yes."

Who is she? Hannah's question rapidly circled back through her mind, and it hit Michelle that she knew who the woman had been, but didn't really know who she *was.*

"Why'd you make her cry?" Hannah said.

"Because I was afraid, honey."

Her daughter glanced away, then seemed to search the crinkly grass before returning her gaze to Michelle. "You were scared?"

"Yes ... but not of her."

"*What* then?"

"Sweetie, I was scared to tell you and Joshie."

"Tell us what?"

"Well ... " Michelle offered what she hoped was a reassuring smile. "That she's your Nana."

Hannah blinked for a moment, emotions wrestling in her baffled expression, and Michelle could tell she was mentally connecting the dots of what that meant.

"I didn't know what you kids would think of it."

Her little girl pressed her finger into the center of her chin and traced its curve down her throat to the collar of her soccer shirt.

"But Joshie and I already have two Nanas. Are we allowed to have *three?*"

Michelle couldn't help but grin. *God, I love her.* "Yes."

"Hmm ... " After pondering that for a few heartbeats, Hannah brightened. "Neat!"

Neat. The problem was, Michelle knew life could be anything *but* neat. She soaked up Hannah's wondrous expression before pulling her into a hug. "I love you."

"I love you too, Mommy."

Michelle closed her eyes and they held tight, until Hannah's voice whispered in her ear, "You're sweaty gross."

She turned Hannah loose, grinned and touched her daughter's cheek. "Let's go inside."

"What about your papers?"

Michelle looked at the envelope she'd set on the chair. "Maybe a big ol' rain will wash 'em away."

"You're sweaty gross *and* weird."

Picking up the blackened envelope, Michelle led her daughter into the house. She knew there would be more questions. A lot more.

A realization she couldn't subdue swept her into a riptide of worry—she wasn't sure she could revisit face-to-face the emotional devastation she'd thought she'd left behind, which she knew she must if she were ever to allow this Lennie woman to be anything more than a mystery to her children.

FIFTY-NINE

Nothing Left Unsaid

"T.G.I.T!" Michelle shouted as Hannah trotted off a soccer field at Poinciana Park. They exchanged a high-five and shouted in unison, "Thank goodness it's Thursday!" Their family catchphrase.

The dusky weekday evening was their mother-daughter soccer night, a time when Hannah played with her friends on a community league team while Michelle shot game-video of Hannah as a way to help her improve her skills, and Tommy spent quality father-son time with Josh, who participated on a pee wee T-ball team on the next field over.

Hannah had notched a goal in her team's 4-3 win, and it was time to celebrate with a treat. The community park's concession stand wasn't all that much to talk about. In fact, it seemed a better hurricane bunker than a refreshment facility.

Built of concrete, it was about the size of a pint-sized school bus, with thick wooden awnings that raised and lowered on squeaky hinges to reveal a lumber counter bolted into the cement structure. At least the painted mural of cherry-red Royal Poinci-ana blossoms that wrapped around it gave it a zing of personality.

But what really made the stand endearing were the friendly volunteer hosts who turned out to serve the kids and their fami-lies. The distant referee whistles and shouts of kids were so familiar to Michelle, she barely noticed them as she stepped with Hannah to the counter.

Noticing the three servers were all busy taking orders, Michelle anticipated waiting, but a woman emerged from what appeared to be a supply closet behind the main serving area.

As she approached them, she slipped on the neck strap of a bib apron. She obviously took her hosting duties humorously: a neon-pink flamingo with a goofy smile, gawky wings, and gangly pencil-thin legs ran the apron's length.

"I love your apron," Michelle said with a chortle.

"Me too!" Hannah chimed in. "You're like a flamingo lady!"

Flamingo Lady looked down her torso. "It's quite something, isn't it?" She secured it with the back strap and tucked a last lock of chestnut hair into one of those elastic food-worker hairnets. "I'm new here and thought this would help me fit in."

Michelle wasn't good at estimating ages, but she pegged the woman to be in her forties, maybe fifty, although she immedi-ately second-guessed herself; those gross honeycomb hair-snares could make even Emma Watson look like a frumpy old church lady.

Flamingo Lady flashed a grin. "What can I getcha? Take it easy on me. Nothing too fancy."

Michelle smiled and scanned the options on the back wall's letter-board menus, then gazed down at Hannah. "Honey, what are you gonna have?"

"Um ... a cherry sno-cone," she said to the server.

Michelle frowned. "A cherry sno-cone, *what*?"

"Please."

The woman gave Hannah an approving nod. "A great choice for a young lady with top-notch manners." She gazed at Michelle with a look that seemed a show of parental support. "Is Mom a sno-coner too?"

Michelle grimaced and shimmied her shoulders. "Ugh, no way. The ice gives me one of those ice cream headaches that hurts my molars."

Flamingo Lady nervously smoothed her apron. "Gracious, I don't wanna harm anyone's teeth."

"Just something cold to drink would be great." She gazed at the menu, but before she could decide, Flamingo Lady beat her to the punch.

"I've got just the thing." She turned back to the prep counter and got to work.

"You didn't order, Mommy."

"Well, we'll see what she comes up with. Surprises can be fun, right?" The woman had sure seemed fired up about her idea, so why not take a chance?

Flamingo Lady was back in less than a minute with a glistening, cherry-red sno-cone in one hand and an icy drink in a clear plastic cup in the other.

Handing them over, she clasped her hands in front of her with the air of a nervous hostess who had just served homemade refreshments to special guests.

Michelle grinned at the drink in her hand. "Iced tea? You read my mind."

"Let me know what you think." Flamingo Lady's eyes widened slightly as she watched her.

As Michelle took a sip, a cold bead of condensation from the cup trickled down the inside of her arm. She loved iced tea on a hot day, and it was super tasty. Then again, old bathwater this cold would've tasted good in the dank humidity.

Hannah crunched into her sno-cone, slurping the syrupy ice crystals. "Mmm. Awesome!" She dashed off toward a group of girls Michelle recognized from the team.

"Don't go far," Michelle called after her before taking another sip.

Flamingo Lady raised her eyebrows. "Well?"

Michelle felt a peculiar sensation well up as the refreshing taste of mint beckoned an unsettling memory. The fragrant ingredient was one she'd never thought of adding to her home brew before: having grown up drinking iced tea all her life in Florida's subtropical heat, she'd never tasted it in the drink, not even in a fancy restaurant like Olive Garden.

In fact, the notion of mint in her favorite drink had just recently made its appearance: it was part of the handwritten iced tea recipe her presumptuous biological mother had inserted as a sort of bookmark in the Christmas gift she'd sent.

Never in all the years she'd been drinking iced tea had mint ever entered the picture and—*Wait a minute* ... Come to think of it, she'd had this beverage plenty of times before at this very concession stand and couldn't recall it ever having had the note of mint in it.

"It's delicious," she said. "Mint, huh?"

"Yes."

"I'm a tea geek, but I've never tried adding mint."

"The key is fresh leaves."

She distracted herself from what surely was just a coincidence with a glance at Hannah and her friends, over behind some bleachers. She returned her gaze to Flamingo Lady, who seemed to enjoy watching the girls nudge a soccer ball around a circle as they chatted.

"How old's your little one?"

"Eight, going on thirty."

The faint smile that creased Flamingo Lady's cheeks revealed a petite cleft in her chin. "She's a beautiful child. Full of life and promise."

Michelle sensed the woman had been a young mom like her.

"Thanks. We think she's pretty special."

Michelle noticed a certain look of emptiness cross the woman's face, like a cloud that raced across open water—a look she knew deep down. One she'd seen in herself. It was a memory she'd always carried with her: the yearning in her reflection as she'd stood numbly brushing her teeth the day she learned at seven that her "real" mother had given her up.

Flamingo Lady shooed a moth away from Michelle's cup and watched Hannah laugh with her classmates.

"Treasure these times." Her words were barely above a whisper, as if she hadn't intended to speak them aloud.

Michelle couldn't deny feeling somehow connected to this woman who, just a few breaths ago, was a stranger serving snacks in a funny flamingo apron. She fully intended to pay and leave, but before her hand could dig money out of her shorts pocket, her voice snatched her innermost thoughts.

"Did you lose a child?" Even in the muggy heat, Michelle instantly felt her face grow warm with embarrassment at such a deeply personal question of someone she didn't even know. "Oh my God, I'm... I'm sorry. I—"

"No-no-no." Flamingo Lady gave her a gentle smile. "It's okay."

Michelle grimaced. "It's just that ... I've been going through some family ... some mother-daughter things. But, I'm sorry, I... I had no right to ask you that."

She followed Flamingo Lady's gaze and watched Hannah try her best to braid a friend's hair while the park bustled around them. She noticed a bittersweet grin on the woman's face.

"I did lose a daughter," the woman hostess said. "Younger than yours even."

"I'm so sorry."

Flamingo Lady's eyes found Michelle's. Their depths held a weariness she had seen in own mirror reflections as a girl. The hostess appeared to take a moment to think as she straightened her apron.

"If there's ever anything you want to say to her? Something you may leave unsaid because you think there'll always be time? Promise yourself you won't miss the chance."

Michelle searched the woman's face, noticing for the first time the elegant cheekbones and then the color of her eyes—hazy green irises sprinkled with gold flecks.

Instantly recognizing Hannah's belly-laugh, Michelle looked over to see her daughter toss her hair over her shoulder, as if throwing off every care in the world. Hannah caught her gaze and waved with a playful little smile. Michelle waved back and smiled, taken by the preciousness of the moment.

When she turned back to Flamingo Lady, she was gone. Michelle worried maybe she'd upset the woman with her inconsiderate question. Feeling increasingly awful as the possibility sank in, she just wanted to go home.

"Excuse me," she said to a barrel-chested guy in suspenders as she dug into her pocket for some money. The retiree ambled down to where she stood.

"What can I do yous for?" His accent was pure Brooklyn—Michelle recognized it from the boatloads of transplanted New Yorkers on her client roster, only his was amped a couple notches, like he was auditioning for a mobster-movie wiseguy.

"I need to pay for this iced tea and a sno-cone."

"Bada-boom. Chree Georgies."

She'd picked up a little Brooklynglish at the office, so she handed him three dollars. "When did you start adding mint to the tea?"

"Addin' who?"

"Mint." She lifted her cup. "I get this here all the time and all it ever has is, like, a lemon flavoring. This has mint in it."

Mr. Wiseguy cocked his head and shouted down the counter. "Yo, Shirl! When'd da'mint show up in the tea?"

"No mint!" the woman called back, busy taking orders from a team of pint-sized kids in baseball uniforms. "Just plain ol' tea. With lemon flavoring. From a jug."

He shrugged. "Da boss says it's mintless. Whaddaya gonna do?"

"But it has mint in it. Plain as day."

The way he indicated with four cupped fingers she should turn over her drink, he could've been a retired NYPD cop directing traffic. "Lemme taste." He winked and staccato-clacked his loosey-goosey dentures in rhythm with imitating shaking dice.

OMG. Really dude? She was parched, but her thirst was drowned by her need to prove to herself she wasn't just imagining the taste of mint because of some sorta subconscious or subliminal, or whatever it was called, coincidental brush with the idea. She handed him the cup.

Taking a gulp, he swished it around like mouthwash then swallowed.

"Get outta heeuh!" He shot a sideways look at Shirl. "Breakin' news! We got mint tea!"

"There's no mint tea!" she hollered back.

"I got it from the woman in the flamingo apron," Michelle said.

"Flamingo apron?" He gave her a confused look before gesturing over his shoulder to the concession team. "We're the only ones here. Shirl, Flo and Rita. No flamingo ladies."

"Well then, who served me the mint tea?"

He lifted his hands, palms up. "What am I, a magician? I can't pull an answer outta my hat. I'm tellin' ya what I'm tellin' ya."

"Michelle!" her husband called out before she turned and saw Tommy, Hannah, and Josh behind the bleachers. "You ready to go?" Michelle mustered a grin for Mr. Wiseguy before joining her family.

She couldn't shake a disorienting feeling. She'd been served a cup of mint tea the concession stand apparently didn't have on the menu, a recipe Lennie had coincidentally introduced into her life out of the blue, by a woman with whom she'd had a deeply intimate conversation, but who apparently didn't work there.

On the drive home, she kept her ricocheting thoughts to herself, becoming consumed by the realization that Hannah's scavenger hunt for explanations about their "new Nana" had become more like quicksand pulling her deeper into the unexplainable.

In the last few weeks, her daughter had made a spunky attempt to read "Nana's poetry," and looked and re-looked at the pictures of her and "the other man."

Michelle had done her best to answer Hannah's questions. But she'd grown increasingly troubled, admitting to herself that her explanations were merely shots in the dark.

The truth was, she didn't know anything about her biological mother, and it kept her awake at night, pondering an expanding web of questions for which she had no answers.

There were only guesses and maybes, until her drifting thoughts fused into an image her mind could grasp and that seemed to make sense: the Jenga tower game she and Tommy loved to play with the kids, pulling out block pieces one by one as the tower teetered, and holding their breath, waiting to see if the delicately balanced structure would remain standing or collapse in a heap.

For Michelle, only one cornerstone block loomed large. Lennie. Her mother, the grandmother to her children, had come seeking forgiveness at her door. She wasn't certain she could bear to open it and let her into their lives.

SIXTY

The Always

Cotton candy-colored skies welcomed Lennie home as she wheeled the tow truck into her driveway after a twelve-hour day rescuing motorists from Miami to Key Biscayne, their vehicles in various states of wreckage.

No one had died, so it was a good day—knowing there'd been a fatality at a scene she worked always put her in a funk.

Maybe she'd give Hector a call. She figured he'd be proud to know his trusty ex-wrecker was still hanging in there, nearly a year after she and John had used it to haul their dreams off the mountain.

Lennie was doing her best to hold her own as well. She'd been renting an adorable little 1940s bungalow on a quiet brick street since her disaster at Michelle's. Actually, the brick was more akin to a washboard road because the roots of towering Gumbo Limbo trees that bordered the street had worked their way under the bricks, dislodging them from below.

Hopping out of the cab, she thought about how the topsy-turvy street was about to become some new renter's worry. She'd decided not to renew her lease and was in the middle of packing to leave town.

As she neared the front porch, her boots crunched through grass made crisp from a lingering drought. She keyed into the door and grabbed mail from a wicker basket she kept under a drop-in letter slot—the old-timey feature was one of her favorite things about the house, and she'd used its antique brass cover as an inspiration piece, decorating with a menagerie of post-war, thrift-store furniture.

But that was then. Now, she'd be leaving it all behind to start her new life on the South Carolina coast, including a dancing mobile of vintage hats that adorned the front room.

The house's owner, a sassy elderly lady who'd taken a shine to Lennie, loved what she'd done with the vintage charmer, and she had even asked Lennie halfway through her lease if she might like to buy the property.

Lennie thanked her kindly, but begged off. She didn't want to get locked into anything. She had never owned a home, and getting saddled with one now could be ruinous—things hadn't worked out the way she'd counted on when she chose last summer to stay in Miami.

She had hoped sticking around to be close to Michelle, just in case she had a change of heart, would help ease her heartache. But such wishful thinking put her so close, yet so far, and it simply deepened her grief. Looking back, she saw putting down roots here was nothing more than a temporary bandage on an emotional scar she now understood would never heal. Best to cut clean from Michelle, just as her daughter had plainly been able to do from her.

It was time to start over again, in a place whose history didn't include her. And how could she not be attracted to a town across the historic harbor from Charleston, Mount Pleasant, on the South Carolina coast?

The owner offered to buy Lennie's household possessions if she didn't want to haul everything with her, and Lennie figured she could use the extra cash, so casting off everything she'd done to make the house her home made sense.

She plunked down on a weathered steamer trunk, tugged off her work boots and pondered a scattering of boxes containing things she was taking with her. Pausing a moment to massage her troublesome foot, Lennie let her gaze come to rest on framed photos of Mom and Dad.

She'd taken Mom's picture from his bedroom wall when she had passed through Mosely on her way to visit John last Christmas. The wish she'd once held in the wake of their mysterious intervention had faded away, and she'd come to simply try to console herself with the memory.

Groaning as she hauled herself off the chest, she ordered a pizza and filled the delivery time taking a shower and then throwing in a load of laundry.

Now near seven o'clock, it had been an hour since her pizza call, and her stomach rumbled as she glanced up at the kitchen's cuckoo clock she'd brought back from Dad's workshop. Her pizza should be here any minute. Five a.m. seemed to come earlier every morning, and she needed to eat and hit the hay.

Slumber hadn't come easy lately. She wasn't sure why, but maybe it was the upcoming year anniversary of her crash and burn at Michelle's.

She felt a crestfallen grin tug her face as she watched the lulling motion of the clock's pendulum. Dad had been known for his grandfather clocks but, to Lennie, his adorable cuckoos represented a more innocent time than the stately grandfathers, a wondrous stretch where childhood dreams might still come true.

She opened the cuckoo's spring-loaded door and considered the tiny hand-carved bird sitting there, staring out, biding its time.

A knock at the porch door. Finally! Pizza. She could practically taste the mega-veggie supreme, and she looked forward to a quick visit with her delivery driver, Roberto, a Haitian immigrant working on his American Dream. He always seemed gleeful and had a way of lifting her spirits.

Her bare feet thudded across the wood floor as she scooted to the front door with her Halloween candy corn purse.

She couldn't keep from smiling as she opened the door with an expectant, "Hey, there!" Her face tightened with a sharp breath as she clamped down on the doorknob.

Michelle. Lennie's mind raced to absorb a fragile panic in her eyes, her little girl looking up from her hip.

"I'm ... sorry," Lennie stammered. "I thought ... you were someone else." Her heart ran wild, and she grabbed for the first lifeline she could think of: the girl's name. Hannah.

Unable to corral her lurching thoughts, Lennie waited for Michelle to say something in a tortuous silence as she clenched a charred manila envelope to her chest.

There was a fire?

"Do you have a minute?" Michelle said, her voice wavering.

Pulse pounding her temples, Lennie ran her finger under her nose and, with as much cool as she could muster, slipped her purse strap over her shoulder to free her hands.

"Of course." She barely heard her response, it was so wobbly. *Did she hear me?*

She cleared her throat. "Yes. I have ... unlimited minutes." She glanced in quick succession between Michelle and Hannah. "Would you, um ... like to come in?"

Michelle didn't move a muscle until she stretched her fingers out on the crinkling envelope. "We'd like to ask you some questions."

Lennie rummaged for words to string together in response as she searched the eyes of a daughter she had never known but had unceasingly loved. She could only rally a couple syllables: "Okay."

She needed to catch her breath. To snag her thoughts from the emotional locomotive thundering through her head, as her innermost hopes for a last-gasp homecoming collided with her worst fears: a repeat of her derailment at Michelle's door.

Just breathe.

"Hannah's worried about you because I made you cry."

Lennie was so absorbed taking in every detail of Michelle's face—the way her lips moved, the contour of her chin, the dimples in her cheeks that peeked out when she made the sound of the letter b—she barely registered what Michelle had said.

Lennie pounced on the word Hannah, clinging to that kernel of conversation as she allowed her attention to stray from Michelle to her child's imploring grape-green eyes.

"Are you okay, Nana?"

Nana. The bolt that shot through Lennie found release in her hand as she turned the doorknob a smidge to unleash the quiver in her chest.

Don't cry.

She glanced at Michelle and silently begged for a clue as to how she felt about Hannah's use of such an endearing family name, but her expression was a steel plate.

Hannah's eyebrows pinched at the bridge of her nose as Lennie slowly drew and released a breath she hoped conveyed calm.

"Yes ... I'm okay."

She shifted her gaze to Michelle. "And ... I'm so sorry. About the last time, I ... Showing up like that. I could've handled things better."

"Yes."

Hannah tilted her head like a junior detective seeking clues to a mystery. "Who's the man with you?"

It was only then Lennie realized the young girl held the *Chasing Echoes* book she'd sent to Michelle. She involuntarily pressed her hands to her chest. "That's my brother ... Johnny. Well, John. But his name was Johnny when he was a kid, and I still—"

Stop.

Hannah threw her the life preserver of a smile. "I like the poem about the waterfall best, and the picture of you jumping. Were you scared?"

Lennie eyed Michelle. Hannah seemed intent on having a chat. *How does she feel about Hannah buddying up to me?* Michelle gave her a barely perceptible nod.

"Thank you, Hannah," Lennie said with a hesitant smile. "That's very sweet of you. I was very scared."

Michelle stepped toward Lennie, moving uninvited inside the house, and Hannah followed like a baby duckling.

"I wrote you letters," Michelle said with the tone of a witness making a direct statement of fact to the accused. She clutched the envelope tighter, then extended it to Lennie.

"You need to read them."

Lennie took it with both hands, her thumbs tracing tiny circles on the singed packet. She could nearly hear the words through the paper. Feel their sting. Their anguish.

A blade of dread sliced through her as she raised her eyes to meet Michelle's, the warmth of tears slightly blurring her vision.

She gazed backed down at the envelope, and a tear escaped her cheek, blotting the paper with a tiny smudge that expanded as she cradled it to her body.

Michelle didn't seem to know what to do with her empty hands. She averted her eyes and jammed them in the pockets of her shorts. Her eyes glistened, tears clinging to her bottom eyelashes. "I told myself I wouldn't cry."

Lennie sniffled. "Me too."

"You need to know who I am. Not just now ... but back then. The always."

Lennie slowly nodded. She opened and closed her mouth twice before she finally found the words. "I want it to be the same for you ... with me."

Michelle blinked, and tears scurried down her cheeks. She immediately wiped them away. Then, something caught her attention behind Lennie, reshaping her grief-stricken expression into the exhausted uncertainty of an ocean shipwreck survivor who had just spied an island from her drifting lifeboat.

Lennie followed Michelle's line of focus, and her gaze came to rest on the foyer's jumble of moving boxes. Michelle seemed riveted. Slipping past Lennie, she slowly approached the cartons and picked up Mom's portrait.

Lennie felt frozen to the floor as she nibbled her bottom lip and watched her daughter, captivated by her most precious memory of Mom.

The image of Michelle's tiny hand reaching from her clinic crib flickered her thoughts, and her throat tightened, the salty hint of a tear in the corner of her mouth. She mustered a smile she hoped would reassure Hannah as she waited for Michelle to say something.

The corners of Michelle's eyes pinched, as if she were trying to wrap her mind around a notion just beyond her grasp. Finally, she turned slightly to look at Lennie.

"Does she volunteer at the park." Her question was more of a statement.

"I'm sorry?"

"Poinciana Park. Does she volunteer at the concession stand?"

Lennie finally stepped to Michelle and considered the photo, as if the right answer were locked inside. "No, um ... No?" She could hear the rising confusion in her voice. "She's passed."

A streak of pain crossed Michelle's face. "I'm sorry." She resumed pondering Mom's photo, and Lennie could practically see her gears turning.

"The mint," Michelle said. "The tea recipe in the book. I don't understand why ... "

Lennie shifted her weight and hugged the burnt envelope tighter. "I ... I just thought it would be nice for you to have a little something from her ... your grandmother. The iced tea was hers. I still make it. It kinda ... I don't know, helps me stay close to her in a way."

Michelle faced her and nodded as if she understood a deeper truth. "A woman who could've been, like, her twin at the park."

"You're right, Mommy," Hannah piped up, next to her. "She does look like the flamingo lady."

"She served me some mint tea," Michelle said. "Out of the blue. I mean, they don't serve mint tea, and I'd never had it before. Ever. She might've been a little older than in this photo, but ... the same eyes. The cheekbones. Smile. We talked a bit. About our daughters ... "

Michelle sniffled and wiped her glistening cheeks. "She told me she'd lost hers." Lennie's heartbeats tumbled one over the other as she held fast to Michelle's every word.

"She didn't say how, but ... she told me to promise myself I'd never leave things unsaid with Hannah. To never miss the chance, thinking there'll always be time later."

Michelle cupped Hannah's shoulder and pulled the child to her hip. "That's why we're here. I wanted her to know about you."

When Hannah reached for the hem of Lennie's shorts and pulled her closer, Lennie felt her bare shoulder press against Michelle's, her entire world collapsing into the soft touch, the warmth of her child's skin for the first time.

A shiver ran down the backs of her legs as she tightened her grip on Michelle's envelope and allowed her eyes to close in silent thanksgiving.

Mom.

It was all she could do to keep from falling to her knees as she felt the pressure of Michelle's shoulder increase ever so slightly against hers and—

"Megah-veggie soopreeeeem?"

Lennie turned back toward the lilting Haitian voice that came from the door. Teary Michelle and curious Hannah looked with her at Roberto, who stood awkwardly with a colossal pizza box.

An uncomfortable smile creased his face. "Oh, my. I'll juss ... leave dis heeah," he said as he backed up. "We can settle laytah, Lennie." He set the pizza down inside the door, and Lennie mouthed the words, "thank you."

As the sound of his footsteps scurried away, Lennie sank into the quiet as she searched Michelle's eyes, her churning mind seeking something to say in this boundless moment she couldn't believe was happening and didn't want to end.

She took refuge in a simple politeness from her childhood. "Are y'all hungry?"

"I love pizza!" Hannah proclaimed with a pleading grin, hands clasped angelically under her chin.

Waiting, hoping, for Michelle's answer to her invitation for what seemed an eternity, Lennie noticed for the first time specks of gold in her hazel eyes and how the wisp of a tentative smile favored her cheekbones.

"Um ... y'know? Yes," Michelle said. "I'm kind of hungry."

Lennie glanced into the kitchen she knew was a disaster area, hoping they didn't notice the grimace dash across her face. "Mint tea okay?"

"For sure," Hannah said immediately, her tone indicating it was beyond question. "That's Mom's favorite now."

Lennie smiled and tried like all get out to keep her hands from shaking as she picked up the pizza box. "I'm sorry the place is a bit of a mess. I was trying to, I guess you'd say, get my life together."

"That sounds familiar," Hannah said, nodding sideways at Michelle. "Neat freak Nellie."

"Hey, I'm the only reason anybody can find anything in that house."

Enjoying their quibble, Lennie gestured them to her little kitchen table snugged against the wall under the cuckoo clock. She hoped it would spark Hannah's curiosity so she could tell her all about how her great-grandfather had made it.

As if on cue, the heirloom clock struck seven, and the cuckoo bird burst through its tiny doors, alternating its playful *cuck-ooo* call with the heirloom's tolling bell.

"Wow!" Hannah said, watching the songbird pop in and out. "That's so cool! Where'd you get it?"

"I can't wait to tell you," Lennie said as they sat down at the table for their first family supper. She wasn't sure if the flutter in her stomach would let her eat a single bite, but she was certain of something else: She'd finally found her forever home.

About the Author

First launching his creative writing career as a screenwriter, William's debut novel, *Someone to Watch Over*, based on his original screenplay, won the Women's Fiction Writers Association's 2019 Rising Star Award.

His yet-to-be-produced screenplay of *Someone to Watch Over* has won film festival screenwriting competitions across the country and placed as a Quarterfinalist (top 5%) in the internationally competitive Nicholl Fellowship Program sponsored by the Academy of Motion Picture Arts and Sciences.

His screenplay for the coming-of-age family film *Captiva Island* featured Academy Award-winner Ernest Borgnine. The movie was distributed in thirty-six countries, was translated into four languages, and aired domestically on HBO Family.

William was born in Augusta, Georgia, and grew up in Fort Myers, Florida, along the Gulf of Mexico. He began writing professionally after graduating with honors from the University of Florida's College of Journalism & Communications. He spent his formative writing years living between Georgia and Florida, and he now lives and writes in Seattle, Washington.

Follow him on Twitter @bill_schreiber and on Facebook at williamschreiberauthor.

Special Thanks

Writing a novel is both a solitary and a partnered undertaking. Although I was alone at the keyboard, I had many cherished companions.

With me were my late Mom and Dad. The emotional journey I experienced when asked to write my father's eulogy after he died unexpectedly inspired this story. What began as the healing self-therapy of writing his remembrance became more than I could have ever imagined. Mom knew I was working on the story and, though she passed during its writing, I have felt her presence all along the way.

Also by my side was my love and my best friend, my incredible wife, Pam. Words cannot express what she has meant to my life and to my aspirations as a writer. Her boundless love and support, no matter how far away things seemed at times, continue to inspire me. What you hold in your hands would never have happened without her. *Vous et nul autre.*

Always over my shoulder in spirit were my brother, David, and my sisters Lee, Susan and Pattie. Like children everywhere, we are our parents' legacy, and we now carry on to our own families our belief that every crisis faced together makes the circle grow stronger. I also want to thank my Wisconsin Walter family for all their love through the years.

My heartfelt thanks to editors Thelma Mariano, who helped me transition from telling the story from a screenwriter's perspective to telling it as a novelist; and Paula Hampton, whose attentive final-editing helped me sleep better at night. Thank you Gigi Little for your inspired cover design that so wonderfully captures the multigenerational facet of the story.

Thank you fellow writers at the Women's Fiction Writers Association, and the literary agents who support the association's pitch program, for your supportive generosity. To the Willamette Writers community, which introduced me to author Mikko Azul. I told her about the story during a chance meeting, and she insisted I meet with her (and now my) publisher, Benjamin Gorman. Thank you, Mikko and Ben. Thank you Not a Pipe Publishing family for your warm welcome.

To Bob Scott, who has been steadfast in his belief in the story since reading the screenplay, helping me see how it might, in its own little way, help broken families heal. To my fellow author, screenwriter and, most importantly, friend, Pat White, who's always quick with a smile and encouragement. To Sharon and Bill Calkins, and Joseph L. Courchesne, for their hearts. To Bill and Carolyn Rogers, who have believed in my writing for as long as I can remember. To the PB&Js for all the fun, folly and creative wanderings.

Finally, thank you Ringo and Mr. Beats, my sibling office cats who patiently considered me with snoozy coolness as I found my way in the story.

QUESTIONS AND TOPICS FOR DISCUSSION

1. A primary theme in the book is family dynamics and how people's life trajectories often define their family relationships. When we meet Lennie and John, we realize their lives went in very different directions. Why do you think they were able to reach a better understanding and appreciation of each other?

2. Lennie's journey took her to different places and into many unique experiences. What do you think her life would have been like if she had stayed in Mosely after having her child?

3. Lennie's resolve to reconnect with her father is abruptly interrupted by his death, combining grief with regret. She finds forgiveness, in part, because she believes he is helping her to find Michelle. Do you believe Lennie was helped by her deceased parents and Joella, or were those experiences due to her emotional state and desire to find answers? How does belief in a divine afterlife help people?

4. Lennie describes her encounter with Boone as the first time a boy paid her that type of attention, and she liked it. Given how the encounter played out, how do you think this impacted Lennie's ability to maintain future relationships with men?

5. What part of the story was your favorite and why?

6. Mosley is a fictitious small town in Tennessee with clear power dynamics between those with resources and those reliant on those who possess the resources. What is your experience with this type of situation? What was your reaction to the encounter between Mr. Mosely and Lennie at

the cemetery when she returns to the small town after finding Michelle?

7. John is convinced he will better understand his deceased father by re-creating the family vacation taken many years
earlier. Why do you think he was so adamant about aspects
of the trip such as the car, the route, and the same stops?
Did you find his reaction to events that undermined his goal
understandable or unreasonable?

8. As the story unfolds, we learn about events pertaining to
Michelle's adoption that were unknown to Lennie and her
father. Have you ever unearthed a "family secret" or information that changed your understanding of past events?
How did this make you feel?

9. Knowing a person's backstory can oftentimes change our
perception of him or her. Describe a time when you learned
more about someone else's experiences and how that
changed your feelings about that person.

10. Lennie's car plays an important role in the story. What of
your current or past possessions hold a special place in your
life? What made that connection so important?

11. Both Lennie and Michelle wrote letters to their absent
mothers. How can writing letters, journaling, or creative expression such as poetry or music help people deal with life's
unknowns? Do you write or do you play music, and if so,
how does it help you?

12. Reconciliation is a complicated process. What was your reaction to Michelle's anger the first time she meets Lennie?
What do you think their relationship was like after the story
ends?

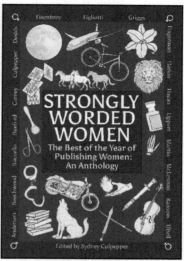

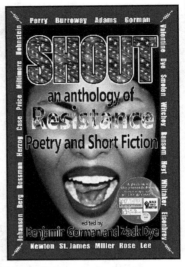

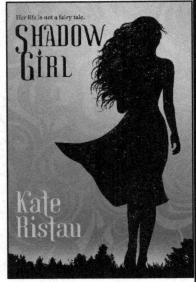

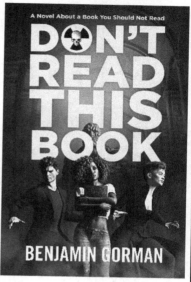

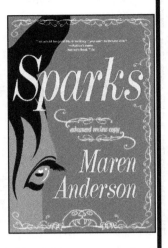

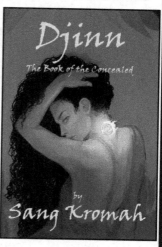

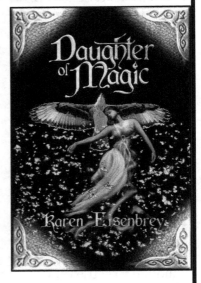

9 781948 120524